a.k.a.
Sheila Doyle

Also by Pat Jordan

Black Coach
A False Spring (*memoir*)
Suitors of Spring
Broken Patterns
Chase the Game
After the Sundown
The Cheat (*novel*)
A Nice Tuesday (*memoir*)

a.k.a.
Sheila Doyle

PAT JORDAN

ORION

First published in Great Britain in 2004 by Orion,
an imprint of the Orion Publishing Group Ltd.

A CIP catalogue record for this book is available from the British Library.

ISBNs 0 75285 602 2 (hardback) 0 75285 603 0 (trade paperback)

Printed in Great Britain by
Clays Ltd, St Ives plc

The Orion Publishing Group Ltd
Orion House
5 Upper Saint Martin's Lane
London, WC2H 9EA

For Susan,

My inspiration for *a.k.a. Sheila Doyle*, as for everthing else in my life.

1

James Raymond Jefferson Washington, III, great-grandson of a Virginia slave; a.k.a Jimmy Ray Washington, convicted car thief; a.k.a Jimmy Wash, convicted dope dealer; a.k.a Baby James to the old bull cons at Stark who turned him out; a.k.a James W., semiretired fag hustler, preferred to think of himself as he was now, in his latest incarnation. Kitty Litter. Sometimes just Miss Kitty. Kit to his closest friends. The most famous gender illusionist on South Beach and the sole proprietress of Kitty's Litter, Funky Rags for Every Puss, on Washington Avenue.

"Named after my ancestors," Kitty said to customers.

The tourists said, "The store?"

"No, sweetheart. The *street!*"

Kitty was hunched over his sewing machine in his back room. He was putting the finishing touches on a white feather boa he'd wear tonight, Ladies' Night, at Club Drip. He was famous for wearing white. It went wonderfully with his Amaretto-colored skin and tight, bleached, yellow afro. He heard the front door bell ring.

"In a *min*ute!" he called out. He finished the boa and then stepped into his boutique. A woman was flipping through a rack of dresses against the wall.

"Can I help you, honey?" he said. He cocked a hip and planted his hand on it.

"Maybe," the woman said. She continued flipping through the dresses. "I'm looking for something a little sexy. Actually, more than sexy. Something kinky."

"Oh, honey! Have you ever come to the right place. Now, let me see." He waited for her to turn around. She had a cute little ass in her tight jeans. Finally, she faced him. He waited for her to smile at him, like most straight ladies did. His yellow hair, his heavy eye makeup, his false eyelashes, his mesh see-through undershirt, and tight red satin pants. But she didn't.

"Well?" she said.

"Let me see," he said. "You're about a size. . . ." He put a long finger to his chin and let his eyes roam up and down her body. She was slim, but not skinny. She wore a black T-shirt with gold script across her chest. "Beyond Bitch." Nice titties, too. Big for such a slim lady. Attractive, older, but he couldn't tell how old because she wore big sunglasses and a Jim Beam trucker's cap pulled over her forehead. Her hair was tucked under her cap.

"Six," he said.

"Very good."

"Honey, I have something you will just cream over."

"You, maybe. Not me."

"I beg your pardon?"

"Cream," she said.

James blinked. Then he got it. His rubbery features rearranged themselves into a big smile. "Oh, right, baby! Cream is only for little boys, isn't it?" He went to the dress rack, fingered his way through the dresses, and pulled one out. He showed it to her.

She looked at it without expression. "I'll take it."

"Baby! Baby! Not so fast! Try it on."

"It's not necessary."

He made a clicking sound with his mouth. "*Well,* at least let me show you how it will look." She shrugged. "Now, turn *around!*" She faced the mirror. He stood behind her and held the dress in front of her body. "Something's not right," he said. He held the dress with one hand and with the other he took off her cap and sunglasses. Her shiny, black hair fell just below her ears. It was cut sharply in bangs at her forehead and sharp angles below her ears. She was *very* attractive, but older than she looked. Maybe 45. A nice tan. A local. She had dark eyes, almost black, and the longest, blood-red fingernails.

"Oh, you look just like Vampira!" he said. "With a tan."

She looked at herself in the mirror for a long moment. The black, wet-looking, latex-rubber minidress was scooped low in front and so short it barely covered her ass.

She nodded. "Yes. This will do nicely." She turned and smiled at him.

He wrapped the dress in tissue paper and put it in one of his shopping bags that had a drawing of him in drag on two sides. She opened her purse and withdrew a wad of bills. She peeled off three new hundred-dollar bills.

"That's way too much, baby," he said. "It's only two hundred."

She put on her sunglasses and trucker's cap. "Tell me, Kitty," she said. "I'll bet you have a lot of ladies who look just like me in your store?"

"Oh, baby! Not like you. Miss Kitty could never forget such a beautiful lady."

"Really?" she said. She peeled off another hundred-dollar bill and handed it to him. "Try."

He looked at the bill in his hand, and then at the woman. She took off her sunglasses and looked at him through her black eyes. Finally, he smiled at her. "Baby, I just forgot you."

"Good girl," she said. She reached for one of his business cards on the counter and put it in her purse. "Because I won't forget you, Kitty." She put on her sunglasses and walked toward the door.

When she opened the door and the little bell tinkled, he called out to her, "Now, you promise Miss Kitty." She turned and looked at him. "You promise her you will wear yerself some frillies under that dress." He smiled. "Don't want to be flashin' our moneymaker now, do we? The way mens are."

"Don't we both know it, baby," she said. She stepped outside into the bright sunlight of a Friday afternoon, and was gone.

Ricardo gave Jessica his party of four at the sidewalk table so he could wait on the lone woman in the Jim Beam trucker's cap. She was sitting at a table under the shade of a date palm in the far back corner of the News Café's outdoor patio. Ricardo straightened his black bow tie, ran his hands over his slicked-back, black hair that ended in a little ponytail, and walked over to her. She looked up at him through her big, dark, sunglasses. He smiled at her.

"Señorita. I can help you?" he said.

She looked at the name tag on his white shirt. "Yes, you can . . . Ricardo. Bring me an espresso. A double. With a lemon peel." She looked down at the bottom of the menu. "And three corona grandes. Gloria Cubanos."

He looked around. "Three? Someone will join the señorita?"

"Just bring the cigars, Ricky, por favor?" She lowered her sunglasses to the bridge of her nose. "And thank you for los complimentos, Ricky. But obviously it's señora."

"Si, señora."

When he returned with her espresso, cigars, and a cutter, she was smoking a cigarette. He stared at her cigarette without putting down her espresso.

"I like my café hot, Ricky," she said. "Or are you posing for me? You *are* a very pretty boy, Ricky. But I'm only interested in my café and my cigars. Comprende?"

"Si, señora. Perdon."

He put down her order and went back to his waiter's stand. He watched her sip her espresso and smoke her cigarette. She stared at the other patrons through her dark glasses. The handsome Cubano boys sitting shirtless in the sun. They talked on their cell phones while their girlfriends sat on their laps, giggling and kicking their legs in the air. The two models sitting side-by-side at a table close to the sidewalk. They looked like those little statues rich Anglos put on their front lawns. One was blanco, with yellow hair, and a white tube top. The other was a frejole negro, with a shaved head and a black tube top. Neither spoke. They just stared at the tourists walking, who stared back at them.

The woman took a drag of her cigarette and stubbed it out in an ashtray. She picked up one of the cigars and held it close to her lips. She peeled back her lips, exposing her teeth, and bit off the end of the cigar. She picked the bits of tobacco from her mouth and examined the end of the cigar. She frowned. She did the same thing with the second cigar, and frowned. After she bit off the end of the third cigar she did not frown. She held the cigar between her thumb and fingers, close to her lips, stuck out the tip of her tongue, and ran it along the sides of the cigar from end to end. Then she held the cigar at one end and put it in her mouth. She wrapped her lips around it and pushed the cigar down her throat until it almost disappeared. She withdrew the wet cigar and lighted it with a silver lighter. She twirled it in her fingers until it was lit, then put it in her mouth. She took a few puffs and then stubbed it out in the ashtray.

"Conyo!" Ricardo said out loud.

"What, Ricky?" said Jessica, balancing a tray of sandwiches on her arm. Ricardo shook his head. "Oh, nothing. It was nothing." Jessica shrugged and walked toward a table of four. When Ricardo looked back at the woman, she was staring at him. She waved him toward her.

"Si, señora."

"These are quite good," she said. Ricky looked at the unsmoked, stubbed-out cigar in the ashtray. "Could you get me a box, please?"

"Certainly, señora."

Ricardo brought her an unopened box of Gloria Cubanos. She opened her purse, took out a wad of bills, and peeled off three one-hundred dollar bills for the $200 box of cigars, the three ten-dollar cigars, and the five-dollar espresso. She got up to leave.

"Your change, señora?" he said.

She put her hand on his cheek and patted it. "For you, Ricky. You worked so hard, didn't you?" She smiled at him and walked away.

He followed her with his eyes as she passed the newsstand and turned the corner toward the ladies' room. She held the box of cigars in one hand, and in the other she held her purse and a shopping bag with a drawing of a mericone negro on it. He called out, "Gracias, señora." Without turning, she raised the box of cigars and wiggled it. Then she was gone down the alleyway that led to the ladies' room. He picked up the ashtray with the stubbed-out cigar and saw that she had left the other two unsmoked cigars.

The woman went into a stall in the ladies' room and closed the door. She sat down on the toilet seat, cut open the tobacco stamp sealing the box of cigars with her fingernail and opened it. She stood over the toilet, flipped up the seat, took a bunch of cigars from the top layer, crushed them in her hands, and flushed them. Then she took another bunch and did the same thing. When she was finished, she had left only half of the cigars on the bottom layer, and only one cigar on the top layer separated from the bottom by the cedar divider. She closed the box and reached down for her purse. She opened it and reached inside.

* * *

The waiters at The Anvil were setting up the tables in the deserted dining room at 5 P.M. on a Friday. They chatted back and forth in Spanish as they took chairs off the tabletops and lined up silverware and plates. The maitre'd, at his lectern in the hallway, glanced over his shoulder at them. Such a vulgar language. For peasants. He was French, raised in Marseilles. A balding man with small eyes, a long nose, and a receding chin. He wore a black tuxedo and patent-leather pumps.

The reservation phone rang. He picked up the receiver, listened a moment, then said, "I am sorry. It ees impossiblé tonight." He hung up and smiled. He looked down his reservation list. He nodded at certain names and shook his head, no, at others. He heard the front door open, and looked up.

A woman was walking down the long, dark hallway toward him. She wore a cap, dark glasses, a T-shirt with something written on it, and those gauche, high-cut, black tennis shoes. She was carrying a purse, a shopping bag, and a box of cigars.

Before she reached him, he said, "I am so sorry, madame, but we are closed until eight o'clock."

"Oh, I know," she said, with an eager smile. She held up the cigar box. "I've just come to rent a humidor, you know, in your Havana Room."

"Certainliment, madame," he said. He opened his humidor reservation book. "Your name, please?" His Mont Blanc pen was poised over the book.

"My name is Mrs. Solomon Bilstein," she said. He began to write. "Oh, no!" she said. "Excuse me. That was before. I mean. . . ." She giggled in that manner of older American women who think giggling makes them seem girlish instead of merely foolish.

He stopped writing and looked up from his book with half-lidded eyes. She was smiling. An attractive woman for her age. "You *do* know your name, madame, I assume?"

She took off her dark glasses and fidgeted with them in her hands. She had very dark eyes, almost black. "Née, Mrs. Solomon Bilstein," she said. "You see, today I go back to just plain old Sheila Ryan." He stared without expression. She smiled again and nodded. "My divorce?" she said. "It came through today. You see?" But he did not see. Nor did he care. It always baffled him why Americans insisted on sharing intimacies with strangers. "I'm celebrating," the woman said. "Treating myself tonight. A new me, you might say." She waited for him to respond. When he didn't, she went on, breathlesly, "He left his cigars, you see. I hated the smell in the house. But after he left, I smoked one. It was kinda nice. It made me feel . . . oh . . . I don't know . . . different." She smiled again, and nodded. He shook his head and sighed. "More in control, you see? Powerful, almost. A *new* me. That's why I went back to my maiden name. I haven't used it in years. That's why I said Mrs. Solomon Bilstein. A habit. We were married, oh, almost ten years, and so now that I . . . well . . . it's something I have to get used to. Using it, I mean. My new name. My old name, really, but new now." She took a deep breath as if she had exhausted herself. Then she said, "Sheila Ryan. That's my name."

He wrote her name, Sheila Ryan, in his book, reached into a drawer and withdrew a key. "That will be two thousand five hundred dollars for the year, madame. How does madame wish to pay? A check, a credit card?"

"Oh, no!" she said. "My new checks haven't come yet. With my new name on them. My old name, I mean." He closed his eyes for a brief moment, then opened them. "He cancelled my credit cards, too," she said. "All I have is. . . ." She opened her purse and began searching inside it. She took out a makeup case and put it on his lectern. Then a lipstick. A lace handkerchief. A pack of cigarettes. "Here it is!" she said. She produced a fistful of bills. She thrust the bills at him. "Cash," she said. "I want to pay cash." When he didn't take the bills, she said, "Oh, I'm sorry." She furrowed her brow and began to count out twenty-five of the bills. "Twenty-two, twenty-three, twenty-four, twenty-five." She looked up at him and handed him the twenty-five hundred-dollar bills. She jammed the rest of the bills back into her purse, and then her makeup case, lipstick, handkerchief, and cigarettes. She squashed them down and closed her purse.

He put the bills into a metal box in his drawer. "This way, madame."

She followed him to a pair of heavy, darkly wooded, double doors halfway between the dining room and the front door. He held open one door for her, and then followed her into the Havana Room. She gasped and put her hand over her mouth.

The walls were all polished, dark wood. There was a pool table in one corner of the room and a circular bar in the middle of the room. Burgundy leather banquettes lined three walls. The banquettes were curved like crescents so that people sitting in them could not be seen by anyone except approaching waiters. On the walls behind the banquettes were little green-shaded gas lamps. Higher on the walls were oil paintings. The paintings above each banquette were different, yet the same. Naked women with huge breasts draped over a motorcycle; lounging on black satin sheets; sprawled, spread-eagle, on the hood of an exotic car. Above the paintings were the stuffed heads of dead animals not commonly found in South Beach. Lions. Tigers. Buffalo. Wolves.

The woman gasped again. "Oh!" she said. "It's sooo classy!" She went over to a banquette and ran the flat of her hand over the leather. "Soft like butter," she said.

"This way," the maitre d' said. She followed him to a corner of the room that was enclosed in glass like one of those TV glass booths that isolated quiz show contestants in the '50s. It was brightly lit by a hanging, cut-glass chandelier. Pale polished wood boxes lined the walls. The maitre'd opened the glass door with a key and ushered her into the stuffy humidor that smelled of tobacco. He opened one of the humidor boxes with her key, turned to the woman, and reached for her cigar box.

"Oh, no!" she said. "Let me do it." She put the box in the humidor, turned the key, and put it in her purse. "There," she said. "I feel better already."

When they were back in the hallway, she leaned toward the dining room and stared. "Can I just look?" she said. "I've heard so much about it. All the beautiful people." She smiled at the maitre'd. "All the rich single men."

"We are booked tonight, I'm afraid," he said.

"Oh, I'm sure you are. I just want a peek."

Before he could stop her, she had walked into the dining room. She stared at the big, open dining room with its round tables set for dinner. Sterling silverware and pearlescent porcelain and cut-glass crystal and white napkins standing up like dunce caps. There was a circular bar and a bandstand at the far end of the room, and private booths along one wall. She walked over to the private booths that were partially hidden by a series of Greek columns.

"Sooo intimate," she sighed. "It would be so much fun to eat here tonight." She looked at the maitre'd.

He shook his head, no. "Out of the question."

"It *is* such a big night for me. I thought I'd celebrate with some champagne, a lobster, or a steak." She pointed to one of the private booths. "That would be perfect. I could see everything without being . . . in the way."

"That one is reserved. Every Friday night. A very special patron."

"Oh." She frowned, then brightened. "What about the ones on either side?"

"Those are always kept deserted. At the request of our patron. He prefers privacy."

"Couldn't you make an exception tonight? Please?" She reached into her purse and withdrew her bills again. She peeled off three of them, and put them in the maitre'd's palm. He glanced around the room, then put the bills in his pocket.

"I'll see, madame. I'm not promising, but I will ask our special patron if he wouldn't make an exception tonight."

She put on her dark glasses. "You do that," she said coldly. "There's another C-note in it for you." He noticed for the first time what was written in gold script on her T-shirt. "Beyond Bitch."

She lay on her back, naked, on a bed in a dirty hotel room at the wrong end of South Beach in the late afternoon's fading light. The room was hot and damp and smelled of mildew from the ocean a block away. There was a slowly turning ceiling fan in the middle of the room. It circulated the musty-smelling air that the loudly humming air conditioner in the window could not cool. The dirty window looked out on the wall of another cheap hotel that had a greenish mold crawling up its faded pink stucco.

The coarse blanket against her back itched her skin. The room was too filthy for her to turn down the sheets. So she just lay there, waiting, not moving, her legs spread. She looked up at the ceiling and saw a mirror directly above her. She stared at her body suspended above her, glistening with sweat. She looked ten years younger than she did two years ago. But harder. Tanned and lightly muscled at forty-seven. Her big breasts, only slightly pendulous, spilled off her chest toward her rib cage. She had faintly defined abs, protruding bones on her slim hips, a trim, blond bush, and long legs. Her currency now, but not always.

She sighed and then took a deep breath. She smelled her own BO. Fear. No, not fear. She wasn't afraid, anymore than she was afraid when she stood in the wings of some little theater years ago, and waited for her cue. It was a nervous anticipation. Almost sexual. That brief instant before she stepped on stage under bright lights in front of an audience. She could feel her heart beating in her breast, her labored breathing, and then she was there, on stage, speaking, and it was all gone. She was conscious of nothing now except the new person she had become at that instant. Laura. Maggie. Blanche. Alma. She became them all, and lost herself. They seemed real to her then. She seemed real when she *was* them, and not real when she was herself. She smiled to herself. She remembered when she told him that plays were real life. He laughed at her. And then he showed her what real life was. That what she was about to do was real life. Final. She either did it right, or didn't. There would be no second takes. No reinterpretation of her lines at rehearsal the next day. No Wednesday matinée performance to make up for her fumbled lines on Tuesday night. Which only heightened her excitement and anticipation. It *was* sexual. She could feel it between her legs. She slid her hand down her sweaty body until it came to her pubic hair. She touched herself and closed her eyes. She began to breathe more heavily as her fingers worked. She put her other hand on her breast and began to massage her nipple with her thumb and forefinger, shivering at her touch. Her mouth was open and she was breathing in gulps of air, her chest rising and falling, her fingers working quickly, bringing her up and up until suddenly her body stiffened, was still. She let out a soft cry, and then her body began to shudder with a chill pleasure that washed over her in waves, the waves bigger at first, one after another, and then smaller, farther apart, and still smaller until they were gone. Her body fell limp against the coarse blanket. Her breathing subsided. She lay there on her back in a dreamy, exhausted haze. She felt herself drifting off, losing consciousness, but not before it came to her that this was how it had all begun. . . .

2

SHEILA WOKE NAKED IN A STRANGE BED. A DOG WAS LICKING HER FACE. "Christ!" she said, and pushed the dog away. The dog sat and stared at her. "I'm sorry, pooch," she said. She reached out a hand and petted him.

She sat up, too quickly, and closed her eyes to the pain behind her forehead. She waited for the pain to subside and then looked over her shoulder at the man in bed beside her. He had a broad, tanned, muscular back. His face was turned away. She saw only his blond ponytail. Bleached blond.

"Oh, Jesus!"

She put the flat of her hand over her throbbing forehead and tried to remember last night. Some women from her theater had taken her to a male strip club to celebrate her divorce. She didn't want to go, but it seemed so important to them, sisterhood and all that crap, so she went. She had no reason not to. The joke was, she wasn't depressed by the divorce at all. It was the end of a long nightmare as Mrs. Scott McKenzie that she hoped to wake from this morning. Now this! She shook her head, and glanced again at the blond ponytail. She remembered what had really depressed her. The strip club was *so* tawdry! Tables of screeching women. Flashing strobe lights. Deafening disco music. They pushed their way through the throngs of women to a round table at the left of the stage. She remembered the soles of her shoes sticking to the floor because of all the spilled sweet drinks.

Sheila ordered a vodka martini, and the others ordered rum collins from a bare-chested waiter. He wore only a tuxedo collar and bow tie like the ones people put on their dogs because they think it's cute. He had three diamond studs in his left ear. Sheila was fixated on those studs. Left ear for gay, right ear for straight. Or was it the other way around? It was different on the East and West Coasts.

"Excuse me," Sheila said to the waiter. He smiled at her. "Your diamond studs." He touched his earrings. "I was wondering. If you fly to L.A., do you change your diamond studs from one ear to the other?" He stopped smiling. "I mean, where do you know to change them? Kansas City? Denver? Or do you have to wait until you're actually *in* L.A.?"

He looked around at her friends to see if they were laughing. They were just staring at Sheila.

"I'll be right back with your drinks," he said, and left.

Sheila turned toward her friends. "I'm serious," she said. "I really am curious."

"Oh, Sheila!" one of the women said, flapping her hand at Sheila. "Just watch the show."

The dancers pranced onstage under an overhead spot that followed them a split second too late. They wore costumes. Tuxedos. Police uniforms. Indian buckskin and head feathers. Sheila laughed at the Indian. Whose fantasy was he?

The men gyrated under the late-trailing spot to deafening music. They whipped their long hair wildly as they stripped down to gold lamé G-strings. They grinned lasciviously at the cheering women. The men had the slimly muscled bodies of male models on South Beach. Their skin was an unnatural orange from painted-on tans. It glistened under the spot and smelled of coconut oil. When they leaped off the stage, close to Sheila's table, she smelled the cheap cologne they used to hide the odor of their sweat.

Sheila watched them dance around the room. They stopped at each table to thrust their hips at the screaming women in a mimicry of sex. They taunted the women to join them. Make fools of themselves. Why not? None of these men had ever loved a woman. They were so obviously gay. Obvious to Sheila *now*, too late.

Some of the women rose out of their chairs, egged on by their friends. They began grinding their hips against the grinding hips of the strippers. One of them stuck a bill in a stripper's G-string, reaching farther down than necessary. The stripper only grinned. It meant nothing to him. Another woman reached her hand behind a stripper's head and pulled his face to hers. She kissed him, sticking her tongue in his mouth, then pulled back a bit so her friends could see her licking the stripper's tongue.

Sheila felt sick to her stomach. She reached for her purse to leave. When she looked up a new stripper was onstage, older than the others. Maybe thirty-five. He'd come onstage already wearing only a G-string. He was right, Sheila thought. He didn't need a silly costume. All he needed was that small, leopard-skin G-string and his huge, dark, muscular body. She sat forward in her chair and watched him. He moved slowly onstage, gracefully, powerfully, like a self-contained animal. His muscles moved inside his dark skin as if they were alive.

When he stepped offstage, women screamed out his name . . . what was it? They waved him toward their table, pleading, begging. He moved through the room as if stalking the women. He eluded their outstretched hands. He never stopped long enough at a table for the women to touch him like they had the other strippers. He didn't taunt them with thrusting hips. But still, he controlled them, like an alpha male controlling his pack. He was like an animal. A dark, powerful, perfectly self-contained, dangerous animal.

Sheila had seen actors control an audience like that, but never that dangerously. She knew the feeling. It had happened to her once. She was in her late thirties, still young enough to play Stella. Stanley was a big, rough boy of twenty-two. So different from her soft, pale, lawyer husband at the time. Ex-husband, now. Stanley had a passionate crush on her. She struggled to fight him off even as she was drawn to his rough passion. "Meet me in the parking lot after rehearsal," he whispered one night. She told the older woman playing Blanche.

"Are you crazy?" the woman said. "Do you know where it will lead?"

Sheila never found out.

Their sexual tension showed onstage during the run of the play. Every night, they fought back and forth, Stanley and Stella, so violently that at the end of each performance Sheila was exhausted, as if what she had gone through was real, not a play. She forgot the audience as they battled onstage. But when the curtain fell each night, and then rose again to thunderous applause, whistles, shouts, she was jolted back to reality. It was the only time in her life that she felt such power over others.

This man, now moving through the room, must know that feeling every day of his life. He was always in control in a way Sheila had known only once, and now, at forty-five, would never know again.

The man was moving toward her table. She kept her eyes fixed on him. But even now, in bed with him, she could not see his face. As he passed her table one of her friends tried to stuff a bill down his G-string. He caught her hand in midair, his big hand circling her wrist. The woman stared, her mouth open. He smiled down at her and shook his head, no. Then he raised her hand to his lips, kissed it, and slipped the bill out of her hand. He moved off, and disappeared behind the stage.

"Jesus Christ!" the woman said. "I'm wet!" The others laughed, except Sheila, and turned their attention to the next stripper, a small man with a trim, brush mustache. They hooted at him. "Come on, shorty! Take it all off!"

Sheila waited a few moments. Then she reached into her purse for some money to call a taxi. She heard a voice from behind her.

"Don't leave." She turned to see him standing there. He was dressed like a cowboy now, pointy-toed boots, jeans, a pink and aqua Hawaiian shirt. "I saw you staring at me," he said.

"I beg your pardon?" Sheila said. He looked at her with a faint smile. Sheila felt her face flush. "I wasn't the only one," she said.

"You were the only one I noticed."

She laughed. "Is that so? Tell me, does that line work with women?"

"I don't know yet. It's the first time I used it. I'll tell you later."

"So how come you only noticed me staring at you?"

"It was the way you were staring."

"How was that?"

"You were appreciating me. Looking for something, too."

"What?"

"You tell me."

"You're very perceptive for a . . ."

"Stripper?" He smiled at her. "We like to say, 'dancer.' Sounds more like an entertainer. Me and Gene Kelly, ya know. Only he wore a rain-coat and carried an umbrella.

"And you wear a leopard-skin G-string."

He shrugged. "Not all the time."

Now Sheila saw his face, close to hers in that club. He was not a hand-some man. Hard-looking, but not handsome. He had narrow black eyes and sharp, upslanting cheekbones and hollows in his cheeks. He had a slightly hooked nose, as if broken in a fight, and a square jaw. He looked almost Slavic, except for his dark coarse skin that was tanned, but dark in itself. His blond hair in a ponytail looked unnatural.

He crouched down beside her. "Now you tell me something. What's a lady like you doing here?"

She laughed. "Are you serious?" He nodded. "What makes you think I'm a 'Lady'?"

"I can tell. I've known enough of the other kind."

"And what kind is that?"

"Strippers mostly. Young. Dumb. No class. Not like you."

Sheila looked at him for a long moment, his dark eyes that drained her of will, and then she saw her hand reaching out, touching his face. "You're sweet?" she said, with a slight tilt of her head. "I'd never have guessed."

"Sweet?" He smiled. "I'll have to remember that. Tell Sol."

"Sol?"

"A friend. You'll meet him someday."

"God, you're awful sure of yourself."

"In my business I have to be."

"I guess so, taking off your clothes in front of screaming women."

"That? That's nothing. I didn't mean that."

"What did you mean?" He shook his head, no. Sheila reached for her purse again. "Listen, this has all been very flattering. But I have to go now."

"Why?"

"Because I want to."

"No, you don't. You want to get to know me."

"Jesus! You're full of yourself." She shook her head. "This is ridiculous!" She made a sweeping gesture with one hand. "There are plenty of women who'd die to get to know you. Why don't you pick one of them?"

"I don't want one of them. I want you."

"Do you always get what you want?"

"Usually."

So that was it, she thought, now in bed with him. He wanted her and no one had wanted her for a long time. They talked and drank a little while longer, and then she left with him because he wanted her and because she couldn't think of a reason not to, and, most of all, because this was the night she had decided to change her life. She remembered telling him about her divorce, and then blurting out, "I just want to change my life." She stunned herself. That was the first moment she had thought such a thing. She was even more stunned that she had shared such a thought with this man, this stranger.

He looked at her, his dark eyes suddenly tired, his grin fading. "Me, too," he said. They didn't speak for a while as if embarassed by their intimacies. Finally, he said, "How bad do you want to change your life?"

"I don't know. I didn't even know I wanted to until a few minutes ago." She laughed, a breath. "Now, it's funny, but the only thing I do know is I want to change my life."

She followed him out to his car at 2 A.M. She waited for him to open her door, but he didn't. She saw over the roof of his car her girlfriends waving at her, giving her the thumbs-up. One of them walked toward his car and called to her.

"Do you know what you're doing, Sheila?"

"No," Sheila said, and got in.

Now she was in bed with him. She was mortified. This was the first time she had done such a thing since she was a struggling actress in New York City twenty years ago. A one-night stand. With a man so much younger than herself. Jesus! *The Roman Spring of Sheila MacKenzie*. She could play that role now. An older woman only too eager, and foolish, to prove that her life was *not* over, that someone, this younger man, could still want her. All that other crap about changing her life, that was just barroom bullshit in a moment of weakness.

She sat up on the edge of the bed, his bed, and stared out the bedroom window. The late morning sunlight glinted off the white sailboats docked alongside his apartment on the canal. She looked back at him one last time before she left, and tried to remember his name. But all she could remember now was being in bed with him last night. The sex. How she fit with him. . . . Why did she think, fit? She meant, felt. . . . Or did she? She had never thought of sex as fitting, physically fitting. Men thought that way. Women thought of feeling. But last night, she didn't feel anything, she only knew she fit with him. Maybe it was the same thing. Men and women just communicated it differently. Then why was she now communicating how she felt the way a man would?

She had been nervous at first. It wasn't her nakedness. She was still slim, with lightly defined abs, and the kind of big breasts some thin, hipless women have if they don't have children. It was her inexperience. She hadn't had sex in almost two years. Not since the miscarriage. The night she found out about her husband. Ex-husband. Which explained why he had had so little interest in sex—with her, anyway. So she lost interest in it, too. It was just something other people gave an importance to she felt it didn't have.

Until last night. Then it seemed the most important thing *in* her life, proof she still *had* a life. She was too aware at first, awkward, reticent . . . not fitting. But he eased her along gently—practiced, she couldn't help thinking. He kissed her face, her breasts, her stomach, and then buried his face between her legs, something her husband, ex-husband, would never do. He brought her out gradually, farther and farther out of herself until she began to lose herself in it, thrusting her hips toward his face so hungrily it shocked her. And then she heard a strange woman's harsh voice, "Now me! Now me!" and she was burying her face between *his* legs now, sucking his cock so hungrily that for a split second she feared she was chewing him up.

"Relax, baby," he whispered to her. "Don't think. Just do it."

He pulled her up to him, kissed her face, and rolled her over onto her back, her legs clamped around the small of his back, pulling him inside her, thrusting to his thrust, and then he was rolling her over again, onto her knees, thrusting behind her now, her face buried in the

pillow, her hands squeezing the bedposts until she came, with a stran-
gled cry, panting, exhausted, soaked with sweat. She fell forward on
her stomach and was instantly asleep.

Now, she didn't even remember his name. Jesus! If only she could
remember it would make everything all right, better anyway, a little.
She saw her clothes scattered on the floor. Her silk blouse and bra
draped over his Hawaiian shirt. Her tan skirt and his jeans. Her Papa-
galo flats near his cowboy boots. Her panties, ripped. *She* had ripped
them off herself, not Bobby. That was it. Bobby. Bobby what? They
were in his car, driving back to his apartment, when she asked him
his name.

"Bobby," he said. "Robert Roberts, actually." He grinned across at
her. "My friends call me Bobby Squared."

Sheila eased herself out of bed, scooped up her clothes, and hurried
into the bathroom. She closed the door and noticed the dog sitting
beside her, staring. "Shooosh!" she whispered, a finger to her lips. The
dog nodded. Or did he? God, there was something eerily human about
this dog. He was so beautiful. Short, reddish-orange fur marked with
white at his face and chest. He had pricked ears and a pointy snout like
a wolf, and a bushy tail that curled over his back like a sickle. He was
wagging his curled tail at her, staring with that eerily human expression in his almond-shaped eyes. She patted his head. How many
women, girls rather, had this pooch seen in the bathroom after a night
of sex with his master?

She looked at herself in the bathroom mirror. Oh, God! Her long,
brown hair, flecked with gray at the temples, looked like a rat's nest
She ran her fingers through it until it calmed down.

She dressed quickly, straightened up, smoothed her skirt, arched
her back the way she always did before taking the stage, and then
stared at herself in the mirror. Jesus! Her clothes were wrinkled, her
face flushed and swollen. She looked like what she was. A one-night

stand who had screwed all night and now, in the harsh glare of a bath-room light, was trying to slink out of his apartment, get home, take a shower, and convince herself this had all been a bad dream.

She opened the bathroom door. He was half-sitting, half-lying in bed, smiling at her.

"Where do you think you're going?" he said.

"I didn't want to disturb you. I just thought I'd. . . ."

"Go home?" She nodded. He shook his head, no. "You haven't had breakfast yet." He patted the bed. "Hosh!" The dog leaped onto the bed so light and agile it distracted Sheila. "Have you met Hoshi?"

"Yes. He introduced himself."

"Licked your face, huh?" He hugged the dog. The dog licked his face. "Did you wake Sheila, Hosh?" The dog wagged his curled tail. "He does that all the time."

"I'll bet."

He smiled at her and shook his head. Then he got out of bed, naked, and began picking up his clothes. Sheila watched him bend over, the muscles in his back and thighs flaring out. Jesus! She was a cat in heat! He faced her, his clothes in his hands, and saw her staring at him. She looked down at his dog.

"Hoshi?" she said. "What kind of a name is that?"

"Japanese. It means, 'Little Star.' Hoshi's a Jap dog, a Shiba Inu. A very tough little bastard."

"He doesn't seem tough." The dog weighed about thirty-five pounds. "He seems more . . . this sounds foolish . . . almost too sensi-tive for a dog."

He nodded. "Good. You know him already. The Hosh, he's beyond dog."

3

THEY WERE SITTING UNDER THE LATE MORNING SUN AT AN OUTDOOR TABLE ON the deck of The Mark's Chickee Bar overlooking Ft. Lauderdale beach and the pale blue-green ocean. He wore a muscle T-shirt, baggy shorts, and flip-flops. Sheila was still wearing her rumpled clothes. The deck was crowded with tourists and a few locals having their breakfast. Fat, pink-skinned women in mumus and their husbands in "Party Naked" T-shirts. Older men with perfect tans and gold chains nestled in their gray chest hair and their women—girls, really—young blondes with big fake tits in G-string bikinis.

Sheila kept glancing around the deck to see if people were staring at her. What must they think? An older, pale-skinned woman in rumpled clothes and a younger stud. Anyone could tell what she and Bobby had done all night. She even smelled of it. Bobby? That was the first time she'd thought of him as Bobby.

"Don't worry," he said. "Nobody at The Mark cares."

"I beg your pardon."

He made a sweeping gesture with his arm to encompass the beach below littered with tanned, young girls in G-string bikinis, their bodies glistening with oil. "They're mostly strippers," he said. "They never pass judgment."

"I don't know what you're talking about."

"Suit yourself."

She felt her face get hot. Finally, she said. "How do you know? What strippers think?"

"I just know."

"I'll bet." He smiled at her. "I'm sorry. I just feel embarrassed."

"At what?"

"You're putting me on?"

"No, I'm not."

She tugged on her wrinkled silk blouse with both hands. "Look at me, for Crissakes! Look at the both of us. It's humiliating. Everyone knows."

He looked around the deck, then back to her. "Maybe. Maybe not. Who cares?"

"I care."

"I don't."

A waitress was standing by their table. Bobby ordered Bloody Marys for them both. He didn't ask her if she wanted one. Then he ordered for them both, scrambled eggs, hash browns for her, grits for himself. Before she could speak up, he said, "A redneck thing. I can't escape it."

"What?"

"Grits," he said.

He was crouched down beside her in the club last night, telling her he was from the mountains of Western North Carolina. "A farmer," he said. She looked at him and laughed. "A farmer! In a leopard G-string?"

"Seriously. I was a farmer."

"What did you grow?"

"Cash crops."

"And what exactly is a 'cash crop'?"

"Just what it sounds like."

"Why did you quit?"

"My crops dried up."

"You mean, in a drought?"

He laughed. "Yeh, a drought. After that there was nothing left for me in the mountains so I came to Lauderdale."

"Where you became a stripper."

He raised a finger and waved it, no, in front of her face. "Dancer, remember?"

"Oh, yes. You and Fred Astaire."

"Gene Kelly. He was more athletic, I think. What about you?"

"What *about* me?"

"What's your story?"

"I don't have 'a story'."

"Yes you do. Everybody in Paradise has a story. That's why we're here. On the run, from a bad check, a bad rap, a bad marriage. What are you running from?"

"I'm sorry to disappoint you, but I'm not running from anything."

"Yes, you are. You're too smart not to know it. Maybe you just don't want to tell me."

So she told him. Not everything, just enough. She'd been a stage actress in New York City, then, as she got older, in regional theaters in New England. When her career didn't pan out like she thought it would, she became a drama teacher at a prestigious New England prep school.

She pointed a finger at herself and said, "*I* taught Martha Stewart's daughter."

"Really?"

She nodded. "Moi."

"Who's Martha Stewart?"

"You're kidding?" He shook his head, no. "She's, well, she's this. . . ." She shook her head. "It was just a joke, anyway. She's nobody. You're right."

"Were you married?" he said.

"Not at first. My husband . . . my ex-husband as of tonight, was the school's legal counsel. Everyone at the school thought it was a perfect match. Both of us were in our late thirties. Neither of us had ever been married. Which should have told me something."

"What do you mean?"

"Nothing. Nothing. Anyway, everyone thought it would be perfect for the school."

"Was it perfect for you?"

"No, I guess not."

"Did you love him?"

"I don't really think so. No, I didn't."

"Then why did you marry him?"

"Everyone . . . I mean, they all thought . . . I couldn't think of a reason not to."

"So, what happened?"

"It didn't work out."

"So you came to Ft. Lauderdale on the run from a bad marriage."

She smiled at him. "You win. Yes, I came to Ft. Lauderdale on the run from a bad marriage. I waited out the divorce for two years. I supported myself by doing TV commercials." She flashed him her 8x10 glossy smile.

"Jesus!" he said. "I hope you never smile at me like that."

"Well," she said, still smiling, "it sold mustard. French's to be exact. I lived off it until the divorce came through."

"What about alimony?"

"I didn't want shit from him!" she said. "Nothing! I just wanted him out of my life." She looked down at her hands in her lap for a long moment. Then she smiled at him again. "Still angry, I guess. Well, anyway I did a part in *Miami Vice*, too, a few roles in local theater, and a low budget HBO movie nobody ever sees unless they're awake at 3 A.M."

"Really? What was the title? I'm awake at 3 A.M."

"I forgot. It was nothing."

"What did you play?"

"A schoolmistress." She didn't tell him it was a soft-porn movie and that she had to dry-hump a student on her desk. "It helped pay the rent and then I quit acting for good."

"A schoolmistress," he said, nodding. "I can see that. A lady like you."

"Why do you keep calling me that?"

"Does it bother you?"

"No. It just makes me sound old."

"Well, you sure aren't old."

"I'm older than you by a bit."

"So what?"

She laughed. "Not very gentlemanly," she said.

"What did you expect me to say?"

"I don't know. Maybe that I didn't look older than you."

"OK. You don't look older than me. Does that make you feel better?"

"No. It makes me feel foolish."

They were both silent for a moment, then he said, "Are you still acting?"

"No, I'm producing. Actually, not really producing. I'm just an assistant for this egomaniacal fag who owns a small theater. He writes, directs, and stars in his own plays. He was Madame Butterfly in the last. The role of his lifetime."

"What do you mean?"

"Don't you know the play?"

He shook his head, no. "I don't know plays. Or books either."

"You know movies. Gene Kelly and *Singin' In The Rain*."

"Yeh, well I watch TV late at night when I can't sleep. I never got into books and plays."

"That's a shame. You can learn a lot from them, especially plays."

"About what?"

"Life. People."

"I already know about life," he said. "Maybe too much. And most people don't interest me." He was silent a moment, then he said, "Is that where you learned about life? From plays?"

"You're making fun of me!"

"Am I?"

She exhaled a deep breath. "You know, it's tiring talking to you."

He shrugged. "Maybe I'm not an interesting guy."

"No. Not that. I mean, it's tiring for me. Guessing wrong all the time. It's the guessing, I think. It takes a lot out of you."

"I wouldn't know."

"No, you wouldn't, would you?" She smiled at him, and said, "Well, in *Madame Butterfly* this male actor plays a man pretending to be a woman to get this straight guy to fall in love with him."

He smiled, too. "I've been there."

"I'm sure."

"Yeh, gay guys come on to me a lot."

"And what do you do?"

"I let them know I'm not interested."

"How? By beating them up?"

"Why would I do that? They don't mean anything. Just taking a shot is all. Maybe it would piss me off if they pretended to be a woman, though. But they don't. I guess they only do that in plays, huh?"

"I'm sorry," she said. "That was a cruel thing to say."

"So, tell me. Does the straight guy ever find out his lover is a man?"

"Only at the end. It becomes a big scandal."

"Too bad. Madame Butterfly shoulda just played it straight. Told the guy from the gitgo."

"But he can't! There wouldn't be a play then."

He nodded. "I see. You mean, there wouldn't be a play about real life?"

"No, I guess there wouldn't, would there?"

"So, what else do you do for this fag who likes to dress up as a woman to seduce straight guys?"

"Mostly, I try to keep his fag snits under control so he doesn't scare off everyone on the set."

"You don't like your job very much."

"No. Do you like yours?"

"You mean, dancing?"

"You have another one?"

"Yeh. Dancing's just a sideline. I like the women."

"Don't you feel it's degrading?"

"Not for me. Not the way I do it. I do it so they'll appreciate me. Like you did." He waited. "You did, didn't you?"

She was silent for a moment, then she said, "Yes . . . yes, I did."

"Then it's worth it, isn't it?" She nodded. Then he said, "If you hate your job, why don't you go back to acting?"

"I'm too old."

"You don't believe that."

"No, I don't. It's a pose, I guess. It gives me an excuse."

"For what?"

"To act old, tired, sorry for myself. It's liberating, in a way, giving up." She laughed, a false laugh. "Self-pity can be very seductive."

"I wouldn't know."

The waitress was laying down their plates of food. Sheila was so famished she immediately began eating her eggs.

"What were you thinking?" he said. "Just now."

"Don't you know? You seemed to know everything I was thinking last night."

"Yeh, sometimes I do. It's a gift."

"A gift?"

"From my ancestors. I'm a Cherokee." He grinned. "A redskin hamster, Sol calls me." His grin faded. He said, "I don't believe all that redman's superstitious shit. But sometimes . . . yeh, I do know things and I don't know why." He raised his eyebrows. "This isn't one of those times."

"I was thinking about last night. What you said about me not being old."

"You aren't. You weren't old last night."

She looked down at her Bloody Mary and swirled her celery stalk. She saw herself looking up from between his legs with his cock in her mouth, his smooth, muscular, dark, hairless body. "So tell me," she said "what's it like being an Indian?"

"You mean, Native American. Indian is some Spanish bullshit name we don't accept."

"I'm sorry. Then Native American."

He glanced over her shoulder. "Another time, Sheila. We got company."

She turned in her chair to see a bald man with a big belly coming toward them. He had a goatee, a button-down collar shirt open to his navel, white tennis shorts, and three beepers on his hip. Sunlight glinted off his gold frame sunglasses, his gold necklaces nestled in his chest hair, his gold bracelets, his gold Rolex. He sat down with them.

"A day late and a dollar short, Solly," Bobby said.

"I had tings ta do," the man said. Sheila stifled a laugh. Nathan Detroit in gold chains. The man tossed a headfake at Sheila without looking at her. "Who's da broad?"

"I beg your pardon?" Sheila said.

"She's OK," Bobby said. "We can talk."

"It ain't us talkin' I'm thinkin'." Sol stared at Sheila without expression. She said nothing, but thought, should I laugh, or be scared?

"Sol!" Bobby said. "Stop playing fucking games and get to it."

Sol leaned toward Bobby across the table and began talking in a strange code that must be particular to men, Sheila thought, or maybe just these men.

"Reverend Jesse tossed me a little sumthin'," the bald man said. "I thought I'd toss it to you. I don't feature dealin' with no sandblasted hamster from Miami." He grinned. "I figure you and da spic have sumthin' in common, Bobby, both a yous being men of color how they say it dese days."

"I thought you Jews were the nigger-spic lovers, Solly." And then, "What's the product?" Sol glanced at Sheila.

"Why don't she take a walk on the beach, get her toes wet?"

"She likes her toes dry," Bobby said.

"You being led around by your dick again, Bobby?"

"My dick appreciates your concern, Solly. But he knows what he's doing."

The bald man shook his head. Sheila said, "Maybe I should go?"

Bobby looked at her. "Only if you want to, baby."

"I don't want to, Bobby."

"See, Solly. The lady wants to stay."

"I don't know, Bobby," Sol said. "She don't look too dumb, not like your usual strippers."

"Oh, I don't know, Solly. She can act pretty dumb. Can't you, baby?" Sheila looked at Sol without blinking, her lips slightly parted. "Scc!"

"She better be deaf, too."

"Excuse me?" Sheila said, wide-eyed, cupping her hand over her ear.

"It's your ass, Bobby." He lowered his voice again and leaned toward Bobby. "The spic needs a few pieces. Small stuff. CZs. AKs. That Israeli shit. They love that foreign shit, the spics. You tink day'd buy American, all dis country's done for them." He shook his head. "Says he already got his big stuff, SAMS, Stingers, from some raghead in Boca."

"So why does he need me and you?"

The waitress appeared at their table. She asked Sol for his order. "Just a vodka tonic, honey," he said. He waited until she left, then leaned close to Bobby again, and said, "He needs us because he can't buy the product in Miami. He's this big-deal fucking exile on the TV all the time screaming how him and his compatriots is gonna take back their fucking island paradise. Building an army, he says, a lotta fat old spics in camouflage out in the 'Glades, huffin' and puffin they don't get a heart attack, blasting gators with grenade launchers like they was Fidel. Fucking asshole calls so much attention to himself he can't even take a piss at Versailles without some ATF faggot holding his dick for him."

"So why doesn't *he* come up here to get his product?" Bobby said.

"You know how dem spics are, Bobby. Like the guineas in the Bronx. Hate to leave their stoop, their fucking exile paradise on Calle Ocho. Besides, a sandblasted hamster like him in Lauderdale, nothing but white people, him sniffing around for product, Jeez, he'd draw more ATF flies than he would in Miami. He needs a buyer. Someone knows his way around up here, got contacts. 'Preferably a white man,' he said."

The bald man grinned at Bobby. "Fucking joke, eh, Bobby? Redskin hamster like you makin' a buy for a sandblasted hamster from Havana." Sol glanced at Sheila. "What day call dat, honey?"

"Excuse me?" she said. Then, "Oh, I think you mean, irony."

"Dat's it, Bobby. Irony. You and him become asshole buddies, maybe he loan you some Stingers so's you can take back the reservation. Do it all over dinner at his hacienda. You and the broad here, she know some Spanish?"

"Her name is Sheila, Sol," Bobby said. "Sheila, this is Sol."

"Charmed, I'm sure," Sheila said. She reached out a limp hand. When Sol didn't take it, she took the tips of his fingers in hers and shook them. "I looove your pinky ring," she said. "And your manicure." She let go of his fingertips and held her hands, fingers spread, over the table. "I can't do anything with mine. Do you know a good manicurist?"

Sol stared at her, as if he couldn't tell if she was serious or putting him on, so he turned to Bobby and said, "There's no rush, Bobby. What da fuck, the guy's been in exile thirty-five years he can wait a few weeks. You call him, make a date, go to his house for dinner, maybe he'll roast ya a fuckin' pig, black beans and rice, that custard shit they like. . . ."

"Flan, I think you mean," Sheila said.

Sol looked at her. "What?"

"Flan. The Cuban custard. It's very. . . ."

"Who gives a shit?" Sol turned back to Bobby. "You go close to midnight, them spics eat late. It's in the Gables." He slid a folded piece of paper across the table. Bobby put it in his shorts' pocket without looking at it. "There's no number on the gate, Bobby, but you can't miss it. Big fucking concrete wall, razor wire on top make sure no one guesses the spic's up to no good. I told him to expect a call from Mr. Bobby Squared. The spics are big on respect. Mr., if it's a white guy, Señor if he's spic."

Sol waited for the waitress to put down his drink and leave, before he added, "One other thing, Bobby. Don't pack. He's fucking paranoid."

Sol glanced at Sheila.

"Very good, Sol," she said.

Sol smiled. "Like I said, par-a-noid. Drives this ten-ton Merc-600, bulletproof glass can take a direct hit from a bazooka not even scratch the paint. He says men in his position gotta fear assassination. Not a hit. Ass-ass-in-a-tion. Like he's Patrick Fucking Henry. Anyway, he's got these guats patrollin' the grounds with MAC 10s and these big fuckin' mutts like in *The Omen*, make a meal of The Hosh."

"Rottweilers," Sheila said.

"Whatever. Dog shit everywhere. I was you, Bobby, I'd wear my cowboy boots. And don't pack. They'll pat you down. They find a piece they'll be very pissed off. You don't wanna piss these guys off, Bobby."

Bobby nodded. "What's my end?"

"All of it. You always stood up for me." Sheila looked at the fat bald man with too much gold jewelery. He wasn't the wise guy now. He was Bobby's friend now. A Jewish gangster from Brooklyn and a Cherokee stripper from North Carolina. Unlike with women, Sheila thought, with men, opposites attract.

Sol was the wise guy again. "What da fuck you care how much? It'll be more than you make them old broads stuffin' bills down your dick."

Sheila's face got hot. Bobby just smiled. "Yeh, but it feels nice, Solly, those long manicured fingers copping a feel. You oughta try it, get your first hard-on. I could get you one of them gold lamé jobs you could stuff a sock in scare the old broads outta their minds."

Sheila stared at Bobby, amazed at how he had slipped into Sol's way of talking as if she were not there. He was a different person now. It surprised her a little, but she'd expected it. What she didn't expect was how annoyed she was over this talk of Bobby's stripping.

Sol was still talking. "The product'll cost ya seventy-five large. The spic'll give you a hunnert. You keep the change. One other thing, Bobby. You know there's only one guy up here deals in that much product."

"The Reverend Tom?" Bobby said. Sol nodded. "I heard of him."

"A fuckin' joke, eh? The two baddest-assed fuckers I ever heard of, Jesse and Tom, and they both call themselves Reverend."

"You think they've been ordained?" Bobby grinned.

"If they are, we're all in big fuckin' trouble. You ever met Rev. Tom?" Bobby shook his head, no. "He's fucking whacko, Bobby. I don't know who's worse, him, Jesse, or our spic friend from Mi-jam-ee. You watch your ass with him. His church, I heard, don't exactly go outta the way to minister to no redskin-hamsters."

"No kike gangsters either, I heard."

"That's a fucking fact. You better go through Machine Gun. He's got the Reverend's ear." Sol shook his head. "God knows why." Sol stood up. "I gotta go." He threw a hundred-dollar bill on the table.

Sheila smiled up at him with her 8x10 glossy smile. "It's been such a pleasure to meet you," she said.

"Yeh," Sol said. "We'll see." And he walked away.

"What a *charming* man!" Sheila said to Bobby.

Bobby laughed, and shook his head. "Yeh, Solly's a real charmer. He keeps getting better and better."

They paid the bill and left. As they were walking to Bobby's car in the parking lot, Sheila said, "Why did you let me hear all that?"

"You said you wanted to stay."

"You know what I mean."

"Maybe it was a test?"

"Did I pass?"

"I hope so."

"What if I didn't?"

"Then I could be in trouble."

Bobby drove her back to her apartment. Sheila was silent, beside him in the front seat, staring out her window. She was both frightened and excited. The frightened Sheila she knew. The excited Sheila was another woman she didn't know. She wondered how long that Sheila had been inside her. She wondered if that Sheila would ever completely come out. And if she did, who would she be?

"What's the matter, baby?" Bobby said.

"Is that what you called your stripper girlfriends?"

"Sometimes. Does it bother you?"

"I don't know yet. No one ever called me baby."

"There's a first time for everything."

"I know. 'Once, a philosopher. Twice, a pervert.'" Bobby looked across at her. "It's from a book, Bobby. A French philosopher."

"What'd he mean by pervert?"

"He meant, the first time you do something, whatever it is, it means you're curious. If you do it a second time it means you like it."

"Yeh, well, I guess it all depends what you like, huh?"

"Yes, it does." Then, after a moment, she said, "Bobby, what exactly does Sol do?"

"Sol? He's a good guy. A little rough, but a good guy."

"That's not what I asked. He's got three beepers on his hip for Crissakes!"

Bobby laughed. "Maybe he's a veterinarian."

Sheila arched her eyebrows and stared at him. "Bobby, you want to call me 'baby' you can answer a straight question."

"You're right. I'm sorry. . . . Me and Sol, well, we move things around."

"Around?"

"Yeh, like them bank couriers, only not exactly."

"A little more specific, please?"

"We move things from one person to another."

"What people?"

"People who got things and people who need things."

"What things?"

"Products."

"Guns?"

"Sometimes."

"What else?"

"Sometimes money."

"Drugs?"

"Not if I can help it."

He stopped his car in front of a small wood-frame carriage house set close to the road in a section of old, wood-frame, Key West cottages. He pointed to a faded-red Hundai in the driveway. "Is that your ride?" She nodded, looking at him, waiting. Finally, he said, "Are you satisfied?"

"For now."

4

BOBBY LOOKED AROUND HER TINY, ONE-ROOM APARTMENT. A SOFA BED. A small, black-and-white TV. Some mismatched plates and glasses. A closet filled with clothes. Pants suits. Summer dresses. Tailored skirts. Low heeled pumps. A single pair of jeans. There were no pictures of family, nothing personal, except, on one wall, three old, yellowed Playbills. He went over to them.

"Is this you?" he said, pointing to a name. Mrs. Sheila Mackenzie.

"Yes."

"I'll bet you were a good actress."

"Pretty good. My husband was a better actor though."

"What do you mean?"

"Nothing. Just, he was a lawyer."

"Yeh, I've known a few lawyers. I know what you mean."

"No you don't." She smiled. "I played Stella in that play ten years ago. Maybe now I could play Blanche."

"Is that supposed to be a joke?"

"You have to know the play. Blanche is older than Stella. A little crazy, sexually frustrated."

Bobby shook his head. "Well, that ain't you." He looked around the room and said, "Sheila, this isn't gonna make it. Pack your things. You're moving in with me." She looked at him. "Did you hear me?"

"I heard you."

"Well?"

"It's ridiculous, Bobby. You don't even know me."

"I know enough."

"I don't know you either."

"You know enough."

She shook her head, no, and sat down on her sofabed. "It's too soon, Bobby. I can't."

He flung the back of his hand at the barren room. "What? All this is too much to leave?"

"No. But it's mine. I don't have to answer to anyone for it."

"Listen. You won't ever have to answer to me. It doesn't work out, you can leave anytime. You think you'll never be able to find another mansion like this?"

She stared at him, her pale, blue eyes opened wide. "What is it, Bobby? Why do you want me?"

He stood over her, looking down at her. "I don't know, Sheila. I don't have a reason I can give you, make it nice and simple, easy for us both. I just know I want you close to me." She looked away from him.

"Listen," he said. "I gotta do some business. It'll take me maybe an hour. At least think about it. I come back, you're not packed, we'll just go out to dinner, that's all."

"I don't know. It's too much. I'm not like you."

"Yes, you are, Sheila. You just don't know it yet."

When he was gone, she was still sitting on her sofabed. She looked around the room to see what he had seen. She saw nothing except her impending old age. A comforting old age. No pressure. A kind of ease she could slip into like an old flannel nightgown on a snowy New

England night. With a fire blazing in the hearth, and a glass of wine. Alone in an old house.

She sat there for an hour, not moving, staring, but not seeing. She was old, and scared, too old and scared to change her life. She had no reason to change her life. People had to have a reason to change their lives. Or did they? Maybe some people change their lives because they don't have a reason not to.

Bobby drove west on Sunrise, toward Black Town. He crossed the railroad tracks at Dixie. He saw the McDonald's where the nigger kid whacked out three employees in broad daylight. He cleaned out the safe, went home, and smoked up all the score with his momma. When the weed ran out, his momma put him on a bus to Shreveport. The next day she ratted him out for the $100,000 reward. Bobby shook his head. How can Jesse deal with them? A redneck Texas farmboy with a posse of rasters and coons. Some people, you could never tell which way they'd jump. Like Sheila. He didn't know what she'd do. He only knew he needed her, he wanted her. It was getting old, all those dumb strippers with hard, fake tits. Dangerous, too. They took his mind off business. Look at me, Bobby! Notice me, Bobby! It was fucking exhausting. They were like pit bulls. He thought dumb chicks would be easier to handle. It was just the fucking opposite. Dumb chicks needed all your attention. You had to baby-sit them, keep them happy because they didn't know how to make themselves happy. Not like Sheila. She could take care of herself. Him, too. She was smart, smarter than him, he knew that much. Smart enough to know she could trust him. He knew it last night when they were in bed. She started slow, scared, protecting herself. Then he brought her around, watching her get into it, liking it, then loving it, not thinking now, outside herself, trusting him. So what if she didn't know things. She could learn. She wanted to learn. He could tell last night in bed how she listened to him when he whispered, "Relax, baby. Don't think. Just do it." And she did. So what if she wasn't a mechanic. He'd had enough of them to last a lifetime. They did it all. They'd hang from the chandelier, all moaning how they loved it, couldn't get enough, shit like that, and still they were lousy fucks. Some of them were even fucking experts, with little tricks, like that twenty-year-old chick from Detroit, who cradled his balls in her silky black hair while she sucked his dick. Where'd she learn that, Bobby thought, even while she was doing it? That was the fucking point. You could never lose yourself in it with them because they never lost themselves in it. They made you be conscious because they were always conscious. They didn't love it, didn't even like it, which was why they'd do anything. What difference did it make?

He saw Jesse's hand-painted sign up ahead. Rev. Jesse's Church of the Good Christian Barbecue. Bobby pulled his black SHO into the dirt parking lot. He parked alongside a rusted-out Cutlass Supreme with Cragar mags and a coat hanger holding up the exhaust to the rear bumper. He reached under his seat and pulled out his CZ-85. He racked the slide, lowered the hammer with his thumb, and stuck the pistol into the back waistband of his pants. He pulled out his muscle T-shirt to cover it, then got out and walked toward a line of niggers at the barbecue stand. An open air grill. A long table to cut the meat. A cash register. And behind it all, Jesse's trailer.

Bobby walked to the head of the line where a nigger was placing his order with the fat nigger kid who worked the register. He looked like that nigger actor in *Good Morning, Vietnam*. Jesse's two raster hitters were curved over the flaming grill, not even noticing the heat, cooking ribs and chicken. They had stoned, hooded eyes, dreadlocks, and long, skinny bodies. They looked like snakes standing on their tails.

Bobby stepped in front of the guy placing his order and said to the fat one, "Tell Jesse, I'm here."

A voice behind him called out, "Heh, home, whatda fuck you think you're doin'?" Bobby waited. Another voice said, "Fuckin' blond faggot!," but not so loud.

The fat kid said, "I ain't your messenger boy."

Bobby leaned close to him. "No. I heard you're Jesse's boy. Now go tell him Bobby's here."

The kid shuffled off, grumbling, and went into the trailer. He came out a few seconds later and gestured with his head toward the door. Bobby went inside. Jesse was seated behind his desk.

"Bobby Squared!" said Jesse with a big smile. "My main man." He reached out a meaty hand and shook Bobby's hand.

Bobby looked at his hand. "Jesus, Jesse! You got grease all over my hand."

Jesse tossed him a piece of paper towel. "Sorry, Bobby. I forgot how fastidious ya'll are." Bobby wiped the grease off his hand and tossed the crumpled towel back at Jesse. He was hugely fat, dressed in black, his black shirt buttoned at the neck, black pants, black pointy-toed boots. He had tiny, yellow eyes, grayish pockmarked skin, and a greasy, slicked-back, Elvis pompadour. He smelled of charred meat and sweet sauce.

"I don't know how you stand it, Jesse. All these coons."

The Reverend shook his head. "Bobby, Bobby, where's your Christian spirit, boy? You make the Reverend sad, man. You, of all people. A man of color hisself."

"Yeh, Jesse, well, it ain't the color I'm talkin' about."

"They can be made to behave, Bobby. You jes gotta remember they's all God's chilluns, jes like you and me. And that's how I treat 'em. Like chilluns." The Reverend laughed, the rolls of fat spilling over his shirt collar and his belt buckle shaking like Jell-O. When he stopped laughing, he said, "Now, the Rasters, Robert, they're a little more difficult. They can be very unpleasant instruments of God's divine plan if you don't know how to handle them."

"And how's that?"

Jesse grinned. "Keep 'em stoned all day and they'll do anythin' I ask."

"I heard," Bobby said. Then, "You said you had a little something for me."

"Bidness! Bidness! It's always bidness with you, Bobby. Jes like a white man." He laughed again, a mean, rednecked fag from the North Texas panhandle. Then he said, "You like Jamaica, Bobby? Lay in the sun a few days, get yerself even darker, drink a little Red Stripe, find you a nice local girl, not too dark, jes a high yeller, and then meet a friend a mine who'll give you a little package to get through MIA customs."

"I told you I don't move that kinda product."

Jesse shook his head. "Bobby, ya'll didn't let me finish. It ain't that kinda product. Jes a hundred large. You get it to me, there's a ten spot in it for ya. Including expenses, of course."

"How will I know your friends?"

"You won't. They'll know you, distinctive man like yerself. You jes hang by the hotel pool until they contact you." He stopped smiling now. "Oh, and Robert, I need it quickly, in four weeks. And one other thing. It would not please me, Robert, if you returned without the money." He smiled again. "Then ya'll'd hafta talk to my rasters, Bobby, and I don't think ya'll find that a pleasing experience."

"I'll bring it back, don't worry."

"Good, Robert." He reached into his desk drawer, took out an envelope, and tossed it to Bobby. "Expense money." Bobby stuffed the envelope into his shorts' back pocket. "Don't wanna count it?" Bobby just looked at him. "Trust me, eh, Bobby? Jes like I trust you."

Bobby turned and opened the door. He heard the Reverend call out to him, "Take yerself some sweet potato pie, Bobby. Tell Reeshaad it's on me." Bobby glanced back over his shoulder at the fat man. "It's an acquired taste, Bobby. Like corn meal."

Bobby could hear the fat man's laughter all the way back to his car.

He saw her the minute he turned the corner onto her street. She was standing up ahead, by the side of the road, three suitcases beside her. When he got closer he saw she had changed into a white T-shirt and jeans. He stopped the car beside her. She opened his back door, threw in her bags, and got in the front beside him. She threw her arms around his neck and kissed him, hard, on the mouth. Then she pulled back, stared at him through narrowed, blue eyes, and said, "You're late! Don't ever let it happen again!" Bobby couldn't tell if she was acting or not, until she began to laugh. Then he laughed, too.

Just before they reached his apartment, Sheila said, "What about my car?"

"We'll trade it in on something nicer."

"But it's not worth anything."

"You got insurance?"

"Yes. More than it's worth."

"Good. I'll have somebody make it go away."

She looked at him. "Just like that?"

"It's already done."

They dropped her bags in his living room and stripped out of their clothes and stepped into the shower. They soaped each other's bodies under the cool spray. She had faint, grayish stretch marks at her belly. She pressed the flat of her palms against his chest and then turned from him. She pushed her ass against his cock, bent half over, and pressed her palms against the shower wall for support.

They finished in bed, soaking the sheets, and fell asleep as Hoshi leaped lightly onto the bed, settling into a ball at their feet.

Sheila woke in darkness. Bobby was still asleep. She got out of bed and stood over him and Hoshi. She smiled at them, then began walking through the apartment, looking. There were some glass and chrome tables, a white leather sofa, a Nagle print on the living-room wall. A stylish Art Deco-looking woman smoking a cigarette through a long cigarette holder, the wide brim of her hat pulled down over one eye. She looked for photographs, books, CDs, anything, but there was nothing. Just the sterile, newly furnished apartment of a man with no past. She went to the kitchenette and opened the refrigerator. A can of Bustello Cuban coffee. A few cans of Coors light beer. A bottle of Carolina mountain spring water. There was a bottle of Jim Beam on the counter. She went back to the living room and sat down on the white leather sofa. The room was dark except for the moonlight that slanted in through the sliding glass doors that led out to his deck over the canal. She looked around again. It was like some futuristic monk's cell. There was nothing of him here. Or maybe there was. Only she couldn't see it yet.

She carried her bags into the bedroom to his dresser. She opened the top drawer, pushed his things aside, his underwear, socks, handkerchiefs, and began laying her things in the drawer, her silk panties, bras, lacy handkerchiefs, panty hose. She opened the second drawer, filled with his shorts and T-shirts. She picked up a pair of his shorts, pressed them to her face, and smelled them. Then she put them back. She felt something hard and bulky under his shorts. She withdrew a pistol. She held it between her thumb and forefinger by the handle. It was heavy, shiny black. She tried to read what was printed on the side. *CZ-85, 9 mm Luger, product of Czechoslovakia.* She remembered Bobby and Sol talking at the Mark. How it had excited her. But this made it more real, dangerous, scary. She put the pistol back and shut the drawer.

She went into the bathroom with her toiletries and perfumes and put on the light. She opened the mirrored medicine cabinet over the sink and put her cosmetics alongside his shaving cream, razor, toothbrush. She picked up his toothbrush, looked at it, then put toothpaste on it. After she finished brushing her teeth and rinsing out her mouth, she put the toothbrush back and closed the cabinet door. She saw her face in the mirror under the harsh bathroom light. The flecks of gray in her brown hair. The lines on her forehead, at the corners of her eyes, the thin stitches around her full lips. She had a little loose skin under her jaw.

She raised an arm, held it suspended, and shook it. Her triceps muscle wobbled. She stared at herself, a good-looking woman once, now aging, with a much younger woman's blue eyes and big breasts. A cruel reminder.

It was over two years ago. She was six months pregnant. Her small breasts had swollen to twice their size. Her husband hadn't wanted children, but then everyone at the school began to talk, and so he relented. She was six months pregnant, when, on a whim, she decided to pack her things for the hospital. It was a stupid thing to do, silly, really, but it made her feel close to her unborn son.

She went through her dresser drawers, pulling out things, folding them carefully, and placing them in her overnight bag. When she held up her Cambrick hankies, trimmed with French lace, she thought, no, not to the hospital where she might lose them.

She put them back. An inconsequential act. She went to her husband's drawer. She opened it and searched her hand under his underwear for one of his hankies. She felt something stiff and withdrew an envelope. It was sealed. She went to put it back, but something stopped her. She pried open the glued flap. She pulled out the first photograph and stared at it. Her husband with another man's cock in his mouth. She pulled out another, then another, and another. They were all the same, only different, different poses, different acts, but the same two men, a stranger and her husband.

She felt the convulsions almost immediately. The pain in her stomach. The vomit in her throat. The beginning of her miscarriage. Her swollen breasts never went back down. They stayed as big and firm as they were now as she stared at herself in the bathroom mirror, tears streaming down her face.

She sat down on the toilet seat. She could not stop crying, but without a sound. The bathroom door opened.

"Baby! What's the matter?" Bobby said. He knelt down in front of her and put his hands on her shaking arms.

Her body was racked with silent convulsions, and then the sound finally came out, gasping, hysterical sobs. "Bobby! I can't! Look at me!"

His hands squeezed her arms hard now, the pressure distracting her from her sobs. "Stop it!" he said. "Stop it!" She was only half-breathing, half-sobbing now. "You can do it, baby!" he said. "I know it."

"I don't know, Bobby!" she said between her sobs. "I'm afraid!"

"Trust me! You can! Just trust me!"

She was nodding now, her sobs subsiding, and then, she pulled her arms from his grasp and grabbed her hair with both hands. "Look at it, Bobby!" she screamed. "What about this?"

He smiled at her. "That? That's nothing, baby. I got just the girl for you."

5

THE GIRL AT THE BEAUTY SALON WAS CHEWING GUM AND CHATTERING WHILE she worked on Sheila's nails.

"So, you're Bobby's new girl," she said. "An improvement over the others, I must say. I told him, I said, Bobby, when you gonna grow up, get outta your stripper phase, find yourself somebody your own age."

Sheila held her hand limp over the table while the girl worked. "Actually," Sheila said, "I'm a bit older than Bobby."

"Not so's you could notice, honey. You just ain't done nuthin' with yourself until now."

"You've known Bobby for a long time?" Sheila said.

The girl nodded, smacking her gum. "We go back a long ways, me and Bobby. Solly, too. You met him?"

"Yes. It was a real experience."

"I'll bet. Solly's a little tough to take at first you don't know him. But he's a good guy. We had a thing once. Solly likes little girls."

The girl was maybe five feet tall, ninety-five pounds, with dark, olive skin and a big, slashing, red mouth. When Sheila walked into the salon, the girl introduced herself as Lucrezia Santucci, and stuck out her hand. She had two rings on every finger, including her thumbs, blood-red nails over an inch long, and jangling bracelets up both arms. Bobby had told Sheila in the car, "You'll like her. A dark, little guinea chick lathers on makeup with a trowel. But she's OK. A good chick. I usta do some things with her husband before he went away."

"What things?" Sheila said.

"Things."

"Where'd he go away to?"

"The slam."

Now the girl was hunched over Sheila's hand, her brows furrowed in concentration, smacking her gum as she worked.

"You actually 'dated' Sol?" Sheila said.

"Yeh, when my husband was away. Solly always treated me like a lady. You gotta understand Solly. He's like most men. They're not like us, honey. They say the opposite of what they mean. Like the time I was sick in bed with the flu. Real bad. Solly comes over with all these pills and shit, who knows how he got 'em, and tosses 'em onto the bed. 'Maybe now you'll get outta that fuckin' bed ya lazy bitch,' he says." She looked up at Sheila and smiled. "It was the sweetest thing."

"I'll bet."

The girl went back to Sheila's nails. She was dressed entirely in fringed suede. "Like a fucking squaw," Bobby had said when he dropped Sheila off at the salon. She wore a fringed vest, fringed miniskirt, six-inch pumps, and feathered earrings.

"So, you were the one who told Bobby he should find someone his own age," Sheila said.

"Yep. I told him, 'Bobby, find yourself a straight lady.'"

"You said that? A lady."

"Uhuh. Bobby listens to me."

Sheila smiled and settled back into her chair while the little girl worked. After a few moments, she said, "Lucrezia, that's a beautiful name. How do you spell it?"

"Just the way it sounds."

"Of course." Then, she said, "I love your outfit. Where did you find it?"

"You do?" The little girl looked up and smiled. Then she went back to Sheila's nails. "Well, one day I was just scrimmaging around the backskirts of this thrift shop, you know, Bitch and Barter, the two fags own it in the Gateway, and there it was."

"You mean 'rummaging'."

"That's what I said."

When Sheila had walked into the salon the little girl had stared at her through her narrowed, dark eyes. Sheila had said, "Bobby said you might be able to do something with my hair. I don't know what. Nothing too drastic. What do you think?"

The girl picked up a strand of Sheila's hair in her hand and looked at it. Then she made a smacking sound with her tongue and shook her head.

"What? What is it?"

"You let yerself go, honey. But I can bring you back."

"Nothing drastic," Sheila said.

"Trust me, honey."

Sheila watched her in the mirror, cutting and snipping, Sheila's hair getting shorter and shorter, until finally the little girl stopped.

"There," she said. Sheila's hair was so short it stood up like spring grass. Sheila stared at her short hair, her mouth open, speechless. The girl said, "Don't panic, honey. I ain't done yet. Too much gray. *Not* attractive. Gimme an hour."

She began bleaching Sheila's new haircut, which she referred to as "Your spikey do," and then put Sheila under a dryer. When Sheila's hair was dry, the little girl unwrapped the tinfoil from it, and then turned Sheila's chair so that she faced the mirror.

"There!" the little girl said. "It's you."

Sheila stared at her image in the mirror. Her short, spikey hair was now ash-blond. It wasn't her. Not the her she'd known all her life. It was someone else. That strange new woman who was coming out of her. Sheila kept staring at this new woman. She was beginning to know her. She was younger than Sheila, maybe late thirties. Harder, too, but in a sexy way.

"I like it," Sheila finally said. "Yes, I like it."

"I ain't done yet, honey. Now your nails."

She led Sheila into the back room to work on her nails that she was now finishing. "There you go," she said. "Finished."

Sheila held up her hands, fingers spread, in front of her eyes. She stared at the inch-long, acrylic nails painted a blood-red. "You don't think . . . maybe . . . it's a bit much," Sheila said.

"What?" the little girl said. "They're perfect." She held up her own fingers. "Just like mine."

Sheila sighed. "If you say so." She got up to leave. "My nails are still wet," she said. "Could you get my wallet out of my purse. Take whatever you need."

The girl rummaged—scrimmaged—through Sheila's purse, took out her wallet, slipped out five twenties, and then put the wallet back.

"Maybe I should have your card," Sheila said. "In case I break a nail."

"Sure, honey. You can call me at home anytime." She took her own purse, a suede, fringed saddlebag, and began pulling things out of it. Her makeup case, packages of gum, lipstick, a silver-plated pistol, her wallet. She took her card out of her wallet and put it in Sheila's purse.

"Is that yours?" Sheila said, pointing to the gun.

The girl looked at it. "Who else's?" she said. "A girl's gotta take care of herself, ain't that right?" She held the gun out for Sheila.

"No, thank you. My nails are still wet."

The girl shrugged and put the gun back into her purse.

"What kind is it?" said Sheila. No, not Sheila. The other woman.

"Smith & Wesson Ladysmith. Nine millimeter. Eight in the clip, one in the chamber. CorBons. Ninety-four percent one-shot stopping power says Evan Marshall in *Guns and Ammo*"

"Really?"

"I got a nice little leather holster, too, you know, when I'm wearing a jacket. Fits right on my hip so's I don't have to waste time scrimmaging around for it in my saddlebag."

"Of course," Sheila said.

"You should ask your old man to get you one. A piece, I mean, honey. The business he's in."

"You know about his business?"

"He ain't told you?"

"Well, he told me he moves things around from one person to another."

The little girl laughed. "That's just like Bobby. A man of few words, ain't he?"

"He doesn't seem to like to talk about himself much."

"Naw. Not his past, anyway. Something about his Indian shit bothers him. He don't wanna tell me, I don't ask."

"There's only one thing I don't understand. What is it between him and Sol? I mean, what makes them so close? They're so different."

Lucrezia looked at her. "Don't kid yourself, honey. They ain't so different."

"But Sol . . . I mean . . . it's obvious. He's a gangster."

Lucrezia laughed. "And what do ya think Bobby is? A stripper? Listen, honey, him and Sol been partners for years. I ain't seen nobody in their business trust each other like they do. It goes back to when Bobby came outta the mountains to Lauderdale in his twenties. He was real raw then. But Sol liked it Bobby didn't say shit. You think he don't say much now, you shoulda known him then. He usta go to Bootlegger's for the Hot Bod contest where all the strippers hung out. He'd stand off by himself, never saying a word, drinking his beer outta a long neck bottle."

She shook her head and smiled. "He looked like a real redneck. Straw cowboy hat, black ponytail, snap-button shirt, jeans, scuffed pointy-toed boots. Then, overnight, that Bobby was gone."

"What do you mean, 'gone'?"

"Gone, honey, like in 'vanished.' Nobody seen him since. The next Saturday at Bootlegger's there was this muscle-beach-lookin' dude. Blond ponytail. Hawaiian shirt. O.P. shorts. Flip-flops. Drinkin' a Cuba Libre. Rappin' with the chicks, introducin' himself now. 'Hi, baby. My name is Robert Roberts.' Then that smile of his. You know it. The little pause, and then, 'But my friends call me Bobby Squared.'"

"That's not his real name?"

"You kiddin'? You didn't know. Baby, your old man is Robert Red-feather off the reservation in Cherokee, North Carolina."

Before Sheila left, Lucrezia went over to her cutting chair. She returned with a bottle of bleach. "On the house," she said. "It's the stuff I used on your hair."

"Oh, thank you," Sheila said. "But I'd rather not take any chances myself. If I need a touch-up I'll just call you."

The little girl put both hands on her hips and stared at Sheila. "Honey," she said. "It ain't for your *head*. It's for your bush. Make you look like a *real* blonde."

"Oh! Of course." Sheila tried to smile at the girl. "I'm afraid I couldn't, though. I mean. . . ."

The girl flapped a limp hand at Sheila. "Trust me, honey. Men love a nice, neat, blond trim. Ain't you ever seen *Basic Instinct*?"

Bobby picked her up in front of the salon. Sheila slid in beside him, and said, "What do you think?" He looked at her, frowning. "Oh, Bobby! *Please!* Don't tell me!"

Finally, he smiled. "I love it," he said. "But I got just one question for you. You think maybe it means something I got a ponytail and you got a crew cut?"

She laughed and hugged him. "Thank God! I was worried." She told him about Lucrezia while he drove. "'Just the way it sounds,' she said. I was afraid to ask her how to spell Santucci."

"Yeh, she's a piecea work. But don't underestimate her, baby. A very tough little chick. She did some things with me and her husband not many chicks could do."

"Like what?" Bobby didn't answer her. "She carries a gun in her purse, Bobby. Did you know that?" He nodded. "She said you should get me one the business you're in." He said nothing. "You think I need a gun, Bobby?"

He shrugged. "Someday. If you want one."

"Did you get all your girls a gun?"

He looked straight ahead. "No. I never got that close to them."

"Are you close to me, Bobby?"

"What do you think?"

"Then why won't you tell me who you are?"

"You mean, who I was, don't you? What difference does it make? That's over with. It don't affect me and you. All you gotta know is what I am now. To you. That should be enough." He looked across at her. "Is it?"

She nodded. "Yes, Bobby."

"The less you know about my past, the better it is for you, Sheila."

"You're protecting me, then?"

"Not only you."

6

SHEILA WOKE ALONE IN BED. SHE CRIED OUT, "BOBBY!" HOSHI LEAPED UP AT her feet and began to growl. Bobby appeared in the bathroom doorway. "Oh, baby!" she said. "I had this terrible dream! You were gone."

"It was just a dream," he said. "I'm right here."

"Don't you believe in dreams, Bobby?"

"Not if they can hurt me."

Sheila sat up and stroked Hoshi behind the ears until he stopped growling. "It's all right, Hosh," she said. "I'm sorry." The dog settled back down, curled at her feet. "Why are you dressed, Bobby?" she said. He was wearing a yellow Hawaiian shirt with green watermelons on it, his good jeans, and his ostrich-skin cowboy boots.

"Gotta hustle, baby. It's almost eleven. Gotta be in the Gables by midnight."

She smiled at him. "You mean, we don't have time?"

"Not now. Business first."

She got out of bed, stretched luxuriantly in front of him, trying to be seductive, acting at first, then really feeling it. "You sure?" He nodded. "Oh, well. Where are we going?"

"Just me. I gotta see the spic, Medina, about the product me and Sol discussed."

"Why not me?" she said, pouting, acting.

"I don't want you mixed up in this. Medina's a bad dude. I don't want him to know you."

She went over to their dresser drawers, bent down, showing him her bare ass, opened the bottom drawer, and stood up to face him with a brown wig on her head. She spread her arms wide, like an actress accepting applause, and smiled. "Tra-la!" The wig was swept up in the back into a bun. It made her look older again, more severe, like she did the night Bobby first met her. "What do you think?" she said. "Can I go?" He hesitated. "Bobby, it's your business then it's mine, too."

"You're the boss." He went back into the bathroom. "Wear something loose, baby. A jumpsuit, pleated. And a panty girdle if you got one."

"What?" She stood in the bathroom doorway, hands on hips, her back arched, tucking in her stomach. "You think I need a girdle, Bobby?"

"Tonight you do."

They drove south on I-95. Sheila stared silently out her window. Finally, Bobby said, "What's the matter?"

"Nothing!" she snapped, not looking at him. Then, turning toward him, she said, "I'm sorry, Bobby. It's not your fault." She looked down at herself dressed in a beige silk jumpsuit. "It's the panty girdle. I don't even know why I kept it. Maybe as a reminder. To punish myself." She told him about her husband, ex-husband, the photographs, the miscarriage. He listened, staring straight ahead. "That's why I can never have children," she said. "That's why my breasts are so big. They never went down after I was pregnant. My stomach stayed bloated, too, like I was still pregnant. 'Filled with fluids,' the doctor said. He made me wear a tampon and this girdle for three months. 'To press out the fluids,' he said. That's what he called it, 'the fluids.' I lost it. I began screaming at him, 'Fluids, asshole! That's my son leaking out of me!'" She was silent now.

"I'm sorry, Sheila. I didn't mean. . . ."

She put her hand on his thigh. "That's all right, Bobby. You didn't know. Besides, that's all behind me now." They passed the Miami skyline, the city's glass skyscrapers illuminated eerily by pastel-colored lights, rose and aqua and pale green, like a fairy-tale city. "I am curious, though." she said. "Why the girdle?"

He reached under his seat with one hand, and withdrew a small silvery-looking pistol. He handed it to her. "Stick this in the front of your girdle."

She looked at the little gun but didn't touch it. "What do I need this for?" she said.

"Nothing, maybe. You ever see that movie, *True Romance*?" She shook her head, no. "There's this kid in it, he's going into a drug sale, and as he sticks a snubby magnum into his belt, he says, 'It's better to have a gun and not need it, then need a gun and not have it.'" He glanced at her. "You gonna take it?"

She took the gun from him. The colored lights of the passing city made it look translucent. "It *is* pretty," she said. "Sooo tiny. It doesn't seem real."

"It's real, all right. Seecamp, .32 acp, chrome-plated, six in the clip, one in the chamber. You just pull the trigger, it'll do the rest."

She unbuttoned her jumpsuit to her navel, stuck the little gun into the front of her girdle. "Oh, it's cold!" She smiled, moved her hips seductively. "Feels good, though."

Bobby shook his head, grinning. "You're something, baby."

When they got off I-95, onto U.S. 1 heading south, the road was darker, without the thruway lights. Sheila stared out of the blacked-out windows of Bobby's SHO. "Jeez, Bobby. You can barely see out of these windows."

"Yeh. And you can't see in, either." He turned left toward Coral Gables, the expensive section, near the ocean. He slowed the car, pulled out Sol's piece of paper, and squinted at the numbers on it. Then he glanced at the numbers on the houses. Sprawling Mediterranian mansions with mission-tile roofs and English Tudors outlined in dark wood. They had lush, tropical grounds and wrought-iron gates. The dark street was lined with royal palms and cypress trees dripping with Spanish moss that hung over the road so that it seemed they were driving through a covered bridge. A soft breeze blew in from the ocean, rustling the big leaves of the royal palms that reflected white in the moonlight.

"We're getting close," Bobby said. Sheila looked out her window at the long driveways that led to parked Mercedes-Benzes, Rolls-Royces, Ferraris, and BMWs. The cars and the houses and the lush grounds were all illuminated by landscape lights.

"You ever fire a gun?" Bobby said.

"No."

"It doesn't matter. At dinner you sit by me. Things start to go bad, you'll know. I'll tap you under the table with my boot. You excuse yourself, go to the ladies' room, powder your nose, take the .32 outta your girdle, put it in your purse. You come back, put the purse under the table near your feet. A few minutes later, you drop your napkin, something, reach under the table, put the .32 in my boot." He glanced at her. "Think you can do that?"

"I think so."

"You sure?"

"I'm sure."

A few minutes later, Bobby muttered, "Jesus!" He stopped the car in front of a towering concrete wall, maybe 12 feet high, topped with razor wire. "You think, maybe, this is it?"

He announced himself at the call box. The big, wrought-iron gate swung open. He drove slowly up the long drive, past shadows moving about in the darkness amid the palms and hibiscus and bougainvillea.

Bobby stopped the car at the front door. There were no lights on around it. Two men, cradling Uzis, stood guard. One of them held a Rottweiler straining at a leash. The one with the dog hurried to Sheila's door and opened it. She reached out her hand for him but he didn't take it. As she stepped out, the dog sniffed her feet, up her legs, smelling Hoshi's scent. The dog began to growl low in his throat. Sheila stood over him, looked down with her blue eyes gone cold, now. She reached down a hand to pet the dog. The dog slunk back, began to whimper. She petted him on the forehead. "Nice pooch," she said.

The other man followed Bobby with his eyes as he got out. He motioned with his head for Bobby to come over to him. He gestured up with his Uzi. Bobby raised his hands over the head. The man patted him down while the other one searched Sheila's handbag. A light went on over the big, hand-carved, wooden door. Then it opened. A pudgy little man in a white linen suit stood in the light of the doorway. He had tiny feet in shiny, black, patent-leather Guccis. His long black hair glistened with grease, like patent leather. It was combed straight back from his soft, pink, round face that looked polished. He had the big, dark eyes of a cruel child.

"Señor Esquared," the man said, smiling. "Señor Rogers told me much about you."

"Señor Rogers?" Bobby said.

The man's smile faded. "Señor Esol Rogers, your associate."

"Oh, yes. Señor Rogers. He told me great things about you, too, Señor Medina."

The man fluttered his eyelashes and nodded. Then he glanced at Sheila. The man who had searched her bag was now patting her down. He ran his hands down her back. The dog on the leash was straining back from Sheila. Medina frowned at the scared dog, then said something in Spanish. The man yanked his hand from Sheila's back.

"Please, excuse the precautions, Señorita," Medina said. "A man in my position, . . ." he shrugged.

"You're too kind, Señor," Sheila said, flashing her 8x10 glossy smile. "But, of course, it's Señora. Señora Sheila Doyle." Bobby looked at her. Doyle? Rogers? Jesus!

Sheila reached out her hand. Medina took it in his fingers and kissed the back of it. He held her fingers close to his face for a long moment, studying her long, blood-red nails, and then he let his eyes roam over her body. He said something in Spanish to his men. A thin smile crossed their lips.

"Gracias, Señor Medina," Sheila said. "Por los bellos complimentos."

"You speak my native tongue, Señora?"

"Un poquito." Sheila wiggled her fingers in front of her face.

Medina looked from her to Bobby and then back to her again. "And you are? . . ."

She smiled. "I am Señor Squared's associate also."

He nodded. "Of course. Come in. Come in. Welcome to my humble compasino home." He held the door open for them. Bobby went inside. Sheila bent down to pet the scared dog. "You have a way with dogs," Medina said.

"Yes. You just have to let them know who's the master." She walked past him and felt a hand brush her ass. Medina followed her, grinning, then glancing one last time at his cowering dog. He muttered under his breath.

Bobby was looking over the foyer. An original Botero on one wall. A gold-gilt mirror on the other. Two security cameras high on the walls at each end.

Medina moved ahead of them into the living room, his tiny heels clicking against the white tile floor. Sheila whispered in Bobby's ear, "That's the only Spanish I know."

Bobby whispered back. "Yeh, but now the little bastard thinks we know Spanish."

The living room was overstuffed with expensive, but gaudy, Mediterranian furniture. A lavender sofa. Two pink armchairs. A heavy, scarred, antique, dark wood coffee table. Medina pointed to the coffee table. "Fourteenth-century Spanish." he said, smiling. "The Inquisition."

"It's lovely," Sheila said. There was Lladro everywhere. China. Figurines. Ashtrays. Spanish kitsche.

Medina gestured with his arm toward an oil painting hanging over the fireplace. "My wife, Lucinda," he said. "Beautiful, no? We have been sweethearts since childhood in Havana."

"She's beautiful," said Bobby. The woman looked about thirty-five, heavily made up, a puff of pinkish-blond hair, like a halo, surrounding her pretty, small-featured face that wouldn't age well.

Medina opened a sliding-glass door and gestured for them to step outside. Sheila followed Bobby again, and again, felt Medina's hand on her ass, not brushing it now, squeezing her cheek. They stepped outside into a warm, humid evening. There was an outdoor bar alongside a heart-shaped swimming pool. A woman was sitting at the bar, nursing a drink. She looked up, wide-eyed, unblinking. She was twenty years older and thirty pounds heavier than her portrait. She looked like a plump pigeon in her flowing, pink kaftan.

"My wife, Lucinda," Medina said. Sheila flashed her 8x10 glossy smile. Bobby bowed slightly and shook the woman's soft, white hand. Lucinda gave them both a quick, nervous, little smile that vanished, but said nothing. A Nicaraguan bartender in white served them drinks.

"Cuba Libres for everyone!" said Medina. "Si?"

"Si," Bobby said. When they all had their drinks, Bobby raised his glass and said, "Cuba Libre!" They raised their glasses and clicked them, except Lucinda, who just sat there, nursing her drink, looking terrified.

Another servant in white appeared with a tray of caviar and crackers.

Medina snapped something in Spanish. One of the servants hovering in the darkness hurried inside and returned with a long box. Medina opened the box and showed it to Bobby and Sheila. Inside was an exact replica of an Uzi machine gun, except it was carved out of ivory.

"Worth maybe forty thousand dollars," said Medina, proudly. "My good friends from the Mossad gave it to me. In gratitude for my assistance."

"And what assistance was that?" Sheila said. Bobby glanced at her.

Medina smiled. "A little matter of a Hamas terrorist. He surfaced in Miami, trying to buy Semtex. Very foolish. Poof!" Medina wiped his palms as if he'd just performed a magic trick.

"It's beautiful," Sheila said. "So intricate."

"Yes, it is," said Medina. "But at times, a patriot needs more than mere artifacts, no, Señora?"

Sheila smiled and nodded.

"Come Señor Esquared. Let the women talk while I show you the grounds."

Bobby and Medina walked off into the darkness, leaving the two women alone at the bar. Bobby glanced back to see Sheila, smiling, trying to make conversation. The plump woman just nodded her head, like one of those fake birds dipping its head for water.

"I have a very Cuban wife," Medina was saying as they walked across the huge expanse of lawn. "I still live a very Cuban life, even here, in exile. I still go to mass every morning, take communion, as I did with my father when I was a boy in Havana. Before that fucking bandit destroyed my country."

He made a sweeping gesture with one arm to point out the six royal palms planted on the grounds. "For the six provinces of Cuba," he said, just as he stepped in something. "Aaaiieee! Fucking dog shit!" He danced aside and began wiping his shoe in the grass. He looked around as if for someone to blame. Finally, he calmed down.

"Come, Señor Esquared, I want to show you something. He led Bobby to a six-car garage and pushed a button. The door rolled up and a light went on. Bobby stared at the beautifully restored, lipstick-red, 1957 Cadillac Coupe de Ville convertible with white leather upholstery.

"Is beautiful, no?" Medina said.

"Very beautiful," Bobby said.

The little man went over to the car and ran his hand along the fender. "It's the same model I used to drive through the streets of Havana. I found this one and restored it myself. A hobby of mine, mechanical things. It took me five years but that did not matter." He looked at Bobby. "Do you know what sustained me, Señor Esquared?" Bobby shook his head, no. "The knowledge that one day Lucinda and I would ride in this car again through the streets of Havana, past cheering crowds welcoming me home from exile." He looked at his car and smiled. "I come here at night to stare at this beautiful thing. I see myself back in Cuba in this car." He looked at Bobby again, but he was not smiling. "I would give it all up, you know, this house, this life, to return."

Bobby nodded. "That's why I'm here, Señor Medina. To help in any small way I can."

"You understand then, what it means to be a patriot?"

"Absolutely," Bobby said. He remembered Sol's warning.

"You gotta understand this guy, Bobby," Sol said over the phone. "He really thinks he's a patriot, not a fucking spic gangster. That's how he can justify the things he does. He's fucking ruthless in ways you and me can't even understand. He's not like the guineas. He wants to take you out, you pissed him off, you don't even know you did, or why, it don't matter, he takes out your wife, your kids, your dog, your fucking goldfish, your parents in a nursing home, everyone, he don't give a shit. He'll sit down to a nice dinner of fried plantains and frijoles negros."

Sol told him about the time this little man with the pouty child's lips and black eyes wanted to make a point. So he blew a Cuban airliner out of the sky, 288 innocent people, some of them exiles from Miami. He didn't care. He just wanted to make his point. Nobody was safe when he was pissed off. And you never knew what pissed him off. Only he did. That's why there were all these exiles in Miami who hired rafters to start their cars. He'd blown up so many cars of his enemies, real or imagined, it made no difference to him, men who hadn't shown him the proper respect, or men *he* didn't think showed him the proper respect, that there's a whole legion of exiles walking around Calle Ocho with one arm, one leg, a disfigured face. "You know what they call them, Bobby?" Sol said. "La Legion del Loco. The Legion of the Crazy One."

Medina was talking now. "Don't misunderstand me, Señor Esquared. I luff America. It's been bery good to me. But a patriot needs something more. Roots. My roots are in Havana. My family. My father is buried there. He was a great patriot. He fought that butcher Cathtro until he was captured. I was a boy. My mother and I were dragged to the prison to watch. We stood in the hot sun in the dusty prison yard that smelled of piss and shit, the walls pockmarked and covered with blood. They brought my father out to Cathtro. Cathtro made him kneel at his feet. He told him to bow his head, but my father refused. He looked up into that butcher's eyes and defied him to kill him man-to-man. And that coward, that bastard. . . ." The little man's finger jabbed the night air, saliva forming in his cheeks, spittle on his lips, as he raged on ". . . that bastard didn't have the courage. He turned to one of his henchmen, an American, a hired assassin, a man I will never forget, this big, fucking gringo, and he handed him his pistola, a P38, a Nazi gun, of course, and said, 'Here, gringo, you do it. He is not worth my time.' And the gringo shot my father between the eyes."

The little man stopped talking. His eyes were glazed over. Finally, he said, "Excuse me, Señor Esquared. But I am a man of passion. A man without passion is nothing. I never forget my enemies." He smiled at Bobby. "Or my friends. Will you be my friend, Señor Esquared?"

Bobby dipped his head slightly and held out his hand. "It would be an honor, Señor Medina." The little man took the tips of Bobby's fingers in his hand. He held them for a moment.

"Good, Señor. Good. Now I know I can trust you. Shall we go back to the women?"

Medina sat at the head of a long dining-room table. He insisted Sheila sit to his right and Bobby to his left. Sheila glanced at Bobby. He gave her a little shake of his head. Lucinda sat at the far end of the table.

During dinner, Medina hardly spoke, except to snap at his servants, or to whisper a few words of Spanish to one of his henchmen. They approached him cautiously from the sliding-glass doors. They bowed to his ear, whispered, waited, bent over, until Medina said a word or two and then dismissed them with a flutter of his fingers. The men backed off slowly, still bowing, turned and disappeared through the sliding doors.

Servants began bringing out the food. Fried plantains and yuca and pieces of roasted pork they carved off a whole pig that lay, on a silver tray, an apple in its mouth, in the center of the table. Medina ate without speaking. He jabbed at his food and shoved it in his mouth, his pouty lips glistening with fat. He smacked his lips as he chewed, tasting in every morsel his revenge.

Only once during dinner did Medina's mood change for a moment. He glanced over at Sheila and smiled. She smiled back at him. Bobby looked at Sheila and gave her a little shrug. She raised her eyebrows and then looked down the table at Lucinda.

"You have a lovely home, Señora Medina," Sheila said. The woman looked up, wide-eyed, unblinking, her fork poised at her lips. She gave Sheila a small, quick smile that vanished and shoved the food into her mouth and began chewing.

When the servants had cleared the dinner dishes, Medina snapped his fingers and a servant appeared with a leather briefcase. Medina handed it to Bobby. Now, smiling, he said, "My grocery list, Señor Esquared. Do you think you can fill it?"

"No problem," said Bobby.

"It is an extensive list, Señor Esquared."

"I can fill it."

"I have heard of only one man in your city who can fill such a list."

"I've heard that, too."

"Very elusive. Suspicious. Difficult to contact."

"I have my sources."

"Yes, that's what I am told." The man was silent for a moment. Then he said, "You know, of course, this man, the man with the groceries, is not sympathetic to my cause."

"No, I didn't know that."

"I have heard this." He smiled. "I, too, have my sources. They tell me it is necessary you exercise, how do you say it, ah, yes . . . discretion with this man."

"It is understood, Señor Medina."

"Good. Than how long will it take you?"

"Maybe a few months. Maybe more."

"A few months is no problem. Let us say six months. More than that. . . ." Medina smiled. "It is agreed then? In six months you will deliver the groceries."

Bobby reached out a hand toward Medina. The little man shook the tips of Bobby's fingers. His fingers were as soft and plump as a baby's, but cold.

"Agreed," said Bobby.

"There's a telephone number and a name on the grocery list. My associate. I would appreciate it if you only contact him from now on. He will explain the details of the transfer of the groceries." Bobby nodded. "The dollars, of course, are there, too."

"Of course."

"Would you like to count them?"

"It's not necessary."

"Good."

Driving back to Lauderdale in the early morning, Bobby told Sheila what happened in the garage, and now, for the first time, what Sol had told him about Medina.

Sheila shuddered. "Brrr! A scary little man."

"Very scary."

"And horny, too." Bobby looked over at her. She smiled, and said, "All through dinner he had his hand on my thigh, touching it at first, than kneading it after a while like it was a piece of meat he was massaging to make it tender for a meal." Sheila laughed. "I felt like a piece of Kobe beef."

"Jesus! Even while he was pissed off?" Sheila nodded. "Fucking prick." He smiled at her. "You didn't even let on."

"I didn't think it was a good idea, Bobby. Tell him get his fucking hand off my thigh, you know." She opened her purse and took out a pack of cigarettes. She lighted one, then exhaled smoke.

Bobby looked across at her again. "I didn't know you smoked?"

"Neither did I."

They were quiet for a while. Finally, Sheila stubbed out her cigarette in the ashtray and began to unbutton her jumpsuit. She took out the little .32. "It was beginning to pinch," she said. She held the little chrome pistol up to the light of a passing car. "It is cute, Bobby. Can I keep it?"

"Why not?"

7

Bobby slept in on their first morning in Montego Bay. "I'm going for a walk on the beach, baby," Sheila said. He mumbled something and rolled over in bed. She went into the bathroom and put on the G-string bikini Bobby had bought at Splish Splash before they left for Jamaica. She looked at herself in the bathroom mirror. She looked firmer than she had a month ago, when she first met Bobby. It had taken him a few days to convince her to go to the gym with him every morning.

"I can't do this," she had said, looking around the gym at the black weights and benches. "I'm too old."

"Bullshit," he said.

So she went with him. The first time she did squats she felt sick to her stomach. She hurried to the ladies' room and threw up. When she came back out looking pale green, Bobby was still standing there by the squat rack.

"Two more sets," he said.

He brought her along slowly, five days a week, with light weights, then heavier, and heavier, until finally she'd begun to like the feeling it gave her to push around those heavy black bars every morning.

"Empowering," she told him one morning as she toweled off sweat.

"Whatever you want to call it," he said. "Now one more set."

But still, in the harsh bathroom light of a hotel room in Jamaica, her pale skin looked untoned. She pulled on a pair of cut-off jeans and a loose T-shirt, and left the room.

She stopped at the front desk. "Excuse me," she said to the light-skinned black girl behind the counter. She was very pretty, maybe twenty-eight, with blue-green eyes that looked sensual behind her wire-rimmed eyeglasses. She wore a brown business suit that fit tight across her big breasts. "I'd like to leave a message for my . . . husband. Room 419."

"Yes," the girl said.

"Tell him I went for a walk on the beach. I'll be back by noon."

The girl smiled at her. "Certainly."

The pool was deserted this early in the morning. A black waiter was setting up tables for breakfast. An old black man in rags was sweeping the tile around the pool. A few small birds hurriedly nibbled crumbs off the tile before the old man swept them up. A hummingbird hovered low to the pool, its tiny wings a blur, and dipped his beak into the water for a drink. The early morning sun was already hot and Sheila could feel the humidity in the air. She crossed a narrow road to the beach and felt the warm sand through her toes. She saw a black family bathing in the pale bluish-green ocean. They soaped their bodies until they were covered with suds, like chocolate sundaes, then dipped below the water to rinse themselves off, and bobbed up again, like seals now. She noticed none of them tried to swim. They just bobbed up and down.

Sheila walked along the water's edge, away from the hotel. To her left, the water stretched out clear and pale, then darker, and darker, as far as she could see, and to her right, the beach gave way to tropical plants, mangroves and coconut palms and banana trees, that rose quickly up the lush, green mountains behind their hotel.

When Bobby had told her he was taking her to Jamaica for a few days, she had said, "Like a honeymoon."

"No," he said. "Like business." He told her about Reverend Jesse and the money he'd have to smuggle through MIA customs.

"Is it dangerous?" she said.

"No. All customs can do is confiscate the money and fine me. It's the Reverend's rasters that's the problem if I lose the money." He told her about the Rasteferians and what they did for Reverend Jesse. "Hitters," he called them.

"You mean, like boxers?" she said.

He smiled at her. "Kinda. But when they hit you you stay down for keeps."

Sheila wanted to tell him not to do it. It was too dangerous. He could get hurt. But before she could say anything, she heard that strange woman's voice say, "How can I help you?"

"I don't know, baby. When the time comes, you'll know what to do. At least I hope so. These things never go the way you plan them. You gotta . . . what's that acting word . . . 'improvise,' yeah, you gotta always be ready to 'improvise.' "

"Actors follow scripts," she said.

"Didn't you ever forget your lines on a stage?"

She shook her head. "I used to have nightmares about it, though. Jeez, I'd wake up in a cold sweat. An actor's worst nightmare. You're standing onstage, naked, and you can't remember your lines."

"I'd have loved to seen that," he said. "What did you do? In your dream, I mean."

"In my nightmare, you mean." She thought a moment, then smiled. "I improvised."

"And if you didn't?"

"The audience would have laughed me off the stage."

"Well, this is sorta like that. You're out there naked, without any script. The only difference is it ain't laughter you gotta worry about."

The hotel was only a small speck in the distance now. She rounded a curve in the beach and came to a rocky, coral cove shaded by a banyan tree. She took off her shorts and T-shirt and waded into the water up to her neck to cool off. Then she returned to the sand and laid down under the hot sun. She heard the gibbering of wild monkeys and parrots in the trees. They lulled her to sleep.

In her sleep, Sheila felt a sudden chill. She shivered, began to stir awake. The monkeys and parrots were silent. She opened her eyes. The sun was gone. A dark form looming over her had blotted out the sun. It cast a shadow across her body. She saw sparks of sunlight shooting off from the edges of the dark form. She sat up.

"So sorry, mo'm," a voice said. "Didn't mean to frighten the nice lady." He was tall, spectrally thin, with wild, reddish Rasteferian braids and purple-black skin. He wore filthy, cut-off jeans, no shirt or shoes. Sheila could see his long cock straining against the leg of his shorts.

"I saw you alone, mo'm," he said in a lilting voice. "I thought to myself, this nice lady might want a date with a nice Jamaican mon." He smiled. Then he unzipped his jeans and pulled out his cock.

Sheila looked around her. She was alone, except for this man standing over, his cock only a few inches from her face. She felt her breathing getting labored. She forced it back down until she was breathing easily, smiling up at the man. "I'm afraid not," she said. "I'm here with my husband."

He kept holding his long cock out for her to see. "Are you sure, madam?" he said.

She forced herself to look into his eyes, pale-green eyes in a ravaged face. "I'm positive," she said, still smiling. "But thank you anyway."

She picked up her clothes and stood up. She used her clothes to wipe off the sand on her body. "I have to go now," she said. "Good-bye." She began to walk back along the sand toward the hotel. She could feel his eyes on her bare ass in her G-string. She fought the urge to run. She listened for the sound of footsteps kicking up sand behind her. Then, she was around the bend and she could see the hotel up ahead. Now, she began to run. When she reached the hotel pool she was panting heavily. She stopped, bent over, to catch her breath, and looked around for Bobby. The tables around the pool were already filled with guests having breakfast. Most of them were black Americans. Then she saw Bobby, off by himself, lying on a lounge chair in his bathing suit. He was wearing his black Wayfarer sunglasses. She hurried over to him.

"Bobby!" she said.

He bolted up, as if awakened, and took off his sunglasses. "What's the matter, baby?" She told him. When she finished, he put his glasses back on and lay down. "The Rasters," he said. "They think every white chick on vacation comes here to fuck them."

"Even the married ones?"

"Especially the married ones."

"That's why the girl at the reception desk smiled at me when I said I was going for a walk on the beach."

"Probably. She smiled at me, too, when she gave me your message."

Sheila stood over him, quiet for a moment. Then she said, "Well, aren't you going to do anything about it?"

"About what?"

"That man! He terrified me, Bobby! I was so scared."

He smiled up at her. "Your worst nightmare, huh? Naked onstage without your lines."

"It's not funny, Bobby! I didn't know what to do!"

He took off his glasses and looked up at her. "Yes, you did, baby. You did what you had to do. Now, lay down and forget it." He put his sunglasses back on. Sheila stood over him for a long moment, staring down at him. Then she laid down in the lounge chair beside him.

"I did, Bobby. Didn't I?"

They passed the next five days lying by the pool under the hot sun, waiting for Jesse's people to contact Bobby. They sipped Bloody Marys with breakfast, wine with lunch, and margaritas in the afternoon. By late afternoon, they staggered up to their room, laughing, slightly drunk. They stripped off their suits, took a cold shower, reviving them just enough to stumble onto the bed, have sex, and then take a nap. They woke around eight and dressed for dinner. Bobby wore his jeans and Hawaiian shirts. Sheila wore the new clothes Bobby had bought for her at Lace-to-Lust. Spandex minidresses and six-inch strippers' pumps from the Wild Pair. The pumps were so tall she was wobbly on them at first, like a schoolgirl, until she got used to them.

They had drinks with dinner, bourbon for Bobby, vodka for Sheila, in the warm darkness by the pool that was illuminated only by little round papier maché Japanese lanterns strung out on wires overhead.

Sheila began to get brown in the sun that tightened her skin. By the third day, she was no longer embarrassed to get up off her lounge chair and walk over to the pool in her G-string. She slipped into the cooling water, swam a few laps, and then stepped out of the pool and walked back toward Bobby. She could feel the eyes of the other guests around the pool staring at her bare, brown ass and her short, ash-blond hair that stood up in little, wet spikes. They were mostly honeymooners, preppy black American couples in their thirties. The women wore one-piece Gortex suits that hid their big asses. The men wore their baggy, college-days shorts that hid their growing stomachs.

When Sheila laid down, facing their stares, they looked away from her. "What's their problem?" she said to Bobby one afternoon.

He took off his sunglasses and looked around the pool. "What do you mean?"

Sheila gestured with her head toward two black couples eating at a table shaded by an umbrella. They were glancing at her and Bobby and then laughing among themselves. "I tried to talk to one of those women," she said, "but she was so rude."

"Which one?"

"It doesn't matter."

"Fuck 'em." Bobby put his sunglasses back on. "They think they're in charge here. Uppity fuckin' niggers. Can't wait to get back to their racquetball club in Atlanta, hurry up take a shower, show their white boss their tan lines."

"You don't like blacks much, do you, Bobby?" He shrugged. "Why not?"

"No reason. They don't bother me, I don't bother them."

"You didn't answer my question."

"Maybe I just don't like people who love being victims."

Sheila was quiet for a while. Then she said, "I went over to her to ask if she and her husband wanted to have a drink with us. The way she blew me off. I felt so foolish."

"That woulda been fun," Bobby said. "You and the black bitch sharing little secrets over piña coladas. You askin' her how she got her nice tan. Maybe her askin' you where you got your hair done. Me and the little man passin' time while you girls chat. 'So, Reggie, what do you do? A stockbroker, eh? Me? I'm a stripper. A little smuggling on the side.' Then we'd swap business cards, baby, only I don't have one really that says, 'Bobby Squared, Inc., You Need It, I'll Move It!'"

He pulled his glasses down to the bridge of his nose so she could see his eyes. "Is that maybe what you were thinking?"

She shook her head and laughed. "Not exactly. But when you put it that way. . . ."

She lay back down beside him, facing the sun. Bobby was right. Her life was different now. She had to remember that. Her only friends were his friends now. Sol. Lucrezia. This guy named Machine Gun, whoever he was. Her world was Bobby's world. It was a world of whispered deals in code. Strange dinners with evil men. Phony names. Guns kept under the seat of his car and in her purse. She remembered when she first began to realize this. Bobby had taken her to "Splish

Splash" to buy her G-string bikini. The clerk was a big, muscular man with a shaved head. He had a German Shepherd with a studded collar lying by his feet at the cash register. Sheila handed him her credit card. Before the man could look at it, Bobby snatched it out of his hand. He handed the man a hundred dollar bill, and waited for his change.

They were driving back to the apartment when Bobby said, "How many credit cards you got?"

"A few," she said.

"Exactly," he said.

She took her wallet out of her purse and counted all her credit cards. "Seven," she said. "Two Visas, an Amoco, Burdines, Searstown, Brands-Mart, and a Winn-Dixie check cashing card."

"Cut 'em up," he said.

"Cut them up?"

"You heard me. And cancel your checking account. From now on, baby, you only deal in cash."

On their sixth day, another white couple appeared at the pool. They sat across the pool from Bobby and Sheila under the shade of an umbrella so as not to burn their milky-white skin. The man wore a panama hat, a wrinkled linen suit like a low level civil servant out of a Graham Greene novel. He smoked a thin cigar. The woman wore a big floppy straw hat that shaded her face, and a gauzy wrap-around the hips of her one-piece bathing suit. They sipped gin and tonics and sat across from Bobby and Sheila for an hour without looking at them. Then the woman got up, walked around the pool, and stood in front of them. She grinned down at Bobby, a neurotically thin woman who had once been pretty but was now shriveling up inside her loose skin.

"Cheers, Robert!" she said with false brightness. She flashed Sheila a brittle smile. "Cheers, Robert's girl!" She leaned over and handed Bobby a folded piece of paper. She brushed her hand across his thigh, straightened up, and walked into the hotel.

"What was *that* all about?" Sheila said.

"It's them."

"You're kidding! *That* woman?"

Bobby smiled. "What'd you think, they'd look like your raster boyfriend?" Bobby unfolded the piece of paper, looked at it, and tossed it to Sheila. He stood up. "I'll be back in a few minutes. You wanna wait here, or in the room?"

"I'll wait in the room. In case you need me. Don't be long, baby."

He shrugged. "However long it takes." He walked into the hotel. Sheila looked at the piece of paper. "Room 333." She gathered up her things and stood up. The man in the panama hat was grinning at her, the same grin the black receptionist had given her. He tipped his panama hat.

Sheila waited in their room. She paced back and forth and checked her watch every few minutes. Finally, she decided to take a shower to make the time pass. When she got out of the shower, she dried herself off. She looked at herself in the mirror. She was tanned, firm, younger-looking with her harsh blond hair. She studied her image for a moment, then went to the medicine cabinet and took out the bottle Lucrezia had given her. She sat on the edge of the toilet seat, her legs spread, and applied the bleach to her bush. It burned for a few seconds, then just smelled of chemicals. She waited until it dried, than washed it off. Her bush was bleached almost the same color as her hair now. But it was still too dense. She got Bobby's razor out of the medicine cabinet and began to shave her bush. She shaved it until it was only a neat thin line, an inch wide, and then she stood up and looked at herself again. She smiled. Bobby would love it. Bobby? She went into the bedroom and checked her watch. He'd been gone over an hour. She felt her breathing getting labored again. She threw on her cut-off jeans and T-shirt and looked around for the piece of paper. She'd left it down by the pool. She sat down on the edge of the bed and forced herself to remember it. . . . Room 333.

She hurried to the stairs, walked up one flight, then walked down the corridor to room 333. She listened, her ear to the door, for a moment, heard nothing, so she knocked.

"Bobby?" she called out.

The woman opened the door, dressed differently now, in a flowered sundress that was too big for her. The woman smiled at her. "Bobby's girl!" she said. "He'll be right out."

Sheila heard the toilet flush in the bathroom, and then saw Bobby walk out, still in his bikini, staring at her.

"Don't forget your briefcase, Bobby," the woman said, smiling at him.

Bobby picked up a briefcase from the bed, the sheets all rumpled, and left the room. He gripped Sheila's arm, hard, at the elbow, and steered her down the corridor.

"Don't ever fucking do that again when I'm doing business!" he said.

"Business?" Sheila said, fighting back tears. "You were fucking her, Bobby! Why? Why?"

"Was I?"

"Yes! I don't have to take that!"

"No you don't. You can't take it you can go home, go back to your one-room fucking cell and your fag director. Is that what you want?"

"No . . . but I don't want this either. I thought I could trust you."

"You can, baby. This was nothing. Just business."

"The Rasteferians?"

"Yeh, the fucking Rasters."

They were at their door now. Bobby waited. She tried to keep herself from crying. "I don't fucking care!" she said. She opened the door and slammed it behind her. Bobby stood in the hallway with the briefcase for a moment and then walked back down the corridor.

The black receptionist got off her shift at midnight. She walked out of the hotel to the pool in darkness. It was deserted. The Japanese lanterns had been put away. Only the light of the moon shone across the pool's water. She walked past the pool toward the road and saw someone sitting at a table in the darkness. It was the big white man with the blond ponytail. His wife—no, she was sure that blond woman wasn't his wife—was nowhere around. She went over to him. He was wearing only his tiny bathing suit that made his body look big and muscular.

"Hello, sir," she said. "Is anything wrong?"

He looked up at her. "No, honey. Just enjoying the night."

She took off her spectacles. "It is a beautiful night, isn't it? A little warm though." She took off her jacket to show him her breasts straining against her white blouse.

"Did your wife enjoy her walk on the beach this morning?" she said.

He smiled at her. "It was interesting," he said.

"I am sure. . . ." She smiled at him. "Is there anything I can do for you, sir?"

He shook his head. "Not tonight, honey."

"I don't mean in my official capacity."

"I know what you mean."

Sheila was silent on the flight back to Miami. Bobby left her alone. Finally, an hour into the flight she laid her hand on his thigh.

"You're right, Bobby," she said. "It was only business."

"That's all it was, baby."

She wanted to throw her arms around him and kiss him, but that strange woman's voice stopped her. "It better be."

Bobby remembered the stripper he lived with when he first came to Lauderdale. She came home early one night, and found him in bed, getting a blow job from one of her girlfriends. Before she could say a word, Bobby said, "Baby, you gonna believe me or your lying eyes?" Before the night was over he'd convinced her a blow job wasn't cheating on her. But he thought Sheila was different.

"You *think* Sheila's different," Sol told him. "But she ain't, Bobby. They're all alike. They ain't like us. They can always find a reason to believe anything. You don't even have to bother helpin' them out. Just throw them back on themselves and let them do it."

Sol was right. Sheila wanted to believe something, so she did. Now she wanted to believe something else. "It was only business, Bobby," she said. He looked across at her. She was still struggling with it, trying to get farther away from that woman he'd met a month ago.

Finally, she said, "You had no choice, Bobby. So let's forget it. It didn't happen."

"Right, baby."

She turned toward him her eyes opened wide. "One last thing, though. You were stupid. You should have known. It was my fault, too. I got all fuzzy and forgot why we were there. You can bet it won't happen again."

She grabbed his hand and pulled him up out of his seat. "Come on!" she said. She led him to the lavoratory door at the rear of the plane. She opened the door in front of a stewardess, pushed him in, followed him, and shut the door. She pulled up her skirt, peeled off her panties, and sat up on the little metal sink. Her face was flushed and she was breathing heavily. She spread her legs, planted one foot against the door and the other against the wall.

"Come on!" she said. "Do it!"

Bobby entered her just as the stewardess began pounding on the door. "You can't do *that* on *my* plane!" she said through the door. Sheila threw back her head and came almost immediately. Then Bobby came. They were both panting now, smiling. Bobby noticed, for the first time, Sheila's blond pussy. He began to laugh.

"I did it for you," Sheila said. "You fuck." Then she laughed, too. The stewardess was still pounding on the door. Sheila picked up her panties, but didn't put them on. She opened the door and stepped out.

The stewardess glared at her. Sheila smiled, held up her panties for the stewardess to see, then walked back up the aisle.

When they got off the plane, Sheila gave the stewardess a big smile. They followed the other passengers down to customs, and stood behind the red line, waiting their turn. Bobby noticed two customs guys standing near a door to the left of the guy checking bags. He whispered in Sheila's ear, "Don't look, but there are two customs guys to the left over there." She took her makeup mirror out of her purse and checked her makeup. She tilted the mirror a bit. "I see them."

"There might be more," Bobby said. He looked around the customs area. When he turned back to Sheila, she was gone. She was standing in front of the customs guy who was checking bags.

"You see anything don't look right," he had told her on the flight. "Get as far away from me as possible."

The customs guy was asking Sheila questions. He went to open her suitcase. She pulled it away from him. Bobby heard a woman's harsh voice say, "What the fuck you think you're doin'?"

The guy checking her bags looked over at the other customs guys near the door. He nodded, and they began walking toward Sheila.

Bobby heard the guy say, "I'm sorry, ma'm, but I have to inspect your luggage."

"Fuck, you do!" Sheila said. She jerked a thumb toward Bobby standing behind the red line. "Go check that asshole's luggage, not mine."

The other two were beside her now. Each one took her by the elbow and tried to steer her toward the door. She pulled her elbows out of their grasp. One of them leaned close to her ear and whispered something.

"Like hell you do!" Sheila said.

Everyone in the lines was staring at her. The two agents grabbed her elbows again and half-led, half-pushed her toward the door. Bobby heard one of them say, "Is that guy with you?"

"Which guy?" she said.

He pointed to Bobby. "That guy."

Sheila looked at Bobby. "Fuck him!" she said. They all disappeared through the door. A few seconds later, one of them reappeared, went over to the guy checking bags, and took Sheila's suitcase. He returned with it to the door.

The agent checking bags was still staring after Sheila when Bobby stood in front of him. He was shaking his head. Finally, he turned to Bobby, and said, "Can I see your passport, sir?" Bobby handed it to him. The agent looked at it, then at Bobby. A big, tanned guy with a blond ponytail. He was wearing a Hawiian shirt, neatly pressed jeans, and ostrich-skin cowboy boots. The agent had seen a lot of guys like Bobby passing through MIA on their way home from the Islands. Personal injury lawyers dressing up to look like smugglers.

"Mr. Roberts?" the agent said. "Mr. Robert Roberts."

Bobby grinned. "Helluva name, ain't it? My buddies just call me Bobby Squared." The agent gave him a blank stare. Bobby kept smiling at him. The guy kept staring. Finally Bobby tossed a headfake toward the door where the agents had taken Sheila.

"That was some crazy lady," Bobby said.

The agent smiled. "We get all kinds, sir." He handed back Bobby's passport. "Do you have anything to declare, Mr. Roberts?"

"Not this trip," Bobby said. The agent waved him through.

Bobby waited for Sheila by his SHO in the Flamingo parking lot. They'd search her bags first, taking their time, trying to make her sweat. Then they'd question her, askin' the same questions over and over, waitin' for her to slip up. The last thing they'd do to humiliate her is call in a female agent to strip search her. Bobby smiled to himself. Naked onstage without her lines. The broad tellin' Sheila to spread her legs, bend over, grab her ankles. Sheila lookin' up through her legs at the broad checkin' her asshole, thinkin' of something to say, something smartass, 'improvising.' "So, honey. Tell me, do you like your job?" Bobby checked his watch. She'd been in there an hour. He'd give her another half-hour. If she wasn't out by then he'd have to call Meyer and get him to bond her out. Then he saw her down the line of cars, walking very fast toward him, her long, flowered skirt swaying. When she got close, she ran to him. She was smiling, her blue eyes wide open.

"Oh, baby!" she said. "You're all right!" She threw her arms around his neck and hugged him. "I was so worried about you."

8

THE TWO WAITRESSES STOOD IN THE SHADE OF THE SERVICE BAR WAITING FOR their drink orders. The brunette sneaked a drag of her cigarette and put it back in the ashtray on the bar.

The blonde said, "You gonna tell them, or me?"

The brunette glanced over her shoulder. The outdoor tables on the deck of The Mark's Chickee Bar were filled mostly with tourists drinking rum runners and piña coladas, and a few older wiseguys sipping champagne with young strippers. The wiseguys and the strippers were laughing, but the tourists didn't talk much, except now and then to whisper to one another and point down below to the male and female strippers lying on the sand, wearing G-strings, their perfectly tanned bodies glistening with oil.

"You mean Spike and the Hunk?" said the brunette. "With the mutt?"

"Who else?"

A man and a woman were seated off by themselves at a table at the far corner of the deck. Only their backs were visible to the waitresses. The man was muscular and tanned in his tiny bikini, a bodybuilder, thought the brunette. The woman was slimly muscled and tanned, too, with close-cropped blond hair that stood up like spring grass. She wore a G-string and smoked a cigarette, very ladylike, limp wristed, while she read a newspaper. With her free hand she had reached down to languidly stroke the fur of the dog sitting at her feet. The dog had reddish-orange and white fur.

"Whaddaya think?" the brunette said. "Tourists?"

The blonde laughed. "Yeh, he's a brain surgeon, she's Mother Theresa."

"Well, it's your table," said the brunette.

The blond waitress walked over to the couple with the dog and set down their drinks. Jim Beam, rocks, for him. Vodka, rocks, for her. The man handed her a twenty. "Keep the change," he said.

"Thank you, sir."

The woman said to the man. "What time is he supposed to get here?"

"Twenty minutes ago," said the man.

The waitress stood there, smiling. Finally, she said, "Excuse me." The woman looked up at her with cool, blue eyes, her hand still absentmindedly stroking the dog at her feet.

"I'm terribly sorry," the waitress said, "but it's against the rules." She pointed at the dog. The dog looked up at her as if he knew what she meant. "No dogs, I'm afraid."

The woman took a drag from her cigarette, and exhaled. "Really?" she said. She smiled down at the dog. "Did you hear that, Hosh? You're not welcome." She poured her glass of water into a tin bowl and laid it down for the dog, then turned back to the man.

"Should we order, Bobby?" the woman said.

"No. We'll wait."

The woman went back to her newspaper. She stubbed out her cigarette. Without looking up, she said to the waitress, "Bring me a pack of Marlboros, honey."

When the blond waitress returned to the service bar, the brunette said, "Well?"

"Well, what?"

"Did you tell them?"

The blonde glanced at the couple, then back to the brunette. "Yeh, I told them."

"Well? What'd they say?"

"They didn't say nuthin'. Except the chick looked at me like I should, maybe, take a fuckin' hike."

"You better tell them again."

"No way. You tell them."

Sheila read something that made her smile. "Bobby, did you see this?" she said. She slid the paper across to him. "Tara Solomon's column, 'Queen of the Night.'" She pointed at a photograph. Bobby looked at it and smiled, too. He shook his head and slid the paper back to Sheila. She studied the photograph. A pudgy little man in a white suit was seated at a dinner table in a restaurant. He was surrounded by an older woman in a low-cut evening gown; a fat bald man who looked like a Roman Empire eunuch; a tall black man wearing a woman's blond wig, heavy makeup, silver glitter on his amaretto-colored skin, and a form-fitting, gold lamé jumpsuit; and a small man wearing a big cowboy hat and grinning a lascivious, comic-book-evil grin at the tiny Cuban girl sitting on his lap with a look of wide-eyed, open-mouthed surprise. The caption read: "Much respected Cuban Exile Politico Juan José Medina holds court as he does every Friday night at his private table at the very chic SoBe eatery, The Anvil. Among Señor Medina's coterie of admirers this night are: Palm Beach socialite Maria Probst von Trapp; SoBe hotel impressario Christian Grubbstein; the world famous gender illusionist, Miss Kitty Litter; and the acclaimed adult film director Tex Pervis, and his newly discovered protegé, the very talented adult actress, Bimini A'Nal.

"He looks like a spic Truman Capote," Sheila said. "At some hallucinating pervert's vision of the Algonquin round table."

"Who does?"

"Our much respected Cuban Exile Politico."

"That what they call him?"

"What'd you expect, Bobby? Fucking Spic Gangster?"

"You forgot, Lech."

"Oh, right. It was so long ago."

"Six months."

"I can still feel his clammy little hand massaging my thigh under the table." She looked at the paper. "Fucking Spic Gangster Lech."

"That's no way to talk about our business partner."

"Jesus! Look at that crew! An old Queen, a fat Queen, a porn Queen, and a black Queen. I was wondering, Bobby, you think the black Queen's got a .32 in *his* girdle?"

Bobby turned the paper around and studied the photo. "Maybe a .45, baby, like your Raster boyfriend in Jamaica."

"Hmmm, yes, that was quite a piece."

"The little spic chick on the cowboy's lap is hot."

Sheila grabbed the paper from him and looked at the photo again. The little girl was wearing a tiny tube top over small breasts, a very short, pleated miniskirt, lacy white ankle socks, and six-inch tall stripper's pumps. Her black hair had been pulled out into two pigtails on either side of her head.

"Oh, Bobby, puh-leeze! She looks like a pedophile's fantasy of a pre-pubescent schoolgirl taking it up the ass for the first time and loving it."

"Pre . . . what?"

"Pre-pub-escent, Robert. A little girl who hasn't gotten her period yet."

Bobby shrugged. "I'll bet Sol would like her."

Sheila didn't hear him. She was looking at the little girl's picture more closely. "But she isn't," she said to herself. "She's in her twenties, her late twenties I'll bet."

"She still looks hot to me."

"Gimme a break! Those pigtails look like Minnie Mouse ears."

"Whatever."

Sheila glared at him. "Forget it, Bobby, if you think I'm going back to Lucrezia's for hair extensions."

A tall stringy man in his thirties was walking toward them. He had dirty-blond, shoulder-length hair, burnt-red skin, and flat blue eyes. He wore a pair of dirty O.P. shorts, flip-flops and no shirt. He had a gold chain with an SS thunderbolt pendant around his neck, and swastika tatoos under each nipple.

"Bobby Squared! How's it hangin', dude?" He slapped Bobby on the back and sat down across from him.

"Baby, say hello to Machine Gun Bob. Bob, this is Sheila."

Sheila flashed him her glossy smile that vanished quickly. "Hello Machine Gun Bob."

"You can call me, Bob, honey." He grinned at her just as Medina had grinned at her six months ago. "Heh, Bobby, dude, your old lady's a fox." He was rubbing one of his nipples with the flat of his hand, his flat blue eyes roaming over Sheila's body in her bikini. "Foxy old lady, dude. I usually don't dig old chicks." His eyes came to rest on Sheila's breasts.

"You see something you like . . . Bob?" Sheila said.

"Smart, too, I heard, that scene she pulled at MIA. Very cool, honey."

"Thank you . . . Bob," Sheila said.

Hoshi stood up on his hind legs and put his paws on the man's arm. He wagged his curled tail. The man pushed him away. Hoshi sat back down and stared at him.

"You don't have to do that . . . *Bob*!" Sheila said. "Just tell him, 'Down!' He'll obey."

"Yeh, well, I hate fuckin' mutts. Can't trust 'em. They'll turn on ya, ya let 'em."

"Not like people," Bobby said.

"Heh, that's right, dude. Not like people." He glanced around.

"Where's our bitch, man? I'm thirsty. Hungry, too." He grinned at Bobby, showing him his green teeth. "Lunch's on you, right, dude?"

"Anything you want," Bobby said.

The man caught the blond waitress's eye. "Yo, bitch! I'm starvin' here!"

The waitress came over to their table, handed out menus, and waited. The man studied his, squinting his eyes, as if the letters were moving. He moved his finger down the list of prices. Sheila glanced at Bobby and shook her head. Bobby smiled.

"You need a little yellow ruler . . . Bob?" Sheila said.

Without looking up at the waitress, he said, "I wanna steak tenderloin sandwich. Well-done. Fries, extra crispy. And a tall Coors." He looked up now, grinning. "Gotta support the brother out in Golden." He slapped his menu shut.

While Bobby and Sheila gave their orders to the waitress, the man looked around the deck, squinting through his flat blue eyes. He saw a fat tourist woman drinking a pink Rum Runner through a straw.

He was still staring at her when the waitress was walking away with their order. Bobby said to him, "She look suspicious to you, Bob? You think she's ATF?"

The man called out to their waitress. "Yo, change my order!" She stopped and looked back at him. "Make it a Rum Runner. Two cherries." He turned back to Bobby and Sheila. "Fuck Golden."

"Rum Runner?" Bobby said. "What are you, a fucking tourist?"

"Yeh, dude. Just a tourist through life." He glanced around the deck one more time, then leaned across the table toward Bobby. "I talked to the man," he said in a low voice. "He said he's got everything you need."

Sheila lighted another cigarette and went back to her newspaper. She reached down a hand and began to stroke Hoshi's fur. She heard the two men's voices as only a low murmur she ignored.

The two men had been talking for a while when the waitress returned with their order. The men stopped talking until the waitress put down their orders and left. Then the man said, "I set it up for ya, dude. Out west State Road 84, past the diner." While he was giving Bobby directions he turned over the top of his bun and looked at the meat. He pushed down on the meat with his dirty fingernails. Sheila pushed her own food away from her. The man looked up, his face flushed, and yelled out to their waitress. "Yo, bitch! Come take this shit!" The waitress finished taking an order from another table and then walked over to him.

"Something wrong, sir?" she said.

"Yeh, there's something wrong! This fucking meat's alive! I can't eat this shit!" He jabbed the meat again with his finger. Blood oozed out. The waitress sighed, and picked up his sandwich. He watched her bringing it back to the kitchen. "Stupid bitch!" he said. He took a sip of his Rum Runner, draining it in one long gulp. "Mmmm, that was fucking good." He stood up. "Get me another one a those, dude. I gotta take a piss."

"You want the little umbrella in it, too?" Sheila said, smiling.

"Yeh, cool, honey."

When he was gone, Sheila looked at Bobby, not smiling now. "Lovely," she said.

Bobby shrugged. "What can I tell ya? Just your average pill-popping, Nazi surfer dude deals in guns."

"Do we need him?"

"Not him. His man. The only guy around deals in as much product as Medina wants. Like Sol said, 'Machine Gun's got the man's ear.'"

"Sol also said, 'God knows why.'" Sheila shook her head. "He looks like a fucking poster boy for the Hitler Youth."

"They're all into that Nazi shit, baby. Gun freaks. You should see what he's got in his van. Nazi helmets, medals, uniforms, that book Hitler wrote."

"You mean, *Mein Kampf*?"

"I guess. They think they're gonna start up another Third Reich in Paradise."

"Maybe they should start in the Jewish condos in Century Village. They can recruit some of those Holocaust survivors who know a few things about the Third Reich." She was quiet, then she said, "What I don't understand, Bobby, is how Sol can deal with this asshole. I mean, Sol's a Jew."

"Way back, maybe. Now he's just a businessman. You gotta learn to deal with who you gotta deal with. Like Michael said in *The Godfather*. It's not personal. It's business."

"Well, he makes me sick to my stomach. You deal with him, Bobby." She went back to her newspaper as the man came walking back to their table. He moved unsteadily now, weaving, knocking into people eating. They looked up at him and saw his wide, unblinking eyes.

He sat down hard on his chair, the chair wobbling, almost tipping over. He flailed his arms to steady himself. "Whoa, man!" he said. When his chair was steady, Hoshi put his paws on the man's arm again and wagged his tail. The man shoved Hoshi's paws away. "Fuckin' mutt doesn't understand!" Hoshi sat back down.

Sheila stared at the man until she caught his eye. She looked into his flat blue eyes with her own cold blue eyes. "*You* don't seem to understand . . . Bob. Keep your fucking hands off my dog." She stood up. "Come on, Hosh."

She walked off the deck onto the beach with Hoshi trotting beside her. Bobby and the man followed her with their eyes. The man's eyes were riveted to her high tight ass that was swiveling left and right with each step in the sand. He began to massage his nipple again.

"Man! What'd I do?" he said.

"You pissed her off, Bob. I were you, I wouldn't."

In the kitchen, the blond waitress slammed down the steak sandwich on the counter next to the young black cook sweating over a flaming grill.

"Whatsa matter?" he said.

The blond waitress tossed her head toward Machine Gun. "The Nazi surfer sent it back."

"Whats he want me to do?"

"Incinerate it."

A college student, a wrestler from the University of Pennsylvania, was walking along the beach, close to the water, on his spring break. He couldn't keep his eyes off of all the beautiful girls in G-strings, sunning themselves everywhere. He was trying to make up his mind which one to talk to, when he saw her, lying on a blanket, across from the Mark's outdoor bar. A small, red-and-white dog was lying beside her, sunning himself, too. The girl was lying on her stomach, close to the water. She was leanly muscled, like he liked them, with a beautiful ass in her G-string. He walked over to her. She was perfectly tanned, with short, blond hair. He hesitated a moment, looked down at his own pink skin, then made up his mind.

"Excuse me," he said. The dog stood up, alert, looking at him with his brown eyes. The girl didn't move. "Excuse me!" he said louder. She rolled over onto her back, shading her eyes from the sun with the flat of her hand. He immediately felt foolish. This woman was in her 30s! "I'm sorry," he said. "I was just wondering what kind of dog you have." He smiled. She said nothing. She just stared at him for a moment, then rolled back onto her stomach.

It had happened a lot to Sheila in the six months she had been living with Bobby. College boys hitting on her. She had no patience with it, now. At first, it had just annoyed her. "I'm old enough to be their mother!" she told Bobby. He laughed. "It's a compliment, baby. Just accept it." So she did. It was just another part of her new life. . . .

They woke in darkness each morning and sat outside on the deck alongside the sailboats rocking in the canal. They listened to the jabbering of the wild monkeys and the cawing of wild parrots coming down the canal from the thick, tropical foliage of Birch Park that separated the canal from the ocean behind it. A soft, warm, insistent breeze blew down the canal rustling the big leaves of the palm trees that hung over the deck. When the sun finally came up, a pinkish-orange ball, over Birch Park, Sheila went inside to get their Cuban coffee and newspapers. Sheila read the *New York Times* book reviews and theater reviews. Every so often she'd see the name of an actor she had worked with who was now famous. Bobby read the *Miami Herald*, crime stories mostly, looking for names of people who could help him, or hurt him. Hoshi chased geckos around the potted plants on the deck. When he caught one he brought it to Sheila, squirming, in his mouth. He looked up at her with his almond-shaped eyes. "Good boy, Hoshi," she said. Only then did he drop the gecko and watch it scamper off. "Come on, Hosh, time for your walk." Sheila led him on a leash down the dock to the little park at the end of the canal alongside Bayview Drive. She watched him sniff and piss everywhere any other dog had pissed. When he was done she led him back to the apartment. She put down his bowl of Eukanuba and watched him eat. He never ate right away like other dogs. He just looked at his bowl of food for a moment, then lay down, and ate with his head draped over the bowl.

"He doesn't eat," Sheila said to Bobby one morning. "He dines."

"Yeh," Bobby said. "That's the way wolves eat."

If his water bowl was empty, Hoshi would sit in front of it, staring at it, until Sheila noticed him.

"I'm sorry, Hosh," she said, and filled his bowl with water and laid it down for him. He looked up at her, nodded his head, and then drank.

They went to the gym early and worked out hard. Bobby didn't have to watch her now. Sheila went straight to the squat rack, loaded up the bar, and did her squats, while Bobby did his biceps curls at the other end of the gym.

After they left the gym, they went to the Dixie Gun Range where Sheila shot Bobby's CZ-85, her Seecamp, and the 12 gauge Mossberg pump shotgun with the pistol grip they kept standing upright in their bedroom closet. Bobby taught her how to strip the guns and clean them, and then put them back together again.

They took a shower as soon as they got home, to wash off the odor of gun powder. Then they had breakfast. It was always the same breakfast, a protein shake with skimmed milk and a banana. Then Bobby drove her out to Route 23, a deserted two-lane black top that cut through the middle of the state to Lake Okechobee. He pulled the car off to the side of the road, got out, and made Sheila drive his SHO, the car squatting down flat to the road at 120 mph, the palm trees and sawgrass flashing by in a blur.

"I set it up that way," he told her. "The faster you drive it, the tighter it hugs the road."

Then he taught her how to downshift coming into a corner, and then brake hard until they were halfway out of the corner before accelerating again so that the car shot out of the corner as if propelled by an unseen hand. She was afraid at first, but he made her go faster and faster into a corner, "Until you see God," he said, "and then you can brake."

She got the hang of it quick, pushing the car faster and faster into a corner until finally even he had to warn her, "Jesus, baby, not that fast!"

She looked across at him with a thin smile. "Whatsa matter, Bobby? You're gonna see God sooner or later."

"Yeah, well, I'd rather later."

He taught her how to drive her used BMW M3 fast, too. "It's different than the SHO," he said. "With a rear wheel drive the rear end kicks out in a corner. You gotta swing it back hitting the gas."

He had bought her the M3 shortly after they'd returned from Jamaica. "You earned it," he said, as they drove west on Oakland toward the flashing baby blue-and-pink neon sign that read: *Uncle Sol's Title Loans. A*

Friend in Deed in Time of Need. Sol was waiting for them in his used-car lot beside the brownish-gray '96 M3 with the red-and-blue insignia on it.

"Some wiseguy wanna be," Sol said, looking at the car. "He had no intention of making a single payment for his $5000 loan, so I repoed it while he was sleeping." Then, to Bobby, he said, "But you already got a ride, Bobby."

"It's for Sheila," Bobby said. He told her what Sheila had done at MIA customs.

Sol listened, but said nothing. Finally, he looked at Sheila and said, "It's about fuckin' time you earned your keep."

"Why, thank you, Sol. That means so much to me." Sol looked at her through narrowed eyes. She flashed him her fake smile.

"Ya know sumthin?" he said. "You're a real smart-ass broad."

"High praise," she said.

When they got the BMW back to the apartment, Bobby got a screwdriver and pried off all the M3 emblems.

In the afternoon, Bobby went out to see people. At first, Sheila asked him where he was going. Then she stopped asking. She went down to the Galleria to shop. Bobby didn't have to buy her clothes for her now. She knew what he liked. Once in a while she drove up to Delray Beach to an art gallery to buy a Haitian painting. She had thrown out Bobby's Nagle print of the woman with the wide-brimmed hat over one eye, and replaced it with colorful Haitian prints of parrots and black Haitians dancing at harvest time. When Sol saw all the colorful paintings and tin works on the walls, he turned to Bobby and said, "Looks like a fucking hamster house, Bobby."

If Sheila didn't go shopping, she went to the beach with Hoshi. She laid out on the sand, close to the water, and felt the warm sun over her body. Her body. Something she had never thought about before. Now it was important to her. Not only because of Bobby, but because of the power it gave her.

They ate dinner out every night that Bobby wasn't working. Bobby dressed as he always did at night, Hawiian shirt, jeans, cowboy boots. Sheila dressed as she always did at night, too. Low-cut, spandex dresses that fit her body like paint. Pink and lime green and white. When she put on a black Betsey Johnson dress one night, Bobby looked at it, and said, "We ain't going to a fucking funeral, baby." She went back to the bedroom and changed.

They followed the maitre'd in his ruffled shirt and tuxedo through the dining room of The Left Bank to their table. The other diners looked up from their food and stared. The women looked at Sheila through narrowed eyes, while their men looked at her, the blond hooker on the arm of the big Imokale cowboy, and smiled.

On those nights that Bobby went to The Crazy Horse, Sheila ate alone at home. Then she washed the dishes and went outside to the deck to sit with Hoshi in the warm darkness. The stars were like pieces of silver tossed onto black velvet. Sheila nursed her drink and smoked a cigarette. Hoshi lay beside her. She stroked Hoshi's fur while Bobby danced in front of strange women in his leopard G-string.

She accepted it. She accepted it all. Spic gangsters and Nazi gun runners and Rastaferian hitters. And a strange Jewish gangster from Brooklyn, who, she was learning, was not exactly what he seemed to be.

She told Bobby one night, "Does he have to work at being so obnoxious?"

"Who?"

"You know who. Sol. Sometimes he's impossible. No, he's impossible *all* the time."

"That's cause you don't know how to deal with him."

"And how's that?"

"That bitch shit of yours doesn't play with Sol."

"What do you mean by that?"

"You know what I mean. Your smart-ass comments. Those threatening looks like you're trying to scare him. Baby, Sol's seen things that are really scary and he never blinked." She was silent for a moment. Then Bobby said, "Sol's easy to deal with. Just be straight with him. You don't like something he said, tell him. 'Fuck you, you little fat Jew bastard.' He understands that."

She must have dozed off under the hot sun. Hoshi was laying beside her on the sand. She shaded her eyes with her hand and looked for Bobby. She saw him up at The Mark's Chickee Bar. He was shaking the Nazi asshole's hand. Then he was walking toward her, the sun at his back in the late afternoon, his big body in shadow. My body, she thought. After we close the Medina deal I'll tell him.

He was standing over her now, his shadow cooling her off in the sun. She looked up into his shadowed face.

"How'd it go," she said.

"All settled, baby. Tomorrow at midnight."

9

Bobby drove west on State Road 84 at midnight. Hoshi sat on the briefcase beside him, staring out the front window with his intelligent eyes. Sheila sat by the passenger window, staring out at the gas stations, the ramshackle barbecue joints, the seedy country-and-western bars, their parking lots filled with pickup trucks.

"Keep your eyes peeled for the diner, baby," Bobby said. "It looks like one of those old-fashioned airstream trailers. That's where Medina's man will be with the van." He'd already told her the plan. They park in back of the diner, take the van out to the ranch while Medina's man waits for them. They load the guns into the van, return it to Medina's man at the diner, and drive home with their twenty-five thousand dollars.

Sheila reached out a hand and began stroking the fur behind Hoshi's ears. It was soft, like cotton. "Bobby," she said. "I still don't know why we brought Hosh. It could be dangerous."

"Hoshi's our burglar alarm once we get the guns." He glanced at her, then back to the road. "He's a member of this family, too, ain't he? Gotta earn his keep, all that Eukanuba he eats. Ain't that right, Hosh?" The dog looked at him as if he understood, then looked intently out the front window down the road.

Sheila reached into her leather satchel for a cigarette. Bobby had bought her the bag at the Thunderbird Swap Shop, along with the jeans and western shirt and cowboy boots she was wearing. "You always gotta go in costume," he told her. "The Reverend might not appreciate you in spandex." She searched through her bag in the dark, felt the cool, hard chrome of her .32, found her cigarettes, and lit one. She inhaled, and exhaled.

"Here, baby, take the wheel," he said. She reached across Hoshi and held the wheel with one hand while Bobby searched under his seat. He withdrew the black CZ-85 pistol Sheila had seen in his dresser drawer. He racked the slide to put a round in the chamber. The metal click chilled Sheila for a moment.

"Is that necessary?" she said. "I thought you trusted Machine Gun."

Bobby lowered the hammer with his thumb, then stuck the gun into his belt in the back of his pants. He took back the steering wheel. "Remember *True Romance?*" he said. She nodded. "I don't know this man personal. Machine Gun said he's OK, but what the fuck does he know, stoned all the time." He glanced at her. "The only person I trust, baby, is you."

They drove in silence for a while, Bobby staring straight ahead, Sheila smoking her cigarette and looking out her window. She stubbed her cigarette out in the ashtray and turned to Bobby. "This Reverend guy, then," she said. "He could be dangerous?"

"I'm not sure. Machine Gun said he's a little crazy but not dangerous. He's some kinda Aryan Nations freak, you know, those rascists live mostly out in Idaho. Except he lives in Davie scrub with his pit bull and enough weapons to start his own revolution. Calls himself the Reverend Tom of the Aryan Mountain Kirk but I don't see any mountains around here, do you? He's got all these skinheads and Nazi wannabes out to his ranch for midnight cross burnings, then a nice church supper prepared by these little old ladies with blue hair.

No pork ribs, though. They don't eat pork 'cause they think they're descendents of the twelve lost tribes of Israel." Bobby laughed. "Maybe they should be living in condos in Plantation, playing mahjong and shuffleboard with the real Jews. The thing about the Reverend, Machine Gun said, is that he hates everybody. Niggers, Spics, Jews, Catholics, Italians, they're all 'mud people' to him, whatever the fuck that means. But he hates Spics the most, Machine Gun said. Something in his past. Machine Gun said, 'Bobby, the dude's awright you don't get on his bad side. Just don't mention the guns are for spics: he might flip out.'"

"There it is." Sheila pointed up ahead to the shiny aluminum diner set back off the road. Bobby turned into the parking lot still deserted close to midnight, the cowboys not yet drunk enough to stagger in for their early morning breakfast. The lot would be crowded when they returned with the guns, though, Bobby thought. Good, all that action in the lot, take the attention off them. He drove around the brightly lit diner to the dark back parking lot until he saw the white van. He parked the black SHO alongside it.

"You wait here," he said, and got out.

Hoshi stood up, alert, now, and followed Bobby with his eyes. "Good boy, Hosh," Sheila said, and stroked his neck. She saw a little man get out of the van. She couldn't make out his face in the darkened lot. She could see only that he was tiny alongside of Bobby's huge bulk. The two men talked for a few moments, then the little man handed Bobby something and walked around to the front of the diner. Bobby waved for Sheila.

Sheila took the briefcase and her bag and got out. Hoshi jumped out, too. She went over to the passenger side of the van and got in alongside Bobby. Hoshi stood outside. He began to bark and back up. "Come on, Hosh!" Sheila said. Hoshi kept barking, backing up.

"What the hell's a matter with him?" Bobby snapped. "Get him in the fucking van!" Sheila reached out, grabbed Hoshi's collar, and yanked him up onto her lap. He wasn't a huge dog, but he was compact, muscular, with a big chest and tiny rear end, like a little bodybuilder. Hoshi squirmed in her lap, whimpering.

"Hoshi! Cut it out, for Crissakes!" Bobby snapped again. The dog calmed down, but only a little. He looked at Bobby and whimpered. "Don't go soft on me now, Hosh. I thought I could rely on you."

Bobby held up the set of keys the little man had given him to the light of the moon through the windshield. "One's to arm the engine burglar alarm," Bobby said. "The other's to arm the rear doors so they can't be opened." Bobby found the remote transmitter with a strip of white tape on it. He pressed the button and all the doors locked with a click, the front lights blinked, and the alarm armed itself with a chirp. Bobby started the engine.

"What about the rear doors?" Sheila said.

Bobby showed her the remote with the red tape on it. "The back door remote only operates with a full load in back. The little spic was very specific. 'Señor Esquared,' he said, 'is muy importante you arm the rear doors the minute the van is loaded with the guns. Not a minute sooner, not a minute later.' Fucking Medina. He's paranoid he'll lose his precious guns for the Revolution." Bobby backed the van out of the space, and drove around the diner. Through the diner's windows, he saw the little man seated at the counter, sipping coffee. "We come back with the guns," Bobby said, "we just hand the little spic the keys, and we're home free."

Ten minutes later they were bouncing over a rutted dirt road so narrow the scrub bushes and palmetto plants brushed against their windows in pitch darkness. Off to the left, Sheila saw tiny green lights flicker a moment, and then disappear.

"Deer," Bobby said. They came into a clearing and a small rise, not even a rise, like a bump in the road, and then a hand-painted sign. "Aryan

Mountain Kirk, Pastor Tom Miller." There was a small, dilapidated, wood-frame cracker house up ahead and beside it a huge quonset-hut-like-barn made out of corrigated alluminum painted green and brown camoflauge.

Bobby parked the van a few yards from the front door and waited. A light came on over the door, then it opened, and a huge man filled the doorway. "Jeezes H. Christ!" Bobby muttered. "He must be six-six, 300." The man was monstrously huge, mythical looking, with a long, scraggily, John Brown spade beard and bib overalls covering his big chest and bigger belly. He wore combat boots.

"Wait here," Bobby said. "I don't come out in ten minutes, you start the engine and drive the fuck outta here."

Sheila looked at him. "You don't come out, I'm going in." She took her little .32 out of her bag.

"Christ. Sheila! That little thing will only piss him off you shoot him, like a mosquito bite. Just do what I told ya."

"Sure, Bobby."

He got out of the van and walked over to the huge man. The man stepped out of the doorway toward Bobby. A dog followed him. The two men shook hands in the darkness, then the huge man wrapped his arms around Bobby as if to hug him. He ran his hands down Bobby's back until he came to the pistol in Bobby's belt. He picked it out, with thumb and forefinger, like it was something rancid. He said something to Bobby, and tossed the gun into the bushes. Then he threw his meaty arm over Bobby's shoulder, the first time Sheila had ever seen Bobby look small next to anyone, and walked him over to the Quonset hut. The man's dog trotted behind them. A small, muscular pit bull Hoshi's size. Hoshi growled low in his throat, the fur on his back bristling, his pricked ears flattened back, as he stared at the pit bull.

Sheila stroked Hoshi's forehead but he seemed not to notice. "That's all right, Hosh. Everything's gonna be all right." The two men and the dog disappeared into the Quonset hut.

Inside the Quonset hut the huge man reached down to pet his dog. "I call him dog-dog," he said in a prophet's booming voice. "He's a loyal guy. An Aryan, too." He winked at Bobby. "White race gotta stick together." He raised his eyebrows and grinned. "Ain't that right Robert Squared?"

"That's right, Reverend."

"Go ahead and pet him, Bobby. He won't bite unless I tell him to."

Bobby reached down with his hand. The small, pale-tan dog looked up at him with mean, yellow eyes. Bobby stroked the dog's fur. His back was covered with lumpy scars. His ears were clipped. His head was too big for his body, all jaws that clamped down and didn't let go.

When Bobby looked up, the man was staring at him. "Bobby Squared, huh? Now what kinda name is that for a full-blood Native American?"

Bobby looked into the huge man's small gray eyes. "It used to be Robert Redfeather on the reservation."

"It did, huh? You shoulda kept it, Bobby. Native Americans are a noble race. They should never have let us in. We ruined the whole damned neighborhood." He threw back his head and roared with laughter. "Come on. Let's see what I got for you."

The Quonset hut was hot. It smelled of mildew and hay and horse shit and gunpowder. The man showed him a card table stacked high with pamphlets, books, newsletters, little plaques that you could hang on the wall, but didn't say, "Home Sweet Home." Bobby looked at it all. *Letters From the Mountain Kirk. The Turner Diaries. The Parabellum Armory* ("We help make war."). *The Brotherhood. The Order. Wenn Alle Bruder Schweigen. No Remorse. The Holy Book of Adolph Hitler.*

The huge man picked up a copy of *The Holy Book of Adolph Hitler*. "Our bible," he said. "He was a great man, eh, Bobby?"

"If you say so Reverend." The man winked at him again, and then, with a sweeping gesture of his big, meaty arm, directed Bobby's eyes to the far end of the hut. There was a barren altar with only a wooden pulpit, and behind it, not a cross, but a huge Nazi flag pinned to the wall.

"The faithful love that shit," the man said. "Hitler, swastikas, burning crosses. Keeps them happy." He shook his head. "They don't even understand National Socialism. But, so what? I figure if they want all that shit, fine, I'll give it to them."

"Where were you ordained, Reverend?"

The man looked at him. "Where?" he said. "WHERE? Right fucking here! I came out here one night and ordained myself." He smiled, then added, "I'm my own fucking God, Bobby."

He walked over to a locked door to the right of his pulpit. He took a set of keys off his belt and opened the door. "After you, Bobby." Bobby stepped into a smaller room filled, floor-to-ceiling, with wooden boxes. They were stamped in black letters: *Brno, Product of Czechoslovakia*; *Israeli Military Industries*; *Llama, Product of Espana*; *Norinco, Product of the People's Republic of China*; *Beretta, Product of Italia*.

The Reverend went over to a box stamped Norinco, opened it, and held up an AK-47. "I believe this is what you're looking for." He racked the slide, aimed the AK at Bobby's forehead, squinted with one eye, and pulled the trigger. Click. He threw back his head and roared again, his booming laughter echoing off the walls. He tossed the AK to Bobby. While Bobby examined it, the Reverend opened boxes and withdrew CZ-75 pistols, Uzis, and a Llama .45.

Bobby handed him back the AK, and smiled. "Everything but the Llama," he said. "My man doesn't like those spic guns."

"A man after my own heart," said the Reverend. "Here, let me show you something." He went over to a closet and opened the door. On the floor were ten big tins labeled, "Survival crackers." On the clothes rack were a dozen different colored satin Ku Klux Klan robes. The man ran the back of his hand down the rack of satin robes. "I got red, I got green, I got yellow," he said. "Robes for every occasion.

Formal, casual, beach wear. They love it." Then he reached up above the robes for a box. He took it down carefully, and turned to Bobby. He took the lid off the box, gently parted the white tissue paper inside, and held the contents out for Bobby to see.

It was a Cuban flag. Three blue stripes, two white stripes, a white star in a red triangle. The flag was dirty and ripped in places, blackened with gunpowder, and stained brown with dried blood. The man watched Bobby as he looked at the flag. Then he looked at it, too, smiling for a moment and then his smile fading, his eyes getting wide, his face flushed.

"I fought for this flag," he said. "I believed in it. It was the only thing I ever believed in. I carried it into battle in the Sierra Madre, and I carried it into Havana after we routed Batista. I was mobbed, like a God. The people shouted my name, 'Gringo! Gringo!' I could have had anything I wanted. Anything! But I only wanted The Revolution to work. They were such good people. They didn't lie, or cheat, and they were so brave. They'd go into battle without any food in their stomachs and fight like a bitch. I made my decision to be with these guys, and they accepted me. I became an outlaw in my own country for them."

He spat on the floor. "And how did that bastard repay me? He put a price on my head, that fucking coward. He wouldn't even enter Havana with us. He was afraid there were still Batista forces there. He waited until we cleaned them out, then he came in two days later. The conquering hero. He pinned a medal on me in a square in Havana with a few hundred thousand people screaming, 'Gringo! Gringo! Gringo!' So Fidel bent over and whispered in my ear, 'You think you're bigger than me, Gringo?' Now, he didn't trust me, see. So he put me in charge of the execution squads, the dirtiest fucking job, to humiliate me. I told him it was a mistake, the Batistas had fought bravely, we should let them in on the Revolution now. But he wouldn't listen. I went around the countryside with a firing squad.

Shot thousands. But I never pulled the trigger myself until one time. Fidel was going to shoot this guy himself, with the guy's wife and little kid watching. They made the guy kneel in front of Fidel but the little bastard had heart. He looked right in Fidel's eyes and dared him to pull the trigger. The fucking coward couldn't do it. He tossed me his gun. 'Here, you do it, Gringo.' I'll never forget it. A chromed, P-38. Fidel was never a Communist. He was a Nazi. He carried a copy of *Mien Kampf* with him everywhere."

The Reverend's eyes went blank. "So I shot him, the little guy. Two weeks later Fidel put out a warrant for my arrest. Treason, it said. I took a slow boat to Miami."

He slammed the lid on the box and shoved it back into the closet. He turned back to Bobby. There were tears in his eyes. "After that, I didn't give a shit. Fuck 'em all. I'll arm everyone, the Jews, Hamas, the IRA, the Ulster Defense Force, both sides. And then I'll sit back and laugh while they kill each other off until there's no one left. God can sort them out." The man smiled again. "So you see, Bobby. I don't give a shit who these guns are for, as long as they're not for spics. Spics *like* to kill their own, they enjoy it. That's why I won't sell to them."

When Bobby and the huge man came out of the Quonset hut, pushing a dolly loaded with boxes, Sheila exhaled a great breath. Bobby signaled her to back the van up to the hut. She slid over Hoshi, started the engine and backed up the van until it was close to them. She heard the back doors open, and the thud of boxes being dropped. Bobby and the man went back into the hut for another load. Sheila lit a cigarette, exhaled, and looked out the driver's side window. The man's dog was sitting there, staring up at her. A mean-looking, muscular little dog. Hoshi climbed onto Sheila's lap and stared down at the dog. He began to growl again, deep in his throat. "It's all right, Hosh. It's all right," she said.

When the van was loaded, Bobby and the man came around to the driver's side window, and stood alongside the man's dog. Sheila opened the window.

"The case, baby," Bobby said. Sheila handed it down to him. Bobby opened it, counted out the Reverend's share, and handed it back up to Sheila. He turned and shook the Reverend's hand.

"Good doing business with you, Reverend."

"You, too, Robert Redfeather." The Reverend raised his eyebrows and smiled. "You oughta come out to a meeting one night, Bobby. I could use someone like you."

Bobby raised his arm to the Reverend's eyes. "I don't think I'm the right color, Reverend. A little muddy, don't ya think?"

"That. That's just bullshit for the assholes, Bobby. I'm not in it for that. I'm in it to fuck the system. Any system. I wanna blow everything up, Bobby. Everything." He looked at Bobby. "Do you *understand*, Bobby?" Bobby nodded his head. The Reverend said, "You think about it, Robert Redfeather. Me and you, we could cry havoc," he winked, "and have a lot of fun doin' it."

"I don't know if I'm that angry, Reverend."

"Sure you are, Bobby. You just don't know it yet."

"I'll think about it." Bobby reached up his hand and opened the van door. But before he could get in, Hoshi leaped out, growling at the Reverend's pit bull. Bobby yelled at him, "Hosh, get back here!"

Hoshi didn't move. He squared off against the pit bull, both of them growling low in their throats, and then they both sprang up on their hind legs, snapping and snarling, their teeth flashing in the darkness. Bobby and the man tried to separate them, both of them screaming at their dogs: "Hosh! Dog-dog! Hosh! Dog-dog!" But the dogs wouldn't stop. The pit bull, less agile, lunged at Hoshi like a clumsy boxer. Hoshi pranced sideways, avoiding the lunge, and as the pit bull passed him, Hoshi took a bite out of the pit bull's rear haunch, drawing blood. The pit bull didn't squeal. He just turned back toward Hoshi with his dead eyes, faked him left, and when Hoshi pranced right, the pit bull caught him, sinking his teeth into the loose ruff of skin around Hoshi's neck, drawing blood.

Three quick shots split the night air, kicking up dirt at the dogs' feet. They separated, whimpering, both glancing up at Sheila holding her .32 steady now on the pit bull. Bobby grabbed Hoshi in his arms. The man dropped to his knees and wrapped his meaty arms around his dog, "Dog-dog! Dog-dog! My baby! Are you all right?" The dog strained against the man's arms to get at Hoshi, but Bobby was already in the van the door closed, with Hoshi beside him still snarling and snapping at the open window. Sheila wrapped her arms around Hoshi and pulled him onto her lap as Bobby started the engine and drove off. She took out a handkerchief from her bag and tried to staunch the flow of blood seeping out of Hoshi's neck.

"Is he all right?" Bobby said.

"I think so. It's just the skin."

Bobby looked back in the outside mirror at the Reverend still on his knees in the dirt, holding his beloved Dog-dog. "The poor old bastard," Bobby muttered.

They drove in silence for a few minutes until they were back on State Road 84, heading east. Sheila was hugging Hoshi to her chest, still inspecting the bite on his neck. "The bleeding's stopped," she said. There was blood all over the front of her shirt. "You're OK, aren't you, Hosh?" The dog looked up at her and licked her face.

"Tough guy, eh, Hosh?" Bobby said, smiling. "Bit off more than you could chew this time."

Sheila was holding the little Seecamp up to the lights of passing cars. "You were right, Bobby."

"About what?"

"It is easy. You just pull the trigger and it does the rest."

"If it was so easy why didn't you kill the fucking pit bull?"

"I don't know. I couldn't. He was just a dog. Only people deserve their own execution."

"Yeah, well a coupla more minutes Hoshi woulda had his own execution."

"Then I woulda killed the pit bull."

They pulled into the diner's parking lot, now crowded with cars and pickup trucks, at 2 A.M. Sheila could see through the diner's windows all the cowboys seated at the counter, having breakfast. Bobby drove around to the back parking lot and parked alongside of his SHO.

"The spic's inside waiting," he said. "I'll be right back."

"I'm going in, too. I want to clean up Hoshi in the ladies' room."

She looked down at her western shirt soaked in blood. "Myself too." Bobby grabbed the briefcase and Sheila hoisted Hoshi into her arms.

The diner was crowded and noisy with rednecks and their girlfriends all dressed up like cowboys with their ten-gallon Stetsons, talking loud, letting out rebel yells, harassing the waitresses. Sheila brushed through the crowd toward the ladies' room. A waitress tried to stop her.

"You can't bring a dog in here, ma'm," she said.

"Watch me."

Bobby looked around for the spic. He walked down the aisle looking along the counter for him. The rednecks glanced over their shoulders at him, his blond ponytail, the briefcase in his hand. Someone said, "Faggot!"

Bobby went over to a waitress balancing three trays of food on her arm. "Honey," he said, "did you see a little Latin guy in here?"

The waitress blew a wisp of hair off her brow. "I got time to look for spics?" She brushed past him.

Bobby asked another waitress. "Give me a fuckin' break?" she said.

The third waitress he asked, said, "Yeh, I seen him a coupla hours ago. Nervous little guy. Had a coffee, made a phone call, and split.

"You got a phone, hon?"

She pointed to the end of the diner. "Sure, baby. In the little boys' room."

Bobby pushed through the crowd to the men's room in back. The telephone was alongside a window looking out onto the back parking lot. He dialed Medina's number, and as it rang, he noticed a cowboy taking a piss. He wore a straw cowboy hat, the brim lovingly curled.

The cowboy glanced over his shoulder at him. "What the fuck you lookin' at?" he said.

"Nothing." Bobby looked out the window. Medina's phone was still ringing. It was dark in the back parking lot, but Bobby could still see his SHO and beside it, the white van . . . with all those guns in it, nobody watching, no alarm turned on. "Oh, shit!" he muttered. He dug out the keys from his pocket, found the remote with the red tape on it, held the remote out the window, aimed it at the van, and pressed the button. The van's rear lights blinked twice, the alarm chirped like a bird, then there was a blinding flash of light, and the whole thing exploded.

The rear doors blew off; the side panels blew off; the guns blew out of the van in pieces hanging a moment in the air, engulfed by flames and black smoke, scattering all over the lot. The van was in flames, twisted out of shape. The left side of his SHO was caved in. There were bits of glass everywhere, gun parts, van doors, the bumper.

"Jesus Fucking Christ, man, what'd ya do?" said the cowboy at the urinal.

Bobby looked at him. He was still holding his dick, turned toward Bobby now, pissing on the floor. Bobby rushed out of the men's room and almost bumped into Sheila holding Hoshi.

"Bobby! Bobby! You all right? What happened?"

He grabbed her hard by the arm and half dragged her out of the diner. Most of the cowboys and waitresses had already gone outside to see what had happened. Bobby dragged Sheila through the crowd toward the highway, and started walking very fast along the side of the road away from the diner. In the distance, he could already hear the sirens of police cars and fire engines. They walked very fast in the darkness, Bobby still dragging Sheila behind him, until finally, she jerked him to a stop.

"*Enough!*" she snapped. They were both breathing heavily. Sheila put Hoshi down on the ground. "What *happened?*"

Bobby could still see the smoke billowing above the diner. Finally, he said, "It was a setup." He told her about the little man's execution by the 'Big Fucking Gringo' in Havana in front of his wife and son almost forty years ago.

"Medina didn't give a shit about the guns," Bobby said. "It was revenge he wanted. 'I never forget my enemies, Señor Esquared.' Yeh, or his friends. The Reverend was right. They kill their own."

Sheila looked at him, her eyes suddenly cold. She said in a flat voice, "You should have known, Bobby. You were careless. Again."

He nodded, but said nothing.

They started walking again in silence. Hoshi trotted beside them. Bobby reached down a hand to pet him. "I shoulda listened to ya, Hosh." He glanced at Sheila. She was staring straight ahead with that cold look in her eyes.

They came to a pay phone by the side of the road. Bobby called for a taxi, then hung up. They waited in darkness for the taxi, illuminated every so often for a brief instant by the light of passing cars.

"Bobby," Sheila said. "I don't know if I can go on like this anymore."

"I know, baby. I'm sorry."

"You're sorry!"

"I mean, I understand."

She stared at him, her face flushed. "*No*, you don't. You don't understand a fucking thing! It drives me crazy every night!"

"What? What drives you crazy?"

She looked at him with her lips pursed, like the schoolmistress she had once been. Finally, she said, "Robert. Hoshi and I have decided. You are going to have to stop stripping."

10

BOBBY AND SOL SIPPED THEIR DRINKS AND STARED AT THE BARBECUE GRILL.

"Maybe you ain't used enough lighter fluid?" Sol said.

"I use any more," Bobby said, "I'll burn down the whole fucking complex."

They were standing on a redwood deck under the shade of a date palm in the front yard of Bobby's apartment building. It was a hot, sunny, Wednesday afternoon. Sheila was floating on a rubber raft in the pool behind them. She was wearing only the bottoms of her bikini. She cradled a drink in a cool glass between her breasts, laid her head back, and closed her eyes to the hot sun.

"Maybe you're not using enough lighter fluid on the briquettes, Bobby?" Sheila said.

Bobby looked over his shoulder. Sol said, "I already told him, Sheila. He's so fucking thick I don't know how you stand it."

Sheila smiled, her eyes closed, and said, "Well, he's got a few things going for him, Solly."

Bobby lit another match and dropped it on the briquettes. They flamed up for a few seconds, then went out.

"We'll be eatin' steaks at midnight," Sol said.

"You think you can do any better," Bobby said. "You light the fucking things." He thrust the matches and lighter fluid at Sol.

Sol doused the briquettes, lit a match, and dropped it into the grill. The brickettes flamed up in their faces. They jumped back.

"Jesus Christ!" Bobby said. "I think you burned my fucking eyebrows off."

"You guys should be in vaudeville," Sheila said.

The briquettes were still flaming. Bobby looked at them and said, "That's how the van went up. What a fucking mess."

Sol shook his head. "I'm sorry about that, Bobby. If I had known. . . . You can't trust nobody these days."

"If it wasn't for the Hosh," Bobby said, "and Sheila, we all woulda been burnt to shit."

"The Hosh awright?" Sol said.

"Just a few bites is all," Bobby said. "Sheila put peroxide on them."

"That shit she uses on her hair?" Sol said.

"*Hydrogen* peroxide, Sol," Sheila said from the raft. "For infections."

The briquettes were still flaming. "Aren't they supposed to stop burning and get red-hot?" Bobby said.

"I think Hoshi's pride was hurt more than anything else," Sheila said.

"I heard you was a real Annie Oakley," Sol said.

"A girl's got to earn her keep," Sheila said. "Someone told me that once."

Sol glanced at her and smiled, the way he did at Bobby sometimes. "Well, you done good, baby," he said.

"Why, thank you, Sol." she said.

". . . For an old, straight broad," he added, grinning.

"Old, maybe," Sheila said. "But not so straight anymore."

Sheila began paddling the water with her free hand. The raft drifted toward the steps that led out of the pool. A UPS truck pulled up in the parking lot behind a low line of hedges that separated it from the pool. Bobby and Sol watched the UPS guy, carrying a box, walking toward them.

The UPS guy smiled at them and said, "I got a package for a . . ." he looked at the label, ". . . a Mr. Chris Brownley. You know what apartment that might be?" Sheila stepped out of the pool and began walking toward them.

"I think he's in eight," Bobby said. "But he ain't home."

The UPS guy was staring over Bobby's shoulder with his mouth half open. Sheila came over to them and laid down on the chaise lounge beside the grill. The UPS guy stared at her huge breasts spilling off her chest.

"Yo, slick!" Sol said. "He said, apartment eight."

The UPS guy looked at Sol, and said, "Oh, yeah, right."

Bobby and Sol watched him leave the package at apartment eight's door, then walk back to his truck and drive off.

Sol turned to Sheila, lying on her back, her eyes closed to the sun. "Didn't nobody ever teach you nothin' about modesty?" he said.

Sheila smiled and opened her eyes. "You see something you've never seen before, Sol?" she said. She closed her eyes again. "I thought you owned The Booby Trap, for crissakes. Home of Stylish Nude Entertainment."

"I'm not talkin' about me," Sol said. "The fucking guy almost had a heart attack."

Bobby smiled. "Good thing Solly and me was here to protect you, baby."

"Besides," Sol said. "I never owned The Trap. I just fronted for Meyer until I got busted on that smuggling rap. I don't own nothin'."

"What about your condo and that black gangster Cadillac you drive?" Sheila said.

"Rented. Everything. Even my jewelery. You own nothin', you lose nothin', Sheila. That's how you get hurt. You got something you're afraid of losing you try to protect it is when you go down."

"Speakin' of going down," Bobby said. "What about Medina?"

"He's a problem, Bobby," Sol said. "You gotta figure out what he wants."

Sheila opened her eyes and sat up. "What *he* wants? The bastard tried to kill us, Sol. He should be worrying about what *we* want."

Sol looked at her. "You know, Sheila, for a smart broad you can be dumb sometimes."

Sheila rolled her eyes. "Oh, please, Sol. Stop with the compliments." She laid back down and closed her eyes.

"Medina ain't like us," Sol said. "He don't think, who's right, who's wrong? How he thinks is, what *he* wants is what's right. You gotta look at things through his eyes. Once you figure out what he wants you can protect yourself . . . maybe."

"So?" Bobby said. "What the fuck does he want? His twenty-five large back? The guns? The Reverend?" He glanced at Sheila, and then back to Sol.

Sol drained his drink. "Sheila, honey. Why dontcha get me and your boyfriend two more drinks?"

Sheila glanced at Sol through half-lidded eyes. "You're pushing it, Sol." She stood up, took their glasses, and went to their apartment.

Sol waited until she was inside, then said to Bobby, "You don't know, Bobby?"

"I got an idea."

"He wants it all, Bobby. He's a pig. He don't want the twenty-five large, he wants the whole hundred. *And* the guns. *And* his revenge. *And* you and Sheila, and maybe even the Hosh, too you made him look foolish." Bobby nodded. "I were you and Sheila, Bobby, I'd get outta Dodge. Take a few months vacation. Go back to the mountains in East-bumfuck, your roots and shit."

"I don't think so."

"Why not?"

"We don't have enough cash to go on ice for a few months."

"You got the twenty-five large, don't you?"

"Not exactly. I spent most of it on Sheila's car."

"You're fuckin' kiddin' me? Before the deal went down?" Sol shook his head. "Jesus, Bobby, either you got balls like watermelons, or you're a stupid prick." Bobby grinned, shrugged. "Or else maybe your old lady been teachin' you things in the sack make your head spin?"

"Maybe you oughta try an old lady sometime, Solly. Instead of those little baby chicks you like. Old ladies are always grateful, ya know. They leave a little note on your pillow the next morning. Fix you breakfast, watch your ass." Bobby looked at the briquettes. "I'll be a sunuvabitch. They're glowing like they're supposed to."

"Fuck the briquettes, Bobby. I were you I wouldn't just be watchin' my ass I'd be usin' it in that G-string of yours so you can make some getaway stash."

Bobby sighed. "Well, I'm not exactly dancin' anymore, Solly."

"What? Why not?"

Bobby tossed a headfake toward his apartment. "Sheila."

"Jesus, Bobby! Who wears the fuckin' pants?"

Sheila came out of the apartment with their drinks and Hoshi on a leash. She was wearing a T-shirt now. She handed them their drinks. Hoshi put his paw on Sol's leg. Sol bent over and petted him.

"The Hosh. How's my man?" Hoshi wagged his tail and licked Sol's face.

Bobby said to Sheila, "Sol thinks we should take a vacation. Maybe go to the mountains for a few months." Sheila looked at him, but said nothing.

Sol said, "The spic won't go lookin' for you there. He won't leave South Florida, not even for you two."

"I don't see why we should let Medina run us out of town, Sol," Sheila said.

"It doesn't matter what *you* 'see,'" Sol said. "That's your only option."

"What about the money to live? Where's that going to come from?" Sheila said.

"We need one more score," Bobby said.

"Me, too," Sol said. He was quiet for a moment, then he said, "I gotta go away for a while. That old smuggling charge. Meyer's been delaying it for years, filing papers, runnin' them around the block till they're exhausted."

"I thought that went away," Bobby said.

"Almost," Sol said. "The judge who sentenced me, an old fucker, forgot to sign the order puttin' me away. Then he retired and took the order home with him nobody could find it for years the judge not tellin' nobody because he's embarrassed, see? He's almost senile. The whole thing woulda gone away except for this hamster parole office I had to report to every week. Fuckin' eighteen thousand dollar-a-year hamster he's wondering how come I'm out on bond all these years and so one day he tells me I can't leave Broward County, can't associate with felons, and can't carry a firearm or else he'll take away my driver's license and I'll be in big trouble. So I tell him, 'Listen, Sambo, I only know felons, I always carry a piece, and I not only leave Broward a lot but the country, too. And if I get caught I won't need a fuckin' driver's license for twenty years.'

"Pissed him off, I guess, 'cause he went to this old judge, gets my papers, and takes 'em to another judge to sign to put me away."

"Well, I guess you showed that parole officer," Sheila said.

"Fucking right I did," Sol said.

"You *really* believe that, don't you Sol?" Sheila said, shaking her head.

"He really does, baby," Bobby said. "He gets off on playing games with the heat, only he plays by different rules than them so that when he loses he can claim he won, ain't that right Solly?"

"Bet your ass," Sol said.

"Where you goin'?" Bobby said.

"Jessup. The Federal slam. I gotta do a year, maybe eight months, six if I'm a good boy."

"Oh, Sol. I'm sorry," Sheila said.

Sol waved a hand at her. "It's nothin'. I been expectin' it. I'll miss the Hosh here, though." They were quiet for a moment. Then Sol said, "I could use a stake when I get out. I thought, maybe a little score now, let you two hold it for me."

Sheila smiled at him. "Then that's what we'll have to do, Sol. A little score for our vacations."

Sol nodded, then took Hoshi's leash from Sheila. "Here, baby, let me take him for a walk. Come on big guy, piss time." Sheila and Bobby watched Sol lead Hoshi toward the little park at the end of the canal.

Sheila said, "Sometimes I watch him with Hoshi and he's like a little boy." She turned to Bobby. "That sounds funny doesn't it?"

"No. Remember *The Wild Bunch* when William Holden takes his gang to that Mexican village. He's watching two of his baddest dudes playing with little Mexican kids and he can't believe it. The old padrone of the village says, 'Why not? Even in the worst of us beats the heart of a child.'" Bobby looked at the glowing briquettes. "Maybe you better go get the steaks, baby."

Sheila went back to their apartment. Bobby pushed the glowing briquettes around with a long fork. He remembered the day Sol decided Hoshi was his "main man." Bobby and Sol were walking Hoshi at the park when a guy came along with a big Rottweiler with a studded collar. The Rotty went up to Hoshi and growled at him. Without a sound, Hoshi leaped at the Rotty's throat, just missing it as the guy pulled his dog back.

The guy laughed at the thirty-pound red dog attacking his hundred-pound dog. "You ought to get that little dog a mirror," the guy said. "Let him see how small he is."

Sol said, "Heh, slick. Don't ever call him a dog. The Hosh is beyond dog."

Sheila came back out with a tray of steaks. Bobby said to her, "I gotta use your car tonight, baby."

"Why?"

"Something I gotta do."

"Bobby!"

"I was thinking I should go out to see Reverend Tom. Have a little talk."

Sheila didn't say anything for a moment. Then she nodded, and said, "Did you tell Sol?"

"No. I already know what he'd say." He smiled, and then, mimicking Sol's voice, he said, "Bobby you gotta leave tings alone don't concern you. You do tings to make yerself feel good it fucks you up. You wanna feel good about yerself, go take the broad here, and Hosh, and go to the fuckin' reservation a few months, show the broad your roots, chop down trees, sit around a fuckin' fire whatever you do there."

Sheila smiled at him. "I'd like that, Bobby. Yes, I'd like that." Then she said, "You know, you would have made a good actor."

11

BOBBY DROVE WEST ON STATE ROAD 84 IN SHEILA'S BMW. IT WAS JUST starting to get dark out at 8 o'clock. He saw the airstream diner up ahead. He slowed the BMW and pulled into the right lane to let the car behind pass him. He looked in his rearview mirror. The car behind him slowed, too, and pulled in behind the BMW. A big, black, Mercedes 600 with blacked-out windows.

As Bobby passed the diner, he stared across the highway. There was a "closed" sign on the diner's front window and yellow crime scene tape all around the parking lot. His SHO was probably still there, all smashed in. Registered to a phony name, thanks to Meyer.

It was dark by the time Bobby reached the dirt road that led to the Reverend's ranch. He slowed the BMW again and looked in his rearview mirror. The Mercedes was still behind him. He picked up speed as he passed the dirt road. A few minutes later he was driving past one of those far west Broward subdivisions that all looked alike. Identical, cheap imitation Spanish-style homes jammed close together around an artificial lake. He could see off to his right, under the lights around the lake, old women with leathery tans power-walking in orange and pink Day-Glo leotards, a few young mothers pushing baby carriages.

When he came to a strip shopping mall he pulled into the parking lot, and waited. He watched in his rearview mirror as the big Merc passed the mall and kept heading down 84 toward Alligator Alley. Bobby waited a few minutes, then pulled the BMW back onto 84, made a U-turn, and headed back toward the Reverend's house. He kept glancing at his rearview mirror for the Merc, but it wasn't there anymore. He saw the Reverend's dirt road up ahead to his left now. He gunned the accelerator until the little BMW was doing almost 70 mph, the narrow dirt road coming up fast to his left, and then, suddenly, Bobby jerked the steering wheel to his left, the BMW shooting across the highway, cutting off a car coming from the opposite direction, the driver jamming on his brakes, his tires smoking, squealing, the car swerving to miss the BMW, the driver nailing his palm into his horn as Bobby shot past him and began bouncing wildly down the bumpy dirt road. . . .

The old man heard the car approaching before he saw its headlights. He called to his wife in bed, "Don't worry, Dot! I'll see who it is." He grabbed his pump 12 gauge with the pistol grip from the kitchen and walked toward the door, a huge bearded man in bib overalls, trailed by a pit bull with mean, yellow eyes and scabs on his flank.

The old man saw the BMW stop in the open space in front of his house. His dog began to growl. A man got out. The old man smiled down at the dog, and said, "It's all right, Dog-dog. It's only the Indian."

He opened the door and smiled at Bobby coming toward him. "Robert Redfeather! What a surprise! I didn't think I'd see you again." The Indian glanced at the pump in his hand, pointed toward the floor, and then the growling dog. "I'm sorry, Robert. This is no way to greet a friend." He put the pump behind the front door, then said to his dog, "Behave yourself. We have a guest. Come in, Robert. Come in."

Bobby hesitated a moment, waiting for the old man to pat him down. When he didn't, Bobby stepped into the house. It smelled musty, from age and dampness and that smell that old poor people have. The living room was sparsely furnished with worn furniture. A drab green cordouroy sofa with stained doilies on each arm. An old rocking chair with a cushion on the seat. A card table in the center of the room that served for a dining-room table. The flowered wallpaper was peeling in places. There were water stains on the cracked ceiling. It could have been the home of any poor old farmer and his wife, living out their lives on Social Security, except that there was nothing personal in it. No family photographs. No mementoes. No reminders of long-dead relatives or grown children and their children. "You go to a guy's house," Sol once told Bobby, "you know right away he's in the business."

"Have a seat, Robert," the old man said, gesturing toward the sofa. Bobby sat on the edge of the sofa, hunched forward, his elbows on his knees. The Reverend sat across from him in his rocking chair.

"So, you've come to tell me something important, Robert."

"How do you know? Maybe I just came for my piece?"

The old man smiled. "No, I think not. But. . . ." He stood up and left the room. He returned with Bobby's CZ and handed it to him.

"Thanks Reverend," Bobby said.

"A commie gun, Robert. Why don't you get yourself a nice Walther? Support the cause."

Bobby stuck the CZ in his pants in the small of his back. "I heard they don't feed hollowpoints."

"No, they don't. There used to be a time when Aryan shit was top of the line. Now, you got your Hondas and AK 47s and Semtex. It's a sad commentary on the Aryan Revolution, Robert."

Bobby said, "You know why I'm here, Reverend?"

"I have an idea. That little trouble you got into at the diner. It was all over the television. Maybe you think I had something to do with it?"

"You did. But not the way you think." Then he told him about

Medina, how he'd set up the whole deal just for revenge. The old man listened, without speaking, nodding every now and then, his mind wandering back to that hot afternoon in Havana years ago.

When Bobby finished, the Reverend was silent for a moment, looking down at his big, callused hands folded between his legs like an old man praying at church. There *was* something religious about this old man, but not like the men Bobby had studied on the reservation. Saints and martyrs who gave up their lives for Christianity. Who let themselves be boiled in oil, crucified on the cross, mutilated, disemboweled, castrated, dismembered, drawn and quartered on the rack. This old man would never let such things happen to him. He was out of the Old Testament. Bitter, avenging, full of fury and blood lust at the weaknesses, betrayals, lies, and cowardices of his puny fellow human beings.

Finally, the old man spoke, "That was the only thing I've ever done in my life I'm ashamed of, Robert. The poor little bastard. His wife and son watching. Now it's come back on me, huh?" He sighed, a great breath.

"A friend of mine knows the spic, said he won't rest till he gets what he wants."

"Of course, Robert. That's the way the game is played. He'll want everything. He deserves it, his chance for revenge. It's not up to me to deprive him of his right."

"You could leave."

"That wouldn't be right, Robert. It would be best for us both to settle this thing once and for all. Besides, I can't leave. My wife, Dot, is sick. She had a stroke a few years ago. I can't run anymore." He brightened, smiled. "But it'll be a good way to go, eh, on top of my shield, maybe a burial at sea like the old Norse warriors, my body laid out on a bed of dried straw on a burning boat drifting out to sea." He winked at Bobby. "Not a bad way to go, Robert. But I'll tell you one thing. I'm going to take a few of those cocksuckers down with me." He threw back his head and laughed, his booming laugh echoing off the walls.

When he stopped laughing, Bobby said, "I could help you. Between the two of us. . . ." The old man cut him off.

"It's not your fight, Robert. Besides, you've got your own set of problems. He'll want you, too, and that smart lady of yours who knows how to think on her feet." He chuckled, and shook his head. "She was something, Robert, the way she saved us all. Temporarily, anyway. Tell her I'm grateful she didn't kill my Dog-dog when she had the chance. I know she could have." He reached down to stroke his pale, yellow dog lying at his feet.

"You and I are lucky men, Robert. We've found good women to stand by us. Now, my Dot, she's been through it all, and she never once complained. Forty-five years of it. She never questioned where I went, how long I was gone, who I returned with. She never asked me why the heat was always knocking on our door, why, one night the FBI, DEA, ATF, came swarming over our farmhouse in Ocala. They came in cars and trucks and helicopters with drawn guns, frightening my wife, those cocksuckers."

His voice became angry now, like an angry, old prophet. "I met them at the door, twenty of them with drawn guns. 'You want me, you cocksuckers,' I told them, 'all you had to do is send one man, not a whole fucking army.' They confiscated my guns and sent me away for seven years." He laughed. "I became the prison handball champion in Marion, partners with a black Muslim. Taught him a lot about his African ancestors, great warriors. While I was inside Dot kept things going. She worked as a domestic cleaning toilets in cheap motels with nigger women. They hated her, a white woman stealing a job from one of their own, but she didn't give a shit. She did what she had to do. Why? Because she was loyal to me. She'd taken an oath, 'through sickness and in health.'

"When I got out, she'd got old, older than me in those seven years. Hell, I was livin' large, three squares, exercise, books to read, good white Aryan fascists to proselytize, while she was struggling. I was only out a few months when she had her stroke. I offered to go into another line of work, but she wouldn't hear it. 'It's what you are,' she said. 'What I married.' They're not like us, Robert. They're tougher than us. They can talk themselves into doing anything for their man. Things even we wouldn't do." He smiled. "The Master Race, you might say. Anyway, I moved down here from Ocala because I thought no one would know me here. It's been a good life. I take care of Dot. I carry her from the bed to the bathroom and put her on the toilet. I wipe her ass, Robert, than carry her back to bed after I wash her and dress her and feed her. My penance, Robert, for the life I lived. But I don't give a shit. It's the life I chose. We both chose, Robert. Once you make a choice you can't second guess yourself. You made the choice, Robert. You know why we're in it. For the action, not the juice. The rest of it is just looking for a reason we can hang it on." He flung out his hand as if to dismiss something. "The other poor bastards. What do they know? Living out their boring death every fucking day. At least we had fun, eh, Robert?"

Bobby smiled. "I never thought of it that way Reverend. Maybe you're right, I don't know."

A woman's shrill voice called out from another room, "Tom! Tom!"

The old man jumped up, smiling. "She's awake. Now, you can meet her." He left the room and returned a few minutes later pushing his wife in her wheelchair. He pushed her up against the card table in the center of the room.

"I'll get your water and your cigarettes, Dot," the old man said, smiling. He left the room with a lighthearted skip, like one of those tap dancers in the old black-and-white movies Sheila insisted Bobby watch.

His wife sat there, staring straight ahead, not looking at Bobby. Her face was without expression, pale, puffy, a plain looking old woman with small, hard, faded blue eyes. She looked small and mortal in contrast to the Reverend's huge, mythological bulk. But not fragile. No, there was nothing fragile about this cold, mean-looking old woman with eyes as dead as her dog's.

The Reverend returned with her water and cigarettes. Camels. She immediately lit a cigarette, took a deep drag, and coughed, a hacking cough. Her husband stood over her, looking down at his wife with the smile of a man doing penance.

"Now, for dinner," he said, rubbing his hands together. "I'm making hamburgers, fried onions, and cottage fries." She said nothing.

He sat back in his rocking chair. "This is the Indian boy I told you about, Dot. A noble savage." She didn't look at Bobby. The old man said, "Dot is my only cause now. My only happiness." He smiled at her. She stared at the far wall. "When I married her I told her all I could promise her was excitement. She knew I was involved in things, but she never asked questions. She was a good wife, isn't that so, Dot?"

"I'm not saying anything," she said in a gravelly voice.

"See! A good wife!"

"All he said to me was, 'I can't promise you anything but excitement.'"

"When I was a boy, all I ever asked from God was that I could have adventures, an exciting life. And he was good to me. He gave me what I asked for." He laughed. "Beware of what you ask for, Robert. Maybe you'll get it."

The old man stood up. "I'll cook dinner now, Dot." Her face was blank as she dragged on her cigarette and coughed. The old man skipped into the kitchen. Bobby could hear him chopping things, than the sizzle of a frying pan on a hot stove. Suddenly, the Reverend appeared in the doorway. He was wearing a woman's apron now, with little frills around it. He wiped his hands on the apron, and said, "Robert, why don't you stay for dinner? Be our guest. We don't get many."

For the first time, the old woman glanced at Bobby with her small, mean, threatening eyes.

Bobby stood up. "Thanks anyway, Reverend, but I have to be going. I just wanted to stop by, say hello." He moved toward the door.

The Reverend called out to him. "You be careful, Robert Redfeather." Bobby glanced back at him, a huge man in a woman's apron. The old man added, "And thank you, Robert."

Bobby sat in Sheila's BMW, too weak to turn the key. He stared through the window, seeing the old woman, and Sheila, himself, and the Reverend. Finally, he started the car and drove back over the rutted dirt road to State Road 84. He waited for a break in traffic, then pulled out onto the highway and headed east toward Lauderdale. He passed a car parked at a gas station. A Mercedes 600 with blacked-out windows. He glanced in his rearview mirror, but the Mercedes didn't follow him.

When he got back to the apartment, Sheila said, "How'd it go?"

He told her about the old man. But he didn't tell her about his wife.

12

THE MEXICAN MAID WAS CLEANING UP THE KITCHEN THAT LOOKED DOWN over the vast white living room, dominated by a yellow leather sofa in Señor Tex's penthouse condominium on Brickell Avenue in Miami. The living room was surrounded on three sides by floor-to-ceiling glass doors that looked out over the pale blue-green waters of Miami Bay below.

Carmalita watched Señor Tex's men setting up their cameras to film the Señor in his unmentionable acts with his Cubano puta. One of Señor's men was talking to a stranger, a pudgy, little man with greased-back hair. He was wearing a white Guayabera and white slacks, with tiny, patent leather shoes as small as a child's.

"It is such an honor, Señor Medina," said Raymon. Medina nodded. "Señor Tex will be ready in a few minutes. Would you like to sit?" Medina moved toward the yellow sofa. "I wouldn't sit there, Señor," said Raymon, grinning. "I have been here two years and I have never sat on that sofa."

Raymon, tall and thin with sallow, pockmarked skin, pushed the sofa against the wall directly underneath the maid in the kitchen. Then he set up his camera in front of the sofa. "It is a simple formula, Señor Medina," he said. "Tex meets girl, Tex fucks girl."

"Yes," said Medina, "simplicity, it is the heart of wisdom."

Another assistant, who looked like the evil Mexican general in *The Wild Bunch*, came into the room pushing a metal pail full of hot, soapy water and a long-handled mop. "Señor Tex wishes you would join him upstairs, Señor Medina, at your pleasure," said the man.

Medina went upstairs. Tex, wearing his trademark cowboy hat and jeans, was waiting for him in the hallway. "An honor, Señor Medina," he said. "To share my artistic vision with you is a great honor."

"And for me, Señor Tex. I so rarely see my business ventures at such close hand."

"Without your support, Señor, I couldn't give the world the pleasure of my vision. Let me show you."

Tex led Medina into his wardrobe room and pointed to all the little schoolgirl outfits on hangers. Pink and baby blue and lime green and mango little tube tops and tiny miniskirts, and white lacy ankle socks alongside row after row of six-inch high strippers' pumps.

"It's a simple philosophy," said Tex. "If a whore lets you fuck her up the ass, it's no shock. But if an innocent little girl lets you, that's the back story." Tex smiled through yellowed teeth. He had small, watery blue eyes and a fringe of yellowish-orange hair beneath his cowboy hat. "I learned there's no limits to the perversions girls are willing to perform."

Medina nodded. "Ah, yes. Perversion." He smiled. "I know something of this. It is what . . . how do you say it . . . makes the world go around."

"Precisely," said Tex. "The more you degrade them, the more they love it." He winked at Medina. "But, heah, Señor, I'm not an evil guy."

Medina threw up his hands as if to dismiss Tex's comment. "Evil," he said, "is overrated, no? There is no such thing. There is only what you want and what you have to do to get it."

Tex smiled through his tiny yellowed teeth. "I knew you'd understand, Señor Medina. Come, let me show you the fruits of your support."

He led Medina into his office. The walls of his office were decorated with plaques that read: Adult Video News, Best Anal; Adult Video News, Best Perversion. One wall was stacked floor to ceiling with colorful video boxes. Tex took one from the stack and handed it to Medina. Medina studied the box cover. Naked, skinny, prepubescent schoolgirls with Tex's cock in their lipstick-smeared mouths and a wide-eyed look of shocked pleasure on their faces.

"So, this is your artistic vision, Señor Tex?"

"I sell fantasies," said Tex, sitting down behind his desk. Medina sat across from him. "We're very forward thinking here at Texicunt. We go places where others are afraid to go."

"We think alike, then," said Medina.

"It takes courage."

"Yes. Courage. Sometimes it is misunderstood, courage, no?"

"Absolutely, Señor. Ignorant people call it other things."

Medina flung the back of his hand in the air. "Fools. They have no understanding of real courage, do they?" Tex shook his head, no. "Only men like you and I, Señor Tex, truly understand it." He smiled at Tex. "Is simple, no? You do the thing everyone else is too afraid to do."

Tex smiled. "I knew you'd understand, Señor Medina." Just then a little girl entered the room. She was dressed like a naughty schoolgirl out of *Clueless*. Pink tube top; tiny pink pleated miniskirt; lacy white ankle socks, and, incongruously, strippers' six-inch high pumps. Her shiny black hair was pulled out into pigtails at either side of her head. She looked very young, almost prepubescent, except for her heavy makeup, blue eye shadow, crimson cheeks, blood-red lips, and the faint lines of aging at her lips and eyes.

Medina stood up and kissed the little girl's hand. "My pleasure, again, Señorita Bimini."

"Oh, thank you, Señor," she said in a lisping Spanish accent. "I'm soooo glad you could join us today. You won't be disappointed."

"I'm sure," said Medina. The little girl sat down beside him.

"Bimini *is* Texicunt," said Tex. "She is a genius, like Meryl Streep, and fearless, too." Bimini smiled and fluttered her long, fake eyelashes. "She had other directors but they never gave her the direction I have."

"Yes, Tex helps me create my character," she said. "Then the character creates me. I become. . . ."

"This living, breathing doll," said Tex.

The little girl frowned. "I don't call myself that. I call myself an actress. I like to be in costume and acting with dialogue."

"Did anyone tell you how cute you look today?" said Tex.

Bimini fluttered her eyelashes. "I try to be."

"Tell Señor Medina what you like best," said Tex.

"I like the peeing part," said Bimini. "That's good."

"What about the anal?" Tex said. Bimini frowned. "You know."

Bimini thought. "Yes, what Tex said."

"You're such a ham, Bimini," Tex said.

Bimini frowned. "What's that?"

"You like to be in front of a camera," Tex said.

"I looove that," she said.

"Our brand of art is very advanced," Tex said to Medina. "Most girls won't do it."

"Not me," said Bimini, smiling. "I love *every*-thing."

"I'm sure," said Medina.

Bimini frowned, a cartoon frown. "Except coming. I don't like that. It's hard work. Why bother? Besides, I'm not a slut. I'm an actress."

"Of course you are," said Medina.

Tex grinned his cartoon grin. "That's my job, isn't it, Bimini?"

"What?"

"Coming."

"Oh, yes." She smiled lasciviously at him. "That's what you're good at, Tex."

"Tell Señor Medina what you learned to do. Her new talent."

Bimini turned toward Medina, her eyes opened wide like a child's and said, "I learned to fist-fuck myself."

Medina blinked, then smiled. "A noteworthy talent. You are to be commended."

Bimini frowned. "It was hard, at first."

"Of course," said Medina, seriously. "Such a tiny girl, you must have a very. . . ."

"I do, I do!" she said. "Look!" She held up one hand in a fist. "I have the biggest hands for a little girl." She looked across the desk at Tex, and smiled. "But Tex helped me until I could do it."

Tex fluttered his eyelashes modestly. "My job as her leader is to inspire confidence." Then he smiled and rubbed his hands together. "Well, baby, it's showtime. Señor Medina is a very busy man."

While Bimini went to touch up her makeup, Tex and Medina went downstairs to the living room.

"We ready?" Tex said to Raymon.

"All set."

Tex went to a cabinet next to the sliding-glass doors that looked out over Miami Bay and opened it. It was filled with bottles of drinking water. Tex opened one and drained it. "I drink a lot of water," he said to Medina with his leering, comic-book grin. "You're gonna see why."

Bimini came clopping onto the white tile floor in her strippers' pumps. She smiled, "I'm ready! I'm soooo ready!"

Tex said, "Are you wearing panties?"

"I dunno." Bimini lifted up her skirt and looked between her legs. "No."

Tex turned to Medina and said, "First, we film the 'meet and greet' shots." Tex and Bimini went to the far corner of the room. When Raymon called, "Action," they began walking toward the center of the room. Medina stood behind Raymon, straining to see over his shoulder on his tip toes.

Tex leered at Bimini and said, "I want to fuck you, little girl."

Bimini stared, wide-eyed, at the camera, and said, "But I don't know how!"

Tex leered even more comically at the camera, and said, "Well, then, I'll just have to teach you, little girl."

Bimini began to take off her tube top slowly until her small, plump breasts were exposed. Then she pulled down her tiny skirt and stepped out of it. She stood there, naked, except for her ankle socks and pumps. She made a feeble attempt at concealing her breasts and her shaved, pink pussy by crossing an arm across her breasts and a hand at her pussy. Tex leered at her nakedness. Then he leered even more comically at the camera. He took off his shirt and his jeans, but not his big cowboy hat or lavender cowboy boots. Then he bent Bimini over the yellow sofa. Raymon moved in for a close up as Tex stuck his cock in Bimini's ass. The Mexican maid looked down from the kitchen for a moment, then went back to her cleaning. Bimini stared, without expression, at the wall, while Tex fucked her. Raymon called out, "Bimini, look shocked." Bimini looked over her shoulder at the camera, with her eyes and mouth wide open in shocked delight. Raymon glanced over his shoulder at Medina and said, "Most girls aren't brain surgeons, but this one can act."

Medina nodded. "I see. It's all about acting, no?"

"You got it," Raymon said.

Now Bimini was lying on her back on the sofa with her head draped over the sofa's arm. Tex stood behind her with his cock in his hand. Bimini opened her mouth and Tex peed down her throat. Just as Bimini gagged, Tex thrust his cock down her throat until she choked. Then he turned toward the camera and flashed his evil, cartoonish, leer.

The maid leaned over the kitchen counter and looked down at Tex throat-fucking Bimini. She called down to him, "Señor Tex, is all right to leave, now?" Still throat-fucking Bimini, Tex waved his hand at the maid. She walked down the stairs, past the yellow sofa, and out of the room.

Bimini was sitting up now, her face and hair soaked with Tex's piss. She smiled brightly at the camera and said, "Look, mommy, what I can do! Tex can fuck my face and make me the center of attention! Look at me, mommy and daddy, I'm a porn star! Aren't you proud of me?"

The scene ended with Bimini saying to Tex, "The next time I come over, Tex, can we order pizza and a Disney movie?"

Tex leered at the camera and said, "The next time I'm gonna cum on your face." When Bimini didn't respond, Tex said, "You're supposed to say, 'Oh, yes, Tex, please cum on my face.'"

Bimini frowned. "I can't remember *every*-thing in my memory box, Tex."

"Try."

"Oh, yes, Tex, please cum on my face."

"Good girl."

"Cut!" said Raymon.

Bimini gathered up her clothes from the floor, scurried across the vast, white room, and ran upstairs. Raymon's assistant pushed the pail of soapy water toward the sofa. He began to mop up Tex's piss from the tile floor, and then from the sofa.

Tex, stroking his cock to keep it hard, walked over to Medina. "Well, Señor. What do you think?"

"You *are* a great artist, Señor Tex."

Tex smiled, not his evil smile, but the smile of a small boy who wanted desperately to please. "I knew you'd appreciate it, Señor." Medina tried not to look down at Tex stroking his cock. Tex said, "Now, the next scene will be the climax. The petite morte."

Medina's brow furrowed. "The, what?"

"Petite morte," Tex said. "What the French call the little death, the climax of love."

Medina nodded. "Of course, of course." Then he lowered his voice so that Raymon and the other one couldn't hear him. "In a way, Señor Tex, that is why I am here today."

Tex nodded. "Oh, yeah. Do you want me to get her back for you?"

Medina waved his hands at him. "No, no, no, that is not what I meant. I have this . . . little problem I thought you maybe could help me with."

"Anything, Señor. I am in your debt."

"It has to do with this . . . cowboy, like you, Señor Tex."

Tex looked confused. "Cowboy? I'm from Milwaukee."

Medina shook his head. "It doesn't matter. The point is, this blond cowboy and his puta girlfriend, they took my money. Even worse, they disrespected me."

"They must be crazy."

"I am not a man to be disrespected, Señor Tex. This is where you come in, and your little one." He tossed a head fake toward the stairway. "I would like the little one to give this cowboy . . . how did you say it?" He smiled. "Ah, yes. A petite morte."

Tex shook his head. "I don't understand. I mean, if this guy disrespected you. . . ."

"He did, Señor Tex, he did, and that is why I want you to teach him and his puta a lesson."

Tex shook his head, once, and said, "But . . . I still. . . ."

"I want *you* to give him the Grande Morte. Do you understand?"

Tex began to nod, slowly, a smile crossing his face that was not like his cartoonish leer. "Yeah," he said, stroking his cock with more enthusiasm now. "A Grande Morte. He'll be comin' and goin' at the same time."

"Ah," said Medina. "And here's the little one."

Bimini, dressed again in her *Clueless* outfit, her face again heavily made up, walked into the living room. Raymon positioned her in the center of the room. Tex, still stroking his cock, went over to Bimini. She knelt down in front of him, her face inches from his cock.

"Before we shoot," said Tex, seriously. "I'd like us all to observe a minute of silence for the death of Dale Earnhardt, my hero." Bimini lowered her head in prayer. Raymon looked down at the floor. His assistant looked down at his mop. Medina shook his head and stared at Tex Pervis in his cowboy hat and boots, his head, too, lowered in silent prayer as he stroked his cock.

Tex looked up. "Thank you all. Now, let's shoot it."

Raymon called, "Action!"

Bimini began to suck Tex's cock. She ran her fingers up and down the side of his cock and said, "Do you play the flute, Professor?" Tex grinned lasciviously at the camera. Bimini sucked his cock again for a few seconds, then looked up at Tex and said, "Professor, I've been studying all the things you taught me real hard." She sucked some more, then said, "Professor, please tell me I'm being a good girl. I sit in front of class in my miniskirt with no panties." She sucked his cock again, for a longer time, then looked up at him, and said, "Professor, your cock is sooo hard. I'll make it shiny and wet." She sucked again, for a long while, as Tex's body began to shudder. She looked up at him, and said, "Please punish me, Professor. Come all over my face." Tex stroked his own cock quickly, his features contorted in a pleasureable pain, until he cried out, "Ahhhh!" and shot a load of cum all over Bimini's face. She smiled up at him with her cum-stained face and said, "Oh, thank you, Professor. Now maybe we can go out to dinner or I won't suck your cock anymore." She stuck out her tongue and licked cum from her lips. "Professor? Can I call you by your first name now?"

Raymon called, "Cut! That's a wrap."

Medina clapped his pudgy hands and called out, "Bravo! Bravo, little one!"

Bimini got up off her knees and rushed over to Medina like an excited schoolgirl. "Did you like me, Señor Medina? Did you?" Tex followed her, wiping off his cock with a baby wipe.

"You were exquisite, Señorita, exquisite. What a talent."

"I was born for porn," said Bimini.

Tex said, "You were radiant, lovely, the most intellectual actress in porn today."

Bimini patted the palms of her hands together in glee. "Oh, thank you!" she said. She leaned her cum-stained face toward Medina's face and kissed him on the lips as a look of horror appeared in his eyes. He began to feverishly wipe his lips with the back of his hand as Bimini walked toward the stairway in her tube top, tiny skirt, ankle socks, and strippers' pumps. She glanced over her shoulder at Medina and smiled. "I *was* good, wasn't I?" Then she gave her hip a cocky little toss that made her miniskirt flounce up, and she was gone.

13

THE LITTLE GIRL ON ROLLERBLADES SAT ALONE AND UNNOTICED AT ONE OF the outdoor tables on the sidewalk in front of Mistral on a hot, brilliantly sunny Sunday morning on Ft. Lauderdale beach. While she waited for the waitress to notice her, she watched the joggers, bicyclists, rollerbladers, and power-walking tourist couples pass by on the sidewalk, and the cars, gleaming in the sunlight, cruise slowly north on AlA past the low, whitewashed beach wall and the palm trees and the bleached-bone sand and the pale blue-green ocean dotted with white boats.

After a long while, she looked around for the waitress. Most of the sidewalk tables were deserted. She saw the waitress standing at a table to her right, flirting with four Yuppie bikers drinking beer out of long-necked bottles. They all wore the same new, black Harley T-shirts with a painting of a naked girl in the arms of the Grim Reaper, and the same black leather vests and leather pants they got from the International Male catalogue. My mother would love *them*, she thought.

One of the bikers looked up at the slim, blonde waitress's bare midriff and the diamond stud in her navel. She heard him say, loudly, for his buddies' benefit, "So honey. You wanna go for a ride on my hog?" His buddies laughed at the waitress who didn't get it.

"Jeez, I can't," she said. "Until my shift is over."

When the waitress left the bikers' table, the little girl raised her hand and called out, "Oh, Miss!" The waitress ignored her and went over to the only other occupied table. Two men talking and an older blonde reading the newspaper.

She was used to being ignored, but it still angered her. Just because of the way she looked. Barely five feet tall, ninety-eight pounds. A dark little girl with big black eyes, sharp cheekbones, and short black hair that fit her head like a stocking cap. If only she was paler, like her mother, she would resemble Audrey Hepburn. But she was too dark, like an Arab street urchin, with the body of a thirteen-year-old in her cutoff jeans and bikini top that was too big for her tiny tits. Even her high black plastic rollerblades looked ridiculously big on her tiny feet and slim legs.

She looked over at the waitress. One of the two men, the younger one with the blonde ponytail, said something to the waitress that made her blush. The older woman looked up from her newspaper, glanced at the man, and went back to her newspaper. She had the coldest blue eyes, with a nice body and spikelike blond hair. She was wearing shorts and a T-shirt with lettering across her chest that read: "It ain't pretty being easy." An older, wise-ass chick. Like my mother.

The big guy with the blond ponytail looked like a Davie redneck. The other guy was short, fat, and bald with a goatee. Not bad looking. He wore a ton of gold jewelry and three beepers on his hip. A loan shark or a bookie or a smuggler. A hard guy.

The blonde gave the waitress their order and she left just as one of the bikers looked up and called over to the blonde. She couldn't hear what he said, but she could see the blonde just looking at him and through him with those eyes. The cowboy grinned at the biker. The bald guy said loudly, "Asshole!"

The biker stood up, red-faced, his buddies looking up at him to see what he'd do. The woman looked at him, raised her eyebrows, glanced at the guy with the goatee, and then back to the biker, and shook her head, no. The guy with the goatee said again, "Asshole!" The biker just stood there, glaring at the fat guy, who didn't even bother to glare back, like he'd already lost interest in the biker, which made the biker even more furious until suddenly a look crossed his face and it dawned on him that whatever he did next didn't matter to the fat guy because he'd been there before.

Finally, the biker said something to his buddies that made them laugh, and he sat down.

The waitress returned with the drinks for the blonde and the two men. She set them down as the little girl called out, "Heh, you gonna wait on me, or what?" The guy with the goatee looked over at her, smiling, something nice in his eyes he was embarrassed to let people see. He raised his drink and nodded at her. She felt herself blushing, smiling, too. She nodded back as the waitress appeared at her table.

"Can I help you?" the waitress said.

"It's about fucking time."

The waitress blinked at the little girl. "I beg your pardon?"

"Just bring me a mimosa."

The waitress stared down at her. "Not until you show me some I.D., sweetheart."

The little girl pulled her driver's license out of her bikini top and showed it to the waitress. The waitress studied it for a long time, then made a disgusted sound with her mouth and walked off. The little girl waited until she disappeared inside the restaurant before she sneaked a look back at the guy with the goatee. He was looking down at something in the newspaper that the blonde was pointing out to him and the guy with the ponytail.

"The most extensive collection of Roy Lichtenstein paintings in the world," Sheila was saying. "Right here on Las Olas."

Sol and Bobby looked at the paper spread out on the table. Sol said, "So what?"

Sheila said, "It's worth millions, Solly. Just hanging there on the walls of this guy's house four blocks from here."

Bobby and Sol looked more closely at the story and photo layout of the collector's house, Big, cartoonish paintings hanging on the guy's living room and dining room walls, and a smaller one on the wall behind his bed. The story mentioned that the collector, Harold Framkin, sixty-five, had accumulated his Lichtensteins over the years with the expert advice of his wife, Sasha Berkowitz-Framkin, an artist in her own right. There were photographs of them. The man was deeply tanned, with small eyes, a big nose and a long, sad, horselike face that was trying to smile. The woman looked androgynous, in her 40s, with pale skin and strong features like those minted on a coin. She was trying to look mysterious and hard behind narrow sunglasses and a military cap pulled down over one side of her face.

"Like that Swedish broad," Sol said. "The old-time actress."

"Greta Garbo," Bobby said.

"Yeh. 'I vant to be alone.'" Sol said.

"Like a guy in drag," Bobby said.

Sheila looked at them through weary, half-lidded eyes. "Marlene Dietrich," she said. "Now, you guys finished playing Trivial Pursuit? Read the rest of it."

The article said that Mr. Framkin, who made his fortune in hurricane shutters, had decided to sell his Lichtensteins at auction in two months because he wanted to exhibit only his wife's paintings at their home. Sasha Berkowitz-Framkin painted in the style of Salvador Dali, only with a persistent sexual motif that prevented the *Miami Herald*, as a family newspaper, from reproducing them for its readers. Before Mr. Framkin sold his Lichtensteins he would have one final viewing of them at his home for prospective buyers.

"Next week," Sheila said.

"By invitation only," Bobby said.

"That's not a problem," Sheila said.

"They look like fucking cartoons with those big dots," Sol said.

"Very expensive cartoons," Sheila said. "The big ones are worth millions."

"So?" Sol, said. "They're too big to snatch. He's probably got security up the ass. And even if we did snatch one, what the fuck would we do with it?"

"Not a problem, Solly," Sheila said. "There's always a market for stolen paintings."

"There's guys in Europe," Bobby said, "they got stolen masterpieces in their cellars just for them to see."

"Jesus!" Sol said. "All that bread for somethin' no one will ever know you got."

"That's the point, Sol," Sheila said. "*They* know they got it. That's how they get off."

Sol shook his head. "There's some sick fuckers out there."

"Not everybody's like you, Solly," said Bobby, grinning. "Three beepers, a diamond Rolex, a gold Star of David weighs maybe a ton hanging from your neck in case there's someone in the world might not get it you're a Jew gangster.

"Understated elegance," Sheila said.

Sol looked down at his Star of David and his Rolex. "Understated?" Sol said. "You think so, Sheila?"

Sheila looked at Bobby and shook her head. Bobby laughed. Sol looked up. "What's so funny?"

Sheila was studying the photo layout now. She said, "But Sol *is* right, Bobby. The big ones are too big to snatch. But that little one over his bed, what's that, maybe 12x12? Worth maybe fifty large. Fit right in a briefcase. . . . What do you think, Bobby?"

She looked at Bobby. He was staring at a big-titted, big-assed, blonde Rollerblader skating past their table. She was wearing an American flag, G-string bikini. Bobby followed her with his narrowed eyes as she headed south toward Las Olas. She had a rose tattoo on each cheek of her big ass.

"Jesus, Bobby," Sheila said. "Where's your fucking taste? You reverting to type, or what?"

"What, baby? Oh, sorry. The tattoo caught my eye."

"That big ass," Sheila said, "she could put a whole fucking rose bush on it." Bobby shrugged. Sheila said, "Can we get back to business?" She looked at Sol. He was whispering something to the waitress. The waitress glanced at one of the other tables, nodded, and left. Sheila said, "Sol? Business?"

"What? Oh, yeah. The pictures."

"Paintings, Sol," Sheila said.

"Whatever. We ain't gonna break in. We ain't got the know-how all that electronic security."

"Right, Solly," Sheila said. "We're just gonna walk in with all those other art dealers."

"Yeh," Sol said. "The guy's gonna welcome us with open arms. 'Let's see, who do we got here? Hmmm . . . Mr. Sol Bass, Jew smuggler. Mr. Bobby Squared, redskin gun runner from east bumfuck Carolina. Oh, yeah, and his old lady, Miss Sheila Doyle or MacKenzie, or whatever the fuck her name is at the moment. A real beauty. Former suburban housewife dresses like a hooker now. You gonna wear your spandex minidress barely covers your ass, maybe your stripper pumps?"

Sheila smiled at Sol. "That might be amusing, Sol," she said. "Bobby in his pink flamingo Hawaiian shirt. You with your understated elegant gold. But actually I had a different idea. How about Ms. Sheila Royce-Jones, art dealer from London?"

Already Sheila had assumed a British accent Sol had heard on that chunky Titanic broad. It always amazed Sol how Sheila could assume any accent she wanted, become a lady right before his eyes, a different person, so that him and Bobby had to look at her twice, remind themselves it was Sheila.

Sheila went on in her British accent. "With her veddy wealthy collector client, Mr. Solomon Weinstein, from Tel Aviv by way of Brooklyn in his Turnbull and Asser suit. And his associate, Mr. Robert Reynolds in maybe a nice, muted Armani."

Bobby smiled. "I like that. Maybe those little guinea loafers with the tassel. No socks. One of those leather fag bags the guineas like to throw over their shoulders so they look. . . ."

"Insouciant is the word I think you're looking for, Robert," Sheila said.

"Yeah," Sol said. "Insou, or whatever. With a fuckin' CZ-85 in his little fag bag with fifteen hollow points in the clip not many guineas carry in Rome I hear. . . . There's still one big problem, Sheila. I don't know nuthin about art. They'll spot me for a phony right off."

"Solly," Sheila said. "Nobody knows anything about art. Everybody fakes it. Like they do wines and cigars these days. You can say anything about any painting and there's always some so-called expert who'll take you seriously."

"Like that nigger kid they made a movie about," Bobby said. "Died of an overdose, people snappin' up his paintings, call him a genius after he died."

"I remember him," Sol said. "A hamster from the Islands. Basket or sumthin'. His pictures looked like hamster graffiti the cons on the work detail wash off the I-95 overpasses."

Sheila was studying the photo layout. "We've gotta find someone to move it for us after we snatch it." She was quiet for a few minutes, then she said, "I think I got it, Sol." She looked at him. He was staring at a dark little girl skating toward their table on Rollerblades. The little girl stopped at their table and smiled down at Sol.

"Thanks for buying my drink," she said.

"It was nothin', honey," Sol said. "My pleasure." Sol was smiling at the little girl the way he did at Bobby sometimes, and Sheila, too.

"Well, thanks anyway," the little girl said.

"The least I could do," Sol said, "I seen the waitress givin' you a hard time."

The little girl shrugged. "I'm used to it."

"You handled it OK."

The little girl smiled at him. "Like you handled the biker?"

"That? It was nothin'. What's your name, honey?"

"Cassandra. My friends call me Cassie."

Sol reached up his hand and shook her hand. "Glad to meetcha, Cassie. I'm Sol."

"Well, thanks again, Sol. I gotta be going." Sol followed the little girl with his eyes as she skated south toward Las Olas.

"Jesus Christ, Sol!" Sheila snapped. "She's in diapers."

Sol kept his eyes on the girl. Bobby said, "She ain't even pretty, Sol. She looks like a rat."

"Whatever you say, Bobby," Sol said.

Sheila shook her head. "For *that* you could do time, Sol. It borders on pedophilia."

The girl disappeared around the corner. Sol turned to Sheila and said, "What?"

"She says you got the same taste as that professor guy in the movies likes little chicks," Bobby said.

"Who?" Sol said.

"Humbert Humbert," Sheila said. "He fell in love with a twelve-year-old. Lolita?"

Sol smiled. "Yeah. The little chick with the lollipop and the heartshaped shades. Real fox. Little helicopter chick."

"What?" Sheila said.

"Helicopter. You sit her on your lap and spin her around." Sheila shook her head. Sol said, "What's that guy's name again?"

"Humbert Humbert," Sheila said.

Sol nodded. "Yeah, a man after my own heart. The guy was on to somethin'. Ahead of his time."

"Oh, Sol!"

"What?" Sol said. "What'd I say?"

Krystal Gayle Fountain, a mountain girl from Robbinsville, North Carolina, who'd reinvented herself as Gaye Fontini, widow of an Italian count, was showing a tourist couple an Erzulli, *The Blue Lady*, in her Delray Beach Haitian Gallery when she heard the bell over her front door tinkle. She glanced over her shoulder at an older blonde who entered the gallery, and then turned back to the tourists.

"It's the artist's finest work," Gaye Fontini said. "Notice the contrast between her blue skin and mango T-shirt."

"That's an awful bright orange," said the wife.

"It's mango," Gaye Fontini said, smiling.

"Her skin doesn't look real," the husband said. "It's too blue."

"All the Erzullis are blue," said Gaye Fontini. "She's the goddess of fertility."

"Fertility!" said the wife.

"No wonder her breasts are too big," said the husband.

"It's the artist's license," Gaye Fontini said. She smiled at the husband and looked directly into his eyes with her own pale blue eyes. She had white skin, like parchment, that showed the pale fibers of her veins, and wild, luxuriant, red hair that fell to her shoulders. "The royal blue and mango and blood-red lips make a stunning contrast, don't you agree?"

The husband and wife looked at each other, and shook their heads, no. "It's just not right," said the wife. "Our motif is beige."

"How much did you say it was?" said the husband.

"Twenty thousand dollars," said Gaye Fontini.

"Twenty thousand dollars!" the husband said. "It doesn't even look like a real person. Her neck's too long."

"It's a primitive," Gaye said, still smiling. "Like Grandma Moses." The couple just shook their heads, no. Gaye stopped smiling. "Maybe something else?" she said, fluttering her fake eyelashes. "An Elvis painting on black velvet?"

She waited until the couple left before she went over to the blonde. "Sheila, honey!" she said now in an easy, mountain drawl. "It's been a long time." The two women hugged. The tall, tanned, hard-looking blonde in jeans and the soft, pale, curvaceous redhead in a pink shirt-waist dress belted tightly at the waist.

When they parted, Sheila tossed a headfake at the departed couple. "No sale, Krystal?"

"I'm afraid not, Shuga. It didn't go with their 'motif.'" The two women laughed. "I missed you, girl. You don't have to be a stranger."

"I missed you, too, Krystal."

"How's that big ole man of yourn?"

"He keeps me busy."

Krystal threw back her head and laughed. "Oh, Shuga, I'll bet he does. Hmmmm. . . . Don't I wish." She shrugged, then she said, "And that unpleasant Jewish gentleman? You still passin' time with him?"

"Still. Solly's all right. He's an acquired taste." Sheila looked around at all the primitive, brilliantly colored paintings of parrots and jungles and black-skinned Haitians on the walls. "Like Haitian art."

Krystal sighed. "I guess so. I'd prefer somethin' more . . . refined, myself. He's sooo . . . vulgar."

Sheila smiled. "A compliment, really, if you knew Sol. But he's loyal, Krystal. Sol and Bobby go back a long way."

"I suppose in your line of endeavor loyalty *is* to be prized. Now tell me, Shuga, what brings you this far north?"

"Business." Sheila looked around the deserted gallery.

Krystal nodded. "I thought so." She went to the front door and flipped over the 'closed' sign and locked the door. "Come on to my office, honey."

Krystal sat behind a brightly colored, handpainted desk, all vivid reds and blues and mangos. Sheila sat across from her in an equally colorful chair with tropical fishes painted on the back and seat. Sheila took out a folded piece of newspaper from her purse and opened it on the desk. Krystal studied the photographs of the Lichtensteins.

"Very nice," Krystal said. "You thinkin' a goin' into the art bidness, Shuga?"

"In a way. See the little one over the bed." Krystal nodded. "What do you think it's worth?"

"At auction?" Krystal said, raising her eyebrows.

Sheila smiled. "Actually, I was thinking more like a . . . private sale."

Krystal smiled. "Of course, Shuga. I shoulda known. Now, let me see." She studied the painting for a long moment, then looked up and said, without her drawl now, "Not one of the artist's finest works, Sheila. Collectors like their Lichtensteins large. To accentuate their 'motif', you might say. This one here, I could get, maybe, two-fifty in an auction. In a 'private sale,' well, I would think fifty-sixty large is not out of the question."

"You could move it, then?"

"Honey, I can move anything . . . for a price. Say twenty percent."

"That seems reasonable," Sheila said. "You realize, of course, there might be an element of risk involved."

Krystal pursed her red lips and flapped a limp hand at Sheila. "Shuga, what's a little risk? Life's a risk, idnit?"

"I guess so."

"But I gotta tell you, Sheila, there's gonna be more risk for you than me."

"What do you mean?"

"I've heard of this guy, Framkin. He's a personal friend of Lichtenstein. His paintings mean everything to him."

"Then why's he getting rid of them?"

"His wife, Shuga. You see her photo? An artist-wannabe. The word is she gave him an ultimatum. Either her paintings go up in place of the Lichtensteins or she's gone."

"Jesus! No wonder the poor bastard looks so miserable."

"Yes, he does, doesn't he? Like that character out of Hemingway. What'd he call him? The Saddest Man in the World."

"Yeah, well, I'm sorry for Mr. Framkin. But as long as his paintings have to go maybe he won't miss the little one if it goes prematurely."

"Sheila, honey, you *are* harsh. But I wouldn't count on that. He does love his Lichtensteins, but he's a businessman, too. He's got a ton of high-tech, electronic security watchin' over those paintings. Very discreet, I heard. No moving overhead cameras like at banks. They all feed into a room in his pool house where a private security guard watches television screens twenty-four hours a day."

Sheila was quiet for a moment. Then she said, "Do you think he'd let some hired stranger watch him on TV in his bedroom?" Sheila shook her head. "I don't think so, Krystal."

"He does so love his paintings."

"Why, Krystal!" Sheila said, batting her eyelashes. "What's a little risk? Life's a risk, idnit?"

Krystal smiled. "I hear, Shuga."

"If he loves his paintings that much, it'll be our problem, not yours. We'll just have to deal with it. Your problem is to move it if we snatch it. You got a buyer in mind?"

"I have a client who might like this little work. He has a very, very private collection in Europe. In the basement of his chateau in Provënce. He's one of those Eye-talian film producers, Shuga. You know, churns out all that Kung Fu shit from Hong Kong." She shook her head in disgust. "No taste in films, but he does appreciate nice art."

"Provënce? That's good. The farther away the better. There's just one other thing. I'm going to need a few things."

"I am at your service, dahlin'."

"I'll need a print of that small one in the exact same frame."

"That's no problem. But it won't fool anyone for very long."

"We'll only need an hour or so," Sheila said. "A print will be better than staring at an empty wall, don't you think?"

"You got a point there, honey."

"Another thing. I'll need some stationery and business cards. Very classy. Embossed, with my name."

"And what might that be, Shuga?"

"Sheila Royce-Jones, purveyor of fine art. With a London address and London telephone number."

"Done, dahlin. Jes give me two weeks."

"Five days, Krystal, that's all you've got."

Krystal frowned. "I dunno, Shuga. That's not much time." She sighed. "Oh, I suppose I might be able to rush it." She batted her false eyelashes at Sheila. "But it'll cost ya."

Sheila fixed her with a look. Krystal stared back at Sheila with her own pale blue eyes opened wide. "Why, Shuga! Does that look really work?"

"Sometimes," Sheila said, batting her own eyelashes. "With men it does." The two women laughed.

14

BOBBY HELD THE LONG NECK OF A BEER BOTTLE BETWEEN TWO FINGERS, LIKE a cigar, at his hip. He stood under a hot sun at Bootleggers' outdoor bar that looked down a small flight of stairs over a swimming pool shaded by palm trees and a few round tables and lounge chairs around the pool. Tourists and locals in bathing suits stood ten rows deep around the pool, were sprawled in the lounge chairs, sat at the tables, and floated in the pool. They were all eating, drinking, laughing, shouting. The tourists were splashing each other in the pool, the couples tonguing each other at the Jacuzzi end of the pool and then glancing around to see if everyone noticed what a great time they were having. The hot air was thick with the smell of coconut oil and sweat and the heavily chlorined pool. Sheila hated to go to Bootleggers with Bobby. "What for?" she said. "To rub elbows with assholes. Besides, it's too hot." When Bobby said she could cool off in the pool, she just looked at him and said, "And get pregnant?" Even he had to laugh.

Bobby looked out beyond the pool to the dock where a line of boats were tied six rows deep, and beyond that to the Intracoastal where boats glided slowly up and down the waterway. Yachts, fishing boats, gofasters. They all gleamed white in the sun, except for the gofasters which were mostly painted black, with their names slashed in red

along the sides. Rum Runner. Smuggler's Blues. Gravy Train. Ménage
à Trois.

Bobby raised the beer bottle to his lips, tipped it up, and sipped,
without taking his eyes off the boats. Recognition, he thought, what
every smuggler wanted even more than the cash. Which was why they
always got caught. They had to flash it around: strippers, bottles of
Dom, Ferrari Fls, all paid for with cash like the Feds were really *that*
stupid. I'll take the cash, Bobby thought, get Medina off our backs and
chill out for a while, maybe go to the mountains like Sol said,
assuming, of course, we can pull off the picture heist. Paintings, Bobby
corrected himself.

"It all depends on Sol," Sheila said this morning.

"He'll do all right," Bobby said.

"I wish I had your confidence, Bobby. He's so fucking stupid."

Jesus! Why'd she have to say that? Sure, she was right, Sol was no
brain surgeon, if it was up to him he'd just go in on the muscle and
snatch the pictures . . . paintings . . . tie everybody up, gag 'em, and
split. Still, it pissed him off.

"Sometimes you can be a bitch, Sheila."

She didn't say anything for a moment. Then, softly, she said, "Isn't
that what you wanted, Bobby?" It was, but sometimes he missed the
Sheila he'd first met. Sweet, scared, trusting.

"Why am I a bitch, Bobby?" He didn't answer. "Because I'm not
afraid to admit the truth? Sol *is* stupid. He's a criminal."

"And what are we, social workers?"

"Not like him. It's a game to him, Bobby. Cops and robbers. He
doesn't even care about the cash. What's he gonna spend it on? He has
no life. We're in it for the cash so we can have a life."

She was right like she always was which was why she pissed him off,
her putting Sol down like that she didn't understand a guy's loyalty to
someone he wasn't fucking, the only loyalty a broad knew, so when she

said she was going to Delray to see if she could fence the pictures . . . paintings, whatever the fuck, he couldn't stop himself.

"And don't bring back any more a that nigger shit for the walls."

She just shook her head. "Jesus, Bobby, you're such a fucking racist." With that Sheila left, slamming the door behind her not even to make a point just glad to get away from him. He couldn't blame her. He knew he was being an asshole but he couldn't stop himself. Like now, hanging around Bootleggers like he used to before Sheila, waiting to pick up a stripper after the Hot Bod Contest, even knowing as he stood here that he wouldn't. But when she came back from Delray he'd tell her where he'd been just to piss her off like that time he'd pissed her off in Jamaica when she thought he'd fucked that skinny broad in the hotel room and he hadn't. He just wanted to see how she'd handle it. She handled it OK and it changed her so that now when he told her he'd spent the afternoon scoping out the chicks at the Hot Bod Contest she'd know what he was doing. "Reverting to type, eh, Robert," she'd say in that prissy way of hers like she was so fucking superior. He smiled. She was. That's why he was with her. He still couldn't figure out why she was with him. He only knew that for both of them there would never be anyone else, which didn't mean they couldn't fuck it up, just that if they did fuck it up it would be their last chance to have someone close to them for the long haul.

Bobby heard a shout go up from the pool and then the crowd hooted and whistled and applauded as two muscular barbacks laid a wooden bridge across the center of the pool. A guy with a hand-held microphone stood at one end of the pool. Off to his left the docked boats rocked gently in the water. On the dock, between the boats and the pool, stood a cluster of perfectly tanned girls in G-string bikinis and strippers' pumps. They looked alike, big girls, like that Rollerblade chick with the rose tattoo on her ass, big-titted, big-assed blonds who looked as if they put on their makeup with a trowel, except for one, a dark-haired little chick who stood off by herself. She looked vaguely familiar, thought Bobby, as the MC began to speak.

"Ladies and gentlemen," he said, "I want to welcome you to the World Famous Bootleggers' Hot Bod Contest down here in sunny South Florida, otherwise known as Paradise, and the Land of Sleeze and Sun. I'll be your host today." He grinned, a pale, hunched-over man with a droopy mustache. He wore a wrinkled, sweat-stained Hawaiian shirt, baggy shorts, and flip-flops. "My name, for all you newcomers, is Jack Mehoff." He cupped a hand to one ear and waited for laughter. There were a few chuckles, some groans, and then someone shouted, "Just bring on the chicks!"

"A tough crowd, I see," he said. "OK, let's get it on." He fished out a stack of file cards from his shorts and squinted at the first one. "Now, our first contestant is Chantelle, a little filly from Boca." He held the card at arm's length, squinted at it, then added, "an aspiring brain surgeon." The crowd laughed. "Let's put our hands together for Chantelle."

One of the big-titted blondes stepped off the dock and stood beside him, facing the crowd. She struck a strippers' pose, legs spread, her back arched like a swaybacked horse so that her massive tits looked like the bullet bumpers of an old Buick, and her big ass looked like two basketballs. Bobby shook his head, bigger is better, I guess.

"Now, tell me, honey," said the MC, "what are your favorite things to do?"

Chantelle made a great production of thinking, and then she brightened, and said in a helium-filled voice, "My very most favorite things in the world are shopping, working out, sunbathing, and . . ." she frowned, then brightened again, ". . . and going on midnight cruises on yachts." She smiled as if proud of herself.

The MC rolled his eyes to the sky, then grinned and said, "You know the rule in Paradise, honey. It's suck or swim." The crowd roared with laughter, drunken tourists with burnt-red skin and local wise guys with perfect tans and too much gold jewelery.

"Well, let's show the crowd your stuff, honey," the MC said.

Chantelle walked very slowly around the pool, thrusting out her tits she was so proud of, her hands on her hips, until she came to the bridge. She stepped carefully onto it and walked to the center of the pool. She stood there for a moment, holding her spread-legged pose, and then she bent over at the waist and grabbed both her ankles. The cheeks of her huge ass flared out. She jiggled them so that they slapped together. The crowd hooted and whistled and applauded. Then she jiggled her massive tits until one of them flopped out of her tiny bra top, and then the other one flopped out. She opened her mouth wide as if shocked and embarrassed, and tucked her tits back into her bra, and stood up. The crowd was screaming and hooting at her. She smiled and waved her hand, a little stiff half wave, and walked very slowly off the bridge, around the pool, to her place on the dock.

"A modest little fillie," said the MC, shaking his head. "You think she's done this kinda thing before? Naww." Then he looked at his next card.

"Our next contestant is a little Cubano chicklet from My-Jami. Let's hear it for . . . Bimini!"

There was a little applause as the dark-haired girl stepped up off the dock and stood beside the MC. She smiled at the crowd and waved. A few people clapped, but most of the crowd just hooted and hissed at her. Someone shouted, "This ain't grammar school." Someone else shouted, "She don't even bleed yet." Still another shouted, "I'll bet it still smells like pee." The little girl kept smiling and waving. Someone in the pool splashed water on her. She backed up a bit away from the pool, a little girl with black pigtails coming out of each side of her head and lacy white ankle socks under her strippers' pumps.

"So, tell me, ah, Bimini, that's such an interesting name," the MC said. "How'd you get it?"

She looked at him very seriously and then said in her lisping Spanish accent, "I was named after the island. It's very beautiful." She fluttered her eyelashes. "Like me. I like it because they dig up bones of those big hairy elephants there."

The MC looked at her. "You're serious?" he said. She nodded. Then he said, "You mean, woolly mammoths."

She shook her head, no. "No. Elephants. I studied them. I was a scientist before I became an actress."

"You're an actress. Why didn't I guess?" He leered at the crowd, and added, "I'll bet you got some talents, Bimini."

"I can do lotsa things."

"Like what?"

"I can cry. When you're an actress, you know, you have to be a good emotioner."

The MC blinked. The audience roared with laughter. Bimini just stood there, smiling. The MC shook his head and said, "OK, baby, you win. Now why dontcha take a little spin and show the folks your stuff."

Bimini walked around the pool, stepped up onto the bridge and walked to the center of the pool. She stood there in a model's pose she'd seen someplace, one leg slightly forward, her hands folded behind her back, smiling, waiting for the applause that didn't come. A guy floated across the pool until he was below her. She bent over and reached out her hand to shake his. He splashed water in her face. She stood up, rubbing the water out of her eyes with the backs of her hands, streaking her mascara all over the face. But still she kept smiling, then waving at the crowd that was laughing at her. She turned to walk off the bridge. Her pointy heel stuck between the boards. She bent over and pulled at her ankle with both hands. The crowd hooted and laughed at her louder. Finally, she yanked her heel free, almost tottering backward into the pool. She stood up, still smiling, tears streaming down her cheeks, trying so hard not lose it, a tough little chick, Bobby thought, and then with as much dignity as she could muster, she walked off the bridge, tears streaming down her face, her mascara streaked, her wet hair plastered to her head. Bobby watched her as she passed a table where a little guy was sitting. He nodded to her. She nodded back and stepped down to her place with the other girls on the dock. Bobby stared at the little guy. He wore jeans, cowboy boots, and a cowboy hat. He looked familiar, but Bobby couldn't place him.

Bobby ordered another beer from the barmaid. "Nice crowd you got here," he said.

The barmaid said, "She shoulda known better."

"Yeah, she shoulda." Bobby turned his back to the pool and the contest and looked out over the parking lot at the valet kids parking all the Ferraris and Lambos and then hustling back to their stand. He heard the crowd cheering again behind him and then the cheers receded as he thought about Sheila and Sol and Medina and he wondered how it all would go down. . . .

When Bobby finally turned back to the pool, the contest was over. The crowd had thinned out. There were only a few people left in the pool and at the tables. One of them was the little guy with the cowboy hat. Jesus, he looked familiar.

Someone tapped him on the shoulder. He turned around to see the little girl standing in front of him. She was still wearing her bikini top over her tiny tits but she had put on a little, pleated miniskirt over her G-string.

"Are you really an Indian?" she said in her Spanish lisp.

"Who told you that?"

"Someone."

"Do I look like an Indian?"

"Yes. Except for your blond hair."

"Why do you wanna know, anyway?"

"Cause I'm an Indian, too."

"I thought you were Cubano."

"No. I just say that so I can get along in Miami. You know how they are down there. If you're not Cuban they don't respect you. If they knew I was a Mexican, from the mountains, well. . . ."

"Yeah, I'm an Indian," Bobby said. "But I know how you feel. I don't like to tell too many people either."

"Will you buy me a drink?" she said.

"Why not?"

"I'll have a rum collins . . . with three cherries."

Bobby ordered her drink, and a Jim Beam rocks for himself. When they came, he touched his glass to hers, and said, "Cheers, honey." She sipped her drink like a child, holding the glass with both hands. Then she put the cherry half in her mouth, toying with it in her lips in a way she thought was sexy, acting at it, but not believable like Sheila.

Bobby watched her, sucking on the cherry, looking up at him, fluttering her false eyelashes, almost making him laugh. Finally, he said, "Did you win?"

She took the cherry out of her mouth. "No. I never win. I'm not a blond anglo." She smiled up at him. "My titties are too small." She cupped her hands under her tits and hefted them. "Do you like small titties?"

"Sometimes." She was working so hard at it he felt sorry for her. Maybe he was just out of practice, chicks coming on to him, or maybe he just never noticed before Sheila how hard chicks worked at coming on to guys like him. Like it was their whole reason for being, a guy, any guy, which was why it was always so easy for him until Sheila. She was never easy because she never worked at it. She just was. He liked that. It kept his head clear.

"If you never win, why do you bother?" Bobby said.

"It's good practice being in front of a crowd." She smiled. "I'm an actress."

"I heard. You're a good crier. Were you acting when you were crying?"

"No. I was acting when I was smiling."

Bobby nodded. "The crowd was rough on you."

"I'm used to it."

"Because you're an actress?" She nodded. "What kind of actress?"

"I'm a porn star." She smiled. "I was born for porn."

Bobby laughed. "I'll bet." Then his smile faded as it came to him. He turned around and looked down at the pool. The little guy in the cowboy hat was staring at him. The little guy with Bimini on his lap at Medina's table at The Anvil. Bobby turned back to Bimini.

"Your friend with the cowboy hat, did he send you to me?"

She looked down for a minute, and then up into his eyes. "Yes. I can't lie. He told me I should get you to like me. Do you like me?"

"Yeah, honey, I like you, but not enough. . . ."

15

BOBBY DROVE THE STRETCH LIMO. SHEILA AND SOL SAT IN BACK BEHIND THE dark glass partition. Sheila pushed a button and the glass went down. She leaned forward in her seat and put her hand on the shoulder of Bobby's beige, loose-fitting, Armani suit that concealed his bulk.

"You look so sexy in that suit, Bobby," she said. "You clean up real nice."

Bobby said nothing. He kept his eyes on Las Olas Boulevard illuminated in darkness by faux, turn-of-the-century streetlamps. The sidewalks were filled with tourists and locals, sitting at outdoor tables, and window shopping. A few of them turned to follow the black stretch Cadillac limousine as it passed by.

"What's the matter, baby?" Sheila said. "Don't you like it?"

Bobby thought about telling her. Bimini, the little cowboy, Medina, but decided against it. Why worry her? So he did what Sheila would do, he acted, curious to see if he could get away with it. He ran the flat of his hand down the back of his head where his ponytail used to be. "What I don't like," he said, "is that I had to cut off my ponytail."

Sheila sat back in her seat. "It was necessary, Bobby," she said. "You want to go in there looking like every tittie bar bouncer in town? We won't get through the door."

Beside her, Sol fidgeted in his tightly fitted, double-breasted, Turn-bull and Asser gray suit with the wide chalk stripes. "I coulda' used Bobby's baggy suit," he mumbled. "This thing's too tight." He unbuttoned his jacket, loosened his tie, and unbuttoned the collar of his blue shirt with its white spread collar.

"Sol, for Crissakes! Button up!" Sheila snapped. "You're supposed to be a wealthy Israeli, not a two-bit smuggler." Sol, grumbling, did as he was told.

Sheila smoothed the skirt of her gray silk Chanel suit. She took out a little mirror from her purse and studied herself. Her sandy colored wig was cut sharply in bangs and at angles at her jawline. She turned to Sol and said, "What do you think, Solly? Businesslike enough?"

"You look like a rich dyke from Park Avenue," he said.

She smiled. "Perfect." She reached down to the floor for the attaché case and laid it on her lap. She clicked it open to reveal stacks of hundred-dollar bills.

"Jeez," Sol said, "where'd ya get all that cash?"

Sheila held up a stack of bills and thumbed them, revealing strips of newspaper between the top and bottom bills.

Sol grinned. "A hamster roll."

"Just give him a quick look," Sheila said. "Whet his appetite. Then we look at the paintings. And remember, Solly, don't say anything more than you have to. Just study the paintings like you're thinking." Sol narrowed his eyes and stroked his goatee. "That's it. Perfect. Maybe nod your head once or twice. Make an innocuous comment or two."

"An inocu-what?"

Sheila sighed. "Innocuous. Harmless. Meaningless. Something that can't be misconstrued." She looked at Sol. "Forget that last part."

Sol looked worried. "But like what?"

"Like . . . 'Hmmm. . . Very interesting.' "

"Oh, yeah." Sol nodded. "Very interesting."

Sheila gave Sol a smile she had given to so many of her students. "Very good, Sol. Now when you get the chance, slip upstairs, snatch the painting and we're gone. If necessary, wait 'til the house fills up with dealers and collectors so we can all get lost in the crowd." Sheila leaned forward in her seat and said to Bobby, "Your job is to take out the security cameras, Bobby. We don't want our images on tape for posterity, now do we?"

"For what?" Sol said.

Sheila smiled at him. "So we don't end up washing hamster graffiti off I-95 overpasses, Sol."

"Bet your ass."

"Good." Sheila lifted a piece of cardboard that separated the layers of C-notes from the framed print underneath. "And make sure you make the switch, Solly. We don't want someone wandering up to the bedroom to stare at an empty wall."

"What are you gonna be doin'?"

"Keeping an eye on the stairs. Make sure no one surprises you."

Sol leaned over to look at the print. "Jeez, it looks just like the real one," he said.

"Not quite," Sheila said.

Bobby turned the limo right onto Isle of Capri. They moved past Mediterranian mansions with mission tile roofs until they came to the end of the street that faced the Intracoastal. A huge, neo-modern, gray concrete block house loomed up in front of them. The house was a series of gigantic blocks arranged in haphazard tiers.

"It looks like a fucking warehouse," Sol said.

Bobby stopped the limo at the electronically controlled gate and spoke into the black box. "The Royce-Jones party for Mr. Framkin." The gate swung open. The limo moved down a long drive past formal gardens and back-lit stone fountains.

As the limo approached the front door, Sheila reached into her purse. She withdrew a roll of duct tape and tossed it on the front seat beside Bobby. Then she took out a pair of handcuffs and snapped one on Sol's wrist.

Sol almost leaped out of his seat. "Jesus Christ, Sheila! What the fuck you doin'?"

Sheila snapped the other cuff around the attaché case handle. "There," she said. "A nice little touch, don't you think?"

"Jesus!" Sol was shaking his head, staring at the handcuff on his wrist. "Handcuffs! Jesus, Sheila! That's a bad omen."

A parking valet kid met them at the front entrance. Bobby shooed him away. "I'll park it myself," he told the kid. "We'll be leaving early." He parked the limo a little beyond the entrance. He reached under the seat for his CZ, racked the slide to chamber a round.

"That won't be necessary, Robert. Not now."

He looked back at her. "What if something goes wrong?"

"Bobby, the guy sells storm shutters. He collects paintings. You think he catches us snatching his painting he's gonna pull an Uzi? Just put the piece away."

Bobby shrugged. "You're the boss." He put the CZ back under the seat, got out of the car, and opened the back door for Sheila and Sol.

Sheila held out her hand. Bobby took it and helped her out. "Thank you, Robert," she said in her British accent.

"You're welcome, ma'm."

Sol struggled across the seat with his attaché case. He held his hand out the door for Bobby, too. Bobby swatted it away. Sheila looked at them both. Sol was grinning.

"I thought I was supposta be this big deal guy. Bobby can't even help me outta my limo?"

Sheila hooked her arm in Sol's and they walked to the front door with Bobby behind them. The door was opened by a maid in a shapeless black dress with a lacy white collar.

"Can I help you, mu'm?" the maid said in a thick, Irish brogue. She was maybe twenty, with creamy skin, freckles, pale green eyes and straight shiny black hair. Black Irish, like Sheila, the old Sheila.

Sheila looked at the sweet, pudding-faced girl the way important people do at servants, without interest, and said, in her British accent, "The Royce-Jones party for Mr. Framkin."

"Oh, of course, mu'm," the girl said, blushing, lowering her eyes. "I shouda known, aiy?" She turned and led them through the foyer. Bobby coughed loudly behind Sheila. Sheila glanced over her shoulder at him. He smiled and raised his eyebrows. "Not your type, Robert," Sheila said. "No tattoo."

"No," Bobby said. "But sweet."

"You had sweet, Bobby. Remember?" But even as she said it she could barely remember that woman.

Sol gasped. "Holy shit!"

The foyer walls were covered with Sasha Berkowitz-Framkin's paintings, all variations of the same painting. A naked woman, who looked like Mrs. Framkin, only younger, tied to tall, phallic-looking pink cactuses sticking up out of a pink desert. All the phallic-looking cactuses were limp, listing to one side.

Bobby said in Sheila's ear, "He's gonna hang this shit on his walls?"

Sol whispered, "I like the cartoons better."

Sheila smiled at Sol. "See, Solly. You're becoming a critic already." They walked past the paintings of the naked woman tied to the limp cactuses. Sheila said under her breath, "You think the Framkins' got a sexual problem, or what?"

The maid stepped down two stairs into the living room with Sheila, Sol, and Bobby behind her. Two men and a woman were waiting for them, standing in a line as if for royalty.

"Missus," the maid said to the woman. "This is them." The woman was dressed like a biker chick out of a 50s B movie. Ratty black hair, black eyeliner, purple lips, low-cut black bustier, black leather vest, tight black leather pants, biker's boots. She had a rose tatoo on each of her huge, fake tits bubbling out of her bustier.

"That'll be all, Tara," the woman said. The maid nodded and left.

"Ms. Royce-Jones, I presume," said a tall, stoop-shouldered man dressed in an earthtone jacket and slacks. "Welcome to West Egg." He smiled his hang-dog smile.

"Mr. Framkin," Sheila said. "What a pleasure!" She handed him her card, then introduced him to Mr. Robert Reynolds, an associate, and Mr. Solomon Weinstein. Sol clicked his heels and bowed. Sheila looked at him.

"Allow me to introduce you to Roy Lichtenstein," said the man. He smiled at the little man beside him as if he was a pet he would soon have to put down. "The world's greatest living artist," he added.

Everyone looked at Lichtenstein, dressed in baggy jeans, a sweat-shirt, and Kmart sneakers. He had a pale, impish, taught-skinned face, a hawk's nose, a bird's eyes, and a tiny gray ponytail. He smiled and bowed, but said nothing.

"And my wife, Sasha Berkowitz," the man said.

"Good evening," said the woman, without expression. She looked older than her photograph, maybe 50, softer, her white skin slack, the loose flesh under her unshaven armpits hanging over the sides of her bustier.

"Mrs. Framkin!" Sheila said. "Such an honor. We so admired your paintings in the foyer."

"Berkowitz-Framkin," the woman said, looking into Sheila's eyes the way men did. "And thank you."

"So original," Sheila said. "The paintings . . . and your look."

"Yes," the woman said. "One's look is part of one's art, don't you agree?"

"Absolutely," Sheila said.

"My wife is surrealism in the flesh," said her husband.

Sheila smiled at the woman. "She certainly is." The woman's eyes roamed down over Sheila's body and up again to her eyes.

"Allow me to introduce Mr. Weinstein," Sheila said quickly. Sol stepped forward, bowed, and clicked his heels.

The woman looked Sol up and down, too, but not in the way she looked at Sheila. "Good evening," she said.

"Your pictures," Sol said. Sheila closed her eyes. Paintings, Sol, paintings, for crissakes. Sol put a hand to his goatee and stroked it. "Ver-ry interesting."

"Thank you, Mr. Weinstein."

"Yes, my wife's paintings are exquisite," said Framkin. "She's my muse." He looked at his wife with a loving smile tinged with his perpetual sadness.

"And this is Mr. Reynolds," Sheila said. The woman nodded.

"Now," said Framkin, "before the others arrive, should we look at the paintings of the world's greatest living artist?"

"We should get the formalities out of the way first," Sheila said. She reached for Sol's attache case, opened it, and turned it toward Framkin.

"That's not necessary," he said, with a shake of his head.

"Do you mind?" said Lichtenstein, speaking for the first time. He stood on his tiptoes like a little boy and peeked into the case. He smiled and made a little humming sound. "Sooo beautiful," he said. "A work of art in its own way, isn't it?"

"Yes, I guess you could say that," Sheila said, closing the case.

"Well, if you'll excuse me," the woman said. "I have to see to the preparations for our other guests." She turned and walked away.

Framkin led them into the living room where servants were laying out crystal-glass bowls heaped with stone crab claws in crushed ice and magnum: of Dom Perignon on a glass and chrome coffee table. The room was stark, colorless, all glass-and-chrome and white furniture, except for the many colorful Lichtensteins on the walls.

Framkin pointed to a large triptych over the fireplace. He stared at it for a long moment, then said, "In this *wonderful* painting the world's greatest living artist shows the progression of women through the 20th century. . . . Isn't that so, Roy?"

"I guess so."

"What do you think, Mr. Weinstein?" the man said.

"Please," Sol said. "Call me, Sol."

"Of course, Sol. And call me Harold."

Bobby leaned over and whispered in Sheila's ear, "And call me Ishmael."

Sol studied the painting in silence while everyone stared at him. He stroked his goatee and nodded. "Ver-ry interesting." Framkin smiled. Sheila exhaled a breath.

Framkin led them to another wall where he had hung one of Lichtensteins' huge, blond women done in a cartoonish style. "Now, here," Framkin said, smiling, "the world's greatest living artist shows us, in his inimitable, fun-loving way, the power of women by re-creating a woman's image five times life-size." He turned to Lichtenstein. "Isn't that so, Roy?"

Lichtenstein shrugged. "I dunno. I just paint them."

Sol studied the painting through narrowed eyes. He stroked his goatee. "Ver-ry interesting," he said, nodding. After a long pause, he added, "And big. That's a big fuckin' broad."

Framkin blinked, once, twice, his mouth half-open. Sheila flashed him her glossy smile.

"I think what Mr. Weinstein means. . . ." Sheila started to say.

"That's it precisely, Mr. Weinstein" said Lichtenstein. "Precisely! I just wanted to paint a *big*, fucking broad."

"You done a good job," Sol said.

"Very perceptive, Mr. Weinstein," Lichtenstein said.

"Please," Sol said. "It's Sol. OK, Roy?"

Framkin smiled again. "Well, now to the library."

They went through a doorway into a darkly wooded library, its walls lined with rare, first-edition books. Framkin picked up a slim volume and caressed it with his hands. "Uncle Tom's Cabin," he said. "Signed by the author." He sighed. "Unfortunately, it's not a first edition. Ah, but here we have a *wonder*ful drawing by the world's greatest living artist." Everyone stared at the drawing of a telescope and planets and numbers.

"Sadly," Framkin said, "it was never commissioned as a painting." Lichtenstein nodded. "See the telescope," Framkin said. "And the number six in the distance. The number is really a nine but the telescope sees it inverted. The author's little puzzle, right, Roy?"

Lichtenstein shrugged. "I dunno. I just drew it."

Sol studied the drawing, not bothering to stroke his beard. Everyone was looking at him. Finally, he said, "Not one of your best works, Roy." Sheila closed her eyes. From behind her, she heard Bobby stifle a laugh. When she opened her eyes, Lichtenstein was smiling at Sol.

"Absolutely, right, Sol," Lichtenstein said. "It was just a sketch I was playing with. I could never figure out what to do with it as a painting."

Sol said, "It shows, Roy. It shows."

Framkin looked from Sol to Lichtenstein and back to Sol again. He was trying to smile, but he couldn't. "Shall we move on?" he said.

After Framkin showed them all his paintings on the first floor, he led them back to the living room. "Well, Sol," he said, "what do you think of my collection?"

"You got some nice pictures, Hal."

"Yes, I love them so."

"It must be painful to part with them," Sheila said.

"Beyond belief."

"Excuse, me, Mr. Framkin," Sheila said. "I know this is painful for you . . . but before Mr. Weinstein makes his decision he'd like to be sure he's seen them all."

"But you have. All the big ones."

"Big ones?"

"There are just two small ones upstairs. They're very personal to me. I was hoping my wife . . . that I wouldn't have to part with them."

"But you might have to?" Sheila said. The man looked at her with his hang-dog smile. She heard Krystal's voice, saying, "Sheila, honey, you *are* harsh."

"We'd love to see those," Sheila said. "Wouldn't we, Mr. Weinstein?"

"Yeah, Hal," Sol said.

"If you wish." Framkin led them through the living room toward a metal, circular stairway. The Irish maid came through a door carrying a silver tray of champagne glasses. Bobby smiled at her. She lowered her eyes, her cheeks red.

"If you all will excuse me," Bobby said. "I think I'll step outside for a cigarette."

Sheila looked at him. "You do that, Robert." Bobby nodded and walked toward the door.

As Framkin led them upstairs to his bedroom, Sheila said, "It must be such a responsibility protecting all this wonderful art!"

"I don't like to think of it like that," said Framkin. "As a responsibility. It's more like a cherished trust. Something I felt honored to do."

"Still, it must take extraordinary precautions."

"Yes. We do have extensive security."

"But I hardly noticed a thing," Sheila said.

"It's discreetly hidden," Framkin said. "I wouldn't want to embarrass my guests with an obvious display of security."

"Of course not," Sheila said. "It must be a little intrusive though, all that security in your life."

"It is. But it gives me peace of mind."

"Of course," Sheila said.

Bobby stood outside under the front door light, looking out over the lushly planted grounds, royal palms and elephant palms and bouganvillia, all backlit by ground lights. It was a soft, warm night. Bobby could see the swimming pool off to his right toward the Intracoastal. The lights from the bottom of the pool made the water look an unreal blue, like Sani-Flush. Beside the pool, separating it from the Intracoastal, was a small concrete pool house. Bobby could see a faint flickering light through one of the pool house windows. He took out a pack of cigarettes and lit one. He looked around for the valet kid. He was sitting on a folding chair off to the right of the front steps in darkness. Bobby went to the limo and got into the front seat. He made sure the inside lights were off. He put the duct tape in his Armani jacket pocket, reached under the seat for his CZ, stuck the gun into the back waistband of his slacks, then clicked on the interior lights. He made a big production of studying the dashboard.

He got out and went over to the valet kid. "It's a beautiful night, isn't it?" Bobby said. The kid nodded. Bobby offered him a cigarette. The kid shook his head, no.

"Thank you, sir, but I'm not allowed to smoke on duty."

Bobby looked around at the empty driveway. "You don't seem to have much business."

"No. The others aren't supposed to arrive for an hour or so. Then I'll be jumping."

"Maybe you got time to do me a favor." The kid looked at him. "I think the limo's low on gas. My boss finds out I didn't fill it he'll be pissed. Maybe you could run it down to a gas station, fill it up for me real quick?"

"Oh, I don't know, sir. My boss, Mr. Framkin, he. . . ."

"No problem. I already asked him."

"Well, if he said it's all right."

Bobby handed the kid the keys to the limo and a C-note. The kid looked at the C-note and smiled. "Keep the change," Bobby said. "And take your time. Have a smoke." He gave the kid a cigarette.

Bobby waited until the kid drove the limo through the front gate, then he moved toward the pool. He stayed in the darkness, away from the ground lights. When he reached the pool he went straight to the pool house. He peered in the window. An old guy dressed in a blue security guard's uniform was sitting behind a desk sipping coffee from a styrofoam cup. He was bald, with a blotchy-red face and a swollen nose, an ex-cop, early retirement because of a booze problem. The old guy was staring at a bank of TV monitors against the far wall, a dozen screens, each showing a room in Framkin's house. Bobby could see Tara setting down champagne glasses in the living room. The other rooms were empty, except for Framkin's bedroom where Sheila, Sol, Framkin and Lichtenstein were standing around Framkin's bed staring at something. The camera was in the wall behind the headboard. It showed all their faces, smiling, talking, except for Sol, who was nodding.

Bobby pulled out his CZ and tapped it on the pool house door.

"Yeh," said a gruff voice.

"Mr. Framkin sent me," Bobby said.

When the guard opened the door, Bobby stuck the muzzle of the CZ up against his swollen nose. "Jeezes Christ!" the guy muttered, his eyes staring, cross-eyed, at the muzzle. "What the fuck?"

"Just relax, old-timer, you won't get hurt."

"Jeezes Christ!"

Bobby pushed him back into the room and shut the door. "You got a bathroom, old-timer?"

The guy pointed to a door. "Jeez, you ain't gonna hurt me, are ya?" The old guy was wheezing. "I got grandkids."

"You just do what I tell ya, you'll be bouncin' them on your knee in no time."

Bobby backed him through the bathroom door, turned him around, the muzzle of the CZ at the back of the guy's head now. Bobby took out the duct tape, bit off a piece and taped the old guy's mouth shut. Then he taped his hands behind his back and made him get down on the floor. He taped his ankles together, pulled his legs back behind him and taped his ankles to his hands. The guy laid there, rocking slightly like a live shrimp.

Bobby locked the bathroom door and went over to the bank of TV screens. He ejected each of the tapes, each screen going blank, until he had them all. He went around to the back of the pool house and tossed the tapes into the Intracoastal.

Framkin's bedroom was as big as Bobby's and Sheila's small apartment on Bayview. The walls were lined with art books, but there was only one painting on the wall behind his bed. They all stood around the bed, staring at the small painting that had been in the Herald.

"It's very restful, don't you think?" said Framkin.

Everyone nodded. Sol said, "It's little."

Framkin smiled. "Precisely, Sol. Shall we go back downstairs?"

"You said you had two paintings upstairs," Sheila said.

"Oh, the other's not really a painting. It's just a crayon drawing the world's greatest living artist did for my daughter."

"You have a daughter?" Sol said.

"My beloved," Framkin said. "An extraordinary child. She's a junior at the University of Miami. She's in her room doing homework now, I think. I don't know if we should disturb her."

Sol shook his head. "I *would* like to see them all, Hal."

Framkin sighed. "Of course, Sol. This way."

Framkin knocked on his daughter's closed door. "Darling!" he said. "I have some guests who would like to see your drawing."

A small, light voice called out, "I'm busy."

Framkin smiled at his guests, then turned back to the door. "Just for a moment, dearest." After a long moment, the door opened. A little girl stood in the doorway. She was wearing a floppy Canes sweatshirt almost to her knees, and nothing else. Sheila stared at her with a smile frozen on her face.

"Mrs. Royce-Jones," Framkin said, "this is my darling baby Cassandra." The girl looked at him, her lips pursed.

Sheila reached out her hand. "It's lovely meeting you, Cassandra." The little girl looked at Sheila's hand and then her face.

"Yeah, nice to meet you."

"And this is Mr. Weinstein," said her father.

Sol stepped forward from behind Sheila. The little girl smiled. "Sol! It's you again!"

"How ya doin', honey." He took her hand in his, raised it to his lips and kissed it, all the while staring into her eyes.

"You know Mr. Weinstein?" her father said.

The little girl glanced at Sheila. "Yeah," she said, "we met on the beach."

"Isn't that a coincidence," said her father.

"Yes, it's a small world, isn't it Cassandra?" Sheila said. The little girl looked at her, her wig, Chanel suit, then at Sol, his fancy suit and tie, and then back to Sheila.

"Where's your T-shirt?" the little girl said to Sheila. "It was *so* clever."

"Oh, that," Sheila said. "Just a little beach thing. . . . Now, shall we?"

Framkin ushered them into her bedroom. It wasn't the bedroom of a college girl. There were no clothes strewn everywhere. No bottles of perfume and lipsticks and makeup. There was nothing but books: on shelves, against the wall, stacked on the floor, littered across her bed.

The little girl flopped down on her bed, her sweatshirt hiking up past her thighs. Sol moved to the foot of the bed so that he was directly in front of her. She raised her eyebrows and smiled at him, but didn't pull down her sweatshirt. She pointed over her head, without interest, at the colorful little crayon drawing on the wall behind her.

"There it is," she said.

Everyone, except Sol, stared at the little drawing that looked as if it had been done by a child.

"It's so cute!" Sheila said, brightly. "Oh, Cassandra! It must be so exciting to have your very own Lichtenstein!"

The girl grinned at Sheila. "Is it?"

"It is cute, isn't it?" Framkin said. "Roy did it especially for my baby. It has a lot of childlike whimsy in it, don't you think?" Everyone nodded, except the girl. "There's a lot of whimsy in Roy's work, isn't there, Roy?"

Lichtenstein shrugged. "If you say so."

"Well, then," Framkin said, rubbing his hands together. "Shall we go back downstairs for some champagne?"

Everyone moved toward the door except Sol. Sheila heard Sol's voice behind her. "Tell me, Hal. . . . How much for the little one?"

Everyone looked at Sol. He was staring at the little girl. She was smiling at him. Lichtenstein was grinning.

Framkin stuttered, "But. . . . but. . . ."

"The drawing!" Sheila said. "Yes! The drawing. Shall we go downstairs to discuss it?" She looked at Sol but he was still smiling at the little girl.

"Of course!" said Framkin. "The drawing! But Cassandra couldn't part with it. It was a personal gift from the world's greatest living artist."

Lichtenstein shrugged. "It's OK with me. I do 'em to sell 'em."

"But it's so very dear to my baby," Framkin said. "Isn't that right, sweetheart?"

"Whatever," the girl said.

"Of course you can't sell it, dear," Sheila said. "It must have great sentimental value." She smiled at her. The little bitch flashed Sheila's smile back at her.

Framkin said, "Oh, it does! It does! Now shall we?" He ushered everyone out of the bedroom. Sol stayed behind. He went over to the side of the bed close to the wall to study the drawing.

"I'll join yous in a few minutes," Sol said, stroking his beard, looking down at the girl. "I just wanna study this little one some more. If you don't mind, honey?"

"Sure, Sol. You can look all you want." She patted the bed beside her. Sol sat down.

Framkin stuttered, "But, sweetheart. . . ." She tossed him a look.

"Come, Mr. Framkin," Sheila said, sliding her arm in his. "Mr. Weinstein will join us directly." She smiled at him. "Mr. Weinstein does so have an interest in the little ones." At the stairway, Sheila heard the little girl's voice coming from the bedroom. "So tell me, Sol. What brings you here?"

Downstairs, Bobby was talking to the Irish maid in the living room. Sheila smiled at him. "Mr. Reynolds! Did you enjoy your smoke?" Bobby smiled and nodded. "Too bad you didn't join us after you finished it."

"Yeah, well, I got lost in conversation with Tara here."

"Really?" Sheila said. "Lost? Did you find your way out of it?"

The girl opened her green eyes wide and said, "Oh, it was nothin', mu'm. Just about Cork 'n all where I come from."

Mrs. Framkin came through a door and approached them. "Tara! What did I tell you? The champagne!"

"Oh, sorry, missus. I was just. . .."

"It was my fault," Bobby said, smiling. "I guess I distracted her."

"I'll bet," Sheila said.

The girl poured champagne into tall glasses and handed them to everyone. They stood around the living room, sipping their champagne and making small talk while waiting for Sol. Every few seconds, Framkin glanced toward the stairway.

Mrs. Framkin looked around. "And where's Mr. Weinstein?" she said.

Her husband said, "He's studying the little drawing in Cassandra's room."

"What? Why that little. . . ." The woman began walking toward the stairs. Sheila looked at Bobby. He was talking to the maid. Framkin was talking to Lichtenstein. The woman was at the stairs. Sheila put down her glass.

"Sasha! Do you have a moment!" The woman turned and looked at Sheila as Sheila walked toward her, smiling, looking into the woman's eyes. "I just wanted to tell you," she said, "how exquisite everything is. Your house, the paintings. . . ." She let her eyes roam over the woman's body" . . . seductive, really." Sheila reached out a hand and laid it on the woman's arm.

The woman looked down at Sheila's hand on her arm and then up to Sheila's eyes. She had a faint smile on her lips. "Did you see anything you found especially seductive?" she said.

"I saw a nice piece I wouldn't mind having."

"Maybe you should come back," the woman said. "When you have more time. You can get a closer look at the piece you like."

"I'd like that. Yes, I think I would like that very much."

Sol was coming down the stairs. Everyone turned to look at him.

"Just in time for champagne, Sol," Mr. Framkin said.

Sol said, "No, thanks, Hal. I think we should be goin'."

"So soon!" the woman said, looking at Sheila.

"I tink I seen enough," Sol said. "I gotta lotta tinkin' to do about your pictures, Hal. When I make up my mind, we'll call you." Sheila caught Sol's eye and looked down at the case. He nodded.

"Well, then," Sheila said, "We'd better be going. We don't want to take you away from your other guests."

Mrs. Framkin led them to the door. Sheila looked back at Framkin, standing in the living room with Lichtenstein. He was smiling his sad smile.

Mrs. Framkin stood in the light of the doorway and waved to Sheila as she walked to the limo in darkness. The woman called out, "Don't forget, Ms. Royce-Jones. I'll be expecting your call." Sheila looked back and waved at the woman in her biker chick costume who looked almost as pitiful, at that moment, as her husband.

"What was that about?" Bobby said, as he started up the limo.

"Nothing," Sheila said from the backseat.

They drove in silence up Las Olas in the darkness. Sheila stared at the back of Bobby's head. Finally, she turned to Sol. "Did you get it?" Sol nodded. Sheila unlocked the handcuffs and put the case on her lap. She clicked it open and saw that some of the bills were missing. She looked under the cardboard that separated the bills from the painting.

"Sol! For crissakes!" She held up the crayon drawing that had hung over the little girl's bed. "You were supposed to snatch the one over *Framkin's* bed!"

"I couldn't," Sol said. "The kid knew what we were up to. She said that was the only piece her bitch mother would let her father keep. She couldn't bear to have him lose it." Sol smiled. "So she gave me this one. I gave her a few C-notes. She said she woulda given it to me for nuthin'. She hated it. It reminded her how everyone treated her like a fuckin' child."

"So what?" Sheila said. "It's fucking worthless. It's the other one we wanted."

Sol was quiet in his seat. Finally, he said, "I didn't like the other one. I liked this one better. It's got, ya know, more whimsy."

Bobby laughed out loud. Sheila closed her eyes and shook her head slowly.

"What?" Sol said. "What'd I say?"

Sheila sat across from Krystal Gayle Fountain seated behind her colorfully painted Haitian desk. She put the attaché case on top of the desk and clicked it open.

"We fucked up, Krystal," Sheila said. "Sol snatched the wrong one." She turned the case toward Krystal so she could see the childlike crayon drawing. Krystal studied it for a long moment. Then she looked up.

"It's not much, Shuga."

"I know. Can you get *anything* for it?"

"At auction, I can get maybe a few large. If that. This is one of Lichtenstein's personal drawings. Just scribbling, really. He gives them to his closest friends. They have more sentimental value than anything else."

"So? What are you telling me? You can't move it."

"Oh, I can move it, Shuga." She smiled at Sheila. "My buyer in Provënce, he has a special, you might say, *perverse* interest in these kinds of personal items. Makes him feel he's not just stealing the artist's work, but the artist's friendship, too."

"You mean, he'll pay?"

"Oh, he'll pay, Shuga. Maybe two, three times what I coulda got you for the other one."

16

BOBBY AND SHEILA WERE ASLEEP IN BED, HOSHI CURLED AT THEIR FEET, when the phone rang at 3 A.M. Bobby groaned in his sleep, reached out for the phone, fumbled it and dropped it. Half-awake now, he picked it up. "This better be fuckin' important," he said.

"Turn on the fuckin' TV," Sol's voice said. "Channel Seven."

"What?"

"Just do it."

Bobby searched in the darkness for the remote, found it, and punched the 'on' button. The TV flickered, the image getting clearer, a house in flames. Bobby sat up in bed, staring at the TV.

"You see it?" Sol's voice said.

"Yeh, I see it." It was the Reverend's house burning, and off to the side Bobby could see more flames coming from his barn. The camera panning back from the house now, to a reporter, a good-looking broad in a white blouse and jeans, holding a microphone, looking straight at the camera, talking:

"The Reverend Thomas Miller of the Mountain Kirk in Davie, and his wife of 45 years, Dorothy O'Malley, were found burned to death in their modest ranch home this evening in a suspicious fire the police believe is related to the van explosion at Teddy's Diner six months ago.

The Reverend Miller, known for his racist views, was suspected of dealing in illegal firearms sales by the police. The Reverend's barn *was* filled with firearms before the fire and police believe something ignited them, causing a huge fireball that engulfed both the barn and the house. Apparently, the Reverend Miller had tried to carry his wife, who was handicapped from a stroke two years ago, toward the front door when he tripped and fell, knocking himself unconscious. His wife, still conscious, tried to drag her husband along the floor to the front door. But the Reverend, who weighed 280 pounds, was apparently too much for her, and they both succumbed to smoke inhalation only a few feet from safety. They were found, clutching each other's hand, by the fire and rescue squad—which arrived only minutes after the explosion that could be heard for miles. They managed to pull the two bodies out of the burning inferno before they were burned beyond recognition."

The camera began to pull back even farther now to show the firemen trying to hose down the flames.

"Like pissing on a bonfire, eh, Bobby?" said Sol's voice.

"Jesus Christ!" Bobby said. "Medina!"

"I told ya, Bobby. He's comin' after you and Sheila next. I were you, I wouldn't wait another minute. You got the thirty large from the picture we took. Go back to your roots, Bobby, or else Medina will have you takin' root."

"What about you? Medina might figure out who brokered the deal and want to take you down, too."

"Fuck him. The spic'll hafta go to Jessup to get me. I'll be on ice startin' Tuesday. I'll give my share of the picture money to Meyer to hold until I get out." Sol was quiet a moment. Then he said, "Good luck, Bobby," and hung up.

Bobby was still staring at the television after he hung up the phone. "I led them right to him," he said to himself. "Poor fucking guy."

"Look, Bobby!" Sheila said, pointing to the TV. She had been watching, too, in silence. Bobby saw, close to the burning house, the Reverend's pit bull. He was lunging at the house, the flames driving him back, but not quitting, lunging again and again, until one of the firemen threw a net over him, the dog snarling and ripping at the net with his teeth.

Hoshi was up, too, his eyes mesmerized by the bright light coming from the TV. When he heard the snarling pit bull, he began to growl low in his throat at the TV.

Bobby was out of bed now, awake. "That's it, baby. We're outta here. Pack everything."

Sheila was already throwing her clothes into open suitcases on the floor. She threw Bobby's clothes in with hers. The dresser was empty in minutes. Sheila stood up and looked around.

"That's everything," she said.

"Not everything," Bobby said. He began pulling out all the dresser drawers. He had taped stacks of hundred-dollar bills to the bottom of each drawer. He ripped off the stacks of bills and tossed them into the suitcases until he had it all.

"You never told me, Bobby," she said.

"What you don't know can't hurt you."

After they both got dressed, they carried the suitcases to the front door. Bobby pulled his CZ from the small of his back, racked the slide to chamber a round, and handed the gun to Sheila.

"What about you?" she said.

He went back to their closet, got the pump action shotgun with the pistol grip, racked the slide, and went back to Sheila. Hoshi was sitting beside her.

"Put the leash on him," Bobby said. "He sees somebody he'll go after them." Sheila clipped Hoshi's leash onto his collar and held Hoshi tight to her side. Hoshi began to growl low in his throat.

"It's all right, Hosh," Sheila whispered to him. "It's going to be all right. Shhh."

Bobby held one suitcase under his arm and another in his hand. In his other hand he held the shotgun pointing up beside his face.

"We go out real quiet, straight to the car," Bobby said. "You ready?" She nodded. "One more thing," Bobby said. "You see anything moving you start shooting I don't care it's a fucking possum." He looked at her. "You think you can do that?"

"If I have to," she said.

"And no shootin' into the dirt this time, baby."

Bobby opened the door to darkness. He listened for sounds but heard only the bugs and a frog croaking by the pool.

They moved quickly down the little sidewalk past the swimming pool and the dense foliage until they were in the parking lot. Bobby dropped the suitcases and faced the street, his back to the BMW. Sheila opened the back door, threw in the bags, then got in the passenger's seat with Hoshi. Bobby moved around the car, still facing the street, until he got to the driver's door. Sheila had already opened it. Bobby backed into the car, closed the door gently, and laid the shotgun on the dashboard. He started the engine, backed the car out, but did not put on his lights until they were already heading north on Bayview.

"Do you see anything?" he said.

"Nothing."

There were no headlights behind them so Bobby picked up speed, but not too much, only a few miles over the thirty-five mph limit. When they reached Commercial they turned left, toward I-95, a little traffic now, but still no one behind them.

"We're home free," Bobby said. He exhaled through puffed up cheeks. "You all right, baby?" He turned to look at her. She had thrown one arm over Hoshi's shoulders, like a lover. They were both staring out the front window.

Without looking at Bobby, Sheila said, "I'm fine, Bobby." She reached into her purse and withdrew a pack of cigarettes. She lit one, inhaled, then exhaled. "How long a drive is it?" she said.

"To where?"

"North Carolina, Bobby. That's where we're going, isn't it?"

They followed the real estate woman's car into the valley. The two-lane blacktop wound around the base of mountains that rose up to their left and a rolling valley of tall grass to their right. It was autumn and the trees on the mountains had already turned color—red and yellow and orange—except for the fir trees that were dark green with white bark. They passed a few cows grazing in the valley and then a sagging gray barn and a weathered old farm-house with clear plastic sheeting for windows and a rusted-orange tin roof. An old man in bib overalls was stacking firewood on the front porch of the farmhouse. Without looking up, he waved to their passing car. Bobby waved back.

"Mountain people," he said to Sheila, sitting beside him. Hoshi was sitting up in the backseat, staring out the window. "They always wave to passing cars."

"That's sweet," Sheila said.

"It's their only entertainment," Bobby said.

Sheila stared out Bobby's window at the mountains' patchwork quilt of colors, and then out her window at the rolling green valley and the rocky river that meandered through it parallel to the blacktop. "It's so beautiful," she said.

"Yeah, it is. I forgot."

"I don't know why you ever left."

"I never did get into waving at cars, baby. The mountains get old after a while."

"But it's so peaceful."

"Another way of saying there's nothing here. At least for me there wasn't." He looked across at her. "What do you always say, baby? You know, about changing your life with me."

"I couldn't think of a reason not to."

"Me, too. When it came to leaving the mountains I couldn't think of a reason not to."

They came on a small hill in the middle of the valley. It was shaped like a pyramid except that its top was a flat plateau.

"What's that, Bobby?"

"A Cherokee burial mound."

She looked at him. "Your ancestors?"

"I guess. A few hundred years ago, all the Cherokee Nations would meet in this valley to plan their war strategy against the white man." He shook his head. "A lotta good it did them."

The real estate woman turned her car left onto a narrow dirt road. Bobby followed her car as it wound around and up a mountain. They passed a log cabin with a sign on the front porch that read: Mount Rush-No-More, and then nothing but the forest as the road got narrower and rockier. The branches of trees and bushes brushed against the side of the BMW as they drove up and up.

Halfway up the mountain, the real estate woman turned her car left between two trees. Bobby followed her into a small clearing and stopped in front of a Gambrel-roofed farmhouse that had been built five years ago to look as if it were a hundred years old. They got out and joined the woman on the front porch.

"Is this remote enough for ya?" The woman said. She was built like a fireplug with a halo of tight frizzy curls. She wore polyester maternity pants with a drawstring and a mumu top.

Bobby looked around. The mountains rose up around them, close to the house, on three sides. The front porch faced down the mountain to the valley. He could see the two-lane blacktop and the dirt road leading up to the house.

"No one's gonna surprise ya with a visit up here," the woman said.

"It'll do," Bobby said.

"One thousand five-hundred dollars a month, first, last, and security," the woman said. "The owner will take an outta state check, though."

"I'll pay cash," Bobby said. "For the whole six months."

"Suit yerself."

Sheila went over to a rocking chair on the porch and sat down. She looked out over the valley below. "What a gorgeous view!" she said.

The woman said, "Not like Mi-yam-a, is it?"

They slept on the sofa bed in the living room in front of the fire Bobby had made in the black Franklin stove. Hoshi woke them at 1 A.M. He was running from window to window, growling at the darkness outside. They heard a heavy, grunting noise far up into the mountains, and then the yip of a pack of dogs trailing the grunting noise across the mountains.

Sheila sat up in bed. "Bobby! What's that?"

"Just a bear," he said. "Being tracked by a pack of hounds." He rolled over and put a pillow over his head.

Sheila listened to the bear and the hounds moving across the mountain for a few moments, then she got up and put a leash on Hoshi. She led him outside on the front porch. He ran to the railing and stood up on his hind legs, his front paws on the railing. He threw back his head, his eyes rolling back, and began to howl like a wolf. Sheila stared at this Hoshi she did not know. She shivered, naked, in the cold mountain air. The noises were getting fainter as the bear moved over the mountaintop and began going down the other side. Hoshi continued to howl like a wolf for a few moments, and then he stopped and sat down. He was panting as if he'd just come out of a trance. Sheila petted him, "Reminds you of your ancestors, too, eh,

Hoshi?" Sheila hugged herself against the chill and looked up at the stars and the pale yellow moon in the purple sky. Then she went back inside with Hoshi. The moment she let him off the leash, he jumped onto the bed and curled up at Bobby's feet.

Sheila drifted through the dark house illuminated only by the light from the moon slanting through the windows. The floors and the walls were wide heart-pine boards and the ceiling beams were rough-cut with bark on one side. The house was completely furnished as if someone had been living here only yesterday. Rough-pine coffee tables and dressers. An old pecan farm dining-room table with antique ladderback chairs. Plush sofas and easy chairs. Colorful Impressionist prints in gilt frames on the walls. Hundreds of books on shelves along the walls. There were family photographs everywhere. A husband and wife on their wedding day years ago. Their children as babies. An older husband and wife with their teenaged children on a beach in Florida. A gray-haired couple posing with a boy in a cap and gown. Grandchildren. A child's crayon drawing in a glass frame of two stick figures with the shaky printed words of a child, Happy Anniversary Grandma and Grandpa.

The real estate woman had told them that the husband and wife had been college professors at the University of Florida in Gainesville. When they retired five years ago, they built this cabin as their dream house. Their children and grandchildren visited them at Christmas and Easter and Thanksgiving. Then, a year ago, the husband had been killed in a light-plane crash in the mountains only a few miles from their home. The wife left the house the following day and never returned. She could not bear to look at it, or rent it, for a year, until now. Bobby and Sheila were the first people to live in it in a year.

Sheila threw another log on the fading fire and got in bed with Bobby and Hoshi. She pressed her body against Bobby's back, feeling his warmth, and fell asleep.

They woke in the morning and found coffee in the kitchen with other canned goods. Bobby made their coffee in an old tin pot. Then they went outside to sit in the rocking chairs and wait for the sun to come up.

Sheila looked at the morning clouds hovering around the mountain tops in the distance. "Is it always like this in the morning?" she said to Bobby.

He nodded. "That's why they call them the Smoky Mountains."

"It must have been fun growing up in these mountains, Bobby. Like Chingakook."

"Who?"

"*The Last of the Mohicans*, Bobby. They even filmed the movie in these mountains."

"Yeah, well, I didn't grow up in these mountains. I grew up on the reservation a few miles from town. The mountains were where white people went to hunt and build vacation cabins like this one. I was a city kid, if you can call Cherokee a city. A main street with a few two-story redbrick buildings. A statue of Daniel Boone in front of city hall. A few Cherokee curio shops for the tourists. A nothing town, really."

"What was it like, Bobby? On the reservation?"

She looked at him. He was staring out at the valley and the mountains beyond it through his narrow black eyes that were unreadable. Finally, he said, "You really want to know?"

"Yes."

So he told her about the government-issue shack on the reservation in Cherokee. How it was always silent, and smelled of stale smoke from the wood-burning stove they used for heat in winter, and corn meal his mother boiled on the stove every night, and most of all piss.

His father spent his days dressed in phony Indian buckskins and a feathered headdress, standing in the summer heat in front of a Cherokee curio shop filled with authentic Cherokee artifacts made in

Taiwan. Tourists walked by, smiling at his father, pointing out to the children "The Chief." His father, standing there, sweating in the heat, drinking Dickell from a paper bag, beginning to sway in the late afternoon sun, needing to take a piss so bad, but not allowed to until his shift was over. By then, he'd already pissed in his buckskin pants.

The shack had a rusted tin roof that leaked rain all over their peeling linoleum floors and down the sheetrock walls that were mildewed and so thin that Bobby, a boy of six, could lay in his bed at night, listening to the driving rain beating down on the tin roof like the drumming fingers of a thousand Cherokee ghosts, and *still* he could hear his father in the next room, grunting on top of his mother, his mother silent, bearing it, as she bore everything, until finally his father finished with a louder grunt and a whoosh of breath and spilled off his mother and began to snore. Bobby heard the creak of bedsprings as his mother got out of bed. She went into the bathroom. Bobby heard running water. One night he got up and went to the bathroom, too, half-asleep, to piss. He pushed open the door and saw his mother standing on one leg, the other leg straddling the sink. She was bent over, holding a rubber hose she had stuck between her legs. She turned to look at him with her black eyes that only Bobby could read. She had shiny black hair parted in the middle, and knotted in long braids down either side of her moonlike face that was the color of dirt, the skin pitted and coarse. She looked at him for a moment without expression, and then down at the rubber hose between her legs, and then back to him for a brief instant, and he knew.

Bobby was twelve the first and only time his father ever really spoke to him, had a conversation with him. It was late August, still hot. His father took him in his pickup truck to an ancient Cherokee burial ground that had just been discovered by a construction crew bulldozing the land for a new Industrial Park. The construction crew had stopped bulldozing up the bones of the dead until the city council decided what to do. The Cherokee Nation council offered to buy the land to preserve it as a burial ground. The company building the Industrial Park promised the town 200 jobs if it could have the land. Cherokees from the reservation and from as far away as Oklahoma came to protest the desecration of this hallowed ground. The protest was peaceful and lasted only until the city council voted to give the land to the company. The construction crew began to bulldoze the burial ground again, digging up bones, putting them in cardboard boxes, and sending them to the reservation for reburial.

Bobby's father parked his truck on the soft shoulder of a dirt road behind the UPS depot alongside a highway. He pointed to a deserted field plowed in rows, as if for planting. Every six feet along a row, there was a plastic garbage bag over a hole, as if something that had been planted there had been uprooted. Bobby's father took him by the hand and led him through tall grass, past the "Warning, No Trespassers!" sign out onto the plowed, red earth. They began walking down the rows of empty graves in the summer heat, past the plastic garbage bags and an occasional loose bone bleached from the sun. Bobby's father began to talk to him in a low, droning, sing-songy voice, like the old medicine men late at night over a fire. He told Bobby these were the graves of their ancestors, the last of the great Cherokee warriors who had fought the white man until they could fight no more. The white man rounded up the Cherokees who had not hid in the mountains, and marched them to a reservation in Oklahoma. It took them months. Nine thousand men, women, and children marched through the mountains of North Carolina and Tennessee and then down into the plains of Arkansas until finally they reached that dusty, dried up land that was their new home. White people lined the streets of every small town they passed through. They watched in silence as one after another of the Cherokees fell by the roadside and died from hunger and exposure and

despair. When they reached Oklahoma only six thousand had sur-
vived. The Cherokee called that march "The Trail of Tears," but not
because the Cherokee cried along that march. They never cried,
Bobby's father said. They were brave, stoic in their suffering. No, it was
the white people standing by the side of the road who cried.

Bobby looked up at his father to see if *he* was crying, and when he
saw he wasn't, he felt proud of his father for the first and only time in
his life. Then he heard a voice.

"Hey, Kemasabi! What do ya'll think you're doin'?" Bobby and his
father turned to see a white man in a yellow hard hat standing behind
them, his hands on his hips. He had a red beard, and wore silvery mirrored sunglasses Bobby couldn't see into.

"Can't you read the sign, Chief?" said the man. "No trespassing! I'll
bet your little brave there can read it."

Bobby looked at his father, waited for him to become like these ancestors, a great warrior. But his father only looked down at the dirt, took
Bobby's hand again, and led him silently past the white man out of the
burial ground, through the tall grass, to his truck.

When they got back to the reservation. Bobby's father had to slow
his old truck over the rutted, dusty, dirt road. It shook and rattled as
they entered the reservation. Bobby looked out the window at the flat
scrub land baking in the sun, surrounded on all sides by thickly
forested mountains rich with game, far from the reservation. He
looked out the window at the gray wooden shacks, tar paper stuffed
between the gaps in the siding, clear plastic over the broken windows.
There were old-fashioned, hand-cranking, washing machines on the
sagging front porches. There were rusted-out cars on cinder blocks in
the dirt front yards. Children, like himself, "little braves," dressed in
worn and tattered hand-me-down clothes, were playing in the dirt
with rocks and sticks. Fat mothers, "squaws," were hanging up wet
laundry on a rope strung between two dying trees. Fathers, "the

chiefs," sat under the shade of the porch overhang, doing nothing, staring out over the front yard, their wives, their children, without seeing because they were already drunk in the heat.

These are my ancestors, Bobby thought. Great warriors. Just as those Cherokee who were defeated by the white men were great warriors. Just as those Cherokee whose bones were dug up and shipped back, without a whimper to the reservation, were great warriors. Just as those Cherokee who were herded together like sheep and forced to march across three states to Oklahoma, dying by the hundreds as they walked, were great warriors. All of them great warriors, my ancestors, because they suffered and did not cry. Because they accepted defeat without a whimper and that made them brave.

"I was only twelve," he said now, sitting on the porch alongside of a white woman and his dog in the mountains. "I took a blood oath that night. Really. I cut myself with a piece of broken glass and rubbed dirt in it. Damned thing got infected. I vowed I would die in battle before I'd ever accept defeat." He laughed. "Me and the Reverend Tom, huh? That old bastard knew me, didn't he? He musta made the same vow as a kid, ya know. To die on his shield. Today, I guess, a shrink would say I made a vow never to become a victim."

He turned and looked at her. She was rocking gently in her chair, holding her mug of hot coffee with both hands close to her chest, her long blood-red finger nails wrapped around the cup, her short blond hair resting against the back of the chair, her blue eyes staring out over the valley, tears streaming silently down her cheeks.

"Is that enough?" he said. She nodded. "Don't you want to hear more, baby? How I started lifting weights the next day, a skinny little kid, but not for long. By the time I got to the white high school I was a big dude. The white girls noticed, but not too obvious about it, sitting behind me in class, whispering in my ear, 'Bobby, meet me out in the field by the Industrial Park tonight.' It was never, 'Bobby, come to my house, meet my parents, have dad toss you the keys to his car, tell you to have fun tonight kids, go to a movie, here's a five spot, have a pizza on me.' So what? I used them, too. It was their boyfriends I had to watch out for. They see me in the school corridor, three or four of them, always a crowd, they knew enough not to fuck with me one-on-one, they begin to sing "Half-Breed." You know, that old Cher song, gypsies, tramps, and thieves. I never took the bait. I just waited my time. It came when I was sixteen. I was fuckin' this little blond cheerleader with a big ass, Tammy Sue, somethin' like that, had this football hero boyfriend, mean dude, bigger than me, but beefy, not hard like I was. He didn't understand mean don't stand a chance against angry. He stops me in the corridor one day, pokes a finger in my chest so hard he knocks me against the lockers. 'Ya'll been talkin' to my girl, Kemasabi,' he says. 'I catch ya'll I'll fuck you up good.' I look at him real innocent, and says, 'I ain't been talkin' to your girl, dude. I been fuckin' her.' Then I hit him with a good shot. I felt the cartilidge in his nose collapsing against my first. He went down, blood spurting all over, holding his nose, crying, not so mean now, not thinking about fucking me up *now*.

"That was the last time anyone ever fucked with me. I gave him a kick in the nuts for good measure and then ran away. The sheriff put out a warrant on me, assault and battery, but they couldn't find me. I went up into the mountains for the first time, and hid out. I met these two mean ole rednecks grew pot on government forest land, taught me how to survive in the mountains. They called me 'Buck.' They gave me a rundown cabin so I could watch their pot, make sure no DEA or poachers found it. I worked for them a few years, mostly grunt work, learnin' to like it up in the mountains, all that time to think. When I was in my early twentys, they let me haul the stuff to Ft. Lauderdale in a U-Haul van. I thought it was great. They just figured, why take chances, let Buck take the fall, do time. I delivered the pot to the rear of this tittie bar on Sunrise called The Booby Trap run by this Jew from

New York City named Sol who threw me a stripper now and then. He got to like me cause I worked hard, kept my mouth shut, wasn't afraid to take a risk. 'I could use a kid like you,' he said. 'An outsider.' He meant I was an Indian in a white man's world and he was a Jew worked for a guinea crew in Brooklyn when he was a kid, until he got in some kinda trouble and had to split for Paradise. 'Everybody's new in Paradise, kid,' he said. 'There's no past in Paradise.'

"He offered me a job. While I was thinkin' about it I got a call from the rednecks telling me the DEA helicopters had sniffed out our pot. So I went to work with Sol. Mostly muscle stuff. I was his bouncer at The Trap. The girls gotta big kick outta me, this big Seminole-looking dude with a black ponytail, jeans, boots, straw cowboy hat. I even sucked on a toothpick, no kiddin'. Then I got hooked up with this stripper, Suzanne, not a bad chick, really. One night I saw her dying her pussy blond in the bathroom before she went to work. The next day my ponytail was blond, I'd swapped my snap-button shirts for Hawaiian shirts, my jeans for O.P. shorts, and my boots for flip-flops. I even changed my name, from Robert Redfeather to Robert Roberts." He smiled at her. "But my buddies call me Bobby Squared, ma'm."

He looked across at her. "Is that what you wanted to hear, baby?" he said. She shook her head, no.

After their morning coffee, they put on their jeans and boots and down vests to ward off the early winter chill before they hiked into the mountains.

"Should we take a piece, Bobby?" Sheila said.

"No. There's nothin' gonna hurt us in the mountains."

They crossed an ice cold branch and followed a narrow path up into the mountains. They had to stop every few yards while Hoshi pissed.

"Good boy, Hosh," Bobby said. "Let the neighbors know there's a new gun in town."

They hiked for an hour to only the sounds of the dead leaves crunching under their feet and their labored breathing and the wind whistling eerily through the fir trees. The trail grew narrower and the brush thicker. Bobby pointed to a fir tree with white bark. "Nigger pines," he said.

"Oh, Bobby."

"Really, baby. That's what the locals call them."

"Why?"

"Cause they're worthless. Too soft to build with and too sappy to burn."

They passed a mound of bear scat. Hoshi sniffed around it and then pissed on it. Bobby laughed. "You may be a city dog, Hosh, but you never forget."

The path vanished and they had to fight their way through laurel and rhododendren bushes. Sheila said, "Maybe we should turn back."

"Not yet. I wanna show you somethin'."

They hiked for another half hour until they were drenched with sweat even in the cold and they came to a small open space and a rock-ledged waterfall. There were the remains of a log cabin. The cabin had collapsed over the years and only a few logs from the walls remained standing, and a stone chimney and fireplace, all of it overgrown with kudzu.

"This is where I usta live when I watched the pot for the rednecks," Bobby said.

"It's so peaceful here," Sheila said.

"Yeah. It gave me time to think when I needed it."

Bobby crouched down by the fireplace the way Sheila had seen Indians crouch in movies when they were trying to read the tracks of horses in the dust. He stuck his hands into the fireplace, sifted through the cold gray ashes and rubbed them into his hands as if he was washing them with soap.

"What are you doing?" Sheila said.

"Something I remembered. An old shaman told me, when you come back to your past you have to embrace it so you can leave it behind."

"And if you don't."

"Then it follows you, like a curse." He stood up, wiped his hands on his jeans. "It's all bullshit."

"Don't you believe it?"

"I don't wanna believe it."

They got back to their cabin at noon. Sheila drove thirty minutes into town to buy groceries at Bi-Lo. Bobby wouldn't go with her. "I been there," he said.

Sheila pushed a shopping cart up and down the aisles that smelled of stale body odor. Women with upswept, lacquered hair stared at her, a tall blond tanned woman in tight jeans. They wore polyester pants with a drawstring and brown shoes with laces. After she passed them in the aisle they whispered loudly to each other, "Floridiot."

Sheila came to a moon-faced Cherokee woman, round as a barrel and brown as dirt. Sheila smiled at her. The woman lowered her eyes to the floor until Sheila had passed. Like Bobby's mother, Sheila thought.

Driving back to their cabin, Sheila saw an antique store by the side of the two-lane blacktop. She stopped and went inside. The big room was cold and filled with junk furniture. A voice called out, "Come back here, honey, and warm yerself."

Sheila walked to the back of the room where a tall angular old woman, with short hair dyed burgundy, sat in a rocking chair by an old black Franklin stove. The woman was in her 80s, with a perfectly made-up face—arched, penciled eyebrows, a ghostly white face powdered with talcum powder, and red lipstick. She was smoking a cigarette through a long mother-of-pearl cigarette holder. She picked up a chunk of coal from a pile on the floor, opened the stove door, and tossed it in. Then she smiled up at Sheila and patted the chair beside her.

"Set a spell, honey," she said.

Sheila sat down beside the woman. "I was just passing by," Sheila said. "I'm not really looking for anything."

"Sure you are, honey. Everybody's lookin' for somethin'. Now I got me some chairs and dressers and a nice bedroom suite. Now the suite is dear, but the chairs are only $20 and the dressers $40. A course some a the chairs got the trembles, you wouldn't want none a them."

"Well, I could use a chair. We just rented a cabin up in the mountains and I'd like to have something of my own in it. It feels strange living in a house with other people's things."

"It sure does, I'll bet. But everything was somebody else's at one time, wadn't it?"

Sheila smiled. "I suppose so."

The woman reached under her chair and picked up a jelly jar filled with a white liquid, like water. "You ain't one a them Baptists, are you, honey? This being a dry county and all. Old Hope don't want to spend her old age in some smelly jail." She looked at Sheila and smiled. "No, I expect not." She took a swig from the jar and handed it to Sheila. "Take the chill offin your bones." Sheila took the jar and held it to her nose. She scrunched up her features. "Don't smell like much," the old woman said, "but it'll do the job."

Sheila took a sip. The liquid tasted like rubbing alcohol and burned her throat. She coughed. The old woman laughed. "Take another, honey, real quick, drown out the taste of the first sip. That's the secret."

Sheila took another sip. "That one wasn't so bad," she said.

The woman said, "They get better 'n better." She pushed herself up slowly from the rocking chair. Sheila reached out a hand to help her.

"Thass awright, honey, old Hope can fetch herself. Now, let me see what I got fer ya."

She walked down an aisle, pointing out different pieces of furniture. "Now I got that there dresser from an old woman mean as a strip-ed snake." She winked at Sheila. "But I got a good buy on it. It's pure white ash under all that paint. All you gotta do, honey, is strip it, and it'll be a family heirloom."

"I don't know. I don't think Bobby. . . ."

"Sure, he would. That Bobby Redfeather's a good ole boy. A little hot tempered for a Cherokee, but he had reason."

Sheila looked at the woman. "How do you?. . ."

The woman flung the back of her hand in the air. "Old Hope knows everything goes on in the mountains, ain't Bobby told you that?"

"He doesn't tell me much about the mountains."

"No, I suppose not. Don't blame him none. The mountains weren't for him. Boy wanted to go to the city. He never had nothin' with that daddy a his. I seen his old man onst after he been drinkin' that Dickell all day, walking home holdin' a piece a rope like it was gold. I said, 'Heh, Buck! Either you lost you a mule or you found yerself a piece a rope.'" She stopped in front of a huge steamer trunk with leather straps. "Now this here would make you a nice hope chest, honey, put all yer fancy things in it. I expect you got some fancy thing, dontcha?" She looked at the dusty trunk. "Gotta de-fumigate it first, though."

"I don't know. I wasn't really looking. . . ."

"You gotta put somethin' a yer own in that cabin, honey, keep the ghosts away."

Sheila laughed. "Ghosts?"

"Ghosts everwheres in the mountains jes waitin' ta grab onto a new un. I got me one livin' right downstairs in my apartment. Name a Ronny. He was real peculiar about that. 'With a Y,' he says. Got hisself killed in an auto-mobile accident. When I moved into my apartment he was already wanderin' around lookin' for company. Introduced his-self real proper to me one night while I was lying in my bed. He stood over me, all gauzylike, expectin' me to be scared, I guess. I jes told him, I said, 'Ronny you can stay long as you like long as you don't bring no cold breezes to chill my achin' bones and none a them bad smells come with ghosts. Ya see, I knew a thing a two about ghosts. But he been a good boy. Been with me 30 years now. Keeps me company, an old woman livin' alone. Every onst in a while he can be a bit of a tick, thinkin he gotta act like a ghost, bangin' pots and pans to scare me until I told him onst that business don't unsettle me none, jes makes me feel sorry for a poor, pitiful lost soul tryin' to scare an old woman. Hurt his feelin's, I did. Ghosts got feelin's, too, ya know, and he didn't come around for a spell. But he come back, said he got no place else to go. I said, 'Me, neither, Ronny.' We been together since. Only thing bothers me now is ever onst in a while him insistin' he ain't really dead. I tell him, 'You ain't dead, Ronny, what you doin hangin' round an old woman fer?' He laughed, ghosts laugh, too, honey, at least the good uns, and he said, 'Hope, you got a point.'"

Sheila couldn't stop herself from laughing. Then she said, "I don't think we have any ghosts."

"Maybe not yet, but that poor soul built that cabin for his family died in an aeroplane accident gonna be comin' back home someday, hauntin' that house still thinks is his. You wanna be prepared, honey. He could be a bad ghost, not like Ronny." She shook her head. "Bad ghosts is tiresome in yer life. It takes a lot ta get rid a them."

"How *do* you get rid of a bad ghost?"

"You gotta make a real hard effort to put them outta yer mind. And even when you do, they'll hang around for ages waitin' for you to slip up sos they can creep back in. If you're strong enough, you can keep 'em out so long, they get tired hangin' on, and they'll just wander off to someone else. Ghosts are lazy, honey, otherwise they wouldn't be ghosts, would they, just hangin' around doin' nothin' but tryin' to scare decent folk?"

Hope helped Sheila carry the streamer trunk out to the car. The old woman was so strong Sheila felt foolish struggling with her end of the trunk. They fit it half in, half out of the trunk and the old woman tied the open trunk to the bottom latch so it wouldn't bang around.

"Tell Bobby you found you a piece a rope with a steamer trunk attached," Hope said.

"Thank you, Hope," Sheila said. The woman leaned over and kissed Sheila on the cheek. Her lips were cold and she smelled of alcohol and talcum powder and worn leather.

The old woman pulled back from Sheila, her hands gripping Sheila's arms tightly. "Why, girl," she said, "you already got a ghost in you."

Sheila smiled. "A good ghost or a bad one, Hope?"

The old woman looked at her with a great sadness in her eyes, "Why, both, dear. Didn't you know?"

When Bobby saw the trunk, he said, "Jesus, baby, we don't need this shit. This ain't our house."

"Hope said we needed something to keep the ghosts away."

"Hope? You stopped at Hope's?" He smiled and shook his head. "That old girl's gonna bury us all. She must be a hundred."

"She knew you were back in the mountains."

"She would. She knows everything. But she won't tell nobody."

"She knows a lot about you."

Bobby was quiet for a moment, lost someplace in his past. Then he said, "When I was a kid I usta help her move some of her furniture. Not that she needed me. That old woman is as strong as an ox."

"She still is."

"Buried three husbands, all of them cousins. She had a son, he must be in his fifties now if he ain't dead. He had the mind of a child. She always kept him close to her she was afraid the social workers would find out about him and put him in a state home. He'd sit in a rocking chair on the porch of her store, smiling his child's smile, his eyes all glassy, drool on his lips, while I helped Hope move her furniture. She'd give me a dollar, more money than I ever saw, and then put a finger to her lips and whisper, 'Now, you listen to me, Robert Redfeather. You don't be tellin' your daddy about that dollar. You know how he'll spend it.'"

"She told me—I know it sounds foolish, but she was so serious— she said there were ghosts in the mountains." She waited for Bobby to laugh at her, but he didn't.

Finally, Bobby said, "Cherokee believe that shit." Sheila looked at him. Bobby said, "You think Hope's a white woman?"

"I thought . . . she's so pale."

"Yeah, all that talcum powder she wears. She ain't that pale."

Late in the afternoon, they sat on the floor of the porch, their legs dangling over the side like kids, and sipped their drinks, vodka rocks for Sheila, bourbon rocks for Bobby, in old tin cups, and shot their guns at the tin can Bobby had hung up on a tree in the woods. The gunshots echoed off the mountains around them.

"Not a bad idea to let the folks around here know we're armed and dangerous," Bobby said. He fired off ten rapid rounds in succession with his CZ. "They'll know the difference between a city gun and a country gun."

"What is the difference?" Sheila said.

Bobby racked the slide of the shotgun and blasted the tin can. "That's a country gun." Then he fired off six, quick shots with his CZ. "That's a city gun," he said.

After target practice, Bobby sat in the rocking chair, disassembled their guns, and cleaned them. Sheila went into the front yard to rake up fallen leaves in early December.

Bobby called out to her, "Don't waste your energy, baby. This ain't our house."

"It's not work, Bobby. I like it. It's therapeutic. Gives me a feeling of permanence. It reminds me of when I was a little girl and used to rake up the leaves in Connecticut into a big pile and then dive into them. Didn't you ever do that as a boy?"

"There weren't no leaves on the reservation, baby. Just hard-packed dirt."

They ate supper early. Bobby sat in a worn armchair in the kitchen and watched Sheila prepare dinner. He sipped his bourbon from the tin cup, and said, "What are you cookin', baby?"

She looked up, wide-eyed, and wiped sweat from her brow with the back of her hand. "A country dinner, Bobby," she said. "Biscuits, collard greens, and fried chicken." She went back to stirring the biscuit batter like a woman possessed. Her arms and face were coated with flour.

"Don't wear yourself out, baby," Bobby said, grinning.

She glared at him. "I'm doing it for you!" she said.

"I didn't know you could cook, baby."

"Well, I can. When I have to." She dropped the little patties of biscuit dough on a greased pan and put them in the oven. Then she checked the boiling collard greens and the frying chicken. The chicken crackled and popped and spewed grease all over the stove.

"Watch it you don't start a fire with that grease," Bobby said.

She looked at him through narrowed eyes.

"Just tryin' to be helpful, baby," Bobby said.

Bobby sat at the dining-room table looking out the window at the valley below while Sheila laid down all the food. She put a piece of chicken, some collard greens, and a biscuit on Bobby's plate. She stood over him, her hands on her hips, and waited.

"Well," she said. "Eat."

Bobby picked up the biscuit. It was burned black on one side. He split it open to butter it. Liquidy, white dough ran out of the biscuit.

"Amazin'," he said. "Burnt on the outside and runny on the inside. How'd you manage that, baby?"

"Oh, Bobby! I'm so sorry. I followed the recipe."

"That's all right, baby. I'll just eat the chicken and greens." He cut open a chicken breast. The meat was bright pink. He looked up at her. Tears were streaming down her cheeks. He pulled her down onto his lap and hugged her. "Come on, baby," he said. "It's nuthin'. I'm not with you for your cookin'."

"Now that you're home," she said, "I wanted you to have a nice country dinner."

"This ain't home, baby. This is what I left. Besides, I didn't have the heart to tell ya, but I *hate* country cookin'."

Sheila wiped tears from her cheeks and said, with her phony smile, "Well, Bobby, we can always order out."

"Shoney's don't deliver, baby." They both laughed.

There was no television in the cabin so they read themselves to sleep at night in front of the fire in the black Franklin stove. They sat up in the sofa bed, Hoshi curled at their feet. Sheila read books about the Cherokee nation and the Trail of Tears. Bobby read the plays Sheila had once acted in.

Bobby put his book down one night, and said, "I can see you as Stella. Stanley was a sexy guy. That was why she was with him. But never as Blanche, baby."

"Not now, Bobby. But without you, I could have been Blanche."

Another night, he said, "Maggie musta been pretty close to the bone for you, baby."

"What do you mean?"

He looked across at her. "She was married to a fag who wouldn't fuck her, too."

Sheila waited until Bobby fell asleep, then she got up in the darkness and drifted through the house, looking for signs of a ghost. She heard only the sounds of the animals outside, foraging for food. She studied the prints on the walls: a Fauve landscape and a primitive girl in a red dress. She read the titles of the books on the shelves: Kafka, Camus, Proust. She looked at the family photographs on the end tables as if for a sign. She picked up a photograph of the family vacationing on a Florida beach one night. It looked like a Ft. Lauderdale beach near The Harbor Beach, the expensive tourist hotel. The Harbor Beach had a huge, kidney-shaped swimming pool with a rock waterfall at one end and an outdoor bar that served only guests who produced a room key. Sheila could see the husband, in his baggy boxer bathing suit, and the wife, in her Lily Pulitzer suit with the little skirt at the hips, sitting at the outdoor bar, sipping Margaritas while they kept an eye on their children playing under the waterfall.

That family had never been to The Mark. They didn't even know such a place existed. The husband had never sat at The Mark's Chickee Bar in a bikini and made a gun deal with Machine Gun Bob. The wife had never worn a G-string bikini from Splish Splash and listened to her husband talking in code to a Jewish gangster from Brooklyn. That family took cruises on The Jungle Queen and gushed over Wayne Huizenga's imitation Spanish mansion with its Blockbuster Video flag flying over the mansion just so all the tourists, like this husband and wife, would envy his wealth. They took their kids to Sea World to see the dolphins, and Six Flags, and then put them to bed early while the husband, in his navy blazer and rep tie, and the wife, in her smart Anne Klein summer dress, ate dinner at the Harbor Beach's gourmet restaurant. The husband had never bought chicken and ribs at the Reverend Jesse's Good Christian Barbecue, with a CZ-85, 9 mm, stuck in the back of his jeans, and the wife had never hid a .32 acp Seecamp in her panties before she had dinner with a Cuban madman in his Coral Gables mansion surrounded by armed guards and a twelve-foot-high concrete wall topped with razor wire. That wife had never had that Cuban madman put his hand on her thigh under a dinner table, and then, six months later, put out a contract on their lives.

No wonder the husband never came back to haunt us, Sheila thought. He's too terrified. She put the photograph of the happy family on the Ft. Lauderdale beach back on the end table. "The ghosts of a life we'll never have," Sheila said softly to herself. And then she got back in bed alongside Bobby.

Sheila, dressed in jeans and a down vest, was picking up logs and cradling them in her arms on the porch amid the softly falling snow in February. The ground and the tree branches were blanketed white with snow. The mountains were eerily silent, still, without a wind. Sheila glanced through the window and saw Bobby kneeling in front of the Franklin stove, starting a fire. Hoshi was lying beside him, his nose as close to the warm fire as possible.

Sheila struggled with the logs to the front door. She heard the phone ring, and Bobby call out, "I'll get it, baby."

She brought the logs into the living room and stacked them beside the stove while Bobby talked in a muffled voice on the phone in the kitchen.

"Who is it, Bobby?" she called out, but he didn't answer.

When Bobby returned to the living room, she said again, "Who was that?"

"Sol. He's gettin' out in a few weeks."

"His time is up already?"

"Meyer got him sprung early. But it cost Sol." He kneeled down and stacked logs in the fire. Without looking at her, he said, "It's time to go home, baby."

"Do we have to?"

"We're runnin' out of money. And we ain't gonna make any up here."

"What about Medina?"

"He's forgotten us by now."

Sheila looked around the cabin at the prints and books and family photographs. "In a way, I hate to leave it," she said. "It was starting to feel like home."

He looked up at her. "This ain't our home. Those aren't our books. That ain't our family in those photographs. We don't have a history, baby. We're lucky if we got a present."

17

"He sounds different," Bobby said. He downshifted for the railroad tracks at Dixie. The black SHO bumped over the tracks, then picked up speed.

"Like how?" Sheila said.

"I don't know. Just different. Not so pissed off." Bobby turned right onto Federal. Two rednecks, a mangy dog lying at their feet, sat in the shade of the Riptide's outdoor bar drinking beer. A skinny hooker walked past them. She wore a miniskirt that barely covered her ass and dirty white fringed cowboy boots. She sashayed down the sidewalk, close to the road, swinging her ass, looking back over her shoulder at passing cars while she talked on a cellular phone.

"Poor thing," Sheila said. "It's too hot to work." Sheila followed the hooker with her eyes. The hooker smiled at her and waved. Sheila shook her head, no. The hooker gave Sheila the finger.

"He's probably just depressed, Bobby," Sheila said. "He's broke. He had to give Meyer his thirty thousand from the painting just so he could get him out early."

"That's not it."

"Well, then maybe he's just tired. He's had to work construction, what, the last three months at the halfway house. He's forty-eight, Bobby. A little late for a career change."

"Not tired like that. Something different. You'll see." The SHO picked up speed as they passed Lauderdale Airport under a hot summer sun at noon. A plane was coming in from the ocean.

"Well, it was his own fault, doing time," Sheila said. "If he hadn't been such a smartass with his parole officer maybe he wouldn't have gone away. Playing his stupid fucking games. Maybe doing his six months at a summer camp didn't agree with him." A 747 passed low overhead. Its shadow, like a prehistoric bird's, enveloped them for a moment, then moved west toward a runway.

"His being different bothers me," Bobby said. "He don't seem angry, you know, the way he was all the time. I don't get it. He only did six months at a fucking camp one step above Club Fed. The place had a fucking chalk line for a fence, like a football field, you cross the line they give you a five-yard penalty. He swept out a warehouse forty minutes a day than spent the rest of the day swapping bullshit stories with embezzeling accountants and money-laundering lawyers, and still it changed him."

"Maybe he got old. They say doing time ages you."

"But it wasn't *hard* time, for Crissakes! He gained twenty pounds. No, he lost something. His edge."

Sheila smiled. "Well, we'll just have to find it for him. Us, too, Bobby. We all got a little slack these last months. We'll just have to tighten up that slack."

Bobby looked across at her. She was staring out her window, smoking a cigarette, holding the cigarette beside her cheek, limp-wristed, in that ladylike way that always amazed Bobby. There was nothing slack about her. She still had those chiseled abs at forty-six, and a little flare to her thighs now that she'd been lifting weights for a year. She was wearing a T-shirt with the words, "Rehab Is For Quitters," across her chest, and tight cutoff jeans shorts. She didn't look like a lady now like she did that night they scammed the painting. Or when she was chopping wood in her jeans and down vest in the mountains, or walking through a fancy restaurant in a spandex dress and six-inch pumps so that everyone assumed she was a hooker.

"There's nothing to it," she had told him once. "The clothes are only a part of it. Mostly, it's the way I see myself. I put on a certain kind of clothes and I become that woman."

Bobby slowed the car as they came into Dania. Sheila said, "Do you think Sol will like my T-shirt?"

"I hope so."

Bobby turned the corner and stopped in front of The Lucky Hotel.

"A misnomer," Sheila said. It was an old, two-story, Cracker hotel made out of Dade County pine, and then stuccoed over over the years. Not even Hurricane Andrew could knock it down, the pine as hard as steel. It just got more and more dilapidated over the years, the stucco peeling, the mission tiles cracking, falling off, until they were replaced with a tin roof. The first floor was reserved for transients one step up from the homeless, $10 a night. The second floor was a halfway house for cons serving out the last six months of their sentence while "acclimating"—Sol's word—themselves back into society. They went to work each morning at six and had to be back in time for supper at six. Today was Sol's last day.

They walked around back. Sol was sitting at a picnic table under the shade of a gumbo limbo tree in a scruffy backyard. He was smoking a cigarette and talking to a woman. Sheila ran over to him. "Sol, baby, we missed you." She bent down and kissed him on the lips. When she straightened up she made a big production of studying him. His bald head was tanned from working in the sun. His van dyke beard was neatly trimmed. He was wearing his Paul Newman-blue contacts. A pressed, long-sleeved, Polo button-down shirt over his big belly. White tennis shorts. Dirty white loafers.

Sheila narrowed her eyes. "You look different, Solly."

"It's the hair," he said, rubbing a hand over his bald head. "I grew it in the slam."

"We *did* miss you, Sol." Sheila said.

"I missed you, too, baby. I like the T-shirt."

Sheila turned to Bobby. "See, I told you."

Sol said, "How's the Hosh?"

"The same now," Sheila said.

"What do ya mean?"

"Well, for a while there up in the mountains he thought he was a big, tough, mountain dog, howling at bears every night."

"You shoulda let him loose. The Hosh can handle himself."

Bobby looked at him. "He's a fuckin' city dog, Sol. Like us. We lose sight of that we're all in trouble."

"Bobby's right," Sheila said. "Hoshi's back in his element now. Chasing geckos."

Bobby said, "You ready, Solly?"

"I gotta check out upstairs." He stood up.

"Where's your jewelery?" Bobby said.

"I got some waitin' for me," Sol said. "Jeez, I feel naked without my Rolex and Star of David."

"You mean, vulnerable," Sheila said.

"Yeah, whatever," Sol said. "I gotta get some real fuckin' cigarettes, too." He tossed his cigarette in the grass. "Prison issue," he said. He held up a pack with "Brand A" written on it. "Brand B's got filters," he said. He crumpled the pack up and tossed it in the grass.

"Aren't you going to introduce us to your friend?" Sheila said.

The woman looked up at them. A tiny, ferret-faced woman with stringy brown hair, a baggy sweatshirt, and baggy jeans.

"Sheila, Bobby, this is Connie." She nodded, gave them a sour smile.

Sheila stayed to talk to Connie while Bobby and Sol went up the back stairs to the halfway house offices. They went through a door, down a narrow sagging corridor, past cons' rooms, cots, chairs, dirty clothes on the floor, to a black guy sitting behind a desk. The black guy was filling out some papers. He didn't bother to lift his head. Bobby and Sol stood there, waiting, silent.

Finally, Bobby said, "Boy, you gonna make us wait all day?" Sol shook his head, no, at Bobby. The black guy raised his head slowly, looking at them finally through half-lidded eyes.

"What's your hurry, cowboy? He goin' nowheres."

"You're mistaken, boy. My friend's going home today."

"Friend? I wouldn't be proud a that."

Sol put his hand on Bobby's arm. "That's all right Mr. Johnson," Sol said. Bobby looked at Sol. "We can wait," Sol said, looking down at the floor.

After Sol signed his release papers, they got Sheila and went to the car. Sol looked at it. "Another fuckin' black Ford," Sol said. "You got a lotta imagination, Bobby."

"What can I say, Sol," Bobby said. "I like something, I stick with it."

"We got it cheap," Sheila said. "We swapped in my BMW for it."

"A BMW for a fuckin' Ford?" Sol said.

"Bobby missed his SHO," Sheila said.

Driving back to Lauderdale, Bobby was quiet. Sol, sitting beside him, stared out the front window. From the backseat, Sheila said, "What's the matter?"

"Nothing," Bobby said.

Sheila gave him a look, then said, "Connie's an interesting girl, Sol. She said she did three years for fraud."

Sol turned around, grinning, and said, "You never heard of her? She's Coupon Connie, was in all the papers. She made millions with a coupon fraud. You know what she did in the slam? Corresponded with male cons. They sent her money, she sent them her dirty undies.

Broad usta get boxes of panties from that Frederick's place, ya know, with no crotch, some a them flavored like candy. Drove the screws nuts tryin to figure out what she was doin with them. If the male cons sent her enough cash, Connie'd send them a dirty letter, too, tellin' them all the nice things she'd like to do to them. 'Whack off Connie's' what they called her.'"

"Good thing none of them saw her," Bobby said.

They passed the Riptide again. The two rednecks and the mangy dog were still there. The hooker was walking back the other way, north now. Sol noticed her. From the backseat, Sheila said, "It's been a long time for you, Solly. Want us to stop for her? A welcome home present."

Sol shook his head. "I just wanna pick up my jewelery."

"We don't have time for the jewelery," Bobby said. Sol looked across at him. "We got something more urgent. A little something Sheila and me put together. Ease your way back into things."

"Yeh?"

"Meyer set it up," Bobby said. "A little something to get you spending money, get you on your feet. No risks. A piece a cake, really."

"Where'd I hear that before?" Sol said.

"Yeh, well this *is* a piece a cake," Bobby said, "Meyer knows this guy runs a limo service, stretches with the bar in back, color TV, cell phone, caters only to high rollers mostly from Europe, some from South America, but we don't want to mess with the spics, could be bad guys."

"You oughtta know, Bobby;" Sol said.

Bobby glanced in the rearview mirror. Sheila shrugged. "Anyway, these guys fly into MIA, businessmen, maybe a little shady, but that's good, kinda guys deal only in cash. They got a wife somewhere, kids, a reputation back home, maybe a little bogus, but still something they got to protect. But they're in South Florida, fucking Paradise, with all these beautiful blond chicks they don't see back home, so after they do their business they wanna have some fun."

"That's where I come in," said Sheila. She flashed her smile. "I'm the fun part."

"Yeh, but not like they think," said Bobby. "What we do is, you pick 'em up at MIA. We got you a nice black suit, skinny black tie, a chauffeur's cap. You talk to them nice, ask about the wife and kids, look at their pictures. Find out where they're staying, how long, for what, get a feel for how much cash they got, jewelery, you know, easy stuff to turn over. Then you start hinting around how much fun Paradise can be if you know where to go, who to be with. Maybe hint around you can get them a guide, you know, like at Disney World. Someone can show them a good time. Very pretty, classy, won't embarrass them in public. Someone they'd be proud to have on their arm."

"Who could that be?" Sol said, glancing back at Sheila. She smiled again, spread her arms wide like an actress accepting applause.

"Ta-da!" Sheila said.

"If they bite," said Bobby, "great. If not, we set it up anyway, by accident. Sheila just happens to bump into the guy at the hotel, a bar, someplace you know the guy's gonna be."

"How do we know the guy's gonna go for it?" Sol said.

"Puh-leeze, Solly!" Sheila said. "Don't insult me."

Sol nodded. "Right. I forgot. I been away too long."

"They have a little dinner, some drinks, go back to his room," said Bobby. "I wait in the lobby, the bar, wherever. Sheila fixes him a drink with a little surprise, makes like Coupon Connie, tells him all the nice things she's gonna do to him. Next thing he knows he's dreamin' what Sheila's doin to him only it ain't the way he thinks. He wakes ten hours later cleaned out."

"Yeah, he likes it so much he don't go to the man," Sol said.

"You ain't been listenin', Sol. I said, the guy's got a wife, kids back home, a rep, don't wanna be embarrassed, tell anybody he's been had by a broad. Plus, he don't miss the money, the jewelery, cause he just wants to finish his business, get outta the country. Which is why we leave him his credit cards. They're iffy anyway, just a way to get caught."

"The guy's humiliated," says Sheila. "He just wants to forget the whole thing, get back to the wife and kids, write it off as a lesson."

"It works right," said Bobby, "we can do it over and over. Make ourselves a few grand a week until we put something bigger together."

"We have to split twenty-five percent with Meyer," Sheila said. "He'll take care of the limo guy."

"Twenty-five percent!" Sol said. "That's a little steep, ain't it?"

"What? We got something better goin'?" Bobby said. "Solly, we all been on ice for a while. This is a nice little thing to get back in again."

"Besides," Sheila said. "Meyer's got you a place to live. One of his motels on the beach. The Royal Palm. Rent free. All you have to do is manage it for him."

"That fuckin' fleabag!" Sol said. "I wouldn't take that hooker there we just saw."

Bobby shook his head. "Like you've been livin' in a Hilton the past six months. We all gotta tighten our belts a little while, Sol. Jesus, me and Sheila and the Hosh are livin' in a little efficiency, a Mom and Pop place, on the beach. Our salad days are a thing of the past, Solly, for a while anyway."

"What do you think, Sol?" Sheila said.

"I think I wanna get my jewelery."

Bobby reached under his seat and took out a small, black pistol. He handed it to Sol. Sol looked at the small gun that had FEG, 9 mm Makarov, SMC 918, Product of Hungary, printed on the slide. He put the pistol in the front pocket of his baggy shorts.

"I still want my jewelery," he said.

Bobby said, "After tonight, Solly, you can go buy a whole shit-load of jewelery. The guy's coming in from New York, by way of Rome, 10 o'clock. Some guinea Ferrari importer, does business with that fancy sports car place out on Sunrise. You remember, with the blonde in the window, sitting behind the antique desk, so everybody passing by can see her nice tits in her low-cut blouse, really classy looking."

"Yeh, Bobby," said Sheila. "Very classy, chewing her fucking gum like a cow."

Sol glanced back at Sheila. She smiled at him. Sol. said. "Jeezus, Bobby, don't ever piss her off, ya know."

"Hell hath no fury, Sol," said Sheila, still smiling.

"Tonight, you're gonna pick up the guinea," said Bobby. "Give him the ride of his life."

"No, that's my job, Bobby," said Sheila. Sol and Bobby looked back at Sheila. She flashed her smile. They all laughed. Sol for the first time since they'd picked him up.

18

SOL STOOD AT GATE 13 AT MIA AT THE BACK OF A CROWD OF PEOPLE WAITING to meet passengers off the New York flight. He wore his black chauffeur's uniform and cap and held up a sign: "Executive Limo—Attn. Señor Paolo Fortunato."

The first-class passengers were passing through the gate. Sol looked for a sleek guinea in a shiny suit, slicked-back, silver hair, tanned from weekends at the Aga Kahn's in Sardinia. When all the first-class passengers had passed through the gate the coach passengers began passing through it. They were mostly Haitians and Jamaicans, carrying big boxes of VCRs, TVs, microwaves they were taking back to relatives in their homeland. Sol turned around to check out the first-class passengers moving down the escalators when someone tapped him on the shoulder.

"Scusi, señor. You are, perhaps, looking for me?"

Sol turned around to see a tall, slightly hunched-over man in a cheap, wrinkled brown suit. He was carrying a small nylon bag.

"Señor Fortunato?" Sol said.

"Si." The man smiled. He had shaggy black hair, a droopy mustache, and bulging eyes.

"Here, let me take that for you, sir."

"No need."

"This way toward baggage claim."

"I have only this," the man said. He held up his little bag. "I travel, how you Americans say, white?"

"Light," Sol said. "Light."

There was little traffic out of the airport at almost midnight.

Soon, they were on State Road 826, through the toll, and then onto I-95 north toward Lauderdale. The mark stared out the window.

"And how was your flight?" Sol said.

"Fine."

"The food OK?"

Sol saw the mark shrug in the rearview mirror. "The food? Not like in Italia," he said.

"You must be tired. Why don't you fix yourself a drink from the bar, señor?"

"A little scotch, maybe." He sat back and sipped his scotch.

"Mind if I smoke?" Sol said.

"Certainly not. Only Americans worry about cigarettes."

Sol lit a cigarette, a Camel. "And what hotel are you staying at, señor? The Harbor Beach? It's the only five-star hotel in South Florida."

"No. The Grand Marquis. I am staying at The Grand Marquis on the ocean. You know it?"

"Yes. A little small, but secluded. Mostly locals stay there. A beautiful view of the beach, though."

"It is simple, yes, but is private and quiet. No tourists. But first I must do some business. A delivery of some cars. Can you take me directly to Paradise Auto Works on Sunset Boulevard?"

"Sunrise," Sol said. "Sunset's in California."

"Of course." The mark settled back in his seat. He sipped his scotch and then looked at it and smiled.

"Have you been to Ft. Lauderdale before?" Sol said.

"Oh, yes. A few times. I love the beautiful sun and ocean and palm trees."

"We have some beautiful sights. We call it, 'Paradise.' Of course, you must know, staying at The Grand Marquis, all the beautiful girls on the beach."

"Ah, si. Very beautiful. Browned and blond."

"Mostly exotic dancers. Very young, though. Beautiful, but not sophisticated, you know what I mean? Not the kind of woman you can take places. Now I know such a woman, very beautiful, more mature, classy, could show you things in Ft. Lauderale you never seen before."

"Yes, that would be wonderful. But I am only here this one night. I fly back to Roma tomorrow, after my business is completed."

"Too bad," Sol said.

They got off at Sunrise, headed east toward black town, past the Swap Shop with its big neon "Circus" sign glowing neon in the darkness, crossed the tracks at Dixie, then slowed at the car place.

"Turn here," the mark said.

Sol turned down a side street alongside the car place's glass showroom window. In the darkness inside, Sol could see the shapes of exotic cars, hump after hump packed close together, like a herd of hippopetamuses in a river.

"Park here," the mark said. Sol parked down the street, alongside an eight-foot high concrete fence topped with razor wire. "Very expensive machines here," the mark said. "I bring in tonight four F-40s, works of art, really. You know such cars?"

"Not really," Sol said. "I'm a Cadillac man myself."

"Oh, yes. The Chevrolet car." He opened his door. "You can wait here, please. I will be only a few minutes."

Sol turned off the engine and waited. The mark went to an iron gate and rang a buzzer. Sol opened his window. He heard voices. The gate was buzzed open and the guy went in. Sol heard the sound of cars being moved with the engines shut off. When the mark was gone five minutes, Sol got out and walked around the wall, looking for an opening. He came to a big garbage Dumpster up against the side of a seedy, mom-and-pop motel, "The Royal Palm." Sol looked, but couldn't see a palm. The dumpster was on wheels so Sol pushed it up against the wall, the wheels creaking from rust. He struggled to climb on top of it. First he tried pushing himself up with his arms then tried to swing a leg up. His knee banged against the dumpster, his big belly stopped him. A light came on in one of the motel rooms. Sol waited a moment, sweating. An old woman's face appeared in the lit window. Sol crouched behind the dumpster smelling of piss from all the home-less who slept behind it. After a few seconds, he peeked out. The woman's face was gone, the lights out again. That's when he saw a con-crete block. He carried it over to the dumpster and used it to climb up. He looked over the wall.

He saw a bunch of guys off-loading Ferraris from a trailer, coasting the cars down a ramp, then pushing them by hand. There were four of them, all red, with fat tires. To the side, Sol could see the mark talking to another guy, shorter than the mark. They talked while they watched the other guys jack up the cars and take off each wheel. They used hand wrenches, not the automatic ones that made wheezing sounds. After they took off each tire, they put on another tire and wheeled the first one over by the mark and his friend. One of the workers took what looked like a knife from his back pocket and cut open the sidewall of the tire. He reached inside and pulled out a square package that looked white in the faint light of the moon. Then he took out another package, and another, until all the tires had been cut open and emptied. There was a neat pile of white packages in front of the mark and his friend, like the beginnings of a block wall, only whiter. The mark's friend kneeled down, and cut open each of the packages. He reached in with his knife and took out something on the blade that looked like powder. He wet his finger, dabbed it on the powder, and tasted it on the tip of his tongue. He nodded to the mark, waved to his men to come and get the packages. They began stuffing the packages back in the tires, then they brought them into the mechanics' bay, and closed the bay door. The last guy out carried two briefcases over to the mark and his friend. The friend took one and opened it. The mark reached in and took out what looked like a wad of bills. He flipped through them, then another wad, and another, and then did the same with the second brief case.

When the mark finished counting he started gesturing with his hands at the little guy. He was talking loudly now, in Italian. The little guy just shrugged, turned his hands palms up. The mark flung his hand at the little guy, grabbed the briefcases and walked toward the iron gate. Sol jumped off the Dumpster with a whoomph, falling forward, facedown in the dirt. The motel light went on again, the woman's face at the window, hissing out, "Who's there? I have a gun. I have a .357 magnum you sunuvabitch!"

Sol ran back to the limo. He was sitting in the driver's seat, smoking a cigarette, when the mark came through the gate. He got in back with his two briefcases.

"We can go to the hotel now," he said.

"Everything all right, sir?"

The mark smiled at Sol. "Everything is fine. Just maybe my plans change. I might have to stay an extra night to tie up, how do you say, tight ends?"

"Loose ends," Sol, said, as he pulled the big limo back onto Sunrise, turned right toward the beach and the Grand Marquis.

When Sol dropped the guy off, about 2 A.M., the guy handed him a C-note. "I need maybe your services tomorrow. Will you be available?" Sol gave him his beeper number, and the limo's cell phone number.

"At your service, Señor Fortunato," Sol said, smiling.

Sol watched the mark go into the hotel carrying his two briefcases like they had maybe dirty laundry. Sol backed the limo onto the street, headed west, and dialed Bobby's number. "Bobby," he said. "You won't fuckin' believe it."

Paolo sat under the shade of an umbrella at a table on the boardwalk a few feet from the beach and the aqua waters beyond The Mark. It was the heat of the day. A yellow sun burned in a cloudless blue sky. He wore a sleeveless ribbed undershirt, baggy khaki shorts, and Birkenstock sandals. His body was white and hairy, his black hair rumpled from sleep. He sipped from a cup of American coffee and wrinkled his nose. He'd asked the young waitress for an espresso, but she only smiled and shrugged. "I'm sorry."

The beach in front of him was already crowded with sunbathers. Young American men and women with beautiful brown bodies. Paolo smelled the sweet coconut oil that made their bodies glisten in the sun. The women wore thong bathing suits, but none of them exposed their breasts. They wore tiny tops that barely covered their nipples. The tops were tied tightly around their necks so that they pushed up their breasts and made them look plumper than they would naked.

He settled back in his chair, lit an American cigarette, and looked out at the beautiful bodies. They were all very young, except for an older woman sitting on her blanket close to the water. The sunlight against her back highlighted her faint muscles. She wore an American baseball hat, the bill pulled low over her eyes, and a thong that exposed her perfectly shaped behind. The woman stood up and walked into the ocean. He watched her cool off, then turn and walk out toward her blanket and past it toward Paolo. The sun was at her back now, her face and body in shadow except at the edges, highlighting her shoulders, her slim hips, her long legs, which glistened with little sparks of golden light. She walked almost up to Paolo and stopped a few feet away at an outdoor shower. She stood under the shower head, took off her cap, and tossed it on the wooden floor near Paolo's feet. She had very short blond hair, almost yellow, like a boy. She pulled the shower chain and washed the salt water off her body. She released the chain and looked for her hat. Paolo picked it up and handed it to her with a smile. She accepted it with a nod, but no smile, and turned to walk back to her blanket.

"Scusi, Señora." She turned to look at him. Pretty in that nondescript American way with her big blue eyes and pleasantly lined face that was without expression. "Would you care to join me for a café? Maybe a cool drink on such a hot day?"

She looked back at her blanket, then at him. Finally, she smiled and stepped up onto the boardwalk. "That would be nice," she said. "Thank you." She sat across from him, sideways in her chair, her legs crossed so that only a tiny patch of her bathing suit was visible at the crotch.

"Do you mind if I have one of your cigarettes?" she said.

"Of course not." She took one. Paolo lit it for her as she held his hand to steady the flame. Paolo raised his arm to summon a waitress. "And now to drink?" he said.

"Vodka collins."

Paolo turned to the waitress behind him. "Due vodka collins." Then he said, "So sorry. Two." Before he turned back to the woman he saw an American cowboy seated behind him at another table. The cowboy was sipping from a bottle of beer and staring out at the ocean. Paolo turned back to the woman.

"You're Roman," she said.

"Yes, I am Italian."

"No. I said, Roman. Your accent." Paolo felt his face get hot. The woman smiled. "That's all right. I've worked in Rome. Accents are my business."

"You are an actress."

"Sometimes. Television commercials mostly. It pays the rent." She reached out her hand. "I'm Sheila."

Paolo shook her hand with a slight nod. "I am Paolo Fortunato."

"You're here on business."

"You can tell." He looked down at his white body.

"Yes. Businessmen have a certain look at the beach. Discomfort, I think you'd call it. They feel powerless out of uniform, do you know what I mean?" He nodded. "Plus, they don't understand what all the fuss is about. The oil and the sand and the heat. It makes no sense to them because there's no profit in it."

"Ah, profit. Yes." He made a backhand gesture toward all the beautiful young exotic dancers sunbathing their bodies. "But for some there is a profit, eh?" He smiled.

"Maybe for some," Sheila said, not smiling. "But not for me. It's just a way to relax."

"Of course," he said. "Forgive me."

"You are right, though. Sex and profit. The American obsessions."

"I have always wondered," he said, "why Americans make such a mystery of sex. On the one hand, you hide your sex with a false coyness, those little tops, and on the other you flaunt it brazenly."

She laughed. "We like to tease."

"But a tease is so boring sometimes, isn't it? It can be frustrating. Like profit. It never gives your people pleasure. Why is that?"

She was quiet for a moment, then she said, "Sex and profit, I think, are only the objects of our desire, not their fulfillment. Does that make sense?"

"Perfectly. I have just done business with such a man. He was not content with the profit we had agreed on. He had to have more than his fair share. It was so boring, really. How many chickens can you eat?"

The woman laughed. "That's not the question," she said. "How many chickens can you have? As many as you can get."

Paolo sighed and shook his head slowly. "Yes, that is this man. He thinks he can cheat me because I have no recourse, no one to help me."

"Maybe he can?"

Paolo smiled. "We shall see."

"What kind of business are you in?" she asked.

"I am an automobile importer."

"Let me guess. Ferraris?" He nodded. "An easy guess. I don't imagine there's much profit in importing Fiats." They both laughed. "I had a Fiat once," she said. "It rusted right out from under me in this salt air."

"Maybe you should try a Ferrari, then."

"That would be nice." She raised her eyebrows. "Do you have a spare one?"

Paolo shrugged, tossed up his hands, palms out. "I am sorry," he said. He pulled out his empty pants pockets. "Nothing at the moment. But I can maybe offer you something else."

The woman looked at him. "You spend a lot of time in Florence, too."

"How do you know?"

"The shrug. Your arms tight to your body the Florentine way. It comes from their tight quarters. The Romans, now, have more space. Their gestures are more expansive."

Paolo threw back his head and laughed. She stubbed out her cigarette in the ashtray, and stood up. "Thank you for the drink," she said.

"Must you leave?"

"Yes. I've had enough sun. There's no profit in any more." She smiled at him.

"You must come to dinner with me tonight. Please! I hate to dine alone." He furrowed his eyebrows in a sad, comical way. "Alone in a foreign country."

Now she frowned. "Poor man. I'm supposed to take pity on you?"

"Not pity. A blessing maybe. Eight o'clock? We can have drinks at the bar." He gestured down the walkway toward the hotel's enclosed bar and restaurant that looked out over the water. "Then we can go dine any where you wish."

"Actually," she said, "The restaurant at the Grand Marquis is quite good. The catch-of-the-day and the water sparkling at night. Very romantic." She turned and walked back toward her blanket. Paolo followed her with his eyes. Then he stood up, paid his bill, and walked back to the hotel past the American cowboy with the blond ponytail.

19

BOBBY SAT IN DARKNESS, AWAY FROM THE SOFT EVENING LIGHTS STRUNG OUT along the boadwalk that ran from The Grand Marquis' restaurant, parallel to the beach, to the outdoor Chickee Bar. It was a warm night, with a strong breeze drifting in from the ocean. A few people walked along the beach, close to shore, couples mostly, holding hands. There was no one else sitting on the boardwalk and just a few people at the outdoor bar.

When the waitress walked past him Bobby called out from the darkness, "Honey, could you get me a beer. A Coronoa."

"Oh! I didn't see you there. Sure."

She returned with his Corona. Bobby sipped it in the soft darkness. He watched Sheila and the mark in the more brightly lit restaurant to his right. They were sitting at a table by a window, close to the beach. He could see their faces by the light of the candle on their table. Sheila was looking into the mark's eyes, laying her hand on his arm, throwing back her head and laughing at something he said.

Bobby had seen Sheila in a TV commercial in the same setting one night. They were lying in bed, watching a movie, when the commercial came on. The guy sitting across from her was older than the mark, but handsomer, too, with silver hair and an actor's deep voice that came from his chest. Sheila wore an off-the-shoulder evening gown. Her brown hair was swept up. She wore dangling earrings. The guy was in a tuxedo. The waiter wore a little white jacket cut at sharp angles at his hips. He hovered over them, the candle on their table lighting their faces, the guy smiling at Sheila, Sheila looking into his eyes, and then the words, "Carribean Princess Cruises," flashed across their faces, and it was gone.

"Jesus!" Bobby said, sitting up in bed. "You were so fucking believable I want to book a cruise right now."

"Yeah, Bobby, me and my handsome lover," she said. "Having a romantic dinner while his fag boyfriend stood off the set, watching us like a hawk, afraid maybe I was going to cop his boyfriend's joint under the table."

"Well, if anybody could make a fag switch, baby, it's you."

"I tried that once, Bobby. Remember?"

Sheila and the mark stood up from the table. The mark held out her chair. He gestured with his hand toward the ceiling. Sheila shook her head, no, and pointed outside to the boardwalk. They stepped outside. Bobby slid his chair farther back into the darkness as Sheila slipped her arm into the mark's and they began walking toward him. They stopped a few feet from him and turned to look at the moon in the purple velvet sky. The mark turned to face her. He put his arms around her and pulled her tight against his body and kissed her. Bobby watched them kissing for a long moment, and then Sheila pulled back a bit, and nodded her head. They turned and walked back to the hotel. Bobby leaned forward to see the mark opening the door, Sheila walking through, the mark turning, glancing down the boardwalk at the soft warm night, and then he followed her.

Sheila had done things like that before, she told him once, in a movie. "It's just acting," she said.

"But you're so fucking believable," Bobby said.

"I'm supposed to be believable," she said. "That's the point."

Then she told him about the soft-porn movie she had made one summer.

"I played this older spinster schoolmarm," she said. "I seduced this young surfer dude in my classroom after the other students left. The director made it very erotic, he thought. I unpin my hair, shake it, take off my eyeglasses, then sit on my desk, and pull the surfer dude on top of me. The asshole kid started dry humping me, with a hard-on no less, grinning down at me, believing it was actually happening. I gave him a slap. Wiped that smart-ass grin off his face. The director yelled, 'Cut! That's not in the script, cunt!' I think he thought he was filming *From Here To Eternity*. So, I pushed the kid off me, stood up, and said to the director, 'Why don't you go lie on the desk with this asshole on top of you, see how you like it. I thought I was in a movie. You know, *acting!*' Well, that pretty much ended my film career."

Bobby went over to the Chickee Bar, sat down, and ordered a coffee. Twenty minutes passed. Thirty. An hour.

The barmaid came over to him. "Excuse me, sir. Are you Mr. Roberts?" Bobby nodded. She handed him a phone. "It's for you."

"Bobby," Sheila said into the phone. "Get up here. Room 218." And hung up.

Bobby hurried out to the parking lot, got his CZ from under the seat, racked the slide, and stuck it into the back of his jeans. He walked back to the hotel, went up two flights of stairs, two steps at a time, walked down the hallway to 218, and listened at the door. He took out his CZ, turned the doorknob, pushed the door open, and stepped through the door with his gun pointed in front of him.

"Buona sera, Señor Squared." The mark was sitting on the sofa, a drink in his hand, smiling at Bobby. The bedroom door opened. Sheila walked into the room smoking a cigarette.

"Put the piece down, Robert," she said. She smiled at the mark. "Say hello to Señor Fortunato." The mark stood up and extended his hand. Bobby looked at it. Sheila said, "Señor Fortunato is our new business partner."

At 5 o'clock on a Saturday afternoon, a white stretch Lincoln Continental limousine pulled up in front of the Paradise Auto Works showroom and parked. Inside, two salesmen walked over to the showroom window and stared out. A chauffeur in a black suit and cap hustled out of the limo and opened the back door. A pair of long tanned legs emerged first, then a woman's hand, long, red fingernails, diamond rings, gold braclets. The chauffeur took the woman's hand and helped her out of the limo. She was wearing gold-rimmed Porsche Carrera sunglasses, a black-and-white Chanel suit with a short skirt and a wide-brimmed black straw hat, the brim pulled down over one eye. She carried a flat black handbag.

The woman walked to the front door and waited. The chauffeur opened it for her and she went inside to the receptionist seated behind the faux oriental black-laquered desk. The blond receptionist was reading a Jacqueline Susann novel and chewing gum. She looked up and said, "Can I help you?"

"I'm here to buy a car," the woman said.

"I'll get you a salesman."

"I don't do business with salesmen. I want to see the owner."

The receptionist shrugged, picked up the phone, and said, "Mr. Kressell, a lady to see you about a car." Then, to the woman, she said, "He'll be with you in a moment."

The woman looked out the showroom window toward Sunrise Boulevard and the 7-Eleven across the street. She took a gold cigarette case out of her bag, opened it, and withdrew a long, brown cigarette. She put it to her lips and waited. The chauffeur was staring at the receptionist's tits. The woman glared at him until he noticed her. He flicked open his cigarette lighter and lit her cigarette. The receptionist was reading her book again, mouthing the words silently. She wrinkled up her nose and looked up. "There's no smoking in here," she said. The woman exhaled smoke and stared out the window. She glanced at the chauffeur and tossed a headfake at the receptionist.

"I told you," the woman said.

A salesman came over to her and smiled. "Mr. Kressel will see you now." He took her by the elbow and steered her through the showroom crowded with cars, Porsche Speedsters, older Dino Ferraris, a Gullwing Mercedes, a Testarossa. The chauffeur followed them. He didn't bother to look at the cars but, instead, glanced up at the security cameras in each corner of the ceiling.

"Whom should I say is calling?" the salesman said. He had an Australian accent, a handsome man with a neat Princeton cut and an Ivy League suit.

"Who," said the woman. "And it's Mrs. Chickie Vantage. From Las Vegas. She gestured toward the tightly packed cars, and added, "It must be difficult to rearrange these when someone wants a test drive."

"We're not in the business of test drives," he said. He opened a door for her, let her pass through, and said, "Mr. Kressell. Mrs. Chickie Vantage to see you. From Las Vegas." The salesman closed the door behind her. The chauffeur waited outside.

She stood in the small office and waited for the little man at the desk to look up. He was eating a tunafish sandwich, his head lowered to the sandwich, chewing with his mouth open, the mayonnaise at the corner of his lips. Finally, he looked up and said, "Have a chair, Mrs. . . ."

"Vantage," she said, but did not move. She stared at him through large, dark sunglasses, a homely man with pockmarked skin, beady eyes, and fat lips, like a troll. Finally, he sighed, stood up, wiping his hands on his pants, and gestured to a chair. She sat down and crossed her legs.

"I'm here to buy one of your cars, Mr . . . ah."

"Kressel," he said.

"Yes. The beige Silver Spirit convertible you advertised in *The Robb Report*. But. I don't see it in the showroom."

"It's in the mechanic's bay out back."

She waited. "Well . . . could I please see it?"

He shrugged. "If you insist."

"I do." He led her through the back door of his office, down a narrow corridor, and outside to the back parking lot crowded with dozens of exotic cars. The concrete wall surrounded the lot on three sides. It had two electronically controlled iron gates, a small one for people and a larger one for cars.

"This way," he said. He led her to the mechanics' bay, pressed a button on the wall, and the garage doors opened. There were six cars in the bay. A Porsche Turbo. The beige Rolls. And four blood-red Ferraris.

The Ferraris were elevated on jacks because they had no tires. Four new sets of racing tires were propped against one wall. They were mounted on magnesium wheels that had a prancing black horse on the hub.

"You like Ferraris?" he said.

"Oh, no, not really. They're not very practical. But they are such beautiful machines. I can appreciate that."

"Yes. I guess. Two hundred and fifty thousand dollars each. Now here's the Silver Spirit. As you can see, it, too, is . . . a beautiful machine."

The woman walked around the car, looked through the window at its leather seats and burled, walnut dashboard. "Yes, it's beautiful. Now shall we fill out the papers."

"You haven't asked the price."

"It doesn't matter. I'm buying it." The little man furrowed his brows. The woman smiled at him. "I'm a widow, Mr. Kressell. My husband had certain business interests in Las Vegas, very complex, some of it tied up in court. I'm sure it'll work out, but still I have this little problem. Mr. Vantage used to keep a little money at home, 'walking around money,' he called it, in case of an emergency." She smiled at him. "Undeclared money, actually, if you know what I mean. If the IRS discovered it, well, there might be a problem. I'd like to convert that money into something tangible, so I thought, why not treat myself to a car after my . . . prolonged period of grieving."

"How long since your husband died?"

"Two weeks."

The little man stared at her through narrowed eyes. She opened her handbag and withdrew a stack of bills. "Would a ten thousand dollar deposit be sufficient?"

The little man smiled. "It would. More than sufficient."

"Shall we fill out the papers, then?"

When the woman finished filling out the papers, she stood up, and placed the ten thousand dollars on his desk. "I'll be by tomorrow evening to pick up the car, and, of course, bring you the rest of the two hundred thousand dollars."

The man looked at the money, then at the woman. "We're closed on Sunday. It'll have to be Monday."

"That's impossible. Mr. Kressell. I'm leaving for Las Vegas Sunday evening."

"I don't know."

"If it's a problem . . . " she said, and reached for the money on his desk. He snatched it up before she could get it. She smiled. "All right, then," she said. "Tomorrow at 9 P.M." She adjusted her sunglasses with a touch of her red nails, turned, and left. The little man went back to his sandwich.

In the limo, Sol turned to Sheila in the backseat. "Did you see all the fucking security?" he said. "Cameras, alarms, like a fucking prison. I don't like it."

Sheila took off her straw hat, unpinned her long sandy hair, lowered her hand, and gave it a shake until it fell around her shoulders and back. "What do you think, Sol? A nice look?" She arched her neck to catch a glimpse of herself in the mirror.

"Yeh, beautiful. I tell ya, Sheila, I got a bad feeling about this."

She settled back into her seat. "Yes, well, we're going to get rid of your bad feeling, Solly. You'll be as good as new again."

"It was that old broad in the motel. Scared the shit outta me. I thought she was gonna ice me with her fucking magnum." He shook his head. "Fuckin' Royal Palm. There must be a dozen of them in town." He was silent for a moment, then he said, "We shoulda just rolled the guinea like we planned."

"I told you, Sol, that was not an option. He'd already stashed the briefcases someplace before I got to his room. Even Bobby waving his CZ in his face didn't rattle him. He's a cool customer. He spotted Bobby in the darkness before we went to his room. He knew the whole scam. There was nothing we could do. We either walked away, or accepted his business proposition. It's not exactly a fucking hardship case, Sol. Twenty thousand dollars each if we pull it off."

"Jeez, I wish I had my jewelery."

Sheila opened her handbag and withdrew a Rolex, two diamond-encrusted pinky rings, diamond bracelets, and a gold chain with a one-ounce gold pendant shaped like a camel. She handed the jewelery to Sol. "The camel is a nice touch, Solly. Like maybe someone'd mistake you for Yassir Fucking Arafat."

Sol examined his jewelery, smiling, his smile beginning to fade. "Hey!" he said. "Where's my Star of David?" Sheila, grinning, handed it to him.

At nine o'clock on Sunday evening, the woman stood at the door of Paradise Auto Works and rang the buzzer. Her chauffeur stood by the limousine parked alongside the showroom window. The showroom was in darkness except for a silver of light under the owner's office door at the far end of the room. The crowded cars looked menacing in the darkness, dark humped shapes waiting to spring.

The little man appeared at the door and buzzed the woman in. He stared at the woman. She still wore her dark sunglasses, but now her hair fell down around her shoulders. She had on a white silk blouse, tight jeans, and black sneakers. She smiled at him and held up a briefcase.

"Ah, yes," the man said. "This way."

Outside in the darkness, the chauffeur lit a cigarette with his lighter. He flicked the lighter on and off three times, the flame sparkling off his gold jewelery and rings. From across the street, parked at the 7-Eleven, a U-Haul truck flicked its lights on and off three times, then started up and moved onto Sunrise. It turned down the side street, past the limo, to the end of the concrete wall, next to the electronic car gates and the Royal Palm Motel. The driver clicked off the lights but left the engine running.

Inside, the woman sat across from the homely little man in his office. He rustled through some papers until he found her contract. The woman put the briefcase on her lap.

"Ah, here they are," the man said. He glanced through them quickly, then handed them to her. "Everything's in order."

"I'm sure," she said. She glanced at the papers, then returned them to the man. She opened the briefcase, and said, "I think I have what you want now, Mr. Kressell." He smiled, and then he stopped smiling as the woman pointed a CZ-85 semiautomatic pistol at his forehead. The man's mouth opened, but he said nothing.

"Now, let's see about some tires, shall we?" the woman said.

The little man didn't move. He stared at the woman with the pistol aimed at his head, asking to see some tires.

"That dago bastard!" he said. "He sent you!"

"Well, yes, as a matter of fact I am a business partner of Mr. Fortunato's. He sent me to tie up some . . . how did he put it . . . oh, yes, some 'tight ends' for him. A charming man, really. Now get your ass up."

The little man sat back in his chair, grinning. "Fuck you," he said. "You're not gonna shoot. The noise will bring every cop in the city. Besides, I got your face on the video camera. How you gonna get away from that!"

The woman looked up at the ceiling of his small office. There were no surveillance cameras. She held the gun on him with one hand, and with the other she took off her sunglasses and then pulled off her wig. The little man stared at her short blond hair, his grin fading.

"You may be right about the noise, however," she said. She put the gun back in the briefcase, then reached inside it with her other hand. She withdrew the pistol a second time, with a silencer screwed onto its threaded barrel. She fired one shot, 'pop,' over the man's shoulder into the wall behind him.

"Jesus Fucking Christ! Awright! Awright!" He jumped out of his chair.

"Now for the tires," she said. She followed him out back to the parking lot and the mechanics' bay. He hesitated buzzing open the bay's doors until she stuck the CZ's barrel into the small of his back, and pulled back the hammer with a 'click'.

"Awright! Awright! Jesus! Be careful with that thing." He buzzed open the door and reached for the lights.

"No lights," she said. "Now buzz open the car gates outside." The man hesitated again, felt the barrel of the gun now pressed against the back of his head. He buzzed open the gates and heard the sound of a truck backing through the gates, saw in the darkness an orange U-Haul backing up to the bay. A big guy with a blond ponytail and cowboy boots jumped out from the driver's side, the chauffeur from the passenger side.

"Everything all right, baby?" the cowboy said.

"No problem, baby."

The chauffeur pushed the little man to the ground into a puddle of engine oil. "Jeezus, what the fuck you doing?" the little man said, just before the chauffeur taped his mouth shut with duct tape. Then he taped the man's hands behind his back, and then his feet.

The cowboy pulled out a flashlight from his back pocket, and shined it around the bay until it landed on the four sets of Ferrari tires. He went over to the tires, pulled a hunting knife from his belt, and sliced open one sidewall. He tugged out the edge of a cellophane package filled with white powder. He turned and smiled at the woman and the chauffeur. "Bingo!" he said.

"Just like on the fucking reservation, eh, Bobby?" said the chauffeur.

The men wheeled the tires into the back of the U-Haul while the woman kept the gun on the little man writhing on the floor. "You keep it up," she said, "you're going to cover yourself with oil."

They buzzed the bay doors shut on the little man and all three got into the U-Haul, drove through the gates and turned on the truck's lights, illuminating an old woman standing in front of the Royal Palm Motel, a nickel-plated .357 magnum at her side.

"I told ya," Sol said. "She's a fucking looney." The woman followed the U-Haul with her eyes, watched it stop at the limo, a man in a dark suit get out, jump into the limo, and then follow the truck onto Sunrise. The old woman went back into the motel.

They drove the U-Haul to the enclosed short-term parking lot at Ft. Lauderdale airport. Bobby pushed the button to get the parking ticket and handed it to Sheila. Sol drove the limo down to the Delta baggage claim area and waited. Bobby parked the truck in a darkened space at the corner of the lot and waited. A figure emerged from the shadows and walked toward them. Sheila raised the CZ to the window.

"Buona serra, amici. Everything went well, eh?"

"Everything went well," said Sheila as she and Bobby climbed out of the truck. They opened the back door and showed the man the tires. He looked at the one with the white bag sticking out. Paolo smiled "Grazia," he said. "And for you." He handed Sheila a briefcase. She didn't bother to open it.

"Open the fucking thing!" Bobby said.

"It isn't necessary," Sheila said. She smiled at the man. "Gratia, Paolo. This is for you." She handed him the parking ticket and the keys to the U-Haul. "Ciao, baby."

"Buono notte, cara mia." He kissed the back of her hand.

The following morning Paolo Fortunato arrived four hours early for his flight to Rome. He waited until the mechanics at the car store had enough time to find their boss in the bay, then called them.

"Señor Kressell. You have lost something, I hear. I have found it. Now you have something for me, maybe?"

A day later, Bobby, Sheila, and Sol were sitting at an outdoor table, under a hot afternoon sun, on the boardwalk next to the Mark. Bobby and Sol sipped beers, while Sheila sipped from a vodka collins, and read the morning's *Sun-Sentinel*. Suddenly, she began to laugh. Bobby and Sol looked at her.

"You won't believe it," she said. "Listen to this:"

"At 2 A.M., Ft. Lauderdale police's elite tactical drug unit raided the Paradise Auto Works. The unit confiscated 160 kilograms of pure heroin with an estimated street value of $10 million. The heroin was concealed in 16 Ferrari racing tires that were in the process of being off-loaded from a U-Haul truck when the police arrived.

"Six people were arrested, among them Mr. Sholomo Kressell, a.k.a. Sonny Kresnick, an Israeli national with dual U.S. citizenship. The police shut down the dealership, pending an investigation, and confiscated over $20 million in exotic cars.

"The police were tipped off to the drug ring by the car dealership's neighbor. Mrs. Estelle Townsend, the proprietor of the Royal Palm Motel. She telephoned 911 when she noticed suspicious activity at the dealership at an early morning hour for the third time in five days. Mrs. Townsend, 76, a widow, who was born in Kansas City, said, 'I knew there were nefarious goings on there. I coulda took them out twice myself with my magnum.' Mrs. Townsend owns a Smith & Wesson .357 magnum revolver. She has a concealed firearm permit and is a member of the National Rifle Association.

"The police have put out an all points bulletin for another member of the ring, a foreign man in his forties of undetermined nationality. It is feared he has fled to Europe.

"Also confiscated at the dealership were Mr. Kressell's records from his office, a 9 mm. bullet lodged in the wall behind his desk, and a woman's sandy-colored wig. The woman is believed to be one of three people Mrs. Townsend saw drive off from the dealership on Sunday evening in separate cars. She claimed to have seen a tall man with a blond ponytail and a woman with short blond hair leave the lot in a U-Haul van. The other suspect was short and fat and drove away in a stretch limousine."

Sheila put down the paper and looked out at the ocean. "I'm glad he got away," she said.

"Fuck him!" said Sol. "What about us? They got descriptions."

"Oh, Sol, you're so fucking dramatic," Sheila said. "Two blondes and a fat guy. In Ft. Lauderdale?"

"It's not only the heat," Bobby said. "There's other people looking for us, too."

"This deal's got you and Bobby written all over it," Sol said. "Medina may be crazy but he ain't fuckin' stupid. He knows you're back in town now."

Sheila looked at them. "You know, you're both getting paranoid."

"Sol's right, baby," Bobby said. "I never forget my enemies, Señor Esquared. Remember?"

"Besides," Sol said. "The heat's got a better description than they let on in the papers. Maybe Kressel didn't get a good look at me and Bobby, but he seen you. He could finger you to make a deal."

Sheila opened her blue eyes wide and pointed a finger at herself. "Moi? I'm a straight lady, Sol. A fucking former schoolteacher. With gray hair for crissakes. That other me, the blonde, they don't even know her name."

"Maybe so," Sol said. "But you shouldn't be so fuckin' sure, Sheila, just because you and Bobby been lucky with that car bomb. You think you're invincible is when it happens to you."

"Yeah, well, *it* is never going to happen to us, Sol. *It* happens to other people who are stupid. I told Bobby once, nothing is ever going to come between us. Isn't that right, baby?"

"You think so," Sol said. "I hope you're right. You don't ever wanna go away, Sheila, so fucking boring why they call it 'doin time.' You learn just how long a day is. Twenty-four fucking hours, one thousand four hundred and forty minutes, eighty-six thousand four hundred fucking seconds, every fucking day." He looked down at his beer. "Takes the heart right outta ya."

Sol glanced over at Bobby. Bobby just shrugged. Sheila was reading the paper again. She shook her head, smiling to herself, and said, softly, "I *am* glad he got away."

Bobby and Sol both glanced at her at the same time. Sol said nothing. Bobby said, "I gotta start kissin' your hand now, Cara Mia?"

"Bobby," Sheila said. "He was just a sweet guy."

"That why you spend a fucking hour in his room, come outta his bedroom smoking a cigarette, a dreamy look in your eyes."

"Oh, Bobby! It was only business." Bobby looked away from her out at the pale blue-green ocean and the hot sun. "Look at me, Bobby," she said. Bobby looked at her, her blue eyes staring into his dark eyes. She laid her hand on his arm. "You've got nothing to be jealous about, baby," she said. "You know that, don't you?"

Bobby looked down at her hand on his arm and then back up to her blue eyes. He smiled, and said, "You know, baby. You are *so* fucking believable."

20

Sol left work at 7 P.M. He locked the door and stepped back into the darkened parking lot to make sure his sign was on. Flashing pink-and-blue neon: *Uncle Sol's Title Loans: A Friend in Deed in Time of Need.* In Deed was Sheila's idea. "A little word-play, Solly," she said. "Like the seventeenth century metaphysical poets."

"Yeah, sure," Sol said. The flashing neon was Sol's idea, a holdover from his days running The Trap, with its flashing blue-and-pink neon sign: *The Booby Trap, Home of Stylish Nude Entertainment.* Stylish was Sol's idea. "Like the broads in The Trap flash their bush more ladylike," Bobby said.

Sol lit a cigarette and walked towards his car. The lights were on in Brian's Auto Security and Stereo Shop next door. The kid worked late a lot and then spent all his free time with his young wife and thirteen-year-old son. He tried to get the kid to go to The Trap with him after work a few times.

"You work too fucking hard," Sol told him. "Let's go stare at some naked pussy."

The kid smiled and shook his head. "Thanks for the invite, Sol," he said. "But I promised my son I'd take him to a Marlins' game."

The kid was always taking his son to a Marlins or a Dolphins game or Little League practice. Every Saturday he took his wife and son to the beach for a cookout. The kid invited Sol to go with him and his family one Saturday.

"Thanks, kid," Sol said. "But I ain't like you. The straight life and all that shit. I never got into it. I missed a sign somewhere and took the wrong turn."

The kid shrugged. "You're missing out," he said.

Sol walked across the parking lot to Brian's shop and went in the front door. The lights were on in the office, but it was empty except for a big old black safe with maybe forty or fifty large in it. The kid only worked on high-end cars, Ferraris, Porsches, installing elaborate stereos in them for smugglers who only paid in cash. Sol told him once, "I were you, kid, I wouldn't keep so much cash in that safe."

The kid flashed him that smile of his Sheila called . . . guileless . . . and said, "Who'd wanna rip me off, Sol? I'm just a working stiff. Besides, you're right next door. I shout and you'll come to my rescue."

"Rescue?" Sol said. "You better watch out I don't hit you over the head with a brick, all that cash."

The kid laughed. "You couldn't do that, Sol."

"In a fucking heartbeat . . . you were somebody else."

"See. That's what I mean."

Sol went through the side door into the work bay. There was a red Testarossa, a black Porsche Carerra, and a Toyota Tercel with the chrome painted gold and a vanity plate, JAKBOYZ. The plate had little blinking lights around it.

Brian was working under the dash of the Toyota. "What're you doin' workin' on that pieceashit hamster car?" Sol said.

The kid pulled up his head. "Hey, Sol." He had long, blond hair pulled into a ponytail and blue eyes. He was thin, wiry and he looked younger than his age, thirty-five. "Is it that late already?"

"Time for you to go home, poke that young wife of yours," Sol said.

"I gotta finish this job first. Two brothers with dreads come in the last minute want me to install an alarm and a boom box with too much bass by tonight."

"Like someone would wanna steal that pieceashit." Brian shrugged. "Maybe they gotta big night planned. Make sure the heat can hear them leavin' after they rip off a 7-Eleven."

"If they don't hear them, they can always follow the license plate."

Sol shook his head. "Jack Boys, Jesus Christ, no wonder they always get caught, so fuckin' stupid."

The kid nodded. "But they pay good, Sol. More than the car is worth."

"What they gonna give you? An outta state check with some white guy's name on it."

"Naw. They're paying cash. They already gave me a $500 deposit."

"Yeh, well make sure that pieceashit don't leave the bay until they pay everything."

"Heh, Sol. I may not be too bright, but I ain't stupid." Sol had to laugh. The kid looked at Sol's cigarette. "At least I ain't stupid enough to smoke them cancer sticks."

Sol looked at his cigarette. "What, you my father now?"

The kid smiled. "Old guys need someone to watch over them, too."

"Not Solly Bilstein, kid. You just watch over yourself. And that young wife of yours. You work too late tonight I'll be poking her before you get home."

"Yeh, Sol. That's her fantasy. She told me, 'Brian,' she said, 'before I die just once I wanna fuck an old, fat, bald Jew gangster with a van dyke beard and a ton of gold jewelery.'"

"Fuck you, Brian." The kid was still laughing when Sol left his shop.

Sol pulled his car into the parking lot of Uncle Sol's Title Loans the following morning at eight. He sat there, staring out the window at the

crowd of people on the sidewalk in front of Brian's shop, the three BSO
squad cars in the kid's lot, the cops all over the place, taking pictures,
searching the lot, going in and out of the shop, ducking under the
yellow crime scene tape that circled the shop. Sol muttered to himself,
"Fucking asshole wouldn't listen." Sol sat there for a long moment. He
lit a cigarette and took a drag. He saw a cop coming toward him, a big,
beefy, freckle-faced redneck, the cop standing by his window now,
waiting, finally tapping on the window with his nightstick, once,
twice, three times, before Sol lowered the window.

"Excuse me, sir," the cop said. "Do you work here?"

"No. I just park here every morning to smoke a cigarette."

The cop looked at him. "A wise guy, huh? What time'd you leave
work last night, wise guy?"

Sol blew smoke out of the window into the cop's face. "Same time
as always."

"You want me to jerk you outta that car, fuckhead?"

"For what? Smokin' in my car, not talkin' nice to you?"

"For impeding a criminal investigation, that's what for."

"I left at seven," Sol finally said.

"You see anything suspicious over there?" He pointed his nightstick
at Brian's shop.

"Nothing, except the kid's light was on."

"He usually work late?"

"How the fuck should I know? I'm supposta be his baby-sitter?"

"Last night the kid coulda used a baby-sitter."

"What happened?"

"You see anyone look suspicious?"

"I ain't seen nothin' since 1947. I thought I was fuckin' blind 'till I
seen you standing there." Sol smiled up at the cop, his face getting red.
"Listen, you gonna tell me what happened or I go into work and you
can go get a warrant?"

The cop looked at him for a long moment, then finally said, "Some-time after 8 P.M., two perps tied up the kid with duct tape, laid him face down in his bay, hog-tied, then riffled his safe and left."

"The kid's alright, then?"

"He woulda been if one of the perps didn't have a brainstorm. A wit-ness across the street saw two figures get into a car, begin to back outta the lot, then stop. One of the perps got out, went back into the shop, like it was an afterthought. The witness heard two pops and then the perp came back out and they drove off." The cop shook his head. "He put two into the back of the kid's head, real neat, like it was his signa-ture, dotting an i."

Sol didn't say anything. The cop shook his head and said, "A fucking mess, dirty oil and blood. Jesus! Some people!"

"You got a description?" Sol said.

"Naw. It was too dark. You got any ideas?" Sol shook his head. The cop said, "The kid keep a lotta cash in that safe?"

"You kiddin'? He was a pain in the ass. Every Friday evening after the banks closed, he was always trying to get me to cash one of his cus-tomer's checks."

"Did you cash any? Remember any names?"

"What, do I look like a fucking bank? But I'll tell you one thing. Those checks were for big numbers. The kid only worked on high-end cars, I hear. Ferraris. Porsches. Maybe that's what they were after."

The cop shook his head, "There was a Ferrari and a Porsche turbo in the bay. The keys in the ignition. They didn't touch them."

"I hear he worked on three, four cars at a time."

"Not last night. We checked his records. A Ferrari and a Porsche turbo, that was it."

Bobby and Sheila were sitting on the deck in the backyard of their rented house, drinking their morning coffee. Sheila was reading the

Times. Bobby was watching Hoshi track a possum walking on top of their wooden privacy fence. The possum froze on top of the fence. Hoshi sat down and stared at him. Then Hoshi began leaping at the fence, shaking it, the possum swaying on top like a sailor on a mast in a storm.

"One of these days Hosh is gonna knock that possum off," Bobby said.

Sheila looked up from her paper. "I think he'll be more shocked than the possum."

The phone rang inside the house.

"I'll get it, baby," Sheila said. She went in the house. Bobby watched Hoshi leaping at the fence, the possum swaying.

"Bobby!" Sheila called from the bedroom. "It's for you. Sol."

Bobby got up and went inside. "What's he want?"

"He wouldn't tell me." Sheila rolled her eyes. "Big fucking secret."

Bobby picked up the phone. He saw Sheila through the bedroom window reading her paper. "Yeh, Sol."

"Bobby. Get over here. I'm at work."

"I'm enjoying my morning coffee. Can't it wait?"

"Not this one. We gotta move quick."

"I'll be there in an hour. Sheila's gotta get dressed."

"Forget Sheila. This one's only for you and me. And Bobby . . . bring your CZ."

Bobby put on his aqua Hawaiian shirt with the pink flamingos, his OP shorts, and his flip-flops. He took his CZ-85 from his underwear drawer and stuck it into the back of his shorts, then pulled his shirt out over his shorts and went back outside.

"What's he want, baby?" Sheila said, not even looking up from her paper.

"Who knows?" Bobby said. "You know, Sol. So fucking dramatic. Probably wants me to help him repo a car." Bobby leaned over and kissed her on the cheek. "I'll call ya."

Bobby turned and went to the Florida room door. Sheila looked up. He was dressed as he always was on a sunny day, except for the bulge beneath the back of his shirt.

Bobby drove west on Oakland Park Boulevard in his '89 black SHO he'd just had painted at Kevin's Auto Body. Kevin had even painted the mag wheels for Bobby.

"Mango," Bobby had said.

Kevin shrugged. "It's your car, Bobby." When Bobby went to pick up the car, Kevin led him out back to his parking lot.

"How do the wheels look?" Bobby said.

"It's a judgment call," Kevin said.

"What do ya mean?"

"Your judgment, not mine."

When Bobby saw the mango-painted, five-star mags he laughed out loud. "Perfect," he said.

Kevin said, "Well, Bobby, you won't need no LoJack with this car."

Bobby pulled into Uncle's Sol's parking lot. Sol was waiting for him outside, smoking a cigarette. Bobby got out of his SHO and said to Sol, "What do ya think? The kid did a nice job, eh?"

Sol looked at the freshly painted black car and then at the mango colored wheels. "Whose idea was the wheels?"

"Mine," Bobby said. "I figured that was just the touch I needed to get a title loan from Uncle Sol."

"Absolutely," Sol said, nodding. "So when I repo it I won't have any trouble finding it."

"Yeh," Bobby said, "But why would you wanna? You couldn't sell it. Not even a hamster wants a car with mango wheels."

"You got a point, Bobby," Sol said, running the flat of his hand over Bobby's fiberglass hood with the big air scoop. "Except for the fucking wheels, Bobby, the kid did a nice job. What'd it cost ya?"

"It started out twelve hundred." Bobby grinned and shrugged. "But it ended up sixteen hundred." Sol looked at him. "Kevin had one of his grunts wash the car for me before I picked it up. The asshole sprayed water down the spark plug holes. It cost me an extra four C-notes to get it running right again."

"What?" Sol said. "You *paid* for the asshole's mistake?"

"The kid cut me some slack on the price to begin with, Sol."

"So what? He fucked up your engine. You shoulda broke his fucking legs."

"Jesus, Sol. Where's your fucking Christian spirit?"

Sol reached inside his shirt and pulled out the gold Star of David on the chain around his neck. He held it out for Bobby to see. "In case you didn't notice, Bobby," Sol said.

Bobby grinned. Then he said, "So what's this big deal you drag me away from my old lady and my dog on a nice sunny morning in Paradise?" Sol pointed across his parking lot to the yellow crime scene tape. Most of the crowd was gone now. Only two cops and one BSO car remained in the parking lot of Brian's Auto Security and Stereo-Shop. Sol told him.

He told Bobby about the forty-fifty large in the safe. The two hamsters with dreadlocks. The pieceashit Toyota. The JAKBOYZ plate. Brian. Hog-tied, facedown in the oil, two neat holes oozing blood out of the back of his head.

"Jeeses," Bobby said. "The poor kid."

"Fucking moron!" Sol said. "I warned him. Him and his fucking straight life. Look what it got him."

"I thought you liked the kid?"

"Fuck him. He deserved what he got. All that cash laying around, the asshole living in a dream world, his wife and kid, like no one'd ever think of snatching it. Well, it's too fucking bad for him, but it's good luck for us. We just got to hurry. Get to those hamsters before the heat does. I already put in a call to McCraw. He's tracin' the car for me now."

"He finds it what're we gonna do?"

"You bring your CZ?"

"Yeah."

Bobby sat with Sol in his small office, behind the bulletproof glass, and waited for McCraw to call. The phone rang.

"Uncle Sol's Title Loans," Sol said into the receiver. Bobby heard a woman's voice screaming. Sol held the receiver away from his ear and grinned at Bobby. When the woman stopped screaming, Sol said, "I'm sorry, Mrs. Briggs, but you knew the contract when you signed it." The woman began screaming again. Sol waited until she was finished. "It's not my fault you didn't read the fine print," Sol said. "Yes, it is 264 percent interest a year. That's perfectly legal." The woman began screaming again. Sol waited. He lit a cigarette and took a drag. When the woman stopped screaming, he said, "What'd you expect me to do? You borrow five thousand dollars on a twenty-thousand dollar Jaguar and miss the first two payments. Then you stash the car in Asheville, NC, so I can't find it. Of course I had it repoed."

When Sol hung up, Bobby said, "What was that all about?"

"You heard it. She had no intention of making a payment, so I snatched the Jag and wholesaled it for fifteen large. But that wasn't even the good part." Bobby waited. Sol grinned. "Her husband's a Broward County Sheriff's deputy." Sol laughed. "Ain't payback a bitch."

"So, what's the bad part?"

"The bad part was the three asshole rednecks in Ashehville I had snatch the car. They drove it to Lauderdale themselves. Took them three fuckin' days for a twelve hour drive. Three motel bills. Fucking steak dinners. A two-day layover in Jacksonville for crissakes! When they get here with the car they hand me a bill for two grand." Sol shook his head. "Three assholes in mountainman beards, army fatigues, and green teeth. I says to them, 'Why didn't you take a fuckin' week? Go to New Orleans for Mardi Gras? Maybe Vegas, do some gambling, get some hookers, send me the bill?' They look at each other with these stupid grins like why didn't they think of that."

The phone rang again. Just before Sol picked it up, he said, "I gave them eight C-notes and they left happy as pigs in shit."

Sol listened for a moment, then said, "Certainly, I'd be interested. Bring it down." He hung up.

The door opened and a fat black woman in her best Sunday dress entered the room holding two small black children. She sat down in a chair, facing Sol through the bulletproof glass.

"Yes, Mrs. Thompson," Sol said. "You're here to make Moisha's payment."

"Yes, sir, Mr. Sol. But I ain't got but. . . ." She opened her purse and pulled out a crumpled wad of bills. She counted them out and straightend them. She held the bills out for Sol to see. ". . . Thirty-seven dollars."

"That's thirteen dollars short," Sol said.

"I know, Mr. Sol, but it be summertime now, and I ain't got as many hotel rooms to clean without tourists."

"What about your daughter? It's her loan. Don't she work?"

The woman sighed. "You know how it is, Mr. Sol. These young' uns, the crack and all. Even I take care of her children here she don't get a job."

Sol nodded. "Yeah. Well, just gimme what you got, Mrs. Thompson." The woman pushed the bills through a half-moon hole in the glass. Sol counted them out and handed her a receipt.

"Thank you, Mr. Sol," the woman said. She struggled to her feet. Bobby and Sol watched her and her two grandchildren walk through the door.

"Jeez, Sol," Bobby said. "How can you stand it all day, listening to these stories?"

"Everybody's got a story, Bobby. It's my job to sort 'em out."

The phone rang again. Sol picked it up and listened for a moment. Then he said, "Come on down, asshole. I'll be waiting for you." He was quiet for a moment, listening. Then he said, "Stop cryin', asshole. Be a fucking man," and slammed down the receiver.

"A real fucking wise guy," Sol said to Bobby. "He knew I was gonna repo his boat, a one hundred thousand dollar Powerplay, so what's he do? He punches holes in the hull. I snatched the fuckin' thing anyway, just for spite."

"So what good is a boat with holes?" Bobby said.

"I puttied them over and sold the boat to a hamster." Sol grinned. "He takes it out on the Intracoastal with all his friends, gonna go down to Bootleggers for the Hot Bod Contest Saturday afternoon, look like a white man docking his big boat. The fucking thing sank right there in front of all those people at the Hot Bod Contest, the hamsters diving overboard, the people at Bootleggers hootin' and laughin'. Fuckin' hamsters couldn't even swim. The dock boys had to dive in to save them. I woulda let 'em drown."

They ate pizza for lunch and Big Macs for dinner and then Sol locked his doors at 7 P.M., and they sat inside waiting. McCraw called them at 9 P.M. with two names and an address. Brothers with different last names and long rap sheets. "Jitterbugs," Sol said to Bobby. "They go in shooting and after everyone's cold they look for somethin' to jack. They probably had no idea what Brian had in that safe. They're probably pissing in their pants their good luck." Sol put on his sports jacket and got the keys to his car. "Well, their luck's run out."

Before they left, Bobby called Sheila. "I might be late tonight, baby." She didn't ask, why. All she said was, "Be careful, Bobby."

Sol was in his car waiting for Bobby. "Can't you make a fuckin' move without checkin' with your old lady?" Sol said. Bobby ignored him. "Her always calling the shots." Bobby looked at him. "This one's my deal." Sol smiled. "The kinda thing I know. Know what I mean, Bobby? No scam, all those fuckin' plans Sheila makes, only she understands, something can go wrong. This one's real simple. We go in on the muscle nothing goes wrong."

21

SHEILA WAITED FOR BOBBY TO CALL FROM SOL'S. SHE PASSED THE TIME PAINTING the living room walls of the old wood-frame Key West-style bungalo they had rented in a gay neighborhood with the money they had made with Paolo. Bobby wasn't crazy about living around "fags and dykes," at first, but after a few months he got used to it, even liked it. When the dyke schoolteacher next door picked up a stray dog with a broken leg in black town and brought him home, Bobby helped her carry the dog into the house. The dog was filthy, flea- and tick-infested.

"You better get him to the vet quick," Bobby said.

"I can't," the dyke said. She was a frail, damaged, little blonde who looked like Sandy Dennis, the actress.

"Why not?"

She looked away from him. "I don't have the money."

Bobby reached into his pants pocket, withdrew a wad of bills, and peeled off three C-notes and gave it to her.

"I can't take this," she said.

"You wanna take care of the dog, or what?"

She took the bills and said, "How can I pay you back?"

Bobby grinned at her. "You can give me a blow job."

She looked at him with her brows furrowed and said, seriously, "But I don't know how. My life has been driven by pussy."

"Mine, too."

Sheila smiled to herself at the thought of Bobby and the schoolteacher he called, "My new dyke girlfriend. You better watch out, baby, she don't beat your time." It was always that way with Bobby. That's why she was with him. No matter how harshly he talked about "fags and dykes and niggers and spics," there was something in him that could never be cruel to an innocent person. Players, now, well, that was a different story. They were in the game, he once told her, they were fair game.

Sheila painted one of the living-room walls Campbell soup-can red to match the red lips of "The Blue Lady" she had bought from Krystal. She painted another wall blue violet to match the sky of a Haitiian harvest scene she had also got from Krystal. There was Haitian art all over the house. Paintings, tin scuptures of Haitian gods and schoolchildren, and little whimsical wood carvings of giraffes and zebras and hippopotamuses.

The rent was exhorbitant, two thousand and five hundred dollars a month. They had paid for a year in advance, cash, which ate up most of their car-scam cash. But Sheila had wanted it so. "I need a sense of permanence," she told Bobby. "A woman needs a nest."

"I never thought of you as the nest-type, baby," Bobby said.

"Well, I am. I do what I have to do for you, Bobby, but there are some things you have to do for me. This is one of them."

So they rented the house and Sheila immediately began making it their own. She planted lariope in the backyard, and key lime trees, and a banana tree, and bouganvillia climbing up the seven-foot high wooden privacy fence that surrounded the backyard. Then she began repainting the walls inside, and hanging her Haitian art. She had track lighting installed in the ceiling to highlight the works that Sol called "Hamster art."

After Sheila finished painting, she took Hoshi for a walk in the afternoon. She led him on a leash down their one-way street past other bungalows like theirs that were owned or rented mostly by gay men. Hoshi stopped to piss every few yards in the hot sun. Sheila waited for him. She saw two men walking toward her with a small dog on a leash. The dog looked like a mop with a rhinestone collar. Hoshi strained at his leash as the little dog came running to him. They sniffed each other's asses.

"She-layh!" said one of the men.

"Olé, Santos," she said. "Hi, Karl," she said to the other man. They were both tiny, in their late fifties. Santos looked like a dark, plump, bald, Latin elf. Karl looked like an aged child with his mischievous blue eyes and austere white beard.

"Where's Robert?" Karl said.

"Working," Sheila said.

"Aie, oh, Bobby can work on me anytime," said Santos, grinning.

"Behave yourself," Karl said.

"I can't help myself," Santos said. "He's soooo beautiful."

"Yes, he is," said Sheila, "but I don't think Bobby does that kind of work."

"He may be straight," Santos said, "but he's not narrow." They all laughed.

Karl sighed. "All the best ones are spoken for."

"Or straight," said Santos. "What a waste."

"Somebody's got to be straight in this neighborhood," Sheila said.

"You're lucky we let you in," said Santos.

"Our token straights," said Karl.

"We keep it from becoming a gay ghetto," Sheila said.

Hoshi and the little dog had stopped sniffing each other and were straining on their leashes to continue their walks.

"Oh, Latrine," Santos said to his dog. "You're so fickle. Just like a woman."

A black Jeep rounded the corner and came toward them. Santos stared at it as it passed them. There were two black men inside. He grinned, "Oh, my, I just luff frijoles negroes."

Karl looked at his partner of twenty years and said, "I can't do anything with him, Sheila."

"He is incorrigible," she said.

"Oh, look, Sheila," Santos said. "They're slowing down in front of your house. They must be admiring it."

Sheila glanced at the Jeep in front of her house, and then it picked up speed again, and went around the corner and was gone.

Both men kissed Sheila on the cheek and walked off with their little dog.

When Sheila got back home with Hoshi, she checked her phone for messages. Bobby still hadn't called. It was three o'clock. She fixed herself a drink and gave Hoshi his biscuits. He sat on the floor, waiting, while she handed him first one, then another, and then his third. He ate slowly and then licked up the crumbs from the floor. He stared at his water dish.

"Oh, I'm sorry, Hosh." Sheila filled his dish with water and put it down for him. He nodded his head, once, then sipped. Sheila smiled at him and shook her head.

"Sometimes, Hosh, you make me feel so inadequate." Then she began to prepare dinner.

She ate alone at the dining-room table, cleaned up the dishes, and then put another coat of paint on the walls. Bobby called at nine to tell her he'd be late tonight.

"Be careful, baby," she said, and hung up. She knew enough, by now, not to ask what Sol was up to. It was dangerous, whatever it was. Sol, like Bobby, was always protecting her from physical danger, even when he knew she could handle it. He had this vision of her that was almost romantic, as if she was some fragile heroine out of a Jane

Austen novel. When she told him that once, Sol said, "Who da fuck is this Austen broad?" She didn't bother to explain.

She went to bed early but had trouble sleeping. She watched TV, flipping from channel to channel until finally she found a movie, *The Last of the Mohicans*, that kept her mind off of whatever it was Bobby and Sol were doing. She couldn't keep herself from crying at the last scene when Chingacook looked out over the mountains and said, "I am Chingacook, the last of the Mohicans." And then she fell asleep with Hoshi lying on the pillow beside her. Bobby's pillow.

Sheila dreamed that they were back in the mountains, sitting on the front porch, sipping their drinks in the late afternoon fading light, when she heard an insistent whining. She opened her eyes to see Hoshi standing on the bed, whining.

"Oh, for crissakes, Hosh!" she said. "You pissed your brains out on your walk." Hoshi looked at her with his eerily human eyes and whimprered. "All right," she said.

Sheila got up and went to the Florida room. She opened the door and left it open so Hoshi could go out and piss, or maybe just chase the possum that walked on their fence late at night, and then come in when he wanted to.

Hoshi ran out into the darkness, straight for the fence. Sheila went back to bed. She fell asleep almost immediately and began to dream again that they were back in the mountains. Suddenly, she was wakened by the sound of gunfire and an explosion. She sat up in bed, her heart beating wildly, only to see Dolph Lundgren shooting his machine gun, an HK-P5, and throwing hand grenades at some Latin-types in army fatigues on the TV screen.

"Oh, for Crissakes!" she said, and flicked it off, She looked around the bedroom, but Hoshi wasn't there. She checked the clock beside the bed. It was 1 A.M.; almost an hour had passed since she'd let him outside. She whistled for him, and waited. Then she called out, "Hosh! Get in here!"

When he didn't come, she got out of bed, went to the closet, and got the pump-action shotgun with the pistol grip and went to the Florida-room door that led out to the deck and the backyard. She waited a moment, listening for the sounds of Hoshi thrashing through the lariope after the possum. The backyard was silent.

"Hoshi!" Her heart was beating wildly again. She forced herself to calm down, listen. She heard nothing at first, and then she heard a muffled noise behind the fence. She stepped onto the deck, naked, with the shotgun aimed in front of her. She moved silently across the deck and down into the lariope. She was breathing so heavily she couldn't hear anything but the sound of her own breathing. She went straight to the huge avocado tree close to the fence and flattened herself against it. She forced herself to stop breathing heavily and listened. She heard nothing at first, and then she heard the faint sound of breathing behind the fence. She raised the shotgun to her face. She remembered something Bobby had told her a year ago when he had first taken her to the Dixie Gun Range.

"You wanna scare the shit outta someone," he had said, "you just rack the slide on this shotgun. That sound will shrivel the balls of the baddest dudes in a heartbeat."

She aimed the shotgun at the sound of breathing behind the fence and racked the slide, click-click. Then she whispered loudly, "Hear that, motherfucker. Come on." She heard footsteps moving very fast away from the fence, the footsteps receding until there was silence.

She stepped out from behind the tree and looked for Hoshi. She moved along the fence, looking down, until she saw him. He was lying on his side, barely breathing, his tongue hanging out, blood oozing from his mouth. His eyes were opened wide, glassy, unseeing. She bent down to him.

"Hoshi, baby, what's wrong?" She saw a piece of raw hamburger meat beside his head. She picked it up and threw it over the fence. Then she scooped up Hoshi in her arms and brought him back into the house. She laid him on the bed. He was barely breathing. She dressed quickly, grabbed her cell phone, and picked him up in her arms again. She carried him and the shotgun outside, and then she realized Bobby had taken the car. If she called a taxi, it might be too late. She ran down the street with Hoshi and the shotgun in her arms until she came to Santos' and Karl's house. She knocked on the door with the butt of her shotgun, and called out, "Santos! Karl! Help!"

The lights went on inside, and then the door opened and the two little men stood there in their boxer shorts, staring at her with Hoshi and the shotgun in her arms.

"It's Hoshi!" she said. "He's eaten something poisonous. I have to get him to the vet."

"Oh, niña!" Santos said. "Certainly." The two men didn't even bother to get dressed. They grabbed their car keys and ran outside. Sheila got in back with Hoshi and immediately telephoned the vet's emergency number on her cell phone. Karl drove while Santos sat beside him, turned in his seat, and tried to calm her, "Don't worry, She-lah. We'll get him there in time."

Sheila got the vet's service, and told them it was an emergency. "My dog's been poisoned," she said. "I'm on the way to his office. Make sure he meets me there."

Karl drove through red lights and stop signs until they reached the vet's office on Commercial. The vet's Explorer was already parked in the lot. Sheila got out with Hoshi in her arms. The two little men opened the door for her and she went inside.

The vet called out, "I'm in the examining room, Mrs. Roberts."

Karl and Santos waited in the outer office while Sheila brought Hoshi to the vet and laid him down on the examining table.

"What did he eat?" the vet said. He was a small Asian man with jet black hair and thick-lensed eyeglasses.

"I don't know," Sheila said. "Some kind of poison. It was in hamburger meat."

The vet opened Hoshi's mouth, saw the blood, and said, "I don't know. It might be too late."

Sheila screamed at him. "It's not too fucking late! You just do something!"

He looked up at her and smiled. "Calm down, Mrs. Roberts. I'll do everything I can. I'll have to pump his stomach. Maybe you'd better wait with your friends."

He picked up Hoshi in his arms and carried him back to his operating room. Sheila stood there for a moment, breathing heavily, and then she went back to the outer office and sat down with Karl and Santos. They sat on either side of her, petting her hand, trying to reassure her.

"He'll be all right," Karl said. "Don't worry, honey."

Sheila began to cry. "If anything happens to him . . . I don't know . . . he's all we have . . ."

"Niña, not to worry," Santos said. "God takes care of the angels."

Sheila looked at him, smiling, and then at Karl, both of them dressed only in their boxer shorts.

Santos grinned at her, "Aie, if it had only been Robert to see me like this. Maybe he switch for me."

Sheila laughed and cried at the same time.

Twenty minutes passed before the vet came out to them. "He's gonna be all right," he said. "I pumped his stomach and got most of it. I'll do some tests to see what it was. But it was poison all right."

She exhaled a great sobbing breath. "Can I see him?" she said.

"He's asleep now. Let him rest overnight. You should be able to pick him up by this afternoon."

Sheila got up to leave. Her legs were shaking and she felt herself collapsing to the floor until Karl and Santos grabbed her by the arms to keep her from falling. They led her back outside to their car and drove her home.

22

Bobby and Sol sat slunk down low in the front seat of Sol's white four-door Pontiac Grand Am across the street from a dilapidated shotgun shack in black town at 11 p.m. A Toyota with a JAKBOYZ plate was parked in the dirt driveway close to the house.

"You sure it's them?" Bobby said.

Sol looked at him. "You think there's another hamster Toyota with a JAKBOYZ plate tooling around black town?"

"You got a point."

"They like to personalize their cars, the hamsters," Sol said. He glanced at Bobby with an evil grin. "Like the fucking redskins off the reservation, I hear. Paint their wheels orange."

Bobby looked around the interior of Sol's plain car. Blue velour bench seats, cigarette butts spilling out of the ashtray, discarded plastic coffee cups on the floor. "This thing could use some personalizing, Solly. Looks like the heat's plain brown wrapper."

"Maybe we shoulda taken your car, Bobby, so two hamsters with fifty large can spot it the minute they step outta their house?"

"So what?" Bobby said. "They'd just think it was another hamster car." Sol grinned.

They sat there in silence for a few minutes, staring out the window into the blackness at the shacks with junked cars on cinder blocks out front and rusted washing machines on the front porches. Groups of old black men sat on discarded sofas under the branches of a tree, sipping out of paper bags. Junk yard dogs prowled the streets, their tails between their legs. Every so often, there was the sound of someone screaming, a gun shot in the distance. A Caddy Seville moved slowly up the street toward them. The car passed their window, a well-dressed white man driving. He stopped the Caddy up ahead beside a thirteen-year-old kid on a bicycle. The man reached his hand out the window. He gave the kid something and then the kid gave him something, and the man drove off.

"Nice neighborhood," Bobby said. "Sheila and me shoulda moved here."

"Remind you of the reservation, Bobby?" Bobby stared out the window but said nothing. Sol took a snubby black .38 special out of his jacket and began loading it with six full metal jackets. He glanced over at Bobby. Bobby took his CZ from the back of his shorts and eased the slide back a bit to make sure there was a round in the chamber.

"Where's the little Makarov we gave you?" Bobby said.

"It's back at my apartment. That's my house gun, Bobby. Besides, I ain't crazy about that little piece."

"Why not? An automatic's the only way to go, Sol. Join the fucking twentieth century for crissakes."

Sol raised his eyebrows. "Like you? Play Russian roulette, wondering when your automatic's gonna jam. Make sure you leave spent shell casings around with your fingerprints so the heat can do forensics, track them to you and your fancy Commie gun. Thirty-eight revolvers don't leave no evidence, Bobby. I were you I'd wipe my prints off the bullets in your piece."

"What for? We ain't gonna shoot anyone, just scare the shit outta the hamsters."

"If you say so, Bobby."

"By the way, we got a plan, or what?"

"No. We're gonna jitterbug it. Go in shooting everything that moves, then see what's there." He looked at Bobby and shook his head. "Of course I got a fucking plan."

"You gonna share it, or just keep it to yourself, surprise me?"

"We wait here for the hamsters to leave, then we follow them, and wait for the right opportunity."

"Then what?"

"We take the money."

"What if they don't leave?"

"They'll leave."

"What if they don't take the cash with them?"

"You think they're gonna leave fifty large in *that* house in *this* neighborhood, like they're Robin Hoods wanna share their score with their hamster neighbors? Hamsters are like chipmunks, Bobby. They keep everything they got in their cheeks."

Bobby was silent for a moment. Then he said, "There's still one thing. How do you know they're gonna leave?"

"They gotta. They gotta flash their score around, let everyone know what they got. You think they're like white boys, gonna invest their score in the stock market, maybe mutual funds? They gotta get rid of it. It's burning a hole in their pocket right now. They won't be happy until they're partyin' in front of a crowd." Sol sat up. "I told ya."

Bobby looked toward the house. Two dark shapes were walking toward the Toyota. One was carrying a gym bag. They stopped by the car's trunk. There was the chirp of a burglar alarm and the trunk swung open. The one carrying the gym bag threw it in the trunk, then they both got in the car. The car began to back out toward the street, its license plate illuminated by little blinking, colored lights.

Sol and Bobby slunk down low in their seats. Sol waited until the

Toyota was up ahead of them before he started his car. He didn't begin to move or turn on his lights.

"We're gonna lose them," Bobby said.

Sol glanced at him. "With that license plate?" When the Toyota turned the corner and headed for Sunrise Boulevard, Sol turned on his lights and began following it. "Party time," he said.

They followed the Toyota's blinking lights west on Sunrise, toward the Thunderbird Swap Shop, to I-95. The Toyota turned right onto I-95, heading north toward West Palm. Sol followed it on the highway, a few cars back.

"Where they going?" Bobby said.

"Where do ya think? Where would you go if you were a hamster with fifty large in the trunk, wanted to party?"

"A strip joint."

"Bingo. The question is, which one? They go to a hamster joint we got a problem. They go to a white joint, we're in."

"They could go to a hamster joint anytime," Bobby said. "With fifty large, now, they can go to a white joint, be very popular with white chicks never gave them the time of day."

"That's what I'm hoping, Bobby."

The Toyota got off at the Atlantic Boulevard exit in Pompano and headed west, then turned north on Powerline and headed toward Martin Luther King Drive.

"Well, waddaya know?" Sol said, smiling. "These hamsters got a little class." Bobby looked at him. "I made this drive a few times myself before I got busted."

The Toyota turned west onto Martin Luther King Drive and then, about a mile up the road, turned left again into the brightly lit dirt parking lot of The Booby Trap, Home of Stylish Nude Entertainment.

Sol said, "They still got my sign."

The lot was filled with cars. Groups of guys were entering the

Trap, leaving, walking to their cars, pulling out onto Martin Luther King Drive.

"A lot of action," Bobby said. "Maybe too much."

The Toyota moved slowly past a row of cars and then turned right into an open space, nose first. Sol drove past the Toyota's trunk to the far end of the lot, near the woods, where there were no overhead lights. He parked in darkness, turned off his lights, and then told Bobby his plan.

Two muscular black guys with dreadlocks got out of the Toyota up ahead. One of them was wearing a Michael Jordan basketball jersey and the other was wearing a Canes T-shirt with Ibis on it. Both of them were wearing stonewashed jeans and Air Jordans. They went to the trunk of their car, looked around, then opened it. The one with the Jordan jersey kept looking around the lot, while the other one reached into the gym bag, took out a fistful of bills, and closed the trunk. Bobby and Sol heard the Toyota's alarm chirp and saw the lights blink.

"Not too much, now," Sol said. "Save some for Uncle Solly."

When the two black guys entered The Trap, Bobby and Sol got out of their car and walked along the rutted dirt road toward the Toyota. When they reached the Toyota's trunk, Sol took a penknife out of his sports jacket, looked around, then bent down quickly and stabbed the knife into the Toyota's rear tire.

Bobby and Sol sat at the end of the bar, nursing their drinks. The Trap was filled with groups of guys sitting at tables, laughing, drinking, staring up at naked girls dancing under pulsating blue- and rose-colored lights at one of the three stages spaced around the room. Dancers wearing see-through negligees and Spandex minidresses only half-covering their asses moved through the room, stopping at tables of men, asking if any of them wanted a lap dance. If one of the guys said yes, the stripper would begin to undulate in front of him, like a snake, peeling off her clothes until she was naked, straddling the guy's lap, grinding her trim bush against the guy's crotch while his buddies laughed. Every so often, after a lap dance, one of the guys would whisper something to a stripper and she would lead him across the room, then up a few steps where they disappeared into the darkened Champagne Room.

The two blacks were sitting at a table close to the main stage, so everyone could see them. They made a big production of ordering a bottle of Dom in a silver bucket from the waitress, and then sticking a bill down the front of her bikini top. Two strippers drifted over to them, both white chicks, one wearing a see-through negligeé, the other a leather-studded bikini. They sat down on the black guys' laps and began drinking champagne with them. After a while, the white chick in the bikini stood up and began dancing for one of the black guys, with her back to Bobby and Sol. She unhooked her leather bra and draped it around the guy's neck. He and his buddy laughed, their white teeth showing in their black faces, and one of them put a bill in her garter.

"I hope those are singles, not C-notes," Bobby said, watching. "They keep spending like that we might as well go home."

Sol wasn't listening. He was staring at the stripper dancing for the two black men. She had a big ass and huge fake tits like round watermelons. Sol kept staring at her, at her long, burgundy-red hair, her purplish-blue eyes.

"Marsha!" Sol said. Bobby looked at him. Sol turned to Bobby and said, "Candy was dancing here when I ran the joint."

"I thought you said Marsha."

"Marsha Jenkins, a good ole redneck chick, a lotta balls, goes by Candy when she dances."

Candy was naked now, her G-string draped over the black guy's head. She turned her back to him so her ass was in his face and then began to grind her ass in his face as she bent over at the waist, her legs spread, showing him some pink now, but not showing him the bored look in her eyes that were staring directly at Sol. Her eyes brightened when she saw Sol. She smiled and mouthed his name, puckered her lips and blew him a kiss. Sol nodded and smiled back, then gave her an almost imperceptible headfake toward him. She nodded, then turned back to the black guy and sat on his lap.

Bobby and Sol waited, nursing their drinks for over an hour, until finally, about 1 A.M., the black guy with Candy got up and went to the men's room. A few seconds later, Candy drifted over to Sol and Bobby.

"Solly!" she said, kissing him on the cheek. Sol wiped off her kiss with a cocktail napkin. Candy threw back her head and laughed, a deep, throaty laugh. "You never change, Sol," she said. "Still a racist."

"Anti-Semite, too," Bobby said. He reached out his hand to shake Candy's. "I'm Bobby."

"Glad to meet ya, Bobby." She studied him a moment, his narrow dark eyes, his high, slashing cheekbones, his dark skin. "Cherokee, huh?" Bobby nodded. "I'm one-quarter Cherokee myself. A little English, Irish, Scottish, and, believe it or not, Italian, too."

"Mostly redneck, though," Sol said.

"Yessiree, Solly. Pure Davie redneck and proud of it." She looked at Sol and shook her head. "Boy, I miss you, Sol. Things never been the same since you left." She jerked her head toward a guy sitting at the end of the bar. He was dressed in a black, collarless shirt buttoned at the throat, jeans, pointy-toed boots with a piece of silver on the toe. "The new manager Meyer hired," she said. "Makes us kick in ten percent. Except me, of course. I told him, 'You want ten percent, you put on this dominatrix bullshit rides up your butthole and go flash your pussy see how much money *you* make.'"

Sol laughed. "I see you ain't changed, either, Marsha."

"Ain't never gonna, either, Sol."

"I woulda thought you'da changed some, though," Sol said, looking around at The Trap. "Leave this business all the money you made and invested."

"I had a few bucks saved up. Stocks, mostly blue chips, mutual funds, not that CD shit for mom and pop." She smiled, shrugged. "Then I met this guy. You know how it is, Solly. I'll always be a stripper at heart." She saw Sol glance at her big ass. "Ya noticed, huh?" She slapped the flat of each hand over each cheek of her ass. "Comes in handy on a horse in Davie, but it's a lot harder to toss around in The Trap. Not a lotta guys like a breezer as big as a quarter horse's ass."

Sol motioned with his head toward the main stage. "Those hamsters seem to like it."

She glanced over her shoulder at them, her eyes narrowed, and then back to Sol. "Scary fucking guys, Sol. All that cash they're tossing around. I don't even wanna know where they got it." She smiled. "But what the hell, a girl's gotta do what a girl's gotta do, ain't that right, Solly?"

Sol leaned closer to her. "You think you can do something for me?"

"Whatever, Solly. You always treated me right."

"You think you can keep those two hamsters occupied until after closing time? Make sure the club is cleared out before they get outta here?"

"I don't know, Solly. You think I still got it in me?"

Sol reached into his pants pocket and took out a wad of bills. He held the wad low to his hip, up against the bar, and counted out some bills. He folded the bills into a small wad and handed them to Candy.

"There's a G-note for you you keep them here until an hour after closing. Then walk them outside, get in your car real quick, and go home forget you ever saw us."

She took the bills and stuffed them down her bra top. Then she went back to the two black guys at the table close to the main stage. At

1:45 A.M., fifteen minutes before The Trap closed, Marsha Jenkins, a.k.a. Candy Kane, thirty-three years old, stood up and led two black men by the hand through The Booby Trap to a set of stairs that led up to the Champagne Room where they all disappeared.

Bobby and Sol sat in Sol's car at the far end of the brightly lit parking lot, watching groups of guys stagger out of The Trap, walk toward their cars, and drive off down Martin Luther King Drive. Sol checked his .38 one last time, and put it in his jacket pocket. Bobby shifted his CZ-85 into the front of his shorts and pulled his Hawaiian shirt over it. They waited.

By 2:45 A.M., there were only a dozen cars left in the lot. Then the dancers began to drift out, get in their cars, and drive off. Fifteen minutes later there were only three cars left, besides Sol's. A pink Miata convertible, a black, Porsche turbo with a Doin OK plate, and a Toyota Tercel with a JAKBOYZ plate and a flat rear tire. Sol started up his car, but kept the lights off.

At 3 A.M., Marsha Jenkins emerged, followed by two black men, one wearing a Michael Jordan jersey, the other a 'Canes' T-shirt. She turned, kissed both black men on the lips, then hurried to the pink Miata. She was out of the lot before the two men reached their Toyota. Suddenly, the overhead lights went out. The black men looked around and saw the Trap's owner, dressed in black, come out, lock the door, and walk to his Porsche Turbo. He was on Martin Luther King Drive when the two men reached their car. Bobby and Sol heard the Toyota's burglar alarm chirp and saw the darkened shapes of the men get in. The Toyota backed up a few feet, then stopped. The two men got out and went around to the back of the car that was still running. They looked down at the flat tire and began to gesture to each other.

"Now," Bobby said.

"Not yet," Sol said.

One of the men opened the trunk and looked inside. He pulled his head out and began gesturing to the other man.

"Now," Sol said. He turned on his lights and slowly drove his car down the rutted, dirt road toward the Toyota. The two black men were still arguing when Sol stopped his car behind the trunk of their Toyota. Sol lowered his window and stuck his head out.

"Hey, guys. Havin' car trouble?" Sol said, smiling.

The two men with dreadlocks looked at him, a fat old bald white guy in a suitcoat. They didn't notice Bobby, slunk low in his seat in the darkened car.

"Yeah, we got trouble, man. Mother fuckin' flat tire my home boy here don't even got a jack."

"You bought the mother fuckin' car! Blame it on me!"

"Hey, guys. Relax. No problem," Sol said. "I got a jack."

"Hey, man, that's cool."

Sol reached under his dash, pulled a lever and the trunk of his car swung open. He got out, leaving the car running, Bobby still inside, and went to his trunk. He pulled out the jack and brought it over to the two guys.

"This oughtta do it, guys," Sol said, handing the jack to the guy in the Jordan jersey. The guy looked at the jack like it was an Erector set without instructions. "What I spose to do with this?" the guy said.

"Here, let me help ya," Sol said, taking back the jack. He looked down at the flat tire. "What'd ya get a nail in it or somethin'?"

"Who the fuck knows, man," said the black guy with the Canes T-shirt. "Just fix the mother fuckin' thing there's a twenty for ya."

Sol bent down, grunting, kneeling in the dirt, and placed the jack against the undercarriage of the car, close to the tire. He began cranking the jack, raising the car slowly. He looked up at the guy who'd offered him twenty dollars. "That won't be necessary," Sol said. "A Friend in Deed in Time of Need, that's what they call me."

The two guys looked at each other. One of them said, "I seen that somewhere."

The other one said, "Me, too."

Sol grunted as he cranked the car up. Finally, he stopped, breathing heavily, mopped sweat from his brow, and stood up. "I must be gettin' old," he said, smiling. "Maybe you can crank it the rest of the way?"

"Aw shit, man, in my new stonewashed," moaned the black guy in the Jordan jersey. He kneeled down in the dirt and began cranking up the car. Sol stood over him in the darkness.

"I hope you guys got a spare," Sol said.

"We got a fucking spare, don't worry," said the black guy in the Canes shirt. He went to the trunk and leaned inside. He was still leaning into the trunk, struggling with the tire, cursing out loud, "Mother fuckin' tire," when Bobby eased himself out of Sol's car, moved quickly and silently around to the trunk of the Toyota, reached in with one hand, grabbed a fistful of the guy's dreadlocks, yanked his head up, banging it against the underside of the trunk, then shoved the muzzle of his CZ, hard, into the guy's mouth, chipping a tooth.

When the guy jacking up the car heard a thunk, he looked up just as Sol slammed his .38 against the side of his head. The guy slumped forward, facedown in the dirt, moaning, drifting in and out of consciousness, blood streaming from his head.

Bobby pulled the other guy by his hair out of the trunk, the guy only stunned, and stuck his face close to the guy's ear. "You like the taste?" Bobby said, keeping the muzzle of his CZ in the guy's mouth. "This is your fucking worthless life flashing in front of your eyes you even blink the wrong way." The guy tried to nod, his eyes white with fear, choking on the muzzle.

Bobby dragged him over to the other guy moaning in the dirt, coming out of it slowly, and kneed him in the small of the back, the guy pitching forward in the dirt beside his brother. He spit out bits of teeth and blood then moaned into the dirt, "Man, why you doin' this?"

Sol leaned over close to his ear and jammed his .38 against his head. "Because, hamster," Sol said, "we wanna steal your pieceashit car. Now shut the fuck up you don't wanna see lights out."

Still leaning over, Sol handed up his gun to Bobby. Bobby held both guns on the two men in the dirt. Sol reached into his jacket pocket and took out a roll of duct tape. He taped both guys' hands behind their backs, taped their ankles together, then bent their legs back and taped their ankles to their hands so that they were hog-tied. Then he bit off two small strips of tape and taped their mouths shut. They squirmed in the dirt, making guttural noises. Bobby and Sol stood over them for a moment, then Sol went to the trunk of the Toyota, grabbed the gym bag and threw it into the trunk of his car. He slammed down the trunk and got in behind the wheel. Bobby was already sitting beside him.

"Pieceacake," Bobby said.

Sol said nothing. He began driving slowly over the rutted dirt road toward Martin Luther King Drive, then stopped. He clicked off the lights.

"What?" Bobby said.

"I forgot the jack," Sol said.

"Fuck the jack. I'll buy you another one."

"My fingerprints are on it," Sol said, and got out of the car. Bobby watched Sol through the rearview mirror. Sol walked back to the Toyota with its blinking little colored lights illuminating the JAKBOYZ plate in the darkness, and the two black guys squirming in the dirt, fully conscious now, trying to free their hands of the duct tape. Sol stood over them, then leaned down. But instead of taking the jack, he pressed his face close to the ear of one guy, then the other and almost immediately the two men began twisting wildly in the dirt now. Sol stood up and watched them thrashing for a moment. Then he took out his .38

and aimed it at the back of the head of the guy in the Jordan shirt. Bobby saw a red flash in the rearview mirror and heard a loud pop. Then Sol aimed his .38 at the back of the other guy's head. There was another flash and loud pop. Both black guys were still now. Sol leaned closer to them and fired a second bullet into the back of each of their heads as if he was dotting an i. Then he reached for the jack.

They drove east on Martin Luther King in silence, then turned south onto Powerline. When they reached Atlantic Boulevard, Bobby said, "Was that necessary?" Sol said nothing. He was staring straight ahead into the darkness. He turned the car east onto Atlantic and headed for I-95. Finally, Bobby said, "What'd you say to them?"

Without looking at Bobby, Sol said, "Nothing. . . . I just told 'em, 'Brian says, good-bye.'"

When Bobby got home at 4 A.M., Sheila was waiting for him on the back deck. She was smoking a cigarette in the fading morning darkness. She was staring at the possum walking on top of their fence.

Sheila looked up at Bobby as he came onto the deck. "How'd it go?"

Bobby shook his head. "You don't wanna know." But he told her anyway. When he finished, she was silent, staring at the possum.

"It was all for nothing," Bobby said. "There was only a few thousand in the bag. They musta stashed the rest of it at their house." He laughed, a breath. "The funny thing is, when Sol opens the bag and sees there ain't hardly anything in it, he didn't give a shit."

"We could have used a score," Sheila said.

"Yeah. But we got enough to get by a coupla months."

"We need more than to get by, Bobby. We need a score, a big one."

Bobby looked at her, staring at the possum. "You think Hoshi's ever going to get that possum, Bobby?" she said

Bobby looked at the possum, then around the yard, then back to Sheila. "Where is he?"

"You don't want to know, Bobby." But she told him anyway.

When she finished, he said, "You sure he's gonna be all right?"

She nodded, then said, "The question is, are we going to be all right?"

"Did you get a look at them?" he said.

She shook her head, no. "But I know who sent them, and so do you."

"Fucking Spic. He's fucking merciless."

"He's never going to stop, Bobby, unless we stop him first."

"Or unless we get outta town again."

"With what?"

"I could go talk to Jesse."

Sheila looked up at him. "I thought you didn't trust him."

"I don't."

23

Sheila drove. Bobby sat beside her, slunk low in his seat, his knees propped against the dashboard. He smoked a cigarette and stared out the window at the swampy marshland and the muddy canal running alongside Alligator Alley. He checked his watch. They were thirty minutes from Imokalee. It was dusk, hot and muggy. Already a mist was forming at the base of the palmetto palms and the cypress trees. By the time they reached Imokalee everything would be shrouded in mist and darkness. A big semi, heading the other way, whooshed past them, almost blowing the black SHO off the two-lane blacktop. Sheila struggled with the wheel, straightened the car out, and speeded up again.

"Can you do it?" he said. Sheila said nothing. Bobby looked at her. "Can you?"

Sheila kept her eyes on the narrow road. "I don't know."

"If you can't. . . ."

"I *said,* I don't know."

Bobby looked out his window and saw a gator slip into a muddy canal. He took another drag on his cigarette. "You shouldn't have to," he said. "He told me not to worry in that shit-kickin' drawl of his. 'Bobby,' he says, 'I set you up in a deal ya'll can take it to the bank . . . or the reservation.'" Bobby laughed, "Fuckin' Jesse. Always jabbin' at me."

Sheila said nothing. Bobby stubbed out his cigarette in the ashtray. "The piece is under your seat," he said. "We get there leave the doors open. Something looks funny you find an excuse, go back to the car, get it and use it." He looked across at her. She was staring out the window. "Like Sol says, baby. You can't trust nobody."

Still staring straight ahead, she said, "Then why are we doing this?"

"Because we have to. You wanna get back to the mountains, don't you? This is our only way out. It could be worth maybe a hundred large to us."

"I thought you didn't make drug deals?"

"Not unless I have to."

"I still don't like it."

Bobby waited a minute, than said, "One other thing, baby." She glanced at him for the first time since they left Lauderdale, then looked back at the road. "I told him you were a hooker."

"Nice," she said.

"I had to, baby. He would never trust my old lady. This way he's gonna be watchin' me, not you."

"So that's why you had me dress like this, to meet a fucking redneck in the swamp." She was wearing rose Spandex pants, a low-cut blouse that exposed the top half of her breasts, and six-inch stripper pumps.

Bobby grinned at her. "You look good to me, baby."

"Fuck you."

Bobby saw the swamp flashing by the car window. "Turn here, baby."

Sheila jerked the steering wheel to her right without even stabbing the brakes. The tires squealed and the big SHO almost tipped over as it swerved onto an even narrower and bumpier two-lane blacktop heading north.

"Christ, Sheila! You tryin to kill us before we even get there?" The canal was a lot narrower now, nothing but a muddy stream, the swamp closer to the car. Bobby saw a dead cow being eaten by a flock of buzzards.

They passed some Seminole burial mounds and then came into the small reservation. "Slow down," Bobby said. "We don't want to get stopped by a Seminole cop. They can be mean sonuvabitches when they get a white person on the reservation."

They passed some moon-faced kids with shiny black hair playing on front lawns of government issue redbrick houses. There was a rusted Chevy SuperSport on cinder blocks in the front yard of one house. A red brick church. A few more houses. An airplane hangar converted to a bingo parlor. Then a rotting wood-frame building with a faded hand-painted sign: *Authentic Seminole Souvenirs,* and then nothing but the swamp.

Brad was waiting for them in his open-air Jeep at the gate to the ranch. He blinked his headlights. They followed him down a rutted dirt road past a few cattle to a cluster of buildings: a farmhouse, a trailer, a few barns, and, farther back in the woods, a cabin. Brad parked in front of the cabin and got out. They parked beside his Jeep. "Don't forget, baby," Bobby said. "The piece is under your seat." They got out and a pack of pit bulls descended on them. Mangy dogs trailed by a cloud of fleas. Sheila glared at the dogs until they backed off, barking. They had old red-rimmed eyes and tiny dark scars on their bodies. Junkyard dogs that had been put together with spare parts.

Brad was laughing. "Donch' all worry. They won't attack unless I tell 'em. Now Corky there, she don't need an excuse." He pointed to a white dog with hundreds of scars on her face and body. Corky wasn't wagging her tail, or barking. She just stared back into Sheila's blue eyes with her own blank yellow eyes. "Ole Corky can chew up a wild hog pretty quick," Brad said, motioning them toward the cabin.

They followed him into a small kitchen. A big man with a .38 in a holster on his hip was waiting for them. "This is Charlie," Brad said, grinning. "He's jes an ole Imokalee cowboy like me." Bobby smiled at Charlie, who didn't smile back. He had the face of a moron, a huge soft-looking man, like an NFL tackle. He kept his hand close to his .38 and his tiny pig's eyes on Bobby. "This is my new bidness pardner, Bobby Squared," Brad said, "and his lady friend."

"Sheila," Bobby said. She smiled at them.

"Nice to meetcha ma'm," Brad said. He was a wiry little man with a red face, a deep scar down one cheek and an even deeper, more jagged scar, on his arm. He wore a dirty T-shirt and jeans. He came over to Bobby, smiling, and threw his arms around him in a hug. "Good ta see ya, buddy," he said. He ran his hands down Bobby's back, patted his ass, then kneeled down and patted his legs. When he stood up, he said, "No offense, Bobby, jes checkin'."

Bobby smiled. "No offense, buddy."

Brad looked at Sheila. She spread her arms wide and smiled. Brad looked her up and down, then said, "That's alright, ma'm. Ya'll can't be hidin' nothin' in that outfit." He smiled at her, then added, "So you're Bobby's ole lady."

"I'm nobody's old lady. I thought Bobby told you."

"Thass right, he did. A workin' gal, huh?" He shook his head. "I plum forgot. Bobby said he was bringin' you along so we could mix bidness with pleasure, ain't that right Bobby?" Bobby smiled and nodded. Sheila was smiling at Brad. Brad looked her up and down again. "Man, you are sweet. How'd ya'll like to see the rest of the cabin, ma'm? If it's all right with you, Bobby, get the pleasure part outta the way first."

"That's why I brought her," Bobby said.

"That's why I'm here," Sheila said.

"Bobby, fix yerself some a that Crown Royal and 7-Up," Brad said. "Charlie, try to be a little sociable with our guest while I show the lady around." He led Sheila down a narrow hallway into a room.

Bobby went over to the Crown Royal and poured some into a dirty glass. "You want one?" he said to Charlie. Charlie just stared at him. Bobby sat at the kitchen table and sipped his drink. He looked around the kitchen. An old white enamel sink filled with dirty dishes. A bare lightbulb hanging from the ceiling that was mildewed from the humidity. The rickety card table he was sitting at. Charlie stood with his back to the sink and stared at Bobby.

Bobby heard the sound of muffled voices from the room down the hallway. Then a woman's laugh and the creaking of bedsprings. A grin passed across Charlie's face and was gone. Bobby drained his drink and poured another. He sat down again and waited. He had another drink. Then he heard footsteps in the hallway. Brad came into the kitchen first.

"Whatever you payin' that girl, it ain't enough, Bobby," he said, grinning. Sheila appeared a moment later, carrying her pumps in her hand. Her face was flushed and her lipstick rubbed off, but she was smiling. Brad looked at Bobby looking at Sheila. "Anything wrong, buddy?" he said.

Bobby smiled at him. "Not a thing, buddy."

Brad tossed a headfake toward Sheila. "Maybe you oughta get yerself a piece a that, Bobby. It's your money."

Bobby looked at Sheila. "I already had my piece, buddy." Sheila smiled at him. Bobby turned to Brad. "Now can we get down to business? Reverend Jesse says you got some product to move, and I'm the man to move it."

"We sure do, Bobby," Brad said. "A lot a product. But don't be in such a hurry, man. Enjoy yerself out here in the country, a city dude like you. I bet you never even went wild hog huntin', did you?"

Bobby looked at him. "What the fuck that's got to do with anything?"

"It's fun, Bobby, out there in the swamp. Peaceful, ya know. I do my best thinkin' out there. We go out in a Jeep, talk some bidness, maybe catch us a wild hog you can bring back some pork to the city."

"Brad, man, it's late," Bobby said. "I got a long drive back. Let's just get. . . ."

Bobby heard Sheila's voice. "I've never been wild-hog hunting. It sounds *exciting!*" Bobby looked at her. She was smiling at Brad. "Is it dangerous?" she said.

"Jes a little," Brad said. "Mostly for the dogs. A wild hog's tusk can tear up a pit bull pretty good." He looked at her with a grin. "You got a lotta surprises in you, lady."

"I'll try anything," she said. "Once, anyway."

"Then, let's go." They all went outside into the cool, damp, darkness. Off in the black swamp, lit by a full moon, the mist hovered low to the ground, wound itself around the bushes and the trunks of trees. Brad whistled for the dogs. They came running, yelping, and leaped onto the back of the Jeep that had no top. One dog hung back. Brad grabbed him by the scruff of his neck and tossed him into the Jeep.

"Just one minute," Sheila said, hugging herself in the cold. "I have to get my sweater in the car. I didn't exactly dress for a night in the swamp."

Brad looked at her, then at the car. "No need. Give me the keys and I'll get it."

"It's open," she said. "The sweater's in back. You might as well take these, too." She handed him her pumps.

Brad went over to the car, searched around in the backseat, and came back empty-handed. "Couldn't find it," he said.

"Damn!" she said. "I must have left it at his place."

"Don't worry, little lady," Brad said. "A little hog huntin' will warm your blood right up."

When all the dogs were loaded in back, Brad chained Corky to the gearshift lever in front. He patted the passenger seat beside Corky. "Sit right here, Bobby. Keep me company." Bobby sat beside Corky, while

Charlie helped Sheila up in back, then stood behind Bobby, looking down at him, while Sheila stood behind Brad as he started the Jeep. "It'll get a little bumpy back there," Brad said. "Best hold tight to that roll bar." Sheila wrapped her arms around the roll bar behind the front seat. It had a big spotlight mounted on it. Brad jammed the Jeep in gear and they took off.

Brad drove slowly without lights through the thick brush and open fields. The mist parted before them, then closed behind them. Charlie and Sheila had to duck under branches. The dogs squirmed around them, except for Corky, who sat perfectly still, staring straight ahead.

The Jeep hit a rut and everyone bounced in the air. "Ooiiee!" Sheila yelled. "This is fun!" Bobby looked back at her. She had her arm around Charlie's waist, her head resting on his shoulder. "What's that?" she said. Far off in the woods, Bobby saw pairs of shining green emeralds, the eyes of deer they'd seen on the road to Reverend Tom's ranch.

"Deer," Brad said. The Jeep flushed a covey of quail. They flapped their wings wildly, then tapered off and lighted farther down in the mist. They passed the top of a fence line, the bottom half covered by the mist. "The man who owned that ranch was the one rolled over on my daddy," Brad said. "They caught him with a lousy two keys." Brad laughed. "Course nobody went away. The guy disappeared before the trial. Ain't that so, Charlie?"

Charlie spoke for the first time. "That's raht." Bobby looked back at him. He was smiling down at Bobby. Sheila's hand was massaging the base of Charlie's neck. A woman's scream pierced the night.

"What was *that?*" Sheila said.

"A panther," Brad said. "Sounds jes like a woman bein raped, don't it?"

"I don't know," Sheila said. "I've never been raped."

Brad glanced back at her. She smiled at him. "I'll bet not, lady," he said.

The dogs stopped squirming and began to sniff the air. "They're on to somethin'," Brad said and slowed the Jeep. Corky was sitting upright now. Brad stopped the Jeep in a clearing and pointed to the woods up ahead in the moonlight. "There," he whispered. The dogs were straining to get out of the Jeep, but Charlie was holding them back. "Turn 'em loose, Charlie," Brad said. Charlie threw the dogs out of the Jeep. They landed on the run in the mist, only the top half of their bodies visible, and headed for the woods. All except Corky, still chained to the gearshift.

The dogs disappeared into the woods. It was still and quiet in the darkness, except for the thrashing of thicket as dogs raced back and forth trying to sniff out the wild hog. Suddenly there was a terrified squeal, then the mad yelping of the dogs, and then the top half of a black hunchbacked hog burst out of the woods, trailed by yelping dogs, and headed across the open field toward the woods. Brad jammed the Jeep in gear. "Hold on!" he shouted, and the Jeep leaped after the dogs and hog. Charlie flicked on the spotlight mounted on the roll bar. The dogs and hog were clearly lit now as the Jeep bounced and rattled across the field. The dogs and hog bounced in and out of the spotlight as if they were being filmed by a handheld camera. When the Jeep hit 60 mph, they passed the dogs, their tongues hanging out, and caught up to the hog. They raced him, side-by-side, like linebackers covering a half-back expecting a pass. They heard his heavy, hog-grunting above the noise of the Jeep's engine, could smell his filthy breath, could even see it, all steamy in the light as he ran with terror in his red eyes. He cut to his right. "Hot damn!" Brad shouted. Sheila was smacking Brad on the shoulder, screaming, "Turn, turn the god-damned wheel, you're gonna lose him!" Brad swerved the Jeep to the right. Bobby felt sick to his stomach, the booze, the careening Jeep, the stench of hog. He leaned over the side of the Jeep and vomited.

"You alright, Bobby," Brad shouted. "This all too much fer ya?" He laughed just as they caught up to the hog. The hog cut across the front of the Jeep and for a split second Bobby saw his eyes as red as hot coals. Then the hog disappeared into the woods. Brad jammed on the brakes. Charlie and Sheila almost fell over the roll bar onto Corky, who sat patiently, waiting. The dogs disappeared into the woods and then everything was quiet, except for the thrashing of thicket.

"God! That was exciting!" Sheila said. "I never had such fun!" Bobby looked back at her. Her eyes were wide and glassy, her forehead damp with sweat. She was breathing heavily. "We're not gonna quit, are we, Brad?" she said. "Can we do it again?"

Brad smiled back at her. "Don't you worry, honey. We ain't done yet."

The thicket exploded with more terrified squeals and mad yelping.

"They got him!" Brad shouted. He unchained Corky, and said, "Go get him, baby!" Corky leaped out of the Jeep and ran into the woods. The squealing grew even shriller now, and then it began to die down, go silent, and all they could hear was the heavy dog-grunting of Corky as she tore the dead hog to pieces.

"We better go in there and pull Corky off," Brad said, "or there won't be nothin' left for you to take back, Bobby." He got out of the Jeep. When Bobby didn't follow him, he waved him on. "Come on, Bobby. It's all over now." Bobby glanced back at Sheila. Her face was flushed and she was still breathing heavily. She had her arm around Charlie's neck, the side of her face against his shoulder. Bobby stepped onto the ground. His legs were shaking. He followed Brad up ahead into the woods. The dogs were tearing at the hog's bloody carcass. Brad pulled them off, one by one, and shooed them back to the Jeep. "Gimme a hand, Bobby," he said. Brad grabbed the hog's front legs and Bobby grabbed his back legs and they began dragging him out of the thicket into the open field. Bobby's back was to the Jeep, but he could still see that the spotlight had been turned off.

"Hold it a minute, Bobby," Brad said, grinning. "Let ole Charlie finish. He's a bashful boy." Bobby turned around to see the Jeep half covered in mist. The dogs were standing around the Jeep, panting, their breath hovering in the air. Charlie, lit by the moon, was leaning back against the roll bar, his head thrown back. For a second, Bobby couldn't see Sheila. Then he saw her, a dark form kneeling on the floor of the Jeep, her head buried below Charlie's waist.

They waited until Charlie came with a low, animal moan they could hear. Sheila began groping around the floor of the Jeep with her hands. She handed Charlie's pants up to him. Then she pushed herself up with her hands and leaned back against the side of the Jeep.

"Come on," Brad said. They dragged the dead hog to the back of the Jeep and tossed it in. The dogs leaped in after it, snorted around it for a moment, than lost interest.

"Y'all had yerselves a time, didn't ya?" Brad said. "While poor Bobby and me was working our ass off." Charlie just grinned, while he buckled his pants. Sheila was leaning against the side of the Jeep, her hands behind her back, breathing heavily. She reached one hand around to wipe off her mouth. Then she smiled at them. Brad chained Corky, her snout all bloody, to the gearshift, and they both got in. Brad started the engine. He let it idle, then turned to Bobby beside him with a grin on his red-leathery face.

"Reverend Jesse said to tell ya he's sorry it had to go down like this, Bobby. He said you'd understand. It's just bidness."

"Can't we talk about it?" Bobby said.

"Fraid not," Brad said. "It ain't only Jesse's decision. He's got partners, ya know. Your Cuban friend in Miami." Brad shook his head. "Man, you musta pissed him off."

"Yeah, well he pissed me off, too."

Brad shrugged. Then he said, "Charlie, do it now."

Bobby heard an explosion in his ear, felt a hot flash, but nothing else. He looked back and saw Charlie's body half slumped over the side of the Jeep. Sheila held Charlie's .38 tight in both hands. Bobby turned back to Brad who was still smiling at him, his smile fading as he looked back and saw Sheila swinging the gun around until it was pointed at his forehead. He opened his mouth. Sheila shot him once between the eyes. His head jerked back, splattering Bobby with blood, hit the front window and fell over the door of the Jeep. Corky began to growl and pull at her chain.

"Oh, baby!" Bobby said. "I didn't know if you were acting or not."

Sheila swung the .38 toward his face now. She held the gun so tightly in her hands that they shook. She stared at Bobby, her breath coming in gasps that made her body shudder.

"You fucking bastard!" she said, and fired the last four bullets into Corky's brain.

24

SOL WAS STANDING BY THE EDGE OF THE ROYAL PALM MOTEL POOL ON FT. Lauderdale beach, fishing leaves off the water with a long-handled net. He held a cigarette and a styrofoam cup of coffee in his free hand. It was early morning. The sun had just come up over the ocean. A few tourists were walking on the beach. An old man with a metal detector was working the sand. Sol watched him. A tall, gaunt, stooped old man with the brim of his dirty golf hat pulled over his eyes swept the metal detector left-right-left-right then stopped every few feet to bend over and pick up . . . a penny? a metal bottle cap? a ten-carat diamond ring?

Sol took the net full of wet leaves to the sand and dumped them out. Then he went back to the pool and sat down on a plastic chair at a round table shaded by an umbrella. He sipped his coffee and smoked his cigarette now that his duties were finished.

"As the manager of the Royal Palm," Meyer had said, "one of your duties will be to keep the pool clean for the guests." They were sitting at the same table Sol was sitting at now. Sol had looked around at the one-story cinder block motel of six efficiency apartments and Sol's one-bedroom manager's apartment, and the swimming pool shaded by a few areca palms, but no royal palms.

"What guests?" Sol said to Meyer that day. "Hardly nobody stays here. And even if they did, why would they use the scummy pool with the ocean only a few feet away?"

"Sol, just clean the fucking pool every day," Meyer said. "It's one of your duties."

So Sol skimmed off the leaves every morning to keep a pool clean that nobody ever swam in. Not even the French girl. She was the Royal Palm's only guest. She arrived with her bags and a Royal Palm Motel brochure in her hand. She stood by the pool and looked around.

"But Mr. Sol," she said, holding up the brochure, "it ees not like the picture." The brochure was an artist's painting of towering royal palms around a kidney-shaped pool. Beautiful women with flipped-up hair were lounging around the pool in 1950s bikinis up to their navels. They were smiling at a bunch of handsome guys playing water polo in the pool.

Sol looked at the brochure, then said, "Musta been taken a while ago. Or maybe it's another Royal Palm."

Sol showed her her room. She looked at the greenish scum on the bathroom floor and the palmetto bugs on the kitchenette counter, but said nothing. She smiled at him, finally, and said, "Is fine."

Sol stubbed out his cigarette on the pool tile, left his cup on the table, and got up to go to his room. He glanced out at the ocean. Dark storm clouds were forming far out to sea. When he turned back he saw Frenchie leaving for work. She was maybe twenty-three, with a different look than Sol was used to. Scrubbed-looking, no makeup, a pale gray business suit, clunky low-heeled shoes. She was maybe 5-6, with muscular thighs and sharply cut sandy-colored hair she was always brushing off her brow with the tips of her fingers.

"A real classy chick," Sol had told Sheila one day. "You know, very French."

Sheila just looked at him. "What do you know about classy chicks, Sol?"

"Nothin'," he said. "I just know one when I see one."

Frenchie was walking toward him now. "Bonjour, Monsieur Sol," she said with a big, wide-eyed smile. She had pale blue eyes that always looked startled because her eyelids were so thin.

"Morning, honey. Your ride here yet?"

"Soon." She was carrying a briefcase. She was a stockbroker trainee with Merrill Lynch on Federal Highway. Her boss picked her up every morning in a cream-colored Rolls Royce convertible. He was a slick-looking guy with wavy black hair, goldframed Porsche sunglasses, a dark suit, a perfect tan. "Too perfect," Sol had said to Bobby. "A rag-head, I think. And a player."

Sol looked out at the ocean and then back to the French girl. "I were you, honey, I'd stay in tonight. Looks like a big blow's coming."

"Blow?"

"Storm."

"Oh, yes. But, my boss, he maybe take me to dinner tonight."

"He takes you to dinner a lot, I see."

She shrugged. "Is part of my job."

"Well, I'd take a rain check tonight, honey." She looked at him. "Just tell him about the storm. He'll understand."

"If you say so, Monsieur Sol. Merci."

Sol watched her walk away from him in the morning sunlight. She went around the motel to the front parking lot. Sol went inside his apartment and went straight to the bathroom. He looked out of the tiny window at the French girl waiting for her boss. She wasn't smiling now. She had that same look on her face she always had when she came home from dinner with her boss late at night. Sol would be sitting out by the pool, smoking a cigarette, when she came around the motel, hurrying toward her room. He called to her one night.

"How ya doin', honey?"

"Oh! Monsieur Sol! You frighten me." She came over to him. He could see in the light of the moon that her eyes were red-rimmed.

"Something the matter, honey?" Sol said.

She made a few quick shakes of her head. "Oh, no. Is nothing."

"You been out with friends?"

"No, I know no one but you, Monsieur Sol. It is just business dinner with my boss."

"Your boss does a lotta business at night, huh?"

She nodded. "Yes. Much business. Excuse me, pleeze." She hurried to her room and disappeared inside.

Sol watched her from his bathroom window. The cream-colored Rolls pulled up alongside her. The passenger side door opened. Sol saw a dark hand open her door. Manicured nails, a Rolex below French cuffs, the Rolex glistening in the morning sunlight. The French girl slid into her seat, her skirt hiking up past her muscular thighs. Sol tried to remember where he'd seen thighs like that. Than he remembered. The Russian broad in the James Bond movie. She fucked guys with her legs wrapped around their backs. Just when they were about to come, she broke their backs with her muscular thighs. A Black Widow.

The car disappeared from Sol's window. He turned and looked at himself in the bathroom mirror. Fat, bald, with a salt-and-pepper goatee. His big hairy belly hung over his dirty white shorts.

He finished putting up the storm shutters when the wind began to blow at dusk. He went inside his apartment that was even darker now than his cell at Jessup. He put a TV dinner in the microwave and made himself a Cuba Libre. The wind was rattling the metal shutters. He put on the TV to drown out the noise, but it got louder and louder, like a freight train passing by his door. The wind whooshed against the door and the shutters as if it were going to cave them in and whoosh right through the apartment and out the back wall, taking Sol with it. Nothing was as loud as a hurricane. It was alive, like one of those dinosaurs in a Spielberg movie.

The rain was beating against the shutters like buckshot. Sol settled back on his sofa in the darkness and tried to watch the seven o'clock news. A broad in a yellow rain slicker was standing on the beach describing the hurricane for her viewers, who were living through it. Big leaves from the palm trees whipped past her, tumbling down the beach. Sol heard a loud banging on his door.

He got up and opened it. The wind whooshed in, blowing Frenchie up against him. He struggled to shut the door. She stayed pressed up against his chest for a moment, then stepped back, drenched, wide-eyed.

"I am so sorry, Monsieur Sol. But the storm, it frightened me." Her wet T-shirt was plastered against her chest so that Sol could see the outline of her small firm breasts and big nipples, like grapes.

"No problem, honey," he said. "Come and get dry. You can wait it out with me."

"Oh, merci," she said, smiling. "I feel safer already." Sol got her a towel. She rubbed her hair dry, the towel covering her face, while Sol stared at her nipples. She handed him back the towel. "Merci, again."

"You better get outta them wet clothes," he said. "You'll catch pnuemonia. I'll get you some things to wear."

She went into the bathroom. Sol handed her a pair of shorts with a drawstring and a T-shirt. She shut the door. Sol put on a pot of coffee. When she came out she was wrapped only in a towel. She handed him his clothes.

"Is alright," she said. "I not need these." She sat down on the sofa, pulling up her legs under her ass, hugging the towel to her.

Sol brought her a cup of black coffee. The wind was beating against the shutters, howling like an animal. She took the coffee from him with a smile and held it with both hands, close to her face, and sipped.

Sol sat across from her in an easy chair. They both listened to the storm for a few minutes.

Finally, Sol said, "You don't have storms like this in Paris?"

"Oh, no," she said, big eyed. "The weather there, it is, how you say it, more prudent."

"Moderate, I think you mean."

"Oh, yes." She giggled. "My English is not so good, is it?"

"It's fine, honey. You just need practice is all."

"I know. I not get much chance to speak English so far."

"What about at work?"

She shook her head, once, and said, "No. My boss, he is French Lebanese. He speak French to me all the time."

"Doesn't help your English much, does it?"

"No." She waited a minute, then said, "Is my boss get me apartment."

Sol smiled. "Tell you the truth, honey, he coulda done better for you."

"Yes. Maybe. But is secluded, he say. Safe for me. No one to bother me."

"Your boss is pretty protective of you, eh?"

"Yes. He say I have to be careful of Americans here. Not to be trusted."

"What about him? Do you trust him?" She just smiled at Sol, without answering. Sol said, "Well, it's a good thing you didn't go to dinner with him tonight. The storm woulda been bad by the time you got home."

"Yes. The storm, it save me."

Sol looked at her. "What do ya mean?"

"Oh, nothing." She smiled brightly. "Just, it give me a chance to see you, Monsieur Sol."

"To see me? You mean, so you can practice your English."

"That, yes. But is nice to talk to someone so kind."

Sol grinned. "Kind?" he said, shaking his head. "I been called a lotta things, honey, but never that."

"Well, maybe people not know you."

"And you do?"

She shrugged. "Maybe." She laid down on the sofa and closed her eyes. "All this English," she said. "It tires me. I think I will go to sleep now."

Sol watched her sleep for a while and then he dozed off sitting up in his chair.

They woke the next morning to sunlight streaming through the thin slits where the shutters didn't quite cover the windows. She sat up, the towel falling from her breasts. She didn't pull it up. She just looked across at Sol staring at her breasts. Then, without looking down, she reached down with a hand and refastened the towel around her breasts.

"How about some breakfast, honey?" Sol said. "I ain't got much but cereal."

"Oh, no. You are too kind. I must get ready for work."

Sol opened the door for her to leave. She stopped, reached up on her bare toes, and kissed him lightly on the cheek. "You are so sweet," she said.

Sol said, "Maybe you might wanna have dinner with me some night?" She gave him a thin smile. "Just a thought."

"Avec pleasure," she said. She laughed. "With pleasure, Monsieur Sol."

"Tomorrow night, then." She nodded and then walked slowly over the wet leaves toward her room, wearing only a towel. Sol followed her with his eyes until she went into her apartment and then he saw all the fallen leaves, the broken branches, the overturned tables and chairs, the sand that had washed up from the beach over the patio. He got his coffee and cigarettes and a few plastic garbage bags and his rake and then went outside to take care of his duties. She had already gone to work.

Sol righted all the overturned furniture first, then began to rake up the leaves around the pool. It was already hot under the early morning sun, as if the hurricane had never happened. He bent over to rake the leaves into the bag and then he saw it floating in the pool. A square, tightly wrapped, cellophane package the size of an airplane carry-on bag. Sol looked around. There was nobody on the beach, no boats on the calm ocean. He grabbed the long-handled net and pulled the package to the lip of the pool. He hoisted it out. It weighed about forty pounds. It was wrapped tightly with waterproof tape.

Sol carried the package to his door, looked around, then went inside. He set the package down on the floor and got a steak knife. He made a slit in the package and stuck the blade in it. He withdrew a flaky, pearlescent powder on the blade of the knife and touched the powder to his tongue. It tasted bitter, then slowly his tongue and lips began to get numb.

"Jesus Fucking Christ!" Sol said, and dialed Bobby's number. The phone rang for a long time before he heard Bobby's voice say, "We're not home. You know the drill," and then a beep. Sol hung up. He sat down on his sofa and stared at the cellophane package for a long time. Then he went to his dresser and took out the little Makarov SMC 918 that Bobby and Sheila had given him. He went to the door with the gun behind his back and looked outside. Nothing. He closed the door and left the shutters up on his window, and sat back down and waited for Bobby to get home.

He waited all day and into the night. He called Bobby every half hour, but he didn't answer. Finally, around midnight, Sol called Meyer at The Booby Trap. "I gotta see ya," Sol said.

"What?" Meyer said. "Something happen to the hotel? You put up the shutters, didn't you? I told you. . . ."

"Fuck the motel, Meyer! This is important."

". . . You see a hurricane coming you put up the shutters or else."

"I put up the fucking shutters awright! The motel is fine, just like in the brochure. This is something else."

"So. . . . Tell me."

"Not over the phone."

"Solly, so conspiratorial. I told ya, those days are over for you. You go away, what, six months on a six-year sentence? You think anybody's gonna do business with you anymore?"

Sol took a deep breath and waited a moment. Then he said, "There's something in this for you, Meyer. A nice piece a cake."

"How big a piece?"

"Big enough."

"Awright. I'll be here."

Meyer was at his usual table in the darkened Champagne Room. A girl was dancing on the table, thrusting her trimmed bush at Meyer's smiling face. Sol sat down across from him. He leaned his head to one side around the broad's ass so he could see his shiny pink face, his thick-lensed eyeglasses like the bottoms of old Coke bottles, smiling up at the girl's bush.

"Meyer, I ain't got time."

"Relax, Solly, relax. In a minute."

Sol sat back and waited. He watched his lawyer smiling up at the naked undulating girl. Meyer was the drug smuggler's lawyer of choice. He paired up his clients—the growers in Medelin, the pilots, the transporters in Miami—and then took ten percent of the action. He also defended them in court when they were caught. That was the only part of his job he didn't like, actually appearing in court with his clients. He stood at the defendant's table, a homely little man, almost a midget, in a wrinkled suit with a string bow tie and elephant-skin cowboy boots with six-inch heels. He muttered to himself, the judge asking him to speak up, pushed papers around on the table, never looking up, objecting to everything, even his client's name. He filed motions, delayed, delayed, delayed, until finally the young prosecutor in his JC Penney suit had had enough, and agreed to cut Meyer's client some slack, which is how Meyer got Sol's six-year sentence reduced to six months in Jessup. Then, when Sol got out, he let him manage the Royal Palm and run Meyer's title loan scam to make up for the heavy fee he'd charged him. Sol had run the Booby Trap for Meyer, too, before he went away, but now as a convicted felon he was no use to Meyer at The Trap.

When the girl finally finished, Meyer reached up his hand and helped her down from the table. He slipped a C-note into her garter. She bent over and kissed him on the lips. Meyer watched her walk off, swinging her bare ass, and then turned to Sol.

"So, what's the big deal, Sol? You got a better offer managing a Holiday Inn?" Sol looked around the deserted room, and then told him.

Meyer didn't say anything for a long while after Sol finished telling him about the cellophane package. Finally, he said, "So, you think you're a player again, Sol?"

Sol didn't say anything. Meyer leaned close to his face and Sol smelled his bad breath. "You know who that parcel belongs to?" Meyer said. Sol waited. "Some very heavy people I am told. They might want it back, I hear. They also might be pissed they find somebody trying to move their parcel."

"Who are these heavies?" Sol said.

"Reverend Jesse. You heard of him, I'm sure."

"Yeah, I heard of him. And his hamster hitters."

"I were you, Solly, I'd take the Reverend a little more seriously."

"I'm not afraid of that fuckin' faggot."

"Well, maybe you should be he finds you trying to move his parcel." Meyer sat back in his seat and took out his gold cigarette holder. He put it in his mouth and began sucking on it.

"You still tryin' to quit, Meyer?" Sol smiled at him. "Bad for your health? Maybe you should make up your mind you're a smoker or not, and just be what you are."

"I know what I am, Solly. It's you don't know what you are. You're not Solomon Billstein, a.k.a. Sol Bass, a.k.a. Sol Rogers, big deal smuggler anymore. Those days are gone forever. Nobody trusts you now you been away. Accept it. You're the manager of The Royal Palm Motel now, and Uncle Sol's Title Loans, and maybe a small-time player in a little scam your two friends come up with every so often. That's all that's left for you, Solly." He leaned toward Sol again, and said, "Listen to me, Sol. It's in your best interest. Give Jesse back his parcel. Maybe he'll toss you a coupla bills finder's fee."

"Fuck Jesse! And fuck you, too, Meyer. After all these years you want me to lay down and play dead. I don't need either of you for this one."

"Who you gonna get to help move it? Bobby and Sheila? I hear they got problems of their own with Jesse."

"Whaddaya mean?"

"You haven't heard? Those two redneck hitters they found dead in the swamp. It was in the papers, Sol. The heat's lookin' for a cowboy with a blond ponytail and a hooker with short blond hair. Sound familiar? Seems somebody dropped a dime on them didn't like that his two redneck hitters ended up dead in the swamp before they fulfilled their contract."

"Jesse?"

"If I were to guess, yeah. Now *you* want to piss him off, too. Jeez, Sol, don't say I didn't warn you."

Sol stood up. "You warned me, Meyer. But I gotta do this one. It's not only for the cash. It's for me. You understand?"

Meyer nodded. "You gotta do what you gotta do, Sol."

Sol got back to his apartment after two in the morning. He called Bobby again. The phone rang and then Sol heard Bobby's voice, "We're not home. You know the drill." He waited for the beep, then said, "Bobby, it's me. Call me. It's important." He hung up.

Sol woke the next morning to a knock on the door. He grabbed his Makarov from under his pillow and went to the door. "Who is it?" he said.

"C'est moi" said a voice.

Sol stuck the gun in the back of his boxer shorts and opened the door.

"Everything is right?" Frenchie said.

"Sure, kid. Why not?" The Makarov began slipping down his shorts. Sol clamped his hand on it in the crack of his ass before it hit the floor.

"The shutters," she said. "They are still on only in your apartment."

"Oh, yeah! I forgot. I been busy is all."

"Too busy for dinner tonight?"

"Of course not, honey. I been looking forward to it. About nine."

She gave him a big smile, leaned toward him, and kissed him on the cheek. Then she walked off toward her ride. Without turning, she reached up a hand and waved to him in that finger-grabbing-air way of Europeans that meant come back. "Au revoir!" And she was gone.

Sol shut the door, took the gun out of his ass, and went to the phone and called Bobby again. "We're not home. You know the drill," Bobby's voice said, and Sol hung up.

25

BOBBY SAT IN THE INTERROGATION ROOM, ALONE, AND WAITED. THERE WERE A few gray metal office chairs, an old metal office table, and a dirty ashtray. The walls were painted a faded peasoup green. The linoleum floor was gray. He faced a two-way mirror. The room smelled of piss and vomit and cigarette smoke.

"Remember one thing," Sol had told him years ago. "You ever go down, the heat always knows less than you think. That's their ace. You tryin' to guess what they know, comin' up wrong, givin' them more credit than they deserve. If they were so fuckin' smart, Bobby, they wouldn't be heat."

Bobby sat there and waited. He stared straight ahead at the two-way mirror. "They'll try to make you sweat, Bobby," Sol had said. "Wait the cocksuckers out. You're a fuckin' Indian, ain't ya? You know how to wait."

Bobby sat there and waited. He stared at the mirror and saw in it Sheila's face contorted in anger. It had taken him a few seconds to ease the gun out of her hand. He wiped it clean of her prints and tossed it into the swamp. He had to pull all three bodies out of the Jeep himself and dump them in the swamp. She wouldn't help him.

Bobby drove the Jeep back to the ranch house, wiped it clean, then made Sheila go inside with him. He wiped down everything he'd touched. The bottle of Crown Royal. The glass. The table. Then he had to half-drag Sheila into the bedroom. She pulled away, screaming, "No fucking way!" But he made her. They stood over the small bed with its dirty, rumpled sheets.

"What'd you touch, baby?" he said.

She pointed to the bedpost. "I was on my knees, holding on to the bedpost," she said. "He was fucking me from behind."

Bobby wiped down the bedpost with a handkerchief, then turned to her. "What else, baby?" he said. She was breathing heavily, her eyes opened wide, glassy. "Come on! What else?"

Her breathing became steadier, a thin smile on her lips, her eyes half-lidded, milky blue. "I touched his dick, Bobby," she said. "But not to worry. I wiped it clean with my mouth."

When they got back to their rented house, she pulled off her clothes, threw them in the garbage can, and took a shower. She was in the shower for almost an hour, while Bobby sat outside on the deck, his face and clothes still splattered with blood. When she finally got out of the shower, Bobby took off his clothes and threw them in the garbage can, too. Then he took a quick shower. When he got out, he dressed again, took the dirty clothes out of the garbage can, and drove to the Gateway Shopping Mall at four in the morning. He threw the clothes in a dumpster and went back home. Sheila was already asleep on the sofa in the Florida room. She was naked, her knees pulled up to her chest like she was in a womb. Bobby went to sleep alone in their bed with Hoshi.

He woke late the next morning. It was almost noon. He went into the Florida room to check on Sheila. She was gone. He went back to the bedroom and opened the dresser drawer. She had taken some of her clothes and most of her underwear. He made himself some coffee and went out onto the back deck to wait for her call. He waited until late in the afternoon, and then he called Sol.

"What's happenin', Bobby?" Sol said.

"Nothing. I was just wondering. Sheila ain't been by, has she?"

"Why should she?"

"I dunno. We had a little thing last night. She got pissed and took off this morning before I got up."

"Ain't you the one always told me don't piss her off, Bobby? What'd she do, catch you with one of those cheap-ass blondes you like, the one with the rose tattoo on her ass?"

"Naw. Nothin' like that. Just a broad thing. She stops by tell her to give me a call."

"Whatever, Bobby."

Bobby stayed in the house all night, waiting for her to return. When she didn't come home by midnight, he went to bed. He woke the next morning to a knock on the door. He hurried to the door, still naked, with Hoshi growling by his side. He opened the door to see two men in suits standing there, flashing their badges. Ft. Lauderdale Homicide.

The two cops came into the interrogation room. The older one was fat, with a drinker's splotchy red face. He tugged his rumpled pants up over his belly and smiled.

"Who do we got here?" he said. He waved Bobby's arrest sheet in his face. "Mr. Robert Roberts, it says."

The younger one, not smiling, said, "Yeh, but his buddies call him Bobby Squared. Ain't that right Bobby Squared?" He was trying to look like a businessman, maybe a stockbroker, in his neat gray suit and Countess Mara tie, with his flip-up cell phone in his jacket pocket. A Gator with freckled pink skin, watery blue eyes, and short, reddish hair with a cowlick. He was already going to fat at thirty-two. Bobby smiled at him.

"Relax, Bobby," the old guy said, "We just wanna ask you a few questions."

"I am relaxed," Bobby said. "Or you too stupid to notice?"

The Gator moved behind Bobby. The drinker put his hands on the table and leaned his face close to Bobby's. "You ever go wild hog hunting, Bobby?"

Bobby wrinkled up his nose. "Vodka, eh? Majorska, comes in those gallon jugs for ninety-nine cents." He smiled up at the drinker. "I'm a bourbon man, myself. Makers Mark. Gentleman Jack."

The Gator behind him grabbed the back of Bobby's chair and yanked it backward, snapping Bobby's neck, but not pulling him over. The Gator leaned over and said in Bobby's ear, "You been drinkin' Gentleman Jack with Brad and Charlie these days?"

"Who?"

"Maybe Crown Royal?" said the drinker.

"I'll bet you like Crown Royal," Bobby said to the drinker. "With sweet Coke in it, maybe some sugar, too."

"Brad and Charlie like Crown Royal," said the Gator.

"I don't know any Brad and Charlie."

"You sure, Bobby?" said the drinker. "Two redneck hitters, use a .38?"

Bobby smiled at him. "I'm a semi-auto man, myself. Collector's items, you know, from the Eastern Bloc."

"Like all that shit blown up at the Reverend Tom Miller's house," said the Gator.

"Who?"

"You know the Reverend," the drinker said. "That Nazi you bought a van full of guns from that blew up. The Reverend, too."

"Oh, yeah. I saw it on TV. Terrible fire. But I don't know nothin' about a van and guns." He smiled. "I'm a dancer, you know, at The Crazy Horse, where your wives go when you're outta town."

"That's not what we heard, Bobby," said the Gator. "We heard you buy guns for people, do them favors, like spics in Miami think they're George Fucking Washington. The same spic, by the way, put out a contract on you and your old lady."

"I don't have an old lady."

"That's not what we hear," said the drinker. "We heard you been seen around town a lot these days with a butch blonde's got this spike-like hair and cold blue eyes."

"I know a lot of blondes."

"Not like this one," said the Gator. "This one's not your usual style. You like 'em young, we hear. This one's an old lady, maybe forties, but lookin fine, nice tits we hear, a real fuckin' mechanic, we hear, too, if we could only ask Brad and Charlie, she done them both. You might say, she had them comin' and goin' at the same time."

"Handy with a piece, too," said the drinker, "the way she put one in the wall behind Sunny Kresnick's head just to make him sit up, pay attention."

"I don't like old ladies."

"No, you went against type this time, Bobby," said the drinker. "Her name is Sheila, we know that much. She's got a lotta different last names, a lotta different looks, too. A real chameleon."

"Maybe she's a hooker I rented once or twice," Bobby said. "You wanna bust me on a solicitation charge?"

"You been renting her long term, we hear," the drinker said. "Like leasing a car, over a year now. What're you gonna do, turn her in she gets too many miles on her? Why don'tcha turn her in now, let us rent her for a while?"

The Gator smiled. "We'll drive her real nice, Bobby, make sure she don't get dented."

"Find your own fucking car."

"By the way," the drinker said, "what're you drivin' these days since your black SHO blew up at the diner?"

"That car registered to me? The one blew up?"

"No," said the drinker, "but we know it was yours."

"Just like the black SHO you're drivin' now," said the Gator.

"See what we mean?" said the drinker. "Your MO is everywhere."

"I'm the only fucking guy in Broward County likes black SHOs?"

"No," said the drinker. "There are ten others to be exact."

"Only three '89s, though, Bobby," said the Gator. "Like yours."

"So go bring in the owners of the other two."

"We did," said the drinker. "One's an orthodontist, the other's a high school principal."

"Yeh," said the Gator, "Neither of them have your kind of friends."

"And what kind is that?"

"Blond hookers, spics in Miami, racist gun runners, and two redneck hitters like .38 specials," said the drinker. "You ever use a .38 special, Bobby?"

Bobby shook his head, no, and made a face. "That's a cop's gun. For old timers like you, don't know how to stay up with the times."

"Somebody used that .38 on your two friends," said the Gator.

Bobby looked back at him as if confused. "Which friends? The old blonde or the spic?"

"You know which friends," said the Gator. "Charlie and Brad."

"Maybe these photographs will help you remember them," said the drinker. He held a photograph in front of Bobby's face. Two bodies lying in swampy grass. Their faces and stomachs half-eaten away.

"Wild hogs," said the Gator. "There wasn't enough of them left to make a positive ID. We had to use their dental charts. Wild hogs don't eat teeth and fillings, ya know Bobby."

Bobby turned around and looked the Gator in the eye. "I didn't know that," he said

"We didn't even know how they died," said the drinker. "We had a good idea, though, with those neat little holes in their foreheads."

"Very professional," said the Gator. "One pop each, right between the eyes. Either you or your girlfriend, Bobby. You didn't do it, then she's as good a shot as she is a piece of ass." The Gator smiled. "Know what else we found, Bobby?"

"Tell me."

"Semen stains. Cum, to you, Bobby. On Brad's thigh and Charlie's pants. Now what do ya think that means?"

"They went out with a smile."

"How'd it feel, Bobby? Know your bitch was ballin' two redneck hitters? Turn you on? Maybe you watched? Did you watch, Bobby? Get a hard-on, then fuck her yourself?" He looked at his partner. "What they call that?"

Bobby smiled and answered first. "I think you mean a buttered bun, Gator. But I like mine fresh from the oven."

"Know what we couldn't find, Bobby?" said the drinker. "The slugs that sent Brad and Charlie off to their just reward. The hogs must a swallowed them when they ate their faces."

"Ya know how we found them, the bullets, Bobby?" said the Gator.

"No. But I have a feeling you're gonna tell me."

"We had to go out there in the fucking swamp in the heat of the day," said the Gator. "In my new suit, pissing me off, scooping up hog shit and bringing it back to forensics. Digging through that shit till we finally found the slugs."

"Must have brought back old times for you, Gator."

26

SOL DRESSED FOR DINNER WITH FRENCHIE. HE PUT ON HIS BLUE OXFORD shirt with the buttons on the collar, his gray slacks, and his loafers with the little tassels. He slapped on some aftershave and looked at himself in the bathroom mirror. He smiled. Then he went to his dresser, put on all his gold jewelery and stuck the little Makarov into his front pants pocket.

They drove south on A1A along the beach in the Taurus he leased from Alamo. They passed Sunrise, and then all the renovated hotels along the strip-The Bahama, The Riviera—and then all the new out-door cafés—Casa Blanca, H2O, Mistral, Evangeline's. The outdoor tables were crowded with tourists and locals eating under the stars and the purple-blue sky. They stared across at the white beach wall with the neon tube in it that was filled with a liquid that kept changing color from pink to blue to green to red and back again. Beyond the wall was the white sand beach and the dark ocean and far out on the ocean the blinking red lights of passing ships.

"Is beautiful, no?" Frenchie said. She was looking across Sol at the beach.

"Yeah. Is beautiful," Sol said. "Paradise." She was wearing a creamy silk blouse and no bra and a tight camel-colored miniskirt that flashed her muscular thighs and the clunky shoes all the broads were wearing these days.

"You hungry, baby?" Sol said.

"No, hurry," she said. She was looking out her window now at the tourists and locals eating at the cafés. "Is like Monaco, a little," she added.

"I wouldn't know. I never been there."

"Oh, you must go one time. I will show you around there."

"Yeah. Some day." Sol turned the Taurus right onto Las Olas and drove over the Intracoastal Bridge. She leaned up in her seat to look down at all the yachts docked in front of the waterfront mansions.

"Is very expensive, no?"

"Very." They came down off the bridge and drove past the fancy shops of Las Olas, the imported guinea men's store Sol could never buy anything from because he couldn't fit into the clothes, and the broads' dress shops, with the wedding gowns so low cut, the broads flashing their tits at the altar the priests had hard-ons. They passed more people eating outside at Mangos and then Sol stopped at the valet stand in front of The Left Bank.

"Is French," she said, turning to Sol with a smile. "For me." She leaned across the seat and kissed him on the cheek. "You are so thoughtful, Monsieur Sol."

The maitre'd, a dark, oily-looking little man in a frilly shirt and tuxedo, stopped them at the dining room entrance. "You have reservations, Monsieur?" He looked Sol up and down and then glanced at Frenchie.

"Hey, Slick, who the fuck. . . ." Sol felt Frenchie's hand on his arm. He looked at her. She was looking at the maitre'd as if she was looking at a bug under a microscope.

Frenchie said something to the maitre'd in French. His eyes opened wide, and then he said, "Certainmont, Mademoiselle." He bowed and made a sweeping gesture with his big menus. Frenchie walked past him, followed by Sol, past the other diners, men Sol's age in dark suits and crisp white shirts with women almost their age in evening dresses and upswept silver hair. They looked up and stared at the older bald man and the young girl.

The maitre'd led them to a banquette against the far wall. Frenchie slid in first, flashing her thighs, and then Sol slid in beside her. The maitre'd handed them each a menu with a flourish and a bow and was gone.

"What'd you say to him?" Sol said.

"Oh, nothing. Just that I recognize his accent. Algerian French." She smiled. "He recognize mine, too. Parisian French."

Sol laughed. "You're somethin' else, baby."

They studied their menus, in French, with no prices. "I order for us," she said.

"You do that, baby." Sol sat back and lit a cigarette.

"For me, too." She reached up her hand, took the cigarette out of his mouth, and put it between her lips. Sol lit another one for himself. A handsome young waiter appeared at their table. She spoke to him in French as she looked down the menu. He nodded, mumbling in French, and wrote in his little black book. He snapped the book shut, gave her a big smile and said something to her. She answered him. His eyes shifted to Sol for an instant, a thin smile on his lips, and then he backed off and was gone.

"What was that about?" Sol said.

"He asked me if mon pere would like something to drink."

"Pear?"

"Father. I said that you were not my father. You were, how do you say, my date."

Sol smiled. "What'd you order, baby?"

"I order the escargots, frogs legs, and a bottle of Pouilly Fuisse, a very good year."

"Those things, the escar . . . what are they?"

"Snails. But very good, Sol. Trust me."

Sol shook his head. "You're the boss."

When the waiter brought the wine, she motioned for him to pour some in her glass first. She sniffed the cork, then took a sip, swirling it around in her mouth before she swallowed. Then she nodded, and the waiter filled their glasses and left. She raised her glass to Sol's with a smile on her beautiful scrubbed face. "To you, Sol, for being such a sweet man." They touched glasses and sipped their wine.

"It's very good," Sol said. "Now, a toast to you. Your stay in America and success in your job." Her smile faded. "Whatsa matter?"

"Is all right. Is nothing."

"Come on, baby. Tell me."

She looked into his eyes with her own pale blue eyes. "Is my boss."

"What about him?"

"He is, how you say, romantic to me."

"And you?"

"Oh, no! He is just my boss."

"Then tell him that."

"I try. But he won't listen."

"You want me to tell him?"

"Oh, no! I have to do it. But is hard. He is kind of man get everything he want. He knows I need this job to keep my visa and stay in America."

"Yeah, America's nice, baby, but I hear Paris ain't the slums."

"For you, maybe. But for me Paris is morte."

"Morte?"

"Death."

Sol laughed. "What, you kiddin'?"

She shook her head, no, and looked down at the table. She was quiet for a moment. When she finally raised her eyes again they were opened wide. She said, "My life in Paris is, how you say it . . . prescribed for me. My father is a diplomat, very important man. He wants me to marry. A boy from old wealthy family. A lawyer."

"You don't love him?"

"That is not the point! You don't understand! I marry him I will live in a big chateau outside of Paris, with servants, and children. My husband will take an apartment in Paris where he works. And a mistress. That is how it is done. Maybe he will visit me on weekends." She shrugged. "Maybe, no. Maybe I be there alone, walking through my garden in my straw hat with my gloves, snipping flowers to put in vases on the dining-room table where I eat alone." She smiled at him. "You see. Worse even than your motel with bugs." She stopped smiling, and said, "That's why I will never go back. Never! Do you understand? I will do anything not to go back to that life."

"So that's why you put up with your boss?"

She nodded. "He knows all this. I make the mistake to tell him one night. That's why he put me in your motel, alone, with no car, no one to see. He have me all to himself."

"He sounds worse than your life in Paris."

"Never! Not even he is worse."

The waiter appeared with their escargots. They ate in silence for a while. Sol struggled with the little plier-like things until he saw how she used them, holding the shells in the pliers and then scooping out . . . worms!

Finally, she looked up at him. "Is not only at work. He takes me to dinner, business, he says, and then goes to la salle du ban every few minutes. By the end of dinner he is aggresseeve."

"He's doing lines in there."

"Lines?"

"Coke. Cocaine. He's a coke-head."

"Yes. I guess that. Is how he makes business. He gives it, the cocaine, to his clients to make the deal. He make very much money."

The waiter brought their frogs legs. Sol looked at them. He forced himself to take a bite of the tiny legs.

"Like chicken," he said.

"Yes, only more delicate flavor." He looked at her, but said nothing. She said, "You have something to tell me? Is what?"

"I was thinking, maybe I got a way you can make a few dollars, baby. A lot of dollars, get your boss off your back."

"Off my back? What is this?"

"Not bother you anymore." She nodded, waiting. "I have something might interest him. A package came into my . . . possession, you might say."

"The package in the swimming pool."

"You know about it?"

"I see when I go to work. Floating. When I come home is gone."

"You know what was in it?"

"No." She shook her head, her hair falling across one eye. "Maybe," she said. She brushed her hair off her eye with the back of her fingertips. "Not then. But now."

"Jeez, kid, you're full of surprises."

"I am not so innocent as you think, Sol. I just not say everything."

"I know. The language must be a problem."

"Is that, too." Then she said, "This package, is expensive?"

"Very. Maybe too steep for your boss."

"Steeeep?"

"Too expensive. Maybe three hundred thousand dollars, which would be a bargain for him. Last him a year to impress his clients, make even more money." She looked at him with her blue eyes blank. "It's a little dangerous, too," Sol said.

"You mean, police?"

"There's that. And your boss. It might be too dangerous for him."

She shook her head, no. "Is not afraid of police. He cheats his clients.

He gives them cocaine at dinner so they won't remember. Next morning he makes stock transfers for big commission. Tells them they agree to the night before. They cannot remember so can do nothing."

"A real sweetheart. But can I trust him? He might want the package without paying for it."

"I can help you. He trusts me."

"You sure you wanna get mixed up in this, baby? You know what you're doing?"

"I know." She leaned close to Sol and put her hand on his thigh. "I not care about the danger, Sol. Is worth it to be free of him. With dollars I can leave him, get another job, with no fear of losing visa." She smiled. "I will be free."

Sol smiled at her. "Me too, baby."

They discussed their plan over dessert, baked Alaska, which they shared, sitting close, talking softly, her hand on his thigh.

They waited in the darkness for the valet to bring the Taurus around. The French girl rested her head against Sol's shoulder, her arm around his waist. Sol saw a black Jeep across the street.

Sol slipped the valet a ten-dollar bill. "Thank you, sir," the valet said, and opened the door for Frenchie. She slid in, Sol walked around the car with his hand in his pants pocket on his Makarov. He got in, turned on the ignition, then the lights, and made a U-turn on Las Olas. The lights of his Taurus shined into the Jeep for an instant, illuminating two dark forms with dreadlocks, and then the Taurus swung past the Jeep and headed east on Las Olas. The Jeep followed them. The Taurus went over the Intracoastal Bridge, then turned north on A1A alongside the ocean. Frenchie sat close to Sol, her head resting on his shoulder. Every so often she gave him a soft kiss in the crook of his neck.

When Sol pulled into the apartment parking lot, he shut off his lights and waited. The Jeep moved past the Taurus and stopped far down the street with its lights off. Frenchie was asleep. Sol shook her and she woke with a smile.

"We home?" she said.

"Yeah, baby."

They walked around the motel to her door. Sol listened for the Jeep to to start up again, but heard nothing. She turned and faced him, put her arms around his neck and kissed him on the mouth. She slipped her tongue into his mouth for only an instant, and then pulled back from him, looking up at him with a half-lidded smile.

"Don't worry, baby," Sol said. "Everything's gonna be OK."

"I not worried, Sol. I trust you." And then she was gone inside.

Sol entered his apartment and immediately called Bobby. He still wasn't home. He made himself a Cuba Libre and sat down on the sofa with the Makarov in his lap.

He didn't like it, Bobby not being there for him. Bobby was always there for him—one of the few things in his life he could count on. Sheila, too. He hated to admit it, the broad was such a bitch sometimes. But he counted on her, too, the way she could see things he couldn't, not only because she was smarter than him—shit, Bobby was smarter than him—but because she didn't have the baggage Sol did, always havin' to prove something, the provin' gettin' in the way of what he knew he should do. Sheila didn't have that. Maybe it was a broad thing, not always havin' to prove somethin'? Maybe it was just Sheila? Whatever the fuck it was, it worked for them, the three of them. Together, they all had things each other needed. Separated, they had gaps in them could get them in trouble. Like now. Sol saw this whole deal goin' down the way it should, but something bothered him, something he was afraid he was missing but couldn't see. Sheila could see right off. But she and Bobby had their own set of problems, the spic still on their ass. Medina would never go away. That's what Sol knew and they didn't. He knew how to take care of the spic, too, the only way to do it make it final. But Sheila probably wouldn't go for it, would try to think up one of her smart-ass schemes that were OK when it came to snatchin' pictures, but not when it came to a crazy fuckin' spic like Medina on their ass.

Sol woke with a start at noon. He was still wearing the clothes he had worn last night with Frenchie. He put the Makarov in his pocket and went around to the parking lot to see if the Jeep was still there. It was gone. He went back to his apartment, changed into his work clothes and busied himself with his duties until she came from work.

He was sitting on the sofa when she burst through the door at six P.M. She ran to him in only her long T-shirt and jumped up on the sofa like a kid, smiling, big-eyed. "He agreed!" she said, jumping up and down like on a trampoline. "He say he will have the dollars by nine o'clock tonight at the Burger King on Sunrise. Near the expensive automobile store." She flopped down on the sofa beside Sol and kissed him hard on the cheek. "Only a few more hours and I will be free," she said.

"We'll both be free," Sol said.

"I go change, Sol. Wait for me."

She went back to her room. Sol put the cellophane package into a black carry-on bag with airline stickers pasted on it. She returned at eight dressed in a white T-shirt, jeans, and white sneakers.

"We ready?" she said, smiling.

"What do you mean, 'we,'?" Sol said. "You ain't goin."

"But I must Sol. My boss will do this only with me."

"I dunno, baby. This is dangerous."

"I can do it, Sol. Is only way."

"OK. We'll both make the swap with him."

She shook her head, no. "Only me or he won't do it."

"I don't like it," Sol said. "You alone with that guy. What if he rips you off, grabs the package without forking over the cash?"

"He won't do that, Sol. You be there in your car. You'll see. If he try to steal package I scream."

Sol laughed. "Great! Bring every cop in town down on us."

"Sol, not to worry. Trust me."

"Awright, baby. I don't like it, but I got no choice."

They left early. Sol drove around for a while to make sure nobody was on his tail. He drove past the Burger King a few times to make sure there were no cars parked too long in the lot. After his third pass by the Burger King he drove over the Intracoastal Bridge to the beach, made a U-turn back onto Sunrise and headed for the bridge again.

"Showtime, baby," Sol said.

She was sitting beside him, the black bag on her lap, holding it tight to her with her arms. "I ready, Sol," she said. "And you?"

Sol didn't say anything for a moment. She said, "Everything is all right, Sol, no?"

"Everything's fine, baby." He smiled. "It feels good, ya know."

She nodded. "I know."

They drove back over the Intracoastal Bridge and headed west on Sunrise toward the Burger King. Sol glanced in the rearview mirror when he stopped at the light at Bayview. He saw the lights of a black Jeep two cars behind him. The light turned green and Sol drove west to the Burger King, and then past it.

She turned her head back toward the Burger King. "Sol, you pass it."

"A little change in plans, baby." He told her not to look around, then he told her about Jesse and his hitters in the Jeep behind them. When he finished he looked across at her. She was chewing on her bottom lip, her eyes narrowed.

"Only a little problem," she said.

"Could be a big fuckin' problem, you understand?"

She shook her head, no, but said nothing.

"Maybe I can shake them." Sol said.

He turned left onto Federal and headed toward the airport with the French girl sitting beside him, holding tight to the black bag, the Makarov in his pants pocket, and the Jeep two cars behind them. Sol drove slowly, looking, until he saw a hooker up ahead, swinging her ass down the sidewalk, looking back over her shoulder at passing cars. Sol pulled the car into the right lane, close to the girl, and gave a little beep of his horn. Then he turned the corner onto Sixth Street that led into black town and stopped. He waited for the hooker to round the corner. The Jeep rounded the corner first, moved past the Taurus, the two men inside staring straight ahead, and then it stopped up ahead. The hooker came by Sol's window. She leaned her arm on his windowsill and said, "You wanna party, hon?" She was skinny, dirty, with missing teeth. When she saw Frenchie, she said, "Cost you more for a threesome, honey."

Sol slammed the car into reverse and nailed the accelerator. The car spun backward onto Federal, just missing another car, the other car swerving, its driver nailing his horn. The hooker screamed, "You prick, you almost tore my arm off!"

Frenchie said nothing. She braced her hands against the dashboard as Sol slammed the gearshift into drive, nailed it again. The tires squealed, smoke and the smell of burning rubber everywhere as the big Taurus launched down Federal. Sol hung a left at Third, then a quick right, and another left until he was deep into Victoria Park with all its narrow one-way streets and dead-ends. He looked in his rearview mirror for the Jeep but couldn't see it. He turned right onto Broward, headed west, and then turned left back onto Federal toward the airport. He was speeding now, past the Riptide bar, the Copa, less than a mile from the airport access road. He looked again into his mirror and still couldn't see the Jeep.

"I think we lost 'em," he said.

"Who?"

"The hamsters in the Jeep."

She turned around in her seat and stared out the rear window for a moment. "No, Sol. I think I see the Jeep. Maybe two cars behind."

"You sure, baby?"

She turned back around. "Yes."

"Shit!" The airport was in front of them. Sol turned onto the access road and headed toward the terminal. "Listen, baby, these guys are dangerous. I don't want you involved. I'll drop you off at the airport, then I'll try to shake 'em again. You catch a cab back to the motel. I'll meet you there. We'll set it up another time with your boss."

She turned to him, wide-eyed, in terror. "No, Sol! You can't! My boss, he will be afraid now. Suspicious. He will not do the deal."

"There's no other way, baby."

She looked straight ahead for a moment, then she said, "I will do it alone."

"Do what alone?"

"Go to the Burger King. Make the swap, the package for the money."

"You outta your fuckin' mind?"

"No. Listen, Sol. You drop me off at the Delta tickets with the black bag. Like I make a trip. You drive away. Let the Jeep follow you until is midnight. Then go back to motel. I take a taxi to Burger King, make the swap, then go to expensive hotel, the Harbor Beach. I call you from there after midnight to tell you everything is well."

"What if everything isn't so fuckin' well?"

"Will be. Trust me, Sol."

He looked at her-her blue eyes, her beautiful, scrubbed face, the bag in her lap. He reached into his pants pocket and withdrew the little Makarov. "Take this," he said, and handed it to her.

She looked at it a moment before she took it in her hands.

"You know how to use that?" Sol said.

She pulled back the slide only a little to see if there was a round in the chamber. "Is loaded," she said.

"You shot a gun before?" he said.

"No. But I see all the time on television."

"Can you use it if you have to?"

"I not want to," she said. "But if I have to I think, maybe, yes."

He stopped at Delta ticketing. She put the gun in the black bag and got out. Sol got out, too, and went around to the sidewalk. They kissed and hugged each other. Sol whispered in her ear, "Make sure the Jeep follows me, baby."

She whispered back, "Not to worry, Sol."

Sol got back in his car. She was standing there, smiling at him, holding the black bag in one hand. Sol waved to her. She raised her hand to the side of her face and waved to him, too, like she had waved to him that morning on her way to work, only somehow different, not the same wave. Then she was gone through the sliding-glass doors.

Sol drove off, looking in the mirror for the Jeep, but he couldn't see it among all the cars circling the airport. He drove back to Federal, busy with traffic now, and headed toward the beach. There were so many headlights behind him he couldn't pick out the Jeep. He slowed down to make sure the Jeep could follow him and then turned east on 17th Street toward the Causeway and the beach.

Sol drove around the beach until midnight, and then drove back to the Royal Palm. He waited a few minutes in the parking lot for the Jeep to pass by and park up ahead, but there was no Jeep. He got out and went to his apartment.

Sol sat on his sofa in the dark, waiting for her to call. He leaned forward and stared down at the floor. The Jeep was following them and Sol tried to shake it but then he didn't see it anymore. When Frenchie saw the Jeep again they stopped at Delta ticketing and hugged on the sidewalk. Sol got back in the car and waved to her through the window. The beautiful French girl waved back, smiling, her hand raised beside her face—waving to him, but not like before, not with that odd, European, finger-grabbing-air wave that meant "Come back." It was a different wave. Familiar. American. Limp-wristed. Hand-flapping. Good-bye.

27

THEY KEPT BOBBY FOR THREE DAYS WITHOUT CHARGING HIM. THEY MOVED him around from one holding cell to another, the Broward County jail, Ft. Lauderdale jail, Miami-Dade Correction, MCI, never letting him use the phone. If Sheila had been there when they collared him, she would have put up a stink, screaming, "Where's your warrant? What's the charge? I'm getting our lawyer," stuff like that, playing the outraged straight lady, threatening a lawsuit, getting Meyer in an hour to bond Bobby out.

But Sheila wasn't there. Only Bobby was there, alone, with a rap sheet, used to the whole process, so he went along without a whimper, the way guys in his line of work did when the heat came knocking. They were just doing their job. Like him. Cops and robbers. Sol was right. It was a game. With rules. Only Sheila didn't accept the rules like Bobby and Sol did, which was why he needed her. She saw through the game and went straight to the fucking point. Medina. That was the fucking point, now, not even the heat; they didn't have a thing on him or they already woulda charged him. Medina was their problem and Bobby knew he couldn't solve it without Sheila.

Finally, they had to let him make a call. He called Meyer at The Trap and two hours later Meyer got him sprung, pulling a Sheila, screaming he was gonna sue the bastards on behalf of his client, "Mr. Robert Roberts."

The Gator grinned, "Y'all mean Mr. Bobby Squared, don'tcha?"

"I don't believe I know that person," said Meyer with a straight face, and then walked Bobby out of the lockup into the bright sunlight of the Ft. Lauderdale jail parking lot.

"Thanks, Meyer," Bobby said.

"Sol's been looking for you," Meyer said.

"What's he want? Sheila with him?"

"I don't know. I just know he's gonna do something stupid maybe you should talk him out of."

"Jesus Christ! I gotta baby-sit him, too?"

"You gotta do what you gotta do, Bobby."

Bobby picked up Hoshi from the dog pound where the heat had brought him and went home. Tree branches littered the front yard from the hurricane that had hit when Bobby was in jail. Inside, the house was deserted. Bobby clicked on his answering machine. There was a message from Sol but nothing from Sheila. He called Sol but there was no answer at his apartment.

The next morning Bobby went outside to clean up the yard. He dragged the fallen palm fronds and broken gumbo limbo branches out to the front and stacked them on the swale across the street for bulk pickup. Then he went in and called Sol again. Still no answer.

He tried to get through the day. He made coffee. He took Hoshi for walks. He did a load of laundry, his clothes stinking of stale piss and vomit from sleeping on the concrete floor in the slam. He made himself dinner, ate it alone, sipped a glass of Jim Beam on the rocks, washed the dishes, dried them, and went outside to the back deck with his glass and a half bottle of Jim Beam and his CZ-85. He sat on a chair in the darkness with Hoshi lying beside him, Hoshi expectant, waiting

for a possum. Bobby put the CZ on his lap and sipped his Jim Beam in
the darkness without a moon, or stars, or even a breeze to ruffle the
leaves of the avocado tree that hung over the backyard.

He sat there in the black silence, waiting, sipping his drink, and then
another, and another, trying to figure it out, where it went wrong,
how it went wrong, what he coulda done to stop it. But he could think
of nothing, except that he had met someone finally he wanted always
to be close to him, and somehow he had pushed her away. He had been
given a gift, and pissed on it, and now it was gone. So he waited, for
whatever. He didn't give a shit. . . .

28

She woke as if from a drugged sleep, naked on a strange bed in a filthy hotel room. She smelled of sweat, and her own sex. She sat up in bed and looked around, breathing heavily, her eyes wide. Then she saw the clock beside the bed. It was 10 P.M. on a Friday night in South Beach. Her breathing grew steadier. She had plenty of time.

She got off the bed and went to a small canvas bag on the floor beside her purse and the shopping bag with the drawing of the black drag queen on it. She took out a pair of six-inch high pumps and laid them beside the bag. Then she took out her black thong panties and her cosmetics case and eyelash curler and went into the bathroom. She put her things on the toilet seat and turned on the shower. She waited for the rusty water to clear up and get warm, and then she stepped in. There was a greenish scum around the tile where it met the bathtub. She soaped herself thoroughly, making sure not to get her hair wet, and then turned the water to cool. The cool spray made her shudder. She made the water colder until her head was clear. Then she stepped out of the shower, toweled herself dry, and stared at her naked body in the sink mirror without expression. She winced, blinked. She adjusted each of her contact lenses with the tip of a finger. Then, satisfied, she began to prepare herself, her makeup, her costume, her props, just as she had done years ago, before she stepped out onto the stage. One performance, she thought, one performance only.

She leaned toward the mirror and put on her brown eye shadow, fluttering first one eye shut, then the other, then her black eyeliner. She curled her eyelashes, holding the curler to each lash for a long moment. Then her mascara. She blinked a few times and looked at her eyes. They looked bigger, blacker, shocking.

She rummaged through her cosmetics case until she found a dark red lipstick. She pressed the lipstick against her lips, then lightly ran her tongue over her lips to moisten them. She added a little blush in a slash along each cheekbone, stepped back, and studied her reflection. Her sharply cut black hair and her outlined black eyes and her harsh red lipstick made her beautiful face look exotic and hard like the faces of those evil androgynous Amazon superwomen in comic books.

She wiggled into her thong panties, turned sideways, cocked a hip to check her ass, and smiled. She went back to the bedroom for her pumps and the dress in the shopping bag. She returned to the bathroom, stepped into her dress and pulled it up. It was so tight she had to wiggle and contort her body until finally it snapped up like an elastic band. She pulled the top over her breasts, adjusted the straps, then bent one leg behind her, slipped on her pump, and then the other. She looked big now, not so slim. Broad shoulders, huge breasts. She pulled down the top of her dress to expose more of her breasts, then bent half over, placed her palms under her breasts, and plumped them up even more. She straightened up and smiled at the woman in the skintight shimmering black latex minidress. She took the Guerlain perfume out of her case, dabbed some behind each ear and in her cleavage, then stepped back to check herself. The dress did barely cover her ass. Miss Kitty was right. She hiked up her skirt over her ass, slipped out of her panties, and pulled down the skirt. She smoothed it with the flat of her hands.

She went back to the bedroom, picked up her canvas bag and purse and left the room. She was halfway down the hall when she stopped. She heard his voice: "What else did you touch, baby?" She went back to the room to the bathroom. She took the wet towel and wiped off the shower knobs, the walls, the edge of the sink, the mirror. Then she picked up her panties and her shopping bag and went to the door, opened it, wiped off the knob with her panties, then closed it and wiped off that knob, too. She walked down the hall to the elevator, pushed the button, and waited for the car to come up. She saw a garbage pail. She stuffed her panties and shopping bag in the pail and stepped into the elevator.

At midnight, The Anvil's upstairs bar and downstairs dining room were crowded with men and women, laughing, drinking, eating, smoking cigarettes and cigars, amid the din and clatter of silverware against china. The women wore tight low-cut dresses, flashing their breasts and ankle bracelets. The men wore sports jackets, pink and baby blue and lime green, and every so often they made a point of letting their jackets swing open, flashing their little Walther PPKs in their Mitch Rosen leather holsters on their hips.

Waiters in white jackets moved through the crowded dining room, slipping sideways between tables like flamenco dancers with silver trays poised above their heads. They tried to avoid the men and women standing beside the various tables, talking and laughing with the seated diners as they stuffed forkfuls of lobster and stone crab and shrimp and chunks of rare beef into their mouths and then washed it down with swallows of Crystal.

The few private tables in darkness along one wall—a step up from the main dining room—were deserted, except for one. A pudgy little man with a pampered child's face sat by himself with his back against the wall. His shiny black hair was slicked back and he wore a white suit and a black silk tie. He looked down over the crowded dining room below him. He was flanked by two tall beefy men in white Guiaberra shirts hanging loose over their pants to conceal the Sigma .40 Smith & Wesson semiautomatic pistols tucked into their pants at the hip. They stood with their backs against the wall, their eyes, behind dark glasses, flitting across the dining room, left-to-right and back again, and again, never coming to rest.

The little man's dark eyes flitted around the dining room, too, as he sipped from a glass of Perrier water. A shimmering black form passed his table and was gone. He had to crane his neck to follow her with his eyes. He saw her only from behind, her sharply cut black hair and her short tight shimmering black dress. He did not see her face until she stood at the upstairs bar and turned toward the dining room. A beautiful face. Sexy. Hard. He watched her order a drink. A man at the bar said something to her. She smiled, shook her head, and paid for her drink. She turned her face slightly. The light over the bar illuminated it so that now he could see it more clearly. The woman looked vaguely familiar, but before he could think of where he'd seen her, he heard a voice adressing him.

"Señor Medina. I'm so sorry to bother you." Medina looked at the maitre d' hovering over his table, bowing slightly. "It's nothing, really. It's just. . . . Do you see the woman at the bar, in the black dress?" Medina glanced at the woman, then back to the maitre d'. "Well, she has made a request. She is celebrating tonight. Her divorce. She would like to dine alone tonight, possibly at one of the tables on either side of you. A harmless woman, señor. A wife, lonely. It would mean so much to her, she said. Of course, only if it meets your approval."

The little man said nothing for a moment, then said, "Such a beautiful woman should not dine alone. Tell her to be my guest."

The maitre d' smiled and bowed, and then walked over to the woman. He said something to her. She nodded, picked up her black purse and walked toward the little man's table. The little man saw her reach into her purse and hand something to the maitre'd, who put it in his pants pocket.

She stood in front of him now, very tall, but with beautiful breasts spilling out of her tight dress. "Thank you so much," she said. "You didn't have to invite me. I'd have been happy dining alone."

"It is my pleasure. Please, sit down."

She pulled out a chair across from him and was about to sit down when one of the men in the Guiaberras stepped forward and put a hand against her chest to stop her. He took her purse before she could stop him.

"Excuse me!" she said. "What do you think you're doing?"

The man was already searching through her purse. Medina smiled at her. "I am so sorry," he said. "My associates are very protective of me. A man in my position." He said something in Spanish to the man, who handed the purse back to the woman. He nodded to Medina and returned to his position against the wall.

"*Please*, sit down," Medina said. "Allow me to explain." She sat across from him, her back to the dining room. "I am José Hor-Hay Medina-Cathtro. You have heard of me, no?"

She thought a moment, then smiled. "Of course. I understand now. A Cuban patriot like yourself, Señor Medina, has enemies."

He shrugged, and fluttered his eyelids. "Communists," he said. "It is the price I must pay for being a patriot." He smiled at her with his heavy-lidded eyes and pouty child's lips. "You do forgive me?" Before she could answer, he glanced over her shoulder at a waiter. "Now, what would you like to drink?" She looked at his Perrier. "It is just another precaution," he said. "But for you, I will break an old habit."

"Stolichnaya on the rocks," she said.

"Two," he said. The waiter backed off, nodding.

"And your name?" he said. "You look so familiar. Have we met before?"

She laughed. "I doubt it. I don't think we move in the same circles. My husband . . . my ex-husband . . . was a lawyer."

"I know many lawyers. In my business, it is a necessity."

"A personal injury lawyer. Not very exciting. Certainly not for a man like you." He nodded. "It used to be Mrs. Solomon Bilstein," she said. "The divorce came through today. Today is the first day of the rest of my life."

"Oh, I'm so sorry."

She waved a hand at him, her long fingernails painted blood-red. "It's a happy day, actually, for Sheila Ryan."

"Such a plain name for such a beautiful Señorita."

She smiled. "That is the second time today I have been called Señorita. I do so love the charm of Latin men."

He fluttered his eyelids and smiled, too. "I would have thought you were Latin, too. The hair, the eyes, so beautiful."

"It's possible," she said. "There's an old tale I heard from my Irish ancestors. In the 1500s the Spanish Armada sailed up to Ireland and anchored off shore. When the Spanish sailors went ashore the Irish girls were very attracted to their dark, sultry good looks. Like yours, Señor Medina."

"Please. José."

"The Spanish sailors and the Irish girls . . . mingled, you might say." She paused, then said, "Too coy a word, perhaps, for a man of action like yourself." She looked directly into his eyes and said softly, "The dark Spanish sailors and the pale Irish girls fucked, José, and produced a lot of little black-haired Irish babies they call 'Black Irish.'"

"Maybe one of my ancestors?"

She laughed. "You mean, we could be related?"

"Oh, Miha, I hope not. It would be such a waste."

"I hope not, too."

The waiter appeared with their drinks, set them down, and backed off. She raised her glass over the table. "To those Spanish sailors and Irish girls." They clicked glasses and sipped their drinks. He leaned forward, closer to her, and put his hand on her knee under the table.

"So, tell me, Miha, what brings you here tonight?" he said.

She looked around the room and then back to him. "The same thing that brings everyone here, José. Possibility."

He raised his eyebrows. "Possibility?"

"Yes. For adventure, romance, a chance to change one's life."

He slid his hand up to her smooth thigh and began to stroke it. "And you would like to change your life tonight, Miha?"

Her eyelids fluttered as his hand stroked her thigh. "Hmmm. Yes," she said softly. "And you, José?"

He grinned. "Maybe just to mingle with an Irish girl like my ancestors." He slid his hand further up her thigh.

She leaned back in her chair, her hips sliding forward, and parted her legs. "You mean, 'fuck,' don't you, José?" she said in a husky voice.

"Yes. That is what I mean. . . . Are you always so direct?"

She looked at him, her eyes half-lidded. "I'm not young enough to be coy, José. Why should I waste time? I wasted twenty years with a man who was more interested in his work than in fucking his Irish wife. I made a vow to myself never to waste time again . . . to get what I want, beginning tonight."

"Should we go, then?" he said.

"Eventually. But I would so like to have dinner tonight. Maybe champagne. I want to experience it all. A romantic dinner, a sexy man, champagne, and then. . . ."

"Of course, Miha." He looked for a waiter.

She looked behind her at the crowded noisy dining room. When she looked back at him she was frowning. "But not here, José. Someplace more intimate. Like the Havana Room."

He stopped stroking her thigh. She put her hand under the table on top of his. "Don't stop," she said.

He stared at her, her black hair, her black eyes, her harsh red lips. "You look so familiar," he said. "Are you sure we have never met before?"

"I would have remembered, José." She smiled at him. "And you would have remembered, too." He began stroking her thigh again. "After tonight you will."

"You are so sure?"

"I'm sure of that."

"So, you wish to eat in the Havana Room. A man's room."

"Yes. It's very sexy. So dark and private in those booths." She looked into his eyes. "Perfect for a little appetizer before the main course."

He smiled again. "Yes. An appetizer. A perfect word. Before the main course." He turned and said something to his men. When he turned back she had stopped smiling.

"Are your associates really necessary?" she said. "I *am* direct, José. But not that direct. I don't like an audience."

He looked at her for a long moment, her purse, her dress, and then he flattened his hand between her legs.

She looked at him with a small smile. "Did you find what you were looking for?"

"Yes," he said. "And no." He turned and said something to his men.

They were sitting close together in a banquette against the wall in the dimly lit Havana Room. There were other couples around them they could not see. Older men with younger women hidden in their booths beneath the erotic paintings of women and the heads of dead animals. In the darkness they could barely see the bar or the occasional waiter moving across the room to stand before a banquette. Only the humidor room was brightly lit by the crystal chandelier.

She sipped from a glass of champagne while he nuzzled her neck, his hand below the table rubbing the trim patch of her pussy. She had her hand between his legs, too, rubbing his cock beneath his linen pants, feeling it grow, smiling, as the waiter approached their table. They did not stop with their hands even as the waiter stood over them, waiting.

"Give us a few minutes, please," she said. "In the meantime." She reached into her purse and took out a small key. She gave it to the waiter. "Would you, please? Number 478 in the humidor room."

The waiter nodded, "Certainly, madame," and went over to the humidor room.

Medina said, "Cigars! Why am I not surprised?"

"Sometimes I surprise myself. It's a recently acquired habit. Something about a cigar in my mouth makes me feel . . . oh . . . so . . . "

"Sexy?"

". . . powerful."

The waiter returned with her box of Gloria Cubanos and her key and handed them to her. She put her key in her purse and centered the box on the white tablecloth.

"Gloria Cubanos!" said Medina. "How appropriate. One day I will make Cuba glorious again."

"I'm sure you will," she said as she opened the box to reveal a single cigar on the cedar divider. She took out the cigar, leaving the box open, and held it close to her lips. She peeled back her lips, baring her teeth, and bit off the end. Medina watched, his hand stilled on her thigh. She stuck out the tip of her tongue and ran it along the sides of the cigar. Then she put the cigar in her mouth, her lips wrapping around it, and pushed it deeper and deeper into her mouth until it almost disappeared. She withdrew the damp cigar, reached into her purse for her silver lighter, and lit it, twirling it between her lips until it was evenly lit. She exhaled smoke toward the ceiling, then, smiling, handed the cigar to Medina.

He shook his head. "I have never seen a woman light a cigar in such a way."

"Practice," she smiled, and reached a hand under the table and unzipped his fly. "Sit back, José, and enjoy. "He put the cigar in his mouth and leaned back, his eyes half-lidded. She looked around the room, then shifted her body toward him and pulled his cock out of his pants. She whispered in his ear, "Save something for the main course, José," and lowered her head below the table.

He felt her moist lips around the head of his cock. Then her lips slid farther and farther down; up again, and down, and up, his eyes fluttering shut as she worked.

He did not see her free hand reach under the cedar divider of the cigar box. He only felt her lips leaving his cock and her hand tightening around it painfully. He opened his eyes wide. She was smiling at him, her face close to his ear now. She whispered, "This is for Señor Esquared, you little prick." He saw that her long fingers with the blood-red nails were wrapped around a small gleaming silver object that she was raising to his forehead. He was about to speak, to tell her now he remembered her, but before a word escaped the woman fired a single bullet into his brain with her tiny Seecamp .32 acp. There was a loud pop, and his head jerked back against the banquette. A small neat hole oozed blood. The cigar dangled from his lips. His limp cock pissed down his leg.

The woman stood up, wiped off the cigar box and her glass with a napkin, picked up her purse, and slid out of the booth. The men and women in the other booths peered out at her, then pulled their heads back when they saw the pistol at her side. The waiters and bartenders were frozen in midpose around the room. She walked past them, not hurrying, out of the room, through the front door and into the darkness outside. Suddenly, she heard women screaming, men shouting. She walked quickly around the corner to her rental car parked in darkness. She reached up with her hand and pulled off her black wig and dropped it in the street. Then she got in, started the car, put the Seecamp on the dashboard, and looked in the rearview mirror. She wet the tip of one finger, dabbed it against each of her eyes, and then dropped both contact lenses into the street.

Bobby was asleep in his bed, dreaming. He was back in the mountains of his ancestors. He saw himself kneeling in front of an old black Franklin stove in a weathered old log cabin high up in the mountains surrounded by the forest. Hoshi sat beside him as Bobby snapped twigs and put them in the stove. He looked outside through a window to the front porch where, amid softly falling snow, Sheila was bent over, picking up logs in the darkness. Bobby watched her in her blue down quilted vest amid the softly falling snow. He turned back to the stove and put in more twigs. He heard the front door open and Sheila walking toward him. He lit the twigs and fanned them with his hands, pulling the smoke toward him the way his ancestors had for hundreds of years. He heard Sheila kneel down beside him. He smelled her perfume and felt her warm breath close to his ear. He heard her soft voice whisper in his ear, "Shhh, baby! Go back to sleep. I'm here now. Everything's all right." Then he heard her voice again, only harder, colder, "I told you, baby, no one would ever come between us. I'd never let anyone hurt you."

In his dream, he reached up a hand to touch her. He felt the silky-smoothness of her dress.